LEGACY OF MASKS

Also by Sallie Bissell

IN THE FOREST OF HARM

A DARKER JUSTICE

CALL THE DEVIL BY HIS OLDEST NAME

LEGACY of MASKS

SALLIE BISSELL

BANTAM BOOKS

LEGACY OF MASKS
A Bantam Book

Published by Bantam Dell
A Division of Random House, Inc.
New York, New York

Book design by Lynn Newmark

Bantam Books is a registered trademark of Random House, Inc.,
and the colophon is a trademark of Random House, Inc.

ISBN: 0-553-80279-8

Printed in the United States of America

For Kate Bissell, my blue-eyed girl

No novel is a solitary achievement; many people aid and abet along the way. My heartfelt thanks to the following friends who were more than generous with their time and expertise.

To Larry Woods of Nashville, Tennessee, who advised me on legal procedure and legal practices; To Susana Vincent of Placitas, New Mexico, who translated the Spanish with great wit and sensitivity; To Lisa Lefler and Jenifer Ross of Sylva, North Carolina, whose sociological insights into the Eastern Band of the Cherokee Indians were invaluable. To Delores Dwyer for another superb job of copyediting; To Kate Miciak, who again held the candle through that spooky old forest of fiction; To Edith Hayes Comer and Betsy Comer Hester, for their love and unquestioning support. And finally, my thanks and love to Margie Lunsford, Sharon Sabo, and Marilyn Meyers, my old Gale Lane pals who inspired much of this book.

AUTHOR'S NOTE

Many of the characters in this novel bear well-known surnames common in the mountains of North Carolina. I did this to add verisimilitude to my story and to convey a stronger sense of place. No character in this novel is based on any real person, living or dead. I would further like to thank the residents of Haywood, Jackson, and Swain Counties, as well as the Cherokee Indians of the Quallah Boundary, who answered the questions of a nosy writer with kindness and generosity.

LEGACY OF MASKS

PROLOGUE

Hartsville, North Carolina
November 30, 1982

Deke! Get your butt up in this truck! We need to help find that little girl!" Harold Craig, assistant scoutmaster of Boy Scout Troop 238, scowled at the wiry, redheaded boy who'd darted across the beams of his headlights.

"Coming, sir." Deke Keener hurried to the rear of Mr. Craig's truck. As he climbed into the back, he saw the rest of 238's Wolf Patrol shivering together, their eyes wide with the urgency of their mission. No camping trip this; not even one of Mr. Craig's beloved forest fire drills. This was *real*. At three o'clock this afternoon, eight-year-old Tracy Foster, daughter of the mayor and Deke's own across-the-street neighbor, had gone missing from Firescald Campground, a skinny finger of cleared land between Tuckaseegee Creek and the five hundred thousand acres of the Nantahalah National Forest. Tracy had gone there on a cookout with her own Brownie Troop 112, and had not shown up when Mrs. Winston, their troop leader, took a final head count before leaving. Deke happened to be fishing right across from the campground when Mrs. Winston had started hollering like someone being skinned alive. He'd looked up to see the woman first gathering the girls inside her minivan, then directing them back out to the edge of the woods to call Tracy's name. When Mrs. Winston spotted him on the other side of the creek, still calmly holding his line in the water, she waved her arms over her head and yelled, "You! Boy! Aren't you Joe Keener's son?"

Deke nodded, pretending that he hadn't been watching them all along.

"Go call the sheriff! Tracy Foster's lost in the woods!"

Dropping his fishing rod, Deke had done what the woman asked, furiously pedaling his bike to Ray Zimmerlee's Texaco station and begging a free phone call off the cheap old bastard, telling him that it was an emergency. That had been six hours ago. The bright copper afternoon had slowly turned into a cold, bristly night, and Tracy had still not shown up. Now, where earlier just the Brownie-packed minivan had stood, the campground was crowded with vehicles and awash with flashing red lights. Police cars, two fire trucks, and an ambulance stood ready to receive the lost Tracy Foster. Deke felt a tingle of excitement as the scouts pulled up beside a police car and he caught a glimpse of the mayor himself standing beside the creek, his arms wrapped around his wife as they both gazed into the dark, rushing water.

"You boys stay put," Mr. Craig ordered as he unfolded his long legs from the driver's seat. "I'll go find out what the sheriff wants us to do."

The boys watched, wide-eyed as young owls, as Mr. Craig strode over to a picnic shelter where Sheriff Stump Logan and a group of Forest Rangers were shining flashlights on a map.

"They won't make us go in the woods, will they?" asked Jerry Cochran. Another neighbor of Deke and Tracy's, Cochran was a skinny bookworm of a boy who was wary of the forest during the day, and feared it mightily at night.

"Probably." Fat-faced Randy Bradley shined his flashlight under his chin. Though he attempted a Frankenstein-like grimace, he looked more like some demonic pumpkin. "They'll probably make you point man, Cockroach."

"No kidding." Cochran pushed his glasses back up on his nose. "What do you think they'll want us to do?"

Deke squelched a laugh. At home, from his bedroom window, he watched Jerry play with Tracy Foster all the time. Once the nerd had even climbed way up a hackberry tree to retrieve her stupid kitten. Now his precious little girlfriend was lost and Cochran was too chicken to go out into the spooky old woods and find her.

"Probably scoop up her body parts." Butch Messer snickered as he unwrapped a piece of bubble gum. "My dad said a bear probably got her. Dragged her off to eat before he caved up for the winter."

"Shoot, I bet she drowned." Floyd Nations, a rangy boy who already kept a wad of tobacco between his lower lip and gum, stood up to scan the dark, hissing creek. "They'll probably find her down in Sley Holler, all swelled-up and green."

Deke was sitting there, relishing Cochran's gaping reaction to all the speculation, when he noticed Mr. Craig give the sheriff a brisk nod and head back toward the truck. "Shut up," he whispered to his pack mates. "Here comes Craig."

"Okay, boys." Mr. Craig hurried up, his usually sallow, hound-dog face now flushed with excitement. "They want us to post a picket line at the entrance of the campground. We're to keep any unauthorized vehicles from coming in."

"Will we have to go into the woods?" Jerry Cochran sounded like the star soprano in an all-boy choir.

"No. We're just going to stand in a line across a slab of asphalt." Mr. Craig, who often regaled them with tales of his European adventures with General Patton's Third Army, sounded vaguely disappointed. "Bear Patrol will spell us at twenty-two hundred hours, unless someone finds that poor little girl."

Minutes later, Mr. Craig had them lined up across the entrance to the campground, flashlights in hand. As the boys spread out, Deke took the end position, to keep the big bad woods away from Cochran. Hiding his smile, he worked hard at feigning concern for Tracy Foster and waited for his chance. It came about an hour later, when the novelty of their duty started to wear off. As the boys began fidgeting and passing bad jokes down the line, Deke made his move.

"Hey, Jerry," he called to Cochran. "Keep watch over here. I gotta go to the latrine."

"Can't you just go behind that stop sign?" Cochran whispered, as if the forest were some huge, living creature that might gobble him up.

"Not for this," said Deke. "I'll be back in five minutes. Get Butch to tell his elephant fart joke. It'll keep your mind off things."

Without waiting for Cochran's consent, he turned and walked toward the latrine at the far edge of the parking area. After he'd gotten about twenty feet behind his friends, he turned left and slipped into the woods, his heart beating like a drum. He'd known the moment the frantic Mrs. Winston had called him that he was going to be the one who found Tracy Foster. After all, he was the one who'd gotten her lost— who better than him to bring her home?

He switched off his flashlight, making his way along a trail where rough pine fingers poked at his cheeks and the ground felt like a sponge beneath his feet. While nameless creatures rattled away through the leaves, he chuckled. Cochran would have shit his pants by now, but nothing underneath this dark lacework of leaves and branches frightened him at all. He felt at home in shadows that moved; in trees that whispered sibilant warnings on the hushed night breeze. No member of Troop 238 was better in the woods than he. Not even those older boys who strutted around with Eagle badges on their chests.

After he'd threaded his way a mile into the forest, he began following a sparkling, moonlit stream that led to a deep ravine guarded by two huge boulders. He'd stumbled upon it three years ago and as far as he knew, was the only person aware of its existence. He walked its quarter-mile length trembling with anticipation. At two o'clock this afternoon, he'd lured Tracy away from her friends with a wild tale about lost Cherokee gold. Now he wondered if she'd found any in the seven hours she'd had to look for it.

He climbed around a big rock he called the mushroom, then turned left. He saw her immediately, lying on a boulder, exactly where he'd left her. She was small and doll-like, her corn-silk hair glowing like foxfire in the dim light. For an instant, he felt a ripple of real fear. Maybe he'd gone over the top, scared her to death with all his bullshit. Then he heard a bawl that sounded like a newborn calf. His heart soared. It was okay! She was still alive! He started to move toward her casually, as if he were just taking a nighttime stroll through the deep woods. Inside, he could barely breathe, he was so excited.

"Hi, Tracy," he said, his voice ringing hollow among the rocks. He had a pins-and-needles feeling in the pit of his stomach and his penis had grown so hard, it hurt. "Find any gold?"

"Deke?" The little girl startled, lifting a tearstained face to peer into the darkness. "Deke, is that you?"

He laughed. "Who'd you think it was? A ghost?"

"Don't say that, Deke. It's really scary out here." Her voice was high and breathy; he could tell she was trying hard not to cry.

He stood still, watching her, savoring her agony. A whole person, right there, totally in his power. He could make her do anything he wanted. Anything at all.

"Have you seen the bear yet?" he asked.

"What bear?"

"The one they call Claw." He quickly invented a new demon to torture her as he took a step closer. "He's the last one to go to his cave. He likes to wait and see if he can get any last morsel of food. Claw has a taste for human blood. Cougars are up here, too. And that maniac who hacked up those kids in Virginia—"

"Stop it!" She clapped her hands over her ears and began to cry for real, tears spilling from her eyes. "Please don't say any more! Please take me home!"

He smiled, wondering if his penis might burst from the sheer pleasure of watching her. "Sure, Tracy. I'll take you home. If you do one thing for me."

"What?"

"Remember last month? That little game I wanted to play in your garage?"

Snuffling, she looked up at him, unspeaking.

"I still want to play that game," he whispered. "I want to play it now."

"But that game isn't nice," she protested. "That game scares me."

"Being left out here to die would scare me more," he said. He stepped closer. "If you ever want to see your parents again, you'll play that game with me, now."

She looked at him like some small trapped animal. He caught a sudden strong whiff of urine and realized she'd wet herself. Jesus, he thought, taken aback by his own power. She's so scared she pissed herself. Right here in front of me.

Crying soundlessly, she got to her feet. "If I do it, will you take me home?"

He looked around. The rocks stood jumbled around them, but he knew of a clearing beneath some pines that would work. He grabbed her hand. "Come on."

He pulled her toward the trees, feeling as if he might explode, wondering if he was going to wind up like those people he'd read about who caught on fire and burned up from the inside out. What a shame that would be, he thought. He'd worked hard at planning this all day, ever since he saw the Brownies drive up this morning. No, he decided. He might well burn someday, but it wouldn't be tonight. Tonight he had Jerry Cochran's precious little playmate to do with as he pleased. He would have to burn up some other time.

Two hours later, he brought her back. As they neared the picnic area, they stopped on a fallen log and surveyed the activity below. The ambulances and fire trucks were still there, only now he could hear distant voices calling his name. He took his official Boy Scout whistle from his pocket, but turned to her before he blew it.

"If you tell what we did up there, you're going to get in tons of trouble. Your parents will really be mad. They'll make you quit the Brownies, and they'll put Mrs. Winston in jail. Then they'll send you to a special school and not let you live at home anymore. You wouldn't want that to happen, would you?"

The little girl gaped at him.

"You've got to promise not to tell, Tracy," he said, giving her wrist a hard squeeze. "If you do, I'll shove a firecracker up your cat's ass."

"I won't tell." Her chin was trembling. "Please don't do anything to Buttons."

"I won't, as long as you keep our secret."

Lowering her eyes, she nodded.

Satisfied about Tracy's cooperation, he blew three sharp blasts on his whistle and started down the mountain. Mr. Craig was the first to reach him, hauling up through the trees like some old coon dog, hot on a trail.

"Where you been, boy?" Mr. Craig's face was ashen. Deke couldn't tell if he was really mad or really scared. Not that it mattered. He'd come back from the forest, holding little Miss Tracy Foster by the hand. "Where'd you find her?"

"Over that way." Deke pointed in the opposite direction from which they'd come. "Near where we camped last winter. I was on my way to the latrine when I heard her calling. She was stuck in a tree. It took me a while to get her down."

Mr. Craig scooped Tracy up in his arms, as if she might disappear all over again if he didn't hang on to her. He frowned at the boy standing in front of him. "Deke, last winter we camped a good mile north. You couldn't have heard anything that far away."

"That's where I went, Mr. Craig. And that's where I found her." Deke's tone brooked no dispute, not even from his scoutmaster.

Mr. Craig frowned at him longer than Deke liked, but then returned his attention to the little girl. "Are you all right, darlin'?" he asked, holding Tracy close. Deke glared up at her, silently reminding her of the terrible consequences the wrong response would carry.

"I'm cold," Tracy whimpered, burying her face in Mr. Craig's plaid shirt. "I want my mama."

"Well, she and your daddy are both waitin' right down there for you, darlin'," said Mr. Craig. "They're gonna be mighty tickled to see you."

Five minutes later, Mr. Craig handed the little girl back to her parents. As Deke's fellow Scouts gathered to congratulate him, a dizzying rush of triumph roared through his body. He'd just broken every law of God and man and the BSA, and everybody was treating him like a hero! He, Deke Keener, had played every one of them as if they were all instruments in his own private orchestra!

Sheriff Logan walked over and shook his hand, as did Mayor Foster and the Forest Rangers. A flashbulb popped as a photographer took a shot of him with Tracy, the mayor, and the rest of the Scouts. When it came out in the paper the next day, his mother wept with pride, and his father peeled off a crisp twenty-dollar bill and told him to go buy something he wanted.

He cut the picture out and framed it, and now keeps it on his office wall. Most every day he leans back in his soft leather armchair and looks at that picture with great longing. Though he's played his game with many others, and even more people now regard him as a hero, he lives for the day when another Tracy Foster will come his way—another innocent, cotton-haired little girl who will follow him deep into those dark, piney woods and do absolutely anything he tells her.

ONE

The Confederate stood on the seventy-first of the one hundred and five concrete steps that led from Hartsville's Main Street to the Pisgah County Courthouse. Rifle at his side, he'd kept a weatherbeaten watch for any encroaching Yankees for as long as Mary Crow could remember. Passing him on her fourth-grade civics field trip, she'd cowered at his towering bronze fierceness. Six years later, as she'd rushed past to apply for her driver's license, she'd found him an embarrassing symbol of the unreconstructed South. Today, nearly twenty-five years after their first acquaintance, the old boy seemed as comforting as a childhood friend. Not much else about Pisgah County did.

"Hey, Johnny Reb." She paused for a moment to look up at the carefully wrought figure of a young private in the Confederate Army. Having been erected in front of the courthouse, he truly faced east, but cut his eyes northward, ever vigilant for an enemy approach. Though birds had roosted on his shoulders and one long strand of spiderweb dangled from his rear, he still looked ready to face whatever challenge the blue bellies might throw at him. Mary wondered if she was in such good shape. Already she was breathing heavily from her climb, and she still had thirty-four steps to go. She'd forgotten how hot the early June sun could be in the Carolina mountains, and she'd foolishly worn Deathwrap, her prosecutorial black suit. Comfortable in the relentlessly air-conditioned courtrooms of Atlanta, here sleek Deathwrap felt like a portable sauna, too close, too heavy, too tight against her skin.

"Damn," she grumbled, leaning against the base of the statue. Already she'd torn her hose and sweated through her underwear. Pretty soon she'd have big damp circles under her arms. In her business it was never good to be visibly nervous; to be both nervous *and* sweating like a pig did not bode well at all.

Nonetheless, she had an appointment with DA George Turpin in four minutes, and she intended to keep it. Squaring her shoulders, she resumed her ascent to the courthouse. As her high heels clicked on the steps, she gave a rueful smile at the irony of her undertaking. When she was eighteen, she'd ached to leave Pisgah County forever. Today, at thirty-five, she couldn't wait to come back home.

The past twelve months had been her year of living dangerously. She'd left her ADA job in Atlanta to go to Peru with archaeologist Gabe Benge. Though it seemed like a wonderful chance for a whole new life, eight months into it she knew she'd made a mistake. One day she was taking a boat ride on Lake Titicaca. As she looked over into the water, a huge fish surfaced next to the boat. For a moment it swam along beside them, its scales flashing in the sun, then it returned to the depths of the lake, the beautiful silver body fading into the translucent green water. Instinctively, she turned to tell Jonathan, then she caught herself. Jonathan was not here. Jonathan was in another country, another hemisphere. Jonathan would never share that singular moment with the silvery fish and the blue sky and green Lake Titicaca. The realization struck her with such a yearning for home that it was all she could do to stay in the boat and not start swimming for shore. *Why are you here,* the lake seemed to whisper, *among mountains you can't name, Indians who will never regard you as anything more than a tourist?* It was then that she knew she had to go home. Not home to Gabe or even home to Atlanta, but back to her true home in the North Carolina mountains, her true home with Jonathan Walkingstick. Somehow everything she didn't need at eighteen, she needed quite desperately now.

But coming home to Pisgah County required money, and for that, she needed a job. She'd called George Turpin two weeks ago, as soon as she stepped off the plane in Atlanta. He'd sounded enthusiastic over the phone—Yes, I'd love to talk to you, love to have a woman of your experience on my staff. In fact, we have a man who's taking early retirement. When could you come up for a talk? They'd made their arrangements, and settled upon today, here, in about three minutes. If she hurried, she would be on time.

She finally reached the hundred and fifth step, and strode into the vaulted lobby of the old courthouse. She passed a gaggle of secretaries clad in frothy print dresses, hurrying to begin their day's work. Suddenly she felt even more out of place. Swathed in black among women clad in the colors of melting sherbet, she realized she must look like the grim reaper seeking her next victim. When she glanced over her shoulder and caught one of the secretaries casting a curious eye back at her, she knew without a doubt that she would be the courthouse's gossip tidbit du jour. *Did y'all see that girl dressed in that fancy black suit? Who was she? You don't see clothes like that around here. She must be some hot shot, over from Raleigh. Don't kid yourself, honey. Didn't you see that hair? She was pure Cherokee. . . .*

Shrugging off the imaginary wags, Mary checked the building directory beside the elevator. Turpin's office was on the third floor. She rode up with two men in seersucker suits, one of whom looked like someone she might have gone to high school with. She considered introducing herself, but both hurried out when they reached the second floor. She rode on, alone, to the next floor, where at the end of the hall stood a frosted glass door with "George H. Turpin, District Attorney" lettered in gold.

She entered to find an older woman seated behind a desk. Gray hair curled on her head like steel wool, and unlike the younger women downstairs, she wore a more decorous linen suit with a simple white blouse. When the woman looked up at Mary, her mouth drew down in a thin line.

"May I help you?"

"I have an appointment with Mr. Turpin at nine o'clock," Mary answered. "My name is Mary Crow."

Her words seemed to frost the woman further. Mary knew her name was not altogether unknown here. She had, three years ago, broken up a conspiracy that had put Pisgah County Sheriff Stump Logan on the FBI's most wanted list. Then, a year later, she had killed that same sheriff near Devil's Fork Gap in Madison County. Though Logan had been found to be a kidnapper, rapist, and murderer, he had also headed a powerful political machine and was still fondly remembered by a number of people on the county payroll. Mary knew that she would have to tread carefully in this courthouse.

Turpin's secretary began writing in some kind of logbook. "Mary C-r-o-w-e," she spelled aloud, using the traditional Cherokee spelling of the name.

"Just C-r-o-w," Mary corrected.

"Really? Most people around here spell it the other way." The woman looked at her with eyes like chips of dark stone.

Mary shrugged. She'd dropped the *e* on the end of her name back when she'd gone to college and simultaneously dropped most all of her Cherokee past. She wasn't sure there was any point in adding it now.

"Have a seat," the secretary said, not bothering to correct her misspelling. "Mr. Turpin'll see you in a moment."

Mary crossed the room and sat by a window that afforded her a view of Johnny Reb's backside, with Hartsville stretched out beyond him. A town of storefronts and sidewalks, Hartsville stood wedged in between a line of the Southern Railroad and the looming Plott Balsam Mountains. It had changed a lot in her seventeen-year absence. Though the west end of Main Street was still somberly comprised of law offices, banks, a motel, and Morehouse's funeral home, trendier, more lighthearted businesses had opened up on east Main. On her way to the courthouse Mary had passed a travel agency, a yoga studio, a massage and nail salon, and a restaurant that proudly displayed its rave review in *Southern Living* magazine. Who would have thought that? Mary wondered, remembering when Hartsville's most exotic restaurant was the Fish Camp Grill, a shack on the river that would fry, for a small fee, whatever you managed to catch off their back deck, hush puppies and coleslaw compliments of the house.

"Ms. Crow?"

A deep voice interrupted her drift into the past. She turned to face a heavyset, balding man dressed in the summer uniform of all Southern

LEGACY OF MASKS   13

attorneys—khaki trousers, navy blazer, striped regimental tie. "George Turpin." He extended his hand, his smile revealing a chipped front tooth that gave him a boyish look that belied his middle age. "I've heard so much about you. It's a real pleasure to meet you."

She rose and shook his hand.

"Come on back to my office," he said. "Would you like some coffee? A Coke?"

"No, thank you," she replied, glancing at the secretary, who again frowned at her over her glasses.

Turpin led her to a corner office that boasted a now-empty fireplace. Where her former boss in Atlanta had decked his walls with basketball memorabilia, George Turpin splattered his personal space with photographs of himself with the prominent and powerful. Turpin golfing with the governor of North Carolina, Turpin hewing down a tree with the local congressman, Turpin shaking hands with the chairman of the new Cherokee gaming commission. Interspersed among the photos were a dozen shadow-box frames displaying the kind of rosette ribbons awarded at county fairs and horse shows. Blues, mostly, with a few reds and yellows thrown in for a touch of humility.

"Do you show horses?" Mary stepped over to get a closer look at one ribbon.

"Honey, any horse I got on would keel over from my excess avoirdupois." Turpin patted his rotund middle. "No, all those ribbons are for barbecue."

"Barbecue?" Mary frowned. Since when had they made barbecue a contact sport?

"Pisgah County DA's office has won the North Carolina Barbecue Championship for the past five years," Turpin explained proudly. "We compete in the vinegar-and-pepper category and the tomato-based group. Best durn stuff you'll ever put in your mouth. Here." Turpin sat down behind his desk and pulled a bottle of dark orange liquid from a drawer. "Take this home with you. Put it on anything—pork, chicken, ribs. Tofu, if you're a tree-hugger. You'll think you've died and gone to heaven."

"Thanks." Mary took the jar the man offered and sat down across from him. "It looks wonderful."

"It is. I tell you, when I retire, I'm gonna open me up a little barbecue shack on 441. Catch all them tourists goin' into the casino before they lose all their money." Turpin laughed heartily, amused by his own future, then he returned to the present, pulling her resume from his drawer.

"Let me say right off it's a real honor to have you in my office. I regarded your mentor, Judge Irene Hannah, as a great legal mind and a true friend." He tapped Mary's resume. "Your record does her proud."

"Thank you." Mary smiled at the memory of the woman in whose footsteps she'd followed, in whose house she now lived. "Irene was a wonderful person."

"She was indeed. Even though that Logan business caught us all with our pants down, we owe you a debt of gratitude for bringing him to justice."

Mary didn't know what to say. She hadn't intended to embarrass Pisgah County law, she'd simply killed a corrupt county sheriff who was trying to kill her. "Who's sheriff here now?" she asked, curious about who might have dared take Logan's place.

"A young man named Jerry Cochran," said Turpin. "Went to high school here—you may know him."

"Actually, I do. We were lab partners in biology." Mary almost laughed. Though she had liked the bookish boy who nearly fainted when they dissected their frog, she couldn't imagine him donning a badge and sidearm to fight crime in Pisgah County.

"I wouldn't have given him a chance in hell to get elected, but the voters seemed to like him. Real high-tech, low-key kind of guy." Turpin shrugged, then turned his attention to her file. "Let's talk a little bit about this, now. Tell me why somebody with this record would want to work here?" His chair squeaked as he leaned back, waiting for her reply.

Mary's tongue felt stuck to the roof of her mouth. What should she say? That in the middle of Lake Titicaca she'd gotten so homesick, she almost cried? That as sweet as the jasmine-scented nights of Miraflores had been, she longed for the smell of pine, the touch of Jonathan Walkingstick instead of Gabe Benge? Why not, she decided. It made as much sense as any other reason.

"I want to come back home," she said simply. "To do that, I need a job. Criminal prosecution is what I do."

Turpin smiled. "You're Cherokee, aren't you?"

"Half," said Mary. "My mother grew up in Snowbird. My father was from Atlanta."

"And you've lived away from here for how long?"

"Seventeen years. I went to live with my grandmother shortly after my mother died." Mary shifted in her chair. She never told new acquaintances that her mother had been murdered; she couldn't bear the cheap sympathy that such a remark evoked.

"Well, I don't know how well you've kept up with things here, but this is about as far from Hot-lanta as you can get. We have one, maybe two murders a year, and most of those are somebody getting drunk and shooting whatever significant other gets on the wrong end of their deer rifles." Turpin sighed. "A trained monkey could get a conviction on most of 'em."

"That's okay," said Mary. "There's more to law than just convicting murderers."

Turpin frowned. "That's true, but I bet if I put you on staff you'd be looking for a new job in six months. I don't mean to be discouraging, honey, but Pisgah County is for lawyers who want nice, quiet careers that allow them time to enter barbecue cook-offs or coach Little League." Again he tapped her resume. "These pages tell me that you eat, breathe, and sleep felony prosecutions. Having you at Pisgah County would be like hitching Seabiscuit up to a plow."

Mary was puzzled. Turpin seemed uncomfortable with the fact that she was good at what she did. "But I gave you my credentials when we talked on the phone. I thought you were excited about the possibility of my joining your staff."

Turpin sighed. "To be honest, Ms. Crow, I'd love to put you in the office right next to mine. But the plain truth is, I don't have an opening anymore."

Mary sat there, stunned. Two weeks ago, Turpin had practically offered her a job over the phone. He explained further.

"When you first called I had Pete Nicholson's resignation on my desk. Three days later, Pete came in and asked if he could stay on. His wife had been diagnosed with breast cancer, and they've still got a boy in college."

"I see." Mary wondered if Turpin's colleague was indeed hanging on to his paycheck, or if Turpin was turning her down for some other reason. Again, she didn't know what to say. She had depended upon getting this job. Irene's little house needed a new well and a new roof and God knows what else. For the last three days, she'd had to haul water in with her car and take sponge baths in the sink. She tried another tack.

"I don't suppose you could give me a trial run? See how I fit in after six months?"

Turpin closed the folder that held her resume. "I'm sorry. I just don't have the budget for that."

"I see," Mary said quietly.

"Tell you what, though. Leave me a number where I can reach you. If and when I get a vacancy, I'll call you right away. I owe Irene Hannah that much."

Mary reached in her purse and handed him one of the business cards she'd made up last night, on her computer. Turpin's brows lifted as he read it.

"This is a local number," he said. "I thought you lived in Atlanta."

"Not anymore. Irene Hannah left me her farm. I'm a full-time resident of Pisgah County, as of a week ago," she replied, hoping that might make a difference.

A look of discomfit flitted across Turpin's face, then vanished as he clipped Mary's card to her folder. "Then welcome to the neighborhood. If anything opens up, I'll be sure to give you a buzz."

Mary gathered her bottle of barbecue sauce and the black leather briefcase she'd brought with her. I can't believe this, she thought, trying to fight the blush of humiliation spreading across her cheeks. She, with her perfect record, turned down by a man who could probably count all his murder convictions on one barbecue-stained hand.

"Thanks for seeing me, Mr. Turpin." She smiled through clenched teeth. "It's been a pleasure."

"Thank you for coming, dear." Turpin took her hand in his. "I promise I'll be in touch. It may be a while, but I won't forget you."

Enduring the openly snide smile of Turpin's secretary, Mary hurried out of the office and into the waiting elevator. Moments later, she was trudging back down the hundred and five steps, dodging two starry-eyed teenagers who were holding hands and giggling. After they passed, she stopped once again by the ever-watchful Confederate.

"I crapped out, Johnny Reb," she whispered, incredulous at Turpin's complete about-face. "They don't want me here."

Swallowing hard, she fought a moment of panic. Two weeks ago she'd left a man who loved her and a potentially promising career in Atlanta for a rural mountain county where the chief legal officer seemed prouder of his barbecue sauce than his conviction rate. Had she totally lost her mind? Was she going through some premature midlife crisis?

She looked up at the statue's face. The sun now cast the eyes in deep shadow, making the mouth a protuberant bulge. Where earlier the young soldier had looked vigilant, now he seemed to gaze at the mountains wistfully, as if longing to be reunited with the companions who'd marched off and left him here to stand watch, so long ago. Mary felt a sudden kinship with the young man. Though both were of Pisgah County, both were now also strangers to it. It occurred to her that what she sought might be just as elusive as the young soldier's dreams.

"Maybe someday you'll find what you're looking for, Johnny Reb," Mary murmured, turning her gaze from the statue to the little mountain town below. "And maybe someday I will, too."

TWO

The size of her breasts surprised him. Looking at her from the back, as she stood in the parking lot, she had such spindly legs and narrow hips, he assumed they'd still be just immature buds, nothing more than fleshy buttons sprouting from an otherwise flat chest. But as he pulled in across from the big orange U-Haul, he could tell that she already wore a small bra; he saw the white straps beneath her T-shirt. He figured her to be around eleven, at that strangely exciting cusp of tomboy and developing woman. She would still have scrapes on her knees and dirt behind her ears, but she would also have skin that felt like velvet and exquisitely soft down on her pudendum. The thought of it made him weak with desire. Martin had said he had a daughter starting junior high school; he'd just never dreamed she'd look so much like his lost Tracy Foster. Trying to ignore the sick heat in his gut, he strode toward the U-Haul and slid in behind his smile.

"Good morning! Y'all sure got here bright and early! I wasn't expecting you till this afternoon."

Earl Martin, the out-of-work foreman he'd just hired down in Greenville, humbly removed the sweat-stained John Deere cap from his head. "We got packed up late yesterday, and just decided to come ahead on. Spent the night in Cherokee."

"Cherokee?" Deke Keener laughed. "Do any good at the casino?"

Martin shook his head apologetically. "I'm not much of a gambler. Never had the money to be one."

"Me, neither," Keener said, pumping Martin's hard, callused hand. "Money spends fast enough on its own. Seems crazy to throw it down a slot machine."

Martin grinned. His hard-hat suntan ended just below his receding blond hairline, revealing skin the color of biscuit dough. Keener wondered if the daughter would be that same color, stretched out naked in the back of his car.

"Let me introduce my family." Martin gestured to a thin corn shuck of a woman, who climbed out of the truck with another child. "That's my wife, Darlene. She's got Chrissy, who's four." He put a hand on the shoulder of the young girl who skipped over to stand beside him. "This here's Avis, who's eleven. Everyone, meet my new boss, Mr. Keener."

"Please call me Deke." He grinned at Martin's family, careful to keep his eyes well away from Avis. "Welcome to Hartsville. Welcome to Keener Construction."

"We're just so happy to be here, Mr. Keener, uh, Deke," the wife said, her voice breathless with gratitude. He'd heard that tone so often, he knew the subtext by heart. *Oh, my God, a job! No more living off the credit card! No more peanut-butter-and-jelly sandwiches for dinner or husbands who can't get it up at night because they can't bring home any money during the day.* "Thank you so much for giving Earl a chance," this one added.

"My pleasure," Deke assured her. "I've got great plans for him." He chucked the younger child under her chin, then, finally, he allowed his gaze to skim across Avis. Beneath her Braves baseball cap he saw that she did, indeed, have her father's blue eyes, her mother's cottony hair. His smile widened. This was too perfect. He couldn't believe his luck. A new family, with one daughter primed and ready for him and a younger one to watch grow.

"So what do you do, short stuff?" He turned and addressed Avis in just the right tone—teasing, yet avuncular.

"Nothing much." She looked down at her cheap Kmart sneakers, uncomfortable under the scrutiny of her father's new boss.

"Oh, come on. You must do something." Giving Earl and his wife a conspiratorial wink, he knelt down to her level. "Talk on the phone? Listen to music? Lie around and eat chocolates all day?"

Earl put a muscular arm around his daughter's shoulders. "Mostly Avis keeps her nose buried in a book," he told Deke. "But last summer she played a little softball."

"No kidding?" Deke grinned. "What position?"

"Third base," Avis whispered, finally lifting her eyes to look at the man who'd so improved her family's fortunes.

"Really? Well, gosh, the Keener Kats need a good third baseman. I don't suppose you'd be willing to play with us, would you? Of course, you'd have to put up with me, since I'm the coach...."

The girl giggled and turned to her father, not knowing what to say.

"I'm sure she'd love to," the mother broke in hastily, lest her daughter's bashfulness offend. "We were worried about her having a bad summer, not knowing anybody here. We figured she'd read herself blind."

"We have a great time on the softball team. After the season, I take all the girls on a trip. Myrtle Beach, Disney World, someplace like that." Deke stood up and returned his attention to the adults. "To me, Keener Construction is a big, extended family. We like to make our new members feel at home right away. Come on in the office. You can meet some of the guys and Linda, my secretary. She's the one who really runs things around here."

The Martins followed him across the parking lot and into the neat brick ranch house that served as headquarters for Keener Construction. They entered through the front door, into a living room that had been converted into a reception area.

"Hi, Deke." A young blond woman looked up from her computer. "The mayor's office has already called twice this morning, and John Thoman needs to talk to you about Acquoni Acres."

"I'll get back to them in a few minutes. Linda, this is Earl Martin and his wife Darlene. Earl's going to foreman the Tsali Trail job. I need to get them going on their house."

"Pleased to meet you." The blonde smiled, revealing deep dimples in both cheeks. "Welcome to Keener Construction."

The Martins nodded shyly, then followed Keener down a long hall, into his private office.

"Darlene, did Earl explain to you about the company houses?" Deke asked as he sat down behind a sprawling desk covered with blueprints.

Mrs. Martin shot her husband a nervous glance. "He said housing would be provided, as long as he worked on this job."

"Well, it's kind of like that." Deke pulled open his lap drawer. "I like to keep up with all the new stuff the industry comes out with. Test it all first in real-life environments, to see what's worth a damn." He fished a set of keys from the drawer. "To do that, I put a few of my more important employees in what I call test houses. We buy some acreage, put up a house, and have a family live there a year before we build any more in that development. We find out a lot about drainage and erosion and how much road maintenance we'll need in the winter."

"So you're out on a lot all by yourself?" Darlene Martin sounded hesitant.

"For a while. And you've also got to put up with us coming in and switching out fixtures and paint and carpeting and such." Deke smiled. "That's the downside. The upside is you get to live free in a brand-new home. At the end of a year, you can buy it from us at cost, or you can move somewhere else entirely. It's totally up to you."

The Martins looked at each other as if they'd washed up on a beach in paradise. "Why are you being so good to us?" Mrs. Martin finally asked. "Earl's never worked for anyone like you."

"Because I want to build the best houses in North Carolina, and I want the best people building them." He smiled at Avis, who was staring at Houdini, a chameleon he kept in a glass cage behind his desk. "And I also want to have the best softball team in the league this year."

"You can depend on me, Mr. Keener," said Earl Martin. "You won't regret the day you hired me."

"I have no doubt about that, Earl." Deke winked at Avis as he handed her father the keys to their new house. "No doubt at all."

Deke watched from the window as the Martins returned to their U-Haul. Avis had once again become all arms and legs, at one point running to jump on her dad's broad back. As Deke pictured her doing that to him in very different circumstances, the hum that had dwelt inside him ever since that night with Tracy Foster kicked into high gear. The notion of Earl Martin hurrying to snug his two daughters into a test house to which he had a key made him laugh. People were such fools. Did they not realize that there's a string attached to everything? You might not see it right off the bat, but it's always there. "And somebody just like me will come along and yank it, every time."

He spent the morning returning his phone calls and meeting with a real estate agent who was trying to broker an out-of-state deal. At noon he left his office to drive downtown for the weekly Rotary Club lunch. Though he found Rotary about as exciting as a horseshoe tournament, he showed up every week, regular as clockwork. He liked to keep an eye on things in town.

He found a parking space in front of the Baptist Church, dug his small gold Rotary pin out of the ashtray, and stuck it in his lapel. Dodging a cement mixer that lumbered down Main Street, he walked over to Layla's restaurant, where the usual crew of Rotarians was gathering in the private dining room at the back. Deke couldn't remember who was scheduled to speak today, but he hoped it would be somebody zippier than the ass-numbing preacher who'd held forth on the moral challenges of Pisgah County at the last meeting.

"Hey, Deke, how's it going?" His old Scout mate Randy Bradley, now the local Ford dealer, waved as he entered the dining room.

"Great!" Deke slapped Randy on the back, smelling the whiskey already on the man's breath. By the time they had reached high school, Randy was sipping moonshine from the back of his pickup. As his taste and income had grown, he now kept a pint of Maker's Mark in the glove box of his Lincoln, augmented by a full case of the stuff stashed in the trunk.

"You wanna play golf with Butch Messer this afternoon?"

Deke shook his head. "Some other time, Randy. I've got softball practice."

"The girls or the men?"

"The girls," he replied, the memory of Avis Martin's rosebud breasts sending a twinge of desire rippling through him.

Bradley snorted. "I don't know why you waste your time, Deke. Them girls ain't even fun to watch. They can't hit, they can't field, and they're too little to have anything jiggle when they run."

"I don't know about that, Randy," Lester Mathis chimed in. "Couple of Deke's older girls jiggle plenty when they run."

Deke was about to respond when another former Scout walked up. Though Jerry Cochran had outgrown his girlish voice, conquered his fear of the woods, and now, amazingly, wore a badge as the newly elected sheriff, Deke still considered him a fool and wondered what in the hell Tracy Foster had ever seen in him.

"Hey, guys, guess who I saw today?"

"Who'd you see, Cockroach?" Randy Bradley now cozied up to the new sheriff by using his old Scout nickname. If Cochran took offense, he never showed it. Mostly he just looked at Bradley as if he were a gnat—annoying, but hardly worth the effort of a swat.

Cochran smiled. "Deke's old nemesis. Mary Crow."

"Mary Crow?" Deke turned, remembering the Cherokee girl he'd never been able to beat in debate. "Are you sure?"

Cochran nodded. "Saw her going into George Turpin's office."

"But I thought she was a big-time DA in Atlanta. That's what they said when she took Logan down."

"Well, she may be, but she was up at the courthouse today, and looking like she meant business. Black suit, black briefcase, legs that stretched from here to Jesus." Cochran raised one eyebrow appreciatively.

"Man, she was hot back in high school." Floyd Nations shook his balding head. "Where was she when I needed a date for the prom?"

"She was with Jonathan Walkingstick, Floyd," Deke reminded him.

"While you were beating your meat in the boys' room!" Randy Bradley bellowed, red-faced, howling with laughter. While the other men hooted at Bradley's joke, Deke noticed that Cochran just lowered his eyes and smiled.

They went into the dining room and sat down at the long table. Sims Buchanan tapped on his glass, bringing the meeting to order. Though

Deke managed to pay attention through the minutes and the treasurer's report, for the rest of the meeting (an earnest young computer geek, urging them to help bring the Internet to the hollers of Appalachia) he considered Mary Crow. She was the only woman he'd ever met who came close to being his intellectual equal. Gorgeous but reserved, she'd moved to Atlanta shortly after her mother died, and had gone to law school there. According to the local paper, she'd earned the nickname "Killer Crow" with a string of high profile convictions. So why was she up here talking with that fat fool Turpin?

The answer to that question came to him so quickly that he nearly choked on his strawberry pie. Mary Crow must be moving back home! She was a prosecutor—naturally she would join Turpin's team. He put his fork down as he remembered the girl's clever wit and persuasive tongue. What would he do if she came up here and got a whiff of his secret life? What would he do if Mary Crow spoiled all the plans he'd made for Avis Martin?

You can't let that happen, he told himself as the geek droned on about how hillbillies deserved a place in cyberspace as much as anybody in New York or California. All your life you've waited for another Tracy Foster. You simply cannot allow Mary Crow to come along and spoil it.

THREE

Two days later, Mary had visited every law office in Pisgah County. Shocked to find the ex-Atlanta DA sitting across their desks inquiring about a job, all the attorneys read her resume with interest, asked a number of encouraging questions, then politely turned her down.

"Your lack of noncriminal litigation bothers me." Marie Bolt, of Bolt and Hughes, shook her head, enormous gold earrings flashing like Spanish doubloons.

"You have no experience in tribal law." Pudgy-faced Orrie Taylor, vice-chief of the Eastern Cherokees, gave a regretful sigh. "I'd love to hire you, but I'm afraid you wouldn't do us much good."

"You've got a fine record, but I've already got two criminal litigators," growled old Ben Bryson, a man who'd argued in front of Irene Hannah many times. "Truth be told, I probably ought to let one of them go. Not that much crime goes on here, thank God."

Mary assured him that she could be up to speed on other areas of law in weeks, but his bristly brows drew down in a frown. "Once you get a taste for criminal prosecution you're spoiled for everything else," the old man declared, jamming a thick cigar in one corner of his mouth.

"Three months here and you'd be back in Atlanta, begging for your old job back."

Bryson's had been the last of ten legal firms and two Cherokee tribal government departments. After his rejection, Mary walked back out into the soupy June afternoon, needing to put some distance between her and the legal establishment of Pisgah County. She trudged down the street and headed to Bayberry's, a small café squeezed in beneath the bookstore. Collapsing at the corner table on an otherwise deserted patio, she ordered a glass of iced tea from a tall mountain flower of a girl who had roses in her cheeks, but a flicker of sadness in her green eyes.

Probably just her aching feet, Mary decided as she slipped off her pumps. Her hours of looking for work had left her with a painful blister on her left heel and a wrinkled blue suit that looked like she'd hiked the Appalachian Trail in it. She sighed. If Bayberry's had served anything stronger than fruit tea, she would have ordered two triples and rolled home drunk.

"No one wants you," she whispered, absently pulling a packet of saccharin from the collection of sweeteners on the table. "You don't know either North Carolina statutes or Indian law and you don't have a clue about figuring billable time." Though she remembered all her grandmother's adages about seeing something funny in any bad situation, the truth stung too sharply for her to see the silver lining in this particular cloud. Here she sat, Atlanta's great Killer Crow, turned down by every practicing attorney in her own hometown.

"And that's just the job scene," she muttered. "I can't wait to see what kind of reception I'll get at Jonathan's." She'd decided early on to reestablish herself in Hartsville before she made the drive to Little Jump Off. Experience had taught her that she needed a functioning home and a viable career to protect herself against the vagaries of her relationship with Jonathan Walkingstick. The last time she'd presented herself to him, he'd taken her in his arms, told her that he would always love her, but he was going to have a baby with Ruth Moon. The memory of that night still made her queasy.

"That's ancient history," she reminded herself. "Concentrate on the now."

Taking a pen from her purse, she began to make a list on a paper napkin. What she had, what she needed, and what she could do without. Though her bank account had not quite plummeted to zero, some major expenses were circling her little nest egg like hungry wolves. When she'd first returned to Irene's house and turned on the water, nothing but a rusty kind of slop oozed from the kitchen faucet. All the bathroom faucets produced the same thing, as did the washer connection. Puzzled, she'd called Irene's closest neighbor, Hugh Kavanagh. "That's a well gone dry, Mary girl," he pronounced, his Irish brogue thick. "You'll have to call Turnipseed."

"Turnipseed?" Mary wondered at the odd un-Cherokee name, but jotted down the number Hugh rattled off. An hour later, a rangy man with no front teeth pulled up in a rusted pickup. When she showed him what was dripping from her faucets, he confirmed Hugh's diagnosis.

"You'll have to find you a new well." He peered out the kitchen window, rubbing a hand over a grizzled chin as he surveyed her land. "Shouldn't be too hard, but you never can tell. . . ."

Though she would have preferred to have a job before making such a major expenditure, she needed a house with functional plumbing. So she'd hired, at a hundred dollars per diem, Mr. J. T. Turnipseed, well digger of note. Add to that Irene's leaky roof and a suspension bridge that needed a new foundation, and she knew she had some major financial hits headed her way.

"You've got to get some money coming in, kiddo," she whispered. "Otherwise Irene's pretty little house is going to fall down around your ears."

She wadded up her napkin and gazed at a honeysuckle vine that curled up a trellis beside the patio. The fragrance reminded her of a section of Lima where jasmine bloomed at night, and she wondered again if she hadn't lost her mind. She'd left an untroubled life with a wonderful man for a waterless house in a backwoods town that regarded her more like Typhoid Mary than Killer Crow. If she had any sense at all, she would book the next flight back to Lima. Gabe would be waiting. Gabe would be thrilled to have her back. But Gabe would also still be Gabe. Never Jonathan. Never the man who'd haunted all of her dreams and a good many of her waking moments ever since she'd left the States. No, this time she was going to see this through. This time she and Jonathan were either going to work it out or she was going to shake the Pisgah County dust from her shoes for good.

The waitress snapped her back to reality, putting a glass of tea and a plate of lacy cookies down in front of her.

"Sorry it took so long," she apologized. "We had to brew a fresh pot. I brought you some cookies to make up for it."

"Thanks." Mary smiled, noticing an unusual pendant hanging from the girl's neck. Intricately carved, it was a cluster of strawberries that curled delicately between her collarbones. "That's a lovely necklace."

"Thank you." The girl took it in her fingers. "My boyfriend carved it for me."

Mary looked closer. Strawberries were the traditional gift given when erring Cherokee males wanted to get back in their girlfriends' good graces. According to legend, the succulent, heart-shaped little berries could mollify the angriest woman. Never, though, had Mary seen anybody wearing them as jewelry. "Your boyfriend's very talented," she said. "Is he Cherokee?"

"Yes. He carves all sorts of things and sells them at the hardware store." The girl smiled shyly. As she turned to go back to the kitchen, Mary suddenly had an idea. If the waitress's Cherokee boyfriend was selling his wares in town, why couldn't she? She called the girl back.

"Say—do you happen to know if there's any office space for rent around here?"

"Office space?" The girl twisted her necklace, thinking. "There's an apartment for rent over the furniture store. And a whole building where the dry cleaners used to be."

Mary shook her head. "No, just an office. A couple of hundred square feet would do."

The girl's face brightened. "Try Main Street. There used to be some space over Sutton's Hardware. A friend of mine tried to rent a room there for his band to practice in, but the landlord freaked out about the noise."

"Do you know who this landlord is?"

"Some kind of therapist," the girl said quickly. "She's got an office up there, too."

"Thanks," Mary said. "Thanks a lot."

"No problem." The girl smiled, but Mary again saw that shadow of sadness cloud her startling green eyes.

Mary finished her tea, and left the girl a nice tip. Feeling a little more hopeful, she jammed her feet back in her shoes and headed down to Main Street. Just as the waitress said, between Sutton's Hardware and the bank stood a freshly painted white door with a brass nameplate beside it. The plate had space for four names, but only two were filled. One by a Dana Smithson Shope, licensed clinical psychologist, the other by something called Smoky Mountain Defenders. Okay, thought Mary as she opened the door and walked up a narrow flight of stairs. Here goes nothin'.

At the top of the steps, four doors opened onto a wide landing. The psychologist had the office directly in front of the stairs, while the Smoky Mountain Defenders were holed up behind the door to the right. Remembering what the waitress had told her, she walked over to the psychologist's door and knocked softly.

"Come in!" came the immediate reply.

Mary opened the door. A small woman with curly dark hair sat on a desk, her short tennis dress revealing tanned, well-toned thighs. Two tennis racquets leaned against the wall, next to a wire basket of practice balls.

"Hi," began Mary, noticing that the rest of the room looked rather like an enormous toy box. An array of stuffed animals was scattered among two huge dollhouses, along with a bookshelf crammed with brightly colored books, and a diminutive artist's easel in one sunny corner. "I understand you might have some office space available?"

"That depends." The woman lifted an eyebrow. "What kind of office are you looking for?"

Mary thought of J. T. Turnipseed, drilling a hundred bucks out of her bank account every day. "I guess inexpensive would be the operative word."

The woman laughed. "No, I mean what kind of business are you in?"

She gestured toward her toy box of an office. "I need to keep it quiet up here. I work with kids a lot, plus I do a bit of hypnotherapy."

"A law practice," Mary ventured, the words feeling foreign on her tongue.

The woman looked doubtful. "I don't know. I've done divorce counseling before. People cry, yell. Once a man said he was going to kill every lesbian in North Carolina, starting with me." She shook her head. "I don't think a law practice would work out."

"But I don't do divorces," said Mary.

"So what kind of law do you do?"

"I don't know." Mary felt her face grow red as the woman waited for a response. "I mean I'm not sure. I'm kind of waiting for a position to open up on the DA's staff. Until then, I thought I might open my own shop. Just do general legal work."

"Like what?"

Mary shrugged. "I don't know. Wills. House closings. Business incorporations. Quiet things. I promise."

The woman frowned at Mary a moment, then she stepped over to a bookshelf and fished a set of keys out of a green ceramic jar marked CARES AND WOES. "I'll show you the space, but I doubt you'll want it."

She led Mary across the landing, to the door next to the Smoky Mountain Defenders.

"The best you can say about this room is that it has a wonderful view," she explained as she fumbled with the key, then pushed the door open.

Mary stepped inside. The room had white stucco walls and wide plank floors, and was lit by a huge bay window that stretched almost floor to ceiling, allowing a panoramic view of the south side of Main Street. A single light fixture dangled from a thick cord in the middle of the twelve-foot ceiling, and though the room probably wouldn't have measured more than twelve by twelve, it had a spacious turn-of-the-century ambiance that brought to mind Model T Fords and Scott Joplin rags. Mary could almost picture Clarence Darrow in a room like this, filling his fountain pen, scribbling notes about how to save Leopold and Loeb from the electric chair.

"It's pretty small," the woman said. "It probably doesn't even have enough space for your books."

"Dana?" A deep male voice boomed into the room. "What's going on?"

Mary turned to see a man standing in the open doorway. Big and pot-bellied, he had gray hair that looked as if he'd combed it with an egg beater. Must be one of the Smoky Mountain Defenders, she thought, noting the standard uniform of Appalachian hippies—faded jeans, a flannel shirt, and nicely battered Merrell boots. This one even carried a walking stick, complete with a little bell on top to scare away bears.

"Hi, Sam." A note of exasperation crept into the psychologist's voice. "I'm showing this office. What can I do for you?"

"You're not renting this space are you?"

She crossed her arms. "I might be. Why?"

"Because I want it. I need it for storage."

She frowned. "Sam, we had this conversation three months ago. You opted out of the deal."

"I did not." The man aimed a withering glare at Mary. "I said I needed to think about it."

"You said my price was outrageous, Sam," said the psychologist.

"How much is it?" Mary interrupted, irked by the man's arrogance.

The woman shrugged. "I told Sam three hundred a month. I suppose I could do the same for you."

"Does that include utilities? Do I have to rent a parking space?"

"Parking's on your own. Utilities are included, plus Sylvia, the clerk from the hardware store downstairs, comes and cleans the landing and delivers our mail."

Mary pulled out her checkbook. "I'll take it."

"But Dana!" the man protested.

"Sorry, Sam." The psychologist held up one hand. "You told me three months ago that you definitely did not want this space. Now meet your new next-door neighbor. I think she might be an attorney."

"Hunnff!" With a single derisive snort, Sam stomped out, slamming the door so hard that a chip of plaster fell from the ceiling.

Mary blinked, stunned by the man's rudeness. "Is he always that friendly?"

The psychologist shrugged again, unperturbed. "That's just Ravenel. Beneath that gruff exterior beats the heart of a fascist pig, but Sam's basically harmless." She glanced at her watch. "Look, I've got to get going.

Shall we sign a lease now, or would you rather think about this overnight? I'm afraid Ravenel comes with the deal."

"I'd like to sign now, if you've got the time." Mary didn't want to risk
the Smoky Mountain Defender talking his way into here, overnight.

They recrossed the landing, returning to the office with the huge
dollhouses.

"So do you treat just kids?" Mary eyed a single long, adult-sized
leather couch.

"Mostly." The woman laughed. "Adult Pisgah Countians seem to regard psychotherapy right up there with witch doctoring and alien ab-
ductions." She rummaged through a drawer, then pulled out a preprinted
lease. "By the way—my name's Dana Shope."

"I'm Mary Crow."

"That's C-r-o-w-e, right?"

"C-r-o-w. No *e* on the end."

"Sorry." Dana crossed out the *e* she'd already written. "I figured you
were from the reservation." She looked at the lease and chuckled. "You
and Sam will make two birds up here, a Raven and a Crow."

"Lucky us," said Mary, without enthusiasm.

Dana filled out the rest of the lease and handed Mary a pen. "Want to
try six months at first, just to see how things work out?"

"Suits me." Mary nodded.

With the exception of the crossed-out *e* at the end of her name, Dana
had filled out everything else in a neat, almost calligraphic hand. Quickly,
Mary read it through twice, then signed it and wrote out a check for
three hundred dollars.

"I really appreciate this." Mary smiled. "I know I kind of twisted your
arm."

"Oh, that's okay," replied Dana cheerfully. "Most of the lawyers keep
to that little tight-ass legal ghetto next to the courthouse. It'll be fun to
have a renegade in the building. You don't happen to play tennis, do
you?"

"A little. But when I grew up here, the nearest courts were over at
the college, in Cullowhee."

"They built two here, last year, behind the high school. They're small and unlit, but they've begun to stock balls and racquets at the hardware store next door. If you ever want to play, give me a call."

"Sure." Mary smiled. "I'd like that."

"Great." Dana grabbed her racquets and headed out the door. "Well, it's been a pleasure, Mary. I'll look forward to having you up here."

"Me, too." Mary watched as Dana hurried down the stairs, then she walked across the landing to survey her new domain. She would need a telephone and a desk, and a couple of chairs for people to sit in, but she might be able to scrounge most of that from Irene's attic. She sighed. Though it wasn't the legal career she'd hoped for, she'd at least gotten herself a base of operations. Now all she had to do was figure out what kind of law to practice and how to get some clients coming in the door.

FOUR

Deke Keener sat on a bench beneath the magnolia tree that bloomed in the front yard of the Baptist Church. Overstuffed with food and camaraderie from the Chamber of Commerce's Beautification Committee luncheon, he was supposed to be taking a walking tour of downtown Hartsville to decide which of the city's trees might need the attention of Sean Doak, their resident arborist. He'd checked the big basswood in front of the bank and the two tulip trees that shaded the front of the funeral home, but when he'd come to First Baptist's magnolia, he'd stopped. The old tree was just beginning to bloom—creamy white blossoms were scenting the air with a heady Southern sweetness that took him back to the summer when he was four.

"Yours is funny-looking! Let me see it up close." Vivian is her name. She is five, visiting from next door. They are playing in his bedroom, with the door shut.

"Only if I can see yours, too." He balks, unwilling to have Vivian boss him around his own house.

"Okay. Come lie down on the bed."

He hops over, his underpants down around his ankles, and stretches out next to her. She still wears her shorts; a green Scooby Doo bandage covers a scrape on her left knee.

"It looks like a little hot dog." She looks at his penis more closely than he himself ever has, then tugs it, as if it were a rubber band. "Does that hurt?"

It does, but he would die before he'd admit that to Vivian. He squirms away from her. "Let me see yours."

He watches, eyes wide, as she wiggles out of her underpants. His heart sinks. She's got nothing to see! Just a slit, as if her butt had cracked far more seriously than normal. He is shocked. He expected a grander version of his own equipment, just the way his mother's full bouncy breasts exaggerated his father's flat chest.

"Where is it?"

"It's inside," Vivian says, as if he's stupid. Hers looks like nothing he's ever seen before—a shriveled little thing that smells like something rotten.

That's it?" he asks, incredulous.

"Yes," she replies, as if he's hopelessly stupid. "Men kiss women down there. I've seen my parents do it."

He stares at it, unable to imagine his mother having one of these, much less his father kissing it.

"Kiss me there, Deke."

"No way!" He is repulsed—her thing reminds him of the tiny end of a slimy asparagus spear his mother once insisted that he eat.

"Go on! I dare you! I double dare you!"

Though the idea makes him want to vomit, his honor is on the line. He leans over and touches her with his tongue. He hears her giggle, then he jumps as someone opens his door.

"What the hell are you two doing?"

He leaps off the bed, sick with fear. His father's brother, his mean uncle Mark, stands there. Mark's home from college, sharing his room for the summer. He points at them and starts laughing. "Look at little Deke! No! Little Dick! Hahahahaha!" His laughter fills the room, the house, the whole world. Soon his mother will come in here and catch them with their pants down. She will spank him for sure, right here in front of Vivian. He drops to the floor, humiliated, scrambling for his shorts, but Mark grabs him and throws him back on the bed. Vivian is terrified, just staring at Mark, not even trying to cover herself. "Since you two are so curious, I'm gonna give you an anatomy lesson." Mark's unzipping his pants. "I'm gonna show you how grownups really do it."

"Coach Keener? Are you okay?"

He opened his eyes. Kayla Daws, a chunky, tomboyish eleven-year-old, stood beside him. She wore shorts and a pink Keener Kats T-shirt, and a look of alarm on her freckled face. He was sweating—the memory of that long-ago day still made his stomach churn. Breathing hard, he held up his hand for a congenial Keener Kats slap, hoping Kayla wouldn't notice the clamminess of his palm. The little girl's small hand banged against his like a bird flying into a pane of glass.

"Hey, Kayla," he said. "What brings you downtown?"

"I had to go to the dentist," Kayla reported, holding up a clear plastic bag that contained a complimentary toothbrush and a small tube of toothpaste. "Got my teeth cleaned."

"Let me see." Deke cupped her chin while she displayed all her teeth to brilliant advantage. He gazed at them with exaggerated scrutiny, peering this way and that, slyly pressing his forearm against the girl's developing breasts. Never would she be as compelling as her sister. Thick-boned where Bethany was slender, brown-haired where she was blond, Kayla was twice the ball player Bethany had been, but none of the junior-high vixen. He'd pictured himself with her a thousand times and never had he felt the slightest twinge of desire. He'd hoped to work his way from sibling to sibling, but the chemistry was just not there. For him, Kayla Daws held as little interest as a full-grown woman. "Man, those choppers are so bright I'm having to squint," he finally told her. "Did you have any cavities?"

"Nope!" said Kayla, dancing backward. "Now I don't have to go back until December."

"Your folks are going to be real proud. Cavities are expensive." Deke held up his hand for another slap, wishing that Kayla looked just a little like her sister Bethany. "I think an accomplishment like that deserves a reward. May I buy you an ice cream?"

Kayla grinned. As always, her smile was too bright, too easily given. "Sure!"

He stood and put an arm around her shoulders. Together they crossed Main Street and walked over to the Dairy Dip that operated March through November. Business had been brisk today, with lots of little girls lining up for chocolate-dipped cones and banana splits. Watching all those long little legs and tight little asses was one of his favorite pastimes.

"What'll it be, Kayla?" he asked when they reached the window.

"A hot fudge sundae?" She looked up at him, coy.

"Absolutely." Deke turned to the boy behind the counter.

A few minutes later, they strolled down Main Street, spooning hot fudge into their mouths. Other kids passed them like a line of ants, ogling Kayla's treat with open envy.

"So what are you up to the rest of this afternoon?" asked Deke.

"I'm supposed to meet Bethany at Bayberry's and wait for Mom to pick us up." Kayla licked chocolate off her plastic spoon.

"I thought Bethany went out with her boyfriend after work."

"No, they broke up."

"Really? How come?" Deke leaned closer. This was a new wrinkle in the Daws' tortuous family saga, though he'd warned Glenn Daws about letting his rebellious daughter spend so much time with that young Cherokee buck. "I know how Bethany has made your lives hell already," he'd told Glenn as they'd played the back nine at Wolf Crossing. "If you let her start bringing a steady boyfriend home, you're just going to double your misery."

"Think so?" Big dumb Glenn had looked at him with the same trust he'd first seen years ago, when he'd hired the guy off the unemployment line in Charlotte.

"Trust me on this one, buddy." Deke had slapped his back before he teed up his ball. "You're too close to see it. If I were you, I'd nip this little romance in the bud."

Apparently, Glenn had done exactly as Deke had suggested.

"Daddy told Ridge not to come around anymore," Kayla was saying as she scraped hot fudge from her ice cream. "Bethany got real mad. Started calling Mom and Dad terrible names. Then she locked herself in her room."

"Sounds bad," Deke commiserated, marveling at how easily he led Glenn Daws around by the nose.

"It was awful," agreed Kayla. "Mom started yelling back at her, telling her how she'd made us all miserable for the last six years and how we were just counting the days before she went to college."

"Is that true?"

"It is for Mom and Dad. I'll miss her, even though all she ever tells me is 'stay away from this' and 'stay away from that.' "

His ears pricked as he struggled to keep his voice neutral. "So what does she want you to stay away from?"

"Everything fun. The softball team, mostly."

"Gosh, I hope you don't do that. I've got big plans for you."

"You do?"

"I sure do." Deke tested Kayla's bottom with three quick, exploratory pats. Still nothing, he noted with disappointment. He and Kayla were simply not meant to be. "I was thinking of moving you off third base. Maybe letting you pitch."

"Really? Cool!"

The two walked on, crossing the street, strolling toward Bayberry's as if by some tacit accord. When they reached the café, they stepped inside the cool, dim dining room. Bethany stood in the far corner with her back to them, rolling setups for the dinner shift. His heart bumped just as always. Bethany Daws, Kayla's sister, was still the most beautiful thing he'd ever seen, and of all the little girls he'd played with, she'd been the only one who'd held his interest past puberty. He had loved her as her breasts swelled; loved her as her hips widened, loved her as coarse dark hair began to hide her charms from him. He kept waiting for the gamier smells of estrus and menstruation to render her repulsive, but in six years, it hadn't happened. He still wanted her just as much as he always had, despite the fact that Bethany regarded him as she would a tarantula. Putting a finger to his lips, he winked at Kayla, and crept up behind her sister.

"Boo!" he cried, lightly poking her in the ribs. "Whatcha doing?"

Bethany gave a little yelp, sending a knife and spoon clattering to the floor. She whirled around, excited, as if she hoped to find her boyfriend Ridge standing there. When she saw her old softball coach instead, her green eyes narrowed.

"What are you doing here?"

"I bought Kayla an ice cream." He smiled. "She got a good report at the dentist's."

"Strange way to celebrate no cavities," Bethany retorted darkly, stooping to retrieve the silverware off the floor.

Deke admired the curve of her hips in her tight waitress uniform. "We can celebrate something else if you'd like. How about I buy you an ice cream for breaking up with your boyfriend?"

Rising, she regarded him as if he were a bug, then tossed the silverware in the dirty dish tub. "I'm done here," she told Kayla. "Go on outside and wait for Mom while I clock out."

"Here." Deke flipped out his cell phone. "Call your mother. Tell her I'll give you a ride."

"In your new SUV?" squealed Kayla.

"It's the only car I've got, sugar."

Kayla grabbed the cell phone and punched in her mother's number.

"Stop, Kayla!" Bethany lunged for the phone. "Don't call—"

"I am, too." Kayla danced away from her sister's grasp. "Who wants to wait for Mom when we can ride in Coach Keener's Lexus?"

As the younger girl spun out the door, Deke gave Bethany a helpless smile. "Sorry. Looks like you're stuck with me."

Bethany started to say something, but then the look he loved so much skittered briefly across her face. For an instant she looked like a trapped little animal who'd thought she'd escaped, only to realize there was no escape. Not now. Not ever.

"Whatever," she muttered bitterly, pulling off her apron.

She disappeared into the kitchen to punch her time card. A moment later she returned with the little calico bag she used as a purse. Following her out into the bright afternoon, he handed Kayla his remote and they walked to his car like a line of discordant ducks—Kayla leading the way, trying to affect the casual sangfroid of girls who rode in sixty-thousand-dollar automobiles every day. Bethany followed, her back stiff, her eyes straight ahead. Deke sauntered along last, hands in his pockets, smiling at the wiggle of Bethany's butt. As they approached his car, Kayla punched the remote and ran the Lexus through all its tricks—lowering windows, beeping alarms, automatically unlocking the doors. When the car's taillights began to wink, Kayla broke into a run, her grown-up pretensions forgotten.

"Shotgun!" she shrieked, then turned to Deke. "Can I ride in the front?"

"Sure," he said.

"No!" Bethany countermanded. "You ride in the back."

"But I called shotgun first. And he said I could—"

"I said ride in the back!" Bethany grabbed her little sister roughly by the arm and opened the rear passenger door. "And don't mess anything up back there."

"Ow!" said Kayla. "You're hurting me!" She wrenched free of Bethany's grasp, then flounced angrily into the backseat. Bethany flashed Deke a little smirk of triumph as she climbed into the front seat beside him; Deke winked back in return.

They roared out of town on Main Street. Bethany sat staring straight ahead, her face expressionless, while Kayla rode in the back busy as a pet raccoon, punching buttons, trying to play the DVD. Deke drove fast, just to remind Bethany who had the power in this car.

"You okay back there, Kayla?" he asked after they'd screeched around a hairpin turn.

"That was so cool!" exclaimed the girl. "Do it again!"

So he did it again, and again. Finally, after a twenty-minute joyride that felt like a downhill slalom, they pulled up in the Daws' driveway, greeted by Darby, their tail-wagging golden Lab.

"Awesome!" Kayla gushed. "That was the best ride I've ever had!"

"Glad you enjoyed it," said Deke. "See you at practice tonight, okay?"

"Okay." Kayla scrambled out of the backseat and ran toward the house, opening the garage door to reveal Paula Daws' white Subaru station wagon.

"Uh-oh." Deke turned to Bethany, his brows drawn with ersatz concern. "Looks like your Mom's home. Should I go in with you? Keep her from yelling at you?"

"Why do you think she'd yell at me?"

"I hear that's about all she does these days," he replied. "When she's not counting the minutes till you leave for college."

"She's a bitch and my dad's a coward." Bethany's words were laced with acid. "And you're the biggest cocksucker of all."

"Bethany." He reached over and patted her thigh. "You shouldn't use such language."

"Oh, really?" She jerked open the car door. "Does it offend you?"

"It's unbecoming. Young ladies shouldn't say things like that."

"I can think of a few other things that young ladies shouldn't do," she said bitterly. She climbed out of the car, then turned back to him. "Look, you son of a bitch. I know what you're up to, and you'd just damn well better stop."

"What do you mean?"

"You know exactly what I mean."

He grinned at her. He knew it was mean to bait her, but sometimes he just couldn't resist. He loved it when her eyes flashed that hot, angry green. "So tell me—I'm confused."

"Kayla," she cried, tearing up. "You try any of your shit with her and I'll tell *everybody* about what's been going on between us! I swear I will! And this time, I won't care if you fire my dad and throw us out of this stupid house."

He leaned against the headrest and started to laugh. "Bethany, don't you know that you can't fuck somebody for six years and then cry rape? Why don't you just admit to yourself that you enjoyed everything we did together? I can still hear you—oh, Coach Keener!" he mocked her in a high falsetto.

"Oh, yeah? Well, I can still hear you, too!" With a fierce look of triumph, Bethany dug in her calico bag. A moment later she pulled out a tape cassette no bigger than a soda cracker. Keener felt his heart stop.

"You know how many of these I've got? You want to guess whose voice is on them, big-time?"

For the first time in his life he couldn't speak, couldn't force his lips and tongue to form words.

"*You,* you stupid jackass! Before I leave for college, you'd better believe that a lot more people than just me are going to hear all about what you've made me do!"

Suddenly he heard someone calling his name. He turned to see Paula Daws smiling, walking toward him from the garage, her left hand shielding her eyes from the bright sun. His frozen brain thawed. Quickly he turned and gave Bethany the look that had never failed to silence all who had ever considered exposing him. "Girlie, you don't want to mess with me. You really, really don't."

For a moment that trapped animal look again flashed across her face, then she slammed the car door shut. He watched as she stormed up the driveway and into the garage, passing her mother without as much as a nod.

"Hi, Deke!" Paula called as she neared his car, so inured to her daughter's fury that it affected her no more than a passing cloud. "Thanks for bringing them home."

"Glad to do it," he replied cheerily, though his voice was tremulous as an old man's. His hands and legs were shaking. He knew he couldn't stay here and chat with Paula Daws. He needed to get away; to go off somewhere by himself and think this tape thing through. "I've got to be going now," he called as he shoved his car into reverse. "Got some plans to look over!"

"So we'll see you at ball practice tonight?" Paula had a wide cheerleader grin that most girls left behind in college.

"Sure will!" He smiled, then with a single wave, started to back out of the driveway. When he finally pulled into the street, he headed straight home, driving as if in a dream, tossed from his Promethean height by a simple girl with a tape recorder, the taste of fear strange and raw in the back of his throat.

FIVE

S o what do you think of my girl?"

Mary Crow watched as the horse loped by. Small by equine standards, she was otter-brown and shiny, with a mane and tail that rippled like silk as she ran. The offspring of Irene Hannah's mare Lady Jane, Cushla McCree had been born the day before Irene died and had lived all but the first few hours of her life here, on Hugh Kavanagh's farm.

"She's beautiful," Mary told Hugh, remembering her as a wobbly, spindle-legged foal. "She's grown up fast."

"Aye, that she has." The old Irishman stood beside her, leaning against the fence. Though his brogue was still thick as oatmeal, he seemed smaller than he had two years ago, as if the loss of Irene had shrunk him. No longer was he the robust horseman who Mary had once interrupted in a moment of passion with her mentor. "She's come along well. I think Irene would be pleased."

"Irene would be thrilled," said Mary, admiring the horse as she sped by. What Mary found almost as impressive as Cushla McCree was the young man riding her. Not only was he riding bareback, in nothing but a pair of cutoff jeans, but he wore his hair in the manner of an eighteenth-century Cherokee: his scalp was totally shaved, except for a single long ponytail that flowed from the crown of his head. Even more curious was the fact that the young man rode like a Commanche. Unlike the Plains Indians, most Eastern Cherokees had affinity only for Mustangs built by Ford. Never had she known any sober person from the Qualla Boundary to jump willingly on the back of anything with four legs. "Who's the rider?"

"Ridge Standingdeer," said Hugh. "He came round looking for work last summer. I'd had a spill off my ladder, so I took him on. He's lived here ever since." The old man leaned closer. "He's an Anti-Galosha," he added in a whisper.

Mary frowned. "An Anti-Galosha?"

"You know, one of the Bear people. They live in the woods and talk to animals."

Mary puzzled a moment, then she realized what Hugh was trying to say. "You mean an Ani Zaguhi?"

"Aye, that's it! Ani Zaguhi!"

Mary laughed, recalling her childhood tales about the legendary group of Cherokees who long ago abandoned village life to live deep in the mountains, by themselves. As the centuries passed, they learned how to divine the future, vanish at will, and converse with bears. Though generally regarded as powerful avengers who made certain their village-bound brothers had plenty of game to hunt, the Ani Zaguhi could also work mischief, if it suited them. *"Watch out for the Bear people tonight,"* Jonathan's Aunt Little Tom used to warn them every Halloween. *"They'll come down from the mountains and change you into skunks, just for fun!"*

"The boy's pulling your leg, Hugh," Mary told him. "The Ani Zaguhi are a myth. Like leprechauns."

Hugh laughed, but wagged an admonishing finger at her. "Don't be calling leprechauns a myth around here, Mary Crow! You'll bring down a curse."

As the boy rode by again, Mary looked at him more closely. Though he was Cherokee handsome, with dark eyes, high cheekbones, and a generous mouth, what was odd about his face was that he looked so at ease on Cushla's back that he seemed to have become part of the horse himself. "How did this boy wind up here, on your farm?"

"Walked into town with his brother from somewhere high up in the mountains. They brought carvings to sell. Ridge ran into Bethany Daws at the hardware store and took such a fancy to her that he decided to stay. Sent his brother back alone to break the news to his family. It's the scandal of all Hartsville. Every time I go to town, all they want to hear about is the Bear boy. The girls at the bank, the chaps at the feed store. It's like havin' a movie star bunking in yer barn."

Mary watched horse and rider glide around the paddock like a singular creation, one body flowing seamlessly into the other. "It seems to me if he were Ani Zaguhi, he'd be having conversations with Cushla McCree, instead of riding around on her back."

Hugh shrugged. "Well, Bear man or no, he's a good lad and doesn't mind putting his shoulder to the wheel. I couldn't have made it through last winter without him."

"Hugh!" The young man's voice rang out from the middle of the paddock. "Want to see my Indian trick?"

"Let's have it, boyo!" called Hugh.

Grinning, the boy turned the little mare in a tight circle, then began galloping clockwise around the ring. At first he rode normally, on top of the horse, but when he reached a point directly opposite Hugh and Mary, he slid down and clung to Cushla's side. Mary winced, expecting him to tumble painfully to the ground, but there he remained, clinging effortlessly to Cushla as she loped around the paddock. When the pair flew by, she saw the boy grinning at them from beneath the horse's neck.

"Bang!" he called, pointing his finger like a gun. "You're dead!"

Hugh roared with laughter. "Ridge, you're every bit the cowboy John Wayne was. Now cool her down and come join us for dinner."

The boy waved in acknowledgment, then righted himself on Cushla's back and jumped her over a low part of the paddock fence, lifting both arms to the sky as they flew through the air.

"Good grief!" cried Mary. "Where did he learn to ride?"

Hugh shook his head. "He'd never seen a horse before he came here, but he does well at everything he tries. Look at what he made me." He held up his cane. A horse's head had been carved into the handle—its nose forming the end of the cane, backswept ears and flying mane blending into the shaft.

"It's beautiful," Mary said, remembering that the Ani Zaguhi were reputedly great weavers and carvers. "What did you say his name was?"

"Ridge Standingdeer. The Bear boy."

A little while later, Mary met the Bear boy in person. She was standing in Hugh's dark-paneled dining room, fishing out three dinner plates from a sideboard filled with horse show silver, when Hugh appeared in the doorway.

"Mary, meet your kinsman, Ridge Standingdeer."

Ridge stepped into the room. Though he'd put on jeans and a white dress shirt for dinner, his clothes could not hide the muscularity of his shoulders, or the old Cherokee symbols tattooed on his forearms. A beaded belt laced through his jeans while a gold nugget studded his left earlobe. In spite of his trendy attire, there was an air of antiquity about the young man's demeanor, and Mary felt as if some time machine had scooped up an ancient Tsalagi warrior and plopped him down in Hugh Kavanagh's dining room.

Remembering all of Aunt Little Tom's fervent admonitions about the Ani Zaguhi, Mary greeted the boy formally, in Cherokee. *"Sheoh. Ahyole deza?"*

"Osta giyalo zadanzo." He gave a deep nod of his head, regarding her with an intensity that bordered on rudeness. His dark eyes drank in her heart, body, and soul in one long draught.

"Hadluh hinel?" Mary stood a bit straighter and asked him where he lived, curious to hear his reply.

At that, he unloosed a torrent of words, as if hungry to converse with someone in his own language. Though most of them spilled out too fast for her to translate, she did manage to pick out "Ziyahi," the old Cherokee name for the little mountain town of Cheowa. Hell, she thought as the boy gushed on, maybe he is Ani Zaguhi. Usually only the most elderly Cherokees could speak the old language with such fluency.

When he stopped talking to draw breath, Mary held up both hands. "Whoa, Ridge. We're going to have to switch to English. You've come to the very end of my Cherokee."

"I have?" His dark brows lifted in surprise.

She nodded. "I haven't lived up here in a long time."

"Okay." He gave the slightest shrug.

"Where did you learn to ride like that?" she asked, certain he would say Tryon or maybe Aiken, South Carolina, nearby towns famous for horse shows and steeplechases.

"I saw it on TV."

"TV?"

"They showed a Western movie festival last New Year's," Hugh chimed in from the kitchen. "Ridge watched the Apaches circle some wagon train. He wanted to give it a try."

"You learn fast," Mary told the boy, impressed in spite of herself. "So what else do you do?"

"I help Hugh," he replied simply. "And I carve things."

"Hugh showed me his cane." Mary noticed that the boy spoke English with a halting rhythm, as if it were a language he knew but seldom used. "It's beautiful."

Ridge smiled, revealing straight, white teeth. "Hugh's taught me a lot. I wanted to give something back."

"Then give me a hand with this, boy," Hugh called, tottering in from the kitchen with a silver tray of beautifully poached salmon. Ridge moved forward to take the tray from the old man's shaky grasp. "Specialty of the house, though I haven't cooked it much lately."

Ridge set the salmon in the middle of Hugh's long mahogany table. While Mary served their plates, Hugh poured the wine, lifting a glass to Irene's memory. As they drank, Mary thought with a pang how much the transplanted Irishman had aged. Though indoors he navigated without his cane, she'd noticed a row of pill bottles lined up like tiny soldiers in his kitchen window.

"Garbage, the lot of 'em," he'd told her. "My doctor doesn't even shave yet. Couldn't tell his arse from his elbow."

"But Hugh, this is nitroglycerin," Mary said, reading one label. "This is heart medicine."

"It's for indigestion." He grabbed the bottle from her hand. "Nothing's wrong with my heart."

But despite the glow from the candles and ruddiness that the wine put back into his cheeks, she could tell that there was a lot wrong with Hugh's heart. She imagined that it had less to do with cholesterol and hypertension and much more with missing his lost Irene.

They feasted on salmon and fried green tomatoes, while birds serenaded them through the long June twilight. Occasionally interrupted by a whinny from the back pasture, Mary told the two men about her disastrous job search, and her rash decision to open a practice of her own.

"Good for you, girl." Hugh gave her a feisty nod. "Set out yer own shingle. Say to hell with the lot of 'em."

"I still hope to get on Turpin's staff," she replied. "But this might work out in the meantime. I rented a small office downtown today. I figure I can furnish it with Irene's law books and some furniture from her attic."

"Where will this office be?" asked Hugh.

"Over Sutton's hardware store. I'm in with a psychologist and some kind of environmental activist." She thought of fat, pompous Sam Ravenel and shuddered inwardly.

"I know that place." Ridge abruptly joined the conversation. "I see people going up there, when I go visit Sylvia."

Mary was puzzled. She thought Hugh had said Ridge's great inamorata was someone named Bethany. "Who's Sylvia?"

"She works at the hardware store," the boy explained. "She buys my things."

Hugh served them both a second slab of salmon. "So when would you be opening for business, Mary girl?"

"As soon as possible. In fact, I was going to ask if might borrow your truck tomorrow."

"Of course. Take Ridge as well, if you'd like." Hugh glanced a bit enviously at the boy who sat intent upon his supper. "That young back's yet to know a mustard plaster."

Mary turned to him. "Ridge, would you help me lug some furniture up a long flight of stairs? I'd be happy to pay you."

"Sure, if Hugh doesn't need me."

Suddenly the doorbell rang. Ridge jumped up from the table. "I'll get it," he said. "I think I know who it is."

"I think I do, too." Hugh looked at Mary as the boy hurried to the front door.

"Who?"

"The lass he fancies," Hugh whispered. "She comes by most every night."

Ridge returned to the dining room, pulling a tall, blond girl dressed in pink shorts behind him.

"This is Bethany." Ridge looked at the girl as if she were an angel, dropped from a low-flying cloud.

"I know." Mary smiled. "We've met." Ridge's Bethany was the waitress with the strawberry necklace.

"You have?" said Hugh.

"Just this afternoon. At Bayberry's." Mary turned to Bethany. "It's nice to see you again."

"Thank you." The girl smiled politely, but Mary noticed that the shadowy sadness that had earlier lurked behind her eyes was tonight even more pronounced, giving her an edgy, haunted look.

Ridge turned to Hugh. "Do you need me for anything more?"

"Not if Mary'll help me clean up in the kitchen."

"Of course I will," Mary replied.

"Then I guess we'll go." Ridge tugged Bethany toward the front door.

"You two have fun." Mary wondered for another moment about the girl's obvious distress, then put it out of her mind. Bethany had a beautiful summer night and a handsome young man to enjoy it with—that would no doubt cure whatever ailed her.

She and Hugh sat at the table as two doors slammed, and a small truck engine roared to life. Gravel crunched in the driveway, then the noise faded away, leaving them in a silence that seemed to underscore the emptiness of their own lives. They sat lost in their own memories, until Hugh gave a great sigh.

"God forgive an old man his foolishness, but sometimes when I see those two together, I miss Irene almost more than I can bear."

"I know what you mean," Mary replied, wondering what Jonathan was doing now and if he ever gave any thought to her at all.

SIX

Bethany sped down Hugh Kavanagh's driveway, eager to escape the social pleasantries of the old man and his dinner guest. Though they seemed nice enough, her encounter that day with Coach Keener had left her both infuriated and terrified, in no frame of mind to chitchat about the weather or her job at Bayberry's. After she'd gotten out of Keener's stupid SUV, she'd slammed inside their house, screaming at her little sister that she must never ride with Coach Keener again. Kayla had thrown her own fit, accusing Bethany of not wanting her to ever have any fun of her own. Then her mother had joined the fray, asking how dare she be so rude to Deke Keener, who by giving them a ride home had saved her a lot of time and a trip to town. Where exactly did Bethany get off, acting so ugly? Nobody (her, her father, Deke Keener, the rest of the known universe) had ever been anything other than kind and generous to her, and look at how she repaid them. She was an embarrassment to the whole family and once she got to college she was going to find out real fast that she wasn't the only pretty girl in the world and that people weren't going to put up with her little prima donna act and if she, Paula Jane Daws, had acted like that to her father's boss her father would have ...

Your father would not have allowed his boss to fuck you, Mom, she'd screamed silently as she slammed her bedroom door in her mother's snarling face. She threw herself on her bed, weeping with frustration. She was not a prima donna! She was not rude! She was just trying to protect her little sister from something that her father had refused to be-lieve was happening! Now she'd blown everything—what had she been thinking of, threatening the master of threats with one of her own tapes? Had she totally lost it?

She lay on the bed a long time, alternately crying and trying to figure out what to do. The house sat cold and silent as an ice cube, but soon she heard her father's truck pull into the driveway. She waited, her hands clenching the bedspread, to see if her mother would send him up here to bitch her out further, but a few moments later she heard the back door close and their voices outside, below her window. Kayla asked her mother if she could go home with Jeannette Peacock after the game, her father muttered something about needing more beer. Then an engine started. She got up from the bed in time to see the three of them driving away in her mother's car, hurrying to Kayla's softball game.

At that point she'd flung open her door, raced downstairs, grabbed the keys to her father's truck, and driven straight to Mr. Kavanagh's farm. She didn't give a shit anymore if her parents caught her sneaking out. Ridge was the only person in the world who truly cared about her. And tonight, she needed him badly.

"So who is that Mary woman?" She turned to him now in the hope that the balm of everyday conversation might lessen her terror at con-fronting Keener.

"She's an old friend of Hugh's." Ridge's hand was warm on the back of her neck. Always, he knew how and how not to touch her. "She's a lawyer."

"A lawyer?" she asked, surprised.

"She rented an office over Sylvia's store. I'm supposed to help her move in tomorrow morning."

"A lawyer." Bethany repeated the words as if they were some se-cret incantation that might make the whole sodden mess of her life disap-pear. Though she'd considered visiting a lawyer after she got her driver's license, she'd never gotten up the nerve to call one. She'd pictured them all as frowning, parchment-faced men in dark suits. She couldn't even imagine making an appointment with one of their secretaries, much less sitting down across from one and telling what Deke Keener had done to her. This Mary Crow, though, seemed different. She acted friendly, had left her a big tip at the café. Plus, she hadn't been in town long enough for Keener to schmooze her. Wonder what Mary Crow would say if she played her some of her tapes?

With her brain spinning at the possibility of a courtroom, a trial, of jurors finding Keener guilty and a judge sentencing him to death, she drove full-speed along the country road. The honey-colored twilight lingered, and the sweet aroma of hay and new-mown grass filled the car. She glanced over at Ridge. He rode with his eyes shut, his face turned to the breeze, as if gleaning aromas from the air. How she loved him! Though his ways were strange, he was good and kind, and when he put his hands on her she realized the true depravity of Keener's caresses.

Ridge must have sensed her gaze upon him, because he opened his eyes and smiled. "Where are we going?"

"Laurel Overlook," she announced as they pulled up at a four-way stop. They used to end their dates there, before her father forbade her to see him. Since their time together now was stolen and therefore more precious, they drove there immediately, hungry for the taste and feel of each other. Tonight, especially, she longed for the safe harbor of Ridge's arms.

She turned left at the four-way and drove on, her heart heavy with her secret. How she wished she could tell Ridge everything! He would believe her, without question; she'd even dreamed the conversation a hundred times in her head.

"He's done this to you for six years? Why didn't you tell someone?"

"I was scared. He said if I told, he'd fire my dad and throw us out of our house."

"But why didn't you tell your parents anyway?"

"I tried to tell my dad once. He wouldn't believe me. He said that I was overreacting, that he'd known Deke Keener for years and the thought of him putting his hands on me was just so crazy that he wasn't even going to dignify it by asking him about it."

"What about your teachers? Or the cops?"

"Every Saturday Keener plays golf with my principal. Every Sunday he takes up the collection at church. He went to high school with the new sheriff. Why should they believe me when my own father wouldn't?"

With that, Ridge's face takes on a look she's glimpsed only once before, when he thought some children were torturing a snake. The planes of his face sharpen and his eyes narrow. If she didn't know better, she would swear the boy she loves has turned into some kind of beast. Though his wild dark eyes are still full of love for her, they hold something quite different for Deke Keener. Finally, Ridge says, "Then I will go and make him sorry for what he's done."

And that was precisely why Bethany hadn't told Ridge Standingdeer what Deke Keener had done. She knew that if she did, that look would return to his face and he would, as naturally and easily as he told her he loved her, walk up to Deke Keener and rip out his throat. She'd seen the strength in his hands, the flashes of wildness in his eyes. Ridge would kill Keener, then it would be Ridge the judge would sentence to death. And her own cowardice would claim yet another victim.

She turned off onto the road that led to Laurel Overlook, the little truck skidding on the slick clay. Higher and higher they climbed, until the road disappeared into a thicket of rhododendron. She drove through them, the branches slapping against the windshield, then fifty yards later the bushes thinned out and they were on a small patch of cleared land on the edge of a mountain, looking out into the valley below. The sky bloomed crimson as the sun sank in the western sky.

She turned off the engine and looked at him. "Ridge, there's something I need you to do for me."

"Sure," he said, kissing the curve of her shoulder. "What?"

Trembling, she leaned forward and pulled an Altoid box from her purse. "I want you to put this in our cache."

He took the box and shook it. Though she'd bound it with several rubber bands, he could tell that something other than breath mints rattled inside. "This is just like those others I buried. What do you keep in these things? Money?"

She knew that this was the moment to play for real the conversation she'd rehearsed so long in her head. She opened her mouth to speak, then closed it. Though Ridge was different from every other boy she'd known, how could she be sure that he would want a girl who'd allowed herself to be pawed and fondled for so many years? She answered his question with one of her own. "What would you say if I told you I was planning to do something that would ruin a lot of people's lives?"

"Whose lives?"

"Mine and all my family's. And some other people's, too. Maybe even yours."

"What are you going to do?"

"I'm going to tell a secret."

"What kind of secret?"

Again she hesitated. She longed to jump into a cleansing sea of admission, yet she was afraid to take the plunge. "A bad secret. A shameful secret."

He frowned, as if trying to fathom her meaning. "You want to know what I would think if you told a bad secret that would ruin a lot of people's lives?"

"Yes." She nodded, eager to test the waters of his reply.

He pondered her question, gazing at the purplish red sunset. "I guess if you did it for a good reason, it would be okay," he said finally. "Why don't you tell me first? Then I could tell you how bad it was."

"You're part of the reason I haven't told it." She blinked away sudden tears.

"Why?"

"Because it would make you crazy. And it would change everything between us."

"Bethany, I——"

"Hush." She pulled him close, shame again overtaking her fledgling courage. This was the boy she loved, the boy whose touch she treasured above all else. She couldn't risk losing him by confessing her relationship with Keener. She would go see Mary Crow, first thing tomorrow. As hard as it would be to tell all that had happened, at least she would still have Ridge. She kissed him. His lips, as always, were soft and sweet. "Forget I said anything. Just put this in our cache, will you?"

"Okay," he said, puzzled.

"And don't look inside. Only one other person in the world knows about this, Ridge. You've got to swear that you will never tell anybody else. Not for the rest of your life."

"Okay." He looked so solemn that she realized he must think this was another strange flatland romantic ritual. She'd already had to explain flowers and Valentines and engagement rings to him.

She watched him take the little box and walk into the nearby woods. One night, he'd dug a hole beneath a beech tree, wrapped a few things he considered needful in a piece of deerskin, and buried it. He'd called it a cache and told her that this was tradition, where he came from. Over time it had become their little private ritual—when either of them had anything significant to contribute, he dug up the deerskin and added it. At first she'd saved mostly sentimental ticket stubs and photographs. Lately, however, she'd wrapped all her Keener tapes in Altoids tins and had passed them along to Ridge, to put in their hiding place. Here they would be safe from Keener's sharp eyes and unremitting inquisitiveness.

Moments later, Ridge walked back to the truck. She spread their red blanket out on the ground and held out her arms for him. "My beautiful bear," she whispered, pulling him close. "I love you so."

Later, they both lay naked beneath a glittering sky. Above them, everything seemed to swirl just like the Van Gogh painting that hung over her bed. The moon, the stars, Ridge's sweet face; then suddenly her mother, her father, and Kayla. All of them seemed to spin and dance beneath Deke Keener's laughing eyes, as if he were some monstrous puppeteer who put them through obscene antics purely for his own amusement. In all the heavens, hers was the only face missing; hers was the only face that could reveal Keener exactly for what he truly was.

SEVEN

He's just celebrated his eighth birthday. He's sneaked into a shed on his father's first golf course. They keep lawn tractors in here; the place is full of weird tools; the sharp smells of compost and machine oil. He loves to climb up on the big machines and pretend he's driving a tank. He heads toward his favorite, a green John Deere tractor, when he hears a noise in one shadowy corner of the shed. An irregular, rustling sound. Wondering if it's one of his father's despised gophers, he tiptoes over to investigate. There, behind some big sacks of grass seed, he finds a rat. It's twice the size of Jeep, his guinea pig, with a long, bare tail. The rat looks up at him, but its small, glittering eyes don't seem to see him. He realizes, then, that something is wrong with the rat. It crouches for a moment, gasping for air, then goes into a fit, scurrying in a tight circle, white foam bubbling from its mouth, its tail whipping like a live wire. He watches, hypnotized. The rat's frothy mouth and gyrating tail make his own penis grow hard, exciting him in a way he's never known before. Suddenly someone grabs him from behind. It's his uncle Mark. "You got a sick little wiggle worm there, boy," Mark says, pointing at his small stiff penis. "Sure hope your dad never finds out that you fuck rats."

He struggles to get away, but Mark is too strong. His big hands pull at his T-shirt, his shorts. Then suddenly Mark changes, his thick arms become slender, his

voice high as a girl's. Now someone else grasps him. Again he tries to wrench him-
self loose, but the arms are sticky, like taffy, and smell like burnt sugar. He hears
Bethany Daws, laughing. "Tapes," she's saying, her voice monstrously loud. "I hope
your dad never finds out about these tapes." Then she loops her taffy arms around
him, over and over, squeezing him like a boa constrictor. "No!" he tries to scream,
but he can't force a single sound from his mouth. "Noooooooooo!"

Deke Keener sat up in bed, his blankets coiled around him, his sheets
damp with sweat. For an instant, he didn't know where he was, and he
sat staring at the dresser that faced his bed, his heartbeat loud in his
ears. Then a nuthatch chirped a loud *bit-bit-bit* outside his window and
he remembered. He was Deke Keener, it was Wednesday, June tenth, in
Pisgah County, North Carolina, and the dream that had haunted him
since he was eight years old had just taken on a new wrinkle.

He untwisted his sheets and stumbled into his sleek spa of a bathroom, peeing loudly into the toilet. His torrential stream of urine reassured him. Though his little wiggle worm was, he supposed, a pretty
sick puppy, at least it still did most of what it was supposed to do. His
uncle Mark's worm hadn't wiggled in years—not since the night somebody cut the brakes on his black Corvette and he'd skidded off the
bridge over Buttersop Creek.

"Got you back, Uncle Mark," Deke muttered as he flushed the toilet.
"You'd probably give your eyeteeth to be able to fuck a rat now."

He crossed the room, to a shower that cost more than most people's
automobiles. He turned the water on hot and stepped into a sizzling del-
uge that issued from twelve different jets. Dreams about Uncle Mark always made him feel dirty. When he was little he used to scrub himself
until the water ran cold, hoping he might emerge from the shower a
normal boy with normal desires. The years, though, had proved that
hope false. However hard he scrubbed, soap and water could not touch
the stain inside him.

Still, he loved bathing his body, and a hot shower might give him a
new perspective on Bethany Daws. He stood under the water, soaping
his arms and legs, a belly that was, thank God, still flat. If he'd had any
sense at all, he would have dumped Bethany five years ago. She had always been the single most troubling girl of his career. Staying skinny

when his other little hillbilly chicks swelled like porkers, remaining zit-free when the others looked leprous with acne, she had sailed through her adolescence gracefully, growing from a child to woman without losing an iota of her allure. Though he'd had to constantly remind her of his power and keep her always afraid, she had endured his caresses with compliant, if sullen, resignation. Then a year ago, when just the sight of her turned his dick to lead, she'd met Ridge Standingdeer. Her sullenness had soured into spite; she'd become hostile and argumentative. Now here she was, threatening him with tapes.

Tapes! He turned off the shower and grabbed a thick Turkish towel from the warmer. Where the fuck had she come up with that? Probably it was just a bluff to protect her stupid little sister. But what if she had taped him? God knows in the past six years she could have recorded hours of stuff. The very idea of it made him sick to his stomach, then her words began to ring in his head. *Before I leave for college, you'd better believe that a lot more people than just me are going to hear it!*

"It's her monthly meltdown." He tried to calm himself with that thought as he crossed over to the sink and lathered his face with shaving cream. "One week out of four, all of them go nuts." Still, she'd never done anything like this before. As he scraped his razor down the left side of his face, he considered his odds. He was, by anyone's account, a huge success. He'd turned his father's small golf-course construction company into a huge development firm. He was a deacon at the First Baptist Church, president of the Hartsville Chamber of Commerce, chairman of the United Way. He'd been married long enough to quiet any gossip about possible homosexuality, and he'd bought his ex-wife's silence about that time she'd found him behaving "inappropriately" with their daughter Stephanie. He lived as the Prince of Pisgah County, doling out playgrounds and ball fields to his grateful little subjects, accepting the mayor's kiss on his ring. Nobody would consider him less than a God-fearing man; nobody would believe that he took anything more than a benign interest in the prepubescent daughters of his employees. Still, as he finished shaving, his hand was shaking so badly that he nicked his chin.

He stuck a piece of tissue on the tiny cut and walked into his closet, a room almost as expensive as his bath. His clothes hung with haberdashery precision—suit jackets hung high, their matching trousers below them. The sight of them made him smile. He loved to go to New York, where he would pick out the wools and cashmeres that complemented his freckled complexion and then stand exquisitely still while an Italian tailor measured everything from the length of his inseam to the circumference of his wrists. How he loved his life! Pulling out a pale blue shirt that countered the sallowness of his complexion, he thrust his arms into the sleeves when Bethany's words reechoed in his head. *Before I leave for college, you'd better believe that a lot more people than just me are going to hear it!*

"Jesus," he whispered, fumbling with the buttons on his shirt. If she truly had tapes of him, she could bring his life down around his ears. Even the Prince of Pisgah County had enemies. Drop one tape off at the mayor's, or with Turpin, or with that idiot Cochran and the sharks would smell blood. *And if Bethany squawked long enough and loud enough, someone would eventually believe her.*

Quickly he buttoned his shirt and pulled on his trousers. Though he usually liked to luxuriate in his clothes and relish the feel of fine cotton and linen against his skin, now was not the time. He needed to figure out how to stop Bethany Daws, and he needed to figure that out fast.

He knotted a yellow paisley tie around his neck, then hurried downstairs. Too antsy to sit still, he got in his car and headed for Big Meat's Pancakes, a small diner between Hartsville and Cherokee that served breakfast twenty-four hours a day. Though Big Meat's was frequented mostly by noisy families of tourists, he found the happy clatter of the place soothing—waitresses shouting out orders, the tink of coffee spoons against coffee cups, the jukebox that Big Meat refused to stock with anybody other than Johnny Cash. He sat at the counter, ordered black coffee, and wondered what to do about Bethany. Even if she was bluffing, he couldn't allow such a gravely mutinous act to go unpunished. Still, even that was a secondary concern. His first order of business was protecting himself from those goddamn tapes.

Big Meat's wife Ora May slid a cup of coffee down in front of him, then hurried over to serve an order of strawberry waffles. Pondering his Bethany dilemma, Deke watched the line cook pluck eggs from two large cartons, opened side by side next to the grill. The remaining eggs looked like chess men scattered across a board, and suddenly he saw his life as a game of chess. He was the king, about to be mated by a lowly pawn. Though he had a good many of his own pawns around him, he needed something powerful—a queen or a rook—to protect him from the infiltrator. As he took a tentative sip of his scalding coffee, the answer came. There was a black queen recently arrived in Hartsville who was easily capable of protecting him from this pawn. She was smart, she was fast, and he had it on good authority that she might be needing some work. All he had to do was enlist her on his side before Bethany went public with her damn tapes.

"Oh, Bethany." He laughed as he rose from his stool and left Ora May five bucks for a single cup of coffee. "You've no idea how badly you've fucked up. No idea at all."

He pulled up under the magnolia tree in front of the Baptist Church, directly across from the hardware store. It was just past eight in the morning. He would give his black queen half an hour to show up. If she didn't appear by then, he'd go over to Cockroach's office and ask him about her. Nothing swelled the new sheriff's pathetic little ego more than being asked a question.

Anxious for his champion to appear, he opened his newspaper, attempting to both read the stock market report and keep watch out the window. Butch Messer drove by in the new Crown Victoria that Randy Bradley sold him, while Sylvia Goins strode out of Sutton's Hardware, carrying a thirty-pound bag of peat moss as it if were a feather pillow. Hastily, Deke slumped down in his seat. Christ, how he hated to see Sylvia Goins. He'd started a game with her the same time he'd started with Bethany, but he'd lost interest when over the course of one summer Sylvia sprouted dark hair in places that had previously been bare and began bursting out of a 34DD bra. He'd tried to disengage himself gently, but for months she'd clung to him like cheap cologne. Finally, when she started high school, her interest in him waned. He'd heard she'd gotten pregnant by some young thug, dropped out of school, and moved away. Then, last spring, he'd gone to Sutton's to order new Kats uniforms and there she stood at the cash register, fifty pounds heavier, with a Mexican boyfriend who looked just like a chimpanzee. From then on, he sent Glenn Daws in to order the uniforms.

Tapping out an edgy tattoo on his steering wheel, he watched Sylvia. She hauled out a dozen more bags of peat moss, piled them neatly in a sidewalk display, then went back inside the store. Then George Turpin waddled out of the snack bar and headed toward the courthouse. Watching him in his rearview mirror, Deke sat up straighter in his seat, wondering if Turpin was actually going to risk a coronary with the hundred-step climb to the courthouse. Suddenly a green pickup truck loaded with office furniture pulled up in front of the hardware store, blocking his view. Two people got out. He blinked in astonishment to see Ridge Standingdeer emerge from the driver's seat, then gaped further at Standingdeer's passenger. She was pretty—taller than average, with an olive complexion. Her shoulder-length hair was definitely Cherokee, but cut with an urban panache rarely seen in downtown Hartsville. He watched her walk to the back of the truck. When she turned to Standingdeer and smiled, he recognized her immediately. Though not dressed as a fashionable teenager circa 1987, the hair, the walk, and that killer smile belonged to the same girl who'd beaten him in debate so many years ago. His black queen had arrived. Quickly, he ditched his newspaper and rolled down his window.

"Mary? Mary Crow?" Deke called, getting out of his car and grinning broadly. "Is that really you?"

EIGHT

Mary jumped at the sound of a male voice calling her name. Dressed in shorts and a tattered blue sweatshirt, she'd been up since daybreak, dragging a bookcase and several chairs down from Irene's attic. Now she was hot and dirty and smelled like lemon Pledge—in no way the clean, fresh-from-Peru woman she wanted Jonathan to see. She turned, mentally scrambling for some excuse as to why she hadn't called him, when she saw with great relief that it wasn't Jonathan at all, but a man with thick auburn hair, getting out of an expensive black SUV.

"Hi." She smiled, hoping he would say some revelatory thing that would tell her who he was. "How are you?"

"I'm great." He loped across the street like a big, friendly dog. Up close she saw that he had bright brown eyes that seemed to seize upon everything at once and skin bronzed by freckles rather than the sun. "I heard you'd moved back."

"Yes, I have." The man looked her age. She must have gone to high school with him, but she didn't have a clue as to who he was. "Hartsville's really grown, hasn't it?"

The man nodded, then started to laugh. "You don't remember me, do you?"

Embarrassed, Mary fudged her reply. "I remember your face. I'm afraid I can't come up with your name."

"Deke Keener." He extended his hand. "Cherokee High, class of eighty-seven. You sat two rows over from me in Miss Cooke's homeroom, and we were on the debate team together. You beat me three times—at the Lions Club meet in Asheville, at the Western Carolina meet, and the All-State tourney, in Raleigh."

Mary didn't know what to say. She barely remembered debate, much less this man who could still rattle off their records. Slowly, though, she began to recall a thinner, redder-headed boy to whom winning was just slightly less important than breathing. She thought he'd pitched on the baseball team, won some kind of scholarship. She remembered that she hadn't liked him very much.

Nonetheless, she shook his hand warmly. "Of course. Deke Keener. How nice to see you again!"

"I read all about you in the paper. You really put it to old Stump Logan. Did you know that Jerry Cochran is sheriff now?"

"I heard that." Mary squelched a sigh, wondering if she would be forever known as the woman who put it to Stump Logan.

Keener eyed the truck full of furniture. "So what are you up to now?"

"I'm opening my own office." She turned to include the Cherokee boy who stood beside her. "This is Ridge Standingdeer. He's helping me move in."

Deke shook hands with the young man, then returned his gaze to Mary. "So where's your office going to be?"

"Up there." Mary pointed to the tall mullioned windows that looked down over the storefront behind them.

"Over the hardware store?" Deke choked back a laugh. "But aren't you a DA? Don't DAs work in the courthouse?"

"They do when they can get jobs," Mary replied, trying hard to keep the bitterness out of her voice. "When they can't, they hang out shingles of their own."

"So you're now going to set criminals free instead of sending them upriver?" Keener gave her a snide little jab, just as he had in debate. The longer they talked, the more she remembered what she hadn't liked about him. He was pushy and aggressive, and his ego was constantly on the line. He reminded her of a few attorneys she'd known and not loved.

She shook her head. "I'm not going to do any criminal work."

"Then what are you going to do?"

"Everything else but divorces."

Deke looked at her as if she were crazy, then gazed up at the tall windows over Sutton's Hardware. "Mind if I come up and have a look?"

She was tempted to tell him yes, she minded quite a bit, that she didn't have time for all his silly verbal sparring, but she couldn't think of a graceful way to decline his company. "Sure," she said reluctantly. "But we have to be quiet. A psychologist holds therapy sessions up there."

She turned and led the two men up the staircase. She walked on tiptoe until she noticed that Dana had tacked a small "In Court Today" sign on her door. Thank God, Mary thought, relieved that she and Ridge wouldn't have to lug her furniture up the stairs and worry about making noise.

"I leased this yesterday," she announced as she crossed the landing to unlock her door. "It's just a closet, but it's a good address."

The opened door revealed the room's whitewashed plaster walls and pine plank floors. As she stepped across the threshold, the feel of the room made Mary smile. Ridge entered and stood close to the door, silently taking everything in, while Keener buzzed around the space like a fly caught in a jar.

"Wow! What a view! You can see all along Main Street." He scurried over to the windows. "There's Groovy Butch, opening the music store late, and old Margaret Stubbs going to get her hair dyed blue. And you can keep an eye on the Mexicans at the Mercado Hispaño, right across the street. This is cool." He turned to her. "What kind of law did you say you were going to practice?"

"Just general stuff. Wills. House closings. I probably won't go to court at all."

"Have you done any real estate work?"

Mary gave an inward groan at the memory of the lease she'd drawn up for her grandmother's house in Atlanta. Long-term in exchange for favorable rent. A year ago, when she'd been in love and in Peru, it had seemed perfect. Now she realized what a financial blunder it had been. "A little," she answered noncommittally. Deke Keener was the last person she'd confess any professional bungling to.

Deke pulled out his wallet and handed her a business card. KEENER CONSTRUCTION was spelled out in raised gold letters shaped like building blocks. "I bill out about sixty mil in construction every year. I'm always looking for good attorneys. You interested?"

"Don't you already have counsel here?" Mary knew nobody could run a business that large without some kind of legal advisor.

"I have several," Deke answered coyly. "All are good for one thing or another, but I'd love to find one person who could handle all of it. You want to give it a shot?"

The thought of having Deke Keener as a client made her stomach churn. He'd come up here and stay for hours, pointing out her windows, jabbering like a magpie. She would have to buy aspirin by the case and keep Sapphire Gin in her desk drawer. "I don't know." She shook her head. "I'm a member of the North Carolina bar, but I'm pretty rusty on my real estate statutes. . . ."

"But if you got up to speed—would you be interested in working for me?" he persisted, in dead earnest. "I pay well."

"I don't know," repeated Mary, feeling the muscles in her neck beginning to tighten. "Let me just get moved in first. I'll be able to think straighter after that."

"Then let's get at it." Deke rolled up his sleeves. "What's that old saying? Many hands make light work?"

"That's really nice of you, Deke, but there's no need for that," Mary said, looking at Keener's creamy linen trousers and Italian loafers. "Ridge and I can handle it."

He grinned at her. "Not a problem—after all, we're old school pals." He thumped Ridge companionably on the shoulder. "Come on, buddy. Let's get this lady unloaded."

An hour later, Mary had learned that Deke had won a baseball scholarship to N.C. State, had been married and divorced, and was the father of a ten-year-old daughter who lived in Colorado with her mother. He'd come back home and expanded his father's golf-course company into subdivision development. He piloted his own plane, went to New York twice a year to buy clothes, and had built a state-of-the-art house on the top of King's Mountain.

"So what have you been up to since Cherokee High?" he asked as he plopped down behind the desk he and Ridge had just lugged up the stairs. "Other than doing in our former sheriff?"

"Oh, just making a living," she replied, wishing Deke Keener would get up from her desk and get the hell out of her office. Ignoring his question further, she stood in the center of the room and looked at what they'd accomplished. She'd brought a smallish desk and three worn leather armchairs from Irene's attic, along with a credenza from her downstairs office. Though none of the pieces matched, they were of good quality, and complemented the room's turn-of-the-century ambiance.

"That everything?" Deke asked, finally rising from Mary's desk as she arranged a small red rug between the two chairs.

"Almost." Mary picked up a plastic sack she'd stashed in the corner. Last night she'd gathered a few personal items to bring from home. One had been the spectacular wall hanging that Irene had commissioned her mother to weave; the other was Winona, a funny little statue of a Cherokee earth mother that Mary kept as a talisman. She loved both pieces, and figured that having them in her office would surely bring her good luck.

She set Winona on her desk and watched as Ridge hung the tapestry on the wall. It looked just as breathtaking here as it had at Irene's—all the colors of the mountains seemed to glow with a luminosity that had not dimmed over the years.

"Dunuhdatluhee," said Ridge, grinning over his shoulder at her.

"Wahdo," Mary answered softly. "My mother was a weaver. She thought the mountains were beautiful, too."

The boy started to say something else, when they heard a knock on the door.

They turned. Bethany Daws stood in the doorway. Dressed in her waitress uniform, she carried a plate covered with a blue-checked napkin.

For an instant, Mary saw the unreserved brightness of the girl's smile. Then Bethany's gaze fell on Deke Keener and all the joy drained from her face as profoundly as if someone had pulled the stopper from a sink.

"I—I'm sorry," she stammered. "I thought just you and Ridge would be here."

"Come on in, Bethany," Mary welcomed her. "This is an old classmate of mine, Deke Keener. We just got the last piece of furniture in place."

"I brought you some muffins from the café. Orange cranberry. They baked them this morning."

"They smell wonderful." Mary passed the plate to her helpers. "Gentlemen?"

"Thanks." Deke stepped forward and grinned at Bethany. "I've eaten these things for years. They're great when they're hot."

Ridge took a muffin, too, but said nothing. An awkward silence sprang up, as if Bethany's entrance had lowered the temperature of the room about thirty degrees. Mary stole a glance at the girl. She remained in the doorway, as if afraid to step inside the room.

"Did you two have fun last night?" Mary tried to boot the conversation onto safer ground.

"Yes," said Ridge. "We—"

"I'd better get back to work," Bethany blurted. "I'll come back later, Mary, when you aren't so busy. Enjoy the muffins!"

Without another word, the girl turned and ran down the stairs, her footsteps resounding sharply. Mary hurried after her, to thank her for the muffins, but by the time she reached the bannister, all that remained of Bethany was the slamming of the street door. Puzzled, Mary returned to her office, wondering why a single glance at goofy Deke Keener would have soured the girl's mood so.

"Gosh, was it something we said?" Deke made a joke, his mouth full of muffin.

"I don't know." Mary looked at Ridge. "Have you two had a fight?"

The boy shrugged. "If we did, I didn't know it."

"That's the trouble with women, son," said Deke. "They get mad at things we've done, and we're too dumb to know we've done 'em. I have an ex-wife to prove that. Here." He put the rest of his muffin down on Mary's desk and extracted a bill from his wallet. "Take this. Buy her a rose. Tell her you love her, and that you're sorry she's upset."

Ridge frowned at the bill Keener had given him. "But this is fifty dollars. . . ."

"A small price to pay to calm the waters of young love." Deke grinned. "Now go on and smooth things over with your girl while I talk to Mary here."

Ridge looked at Mary as if asking for some clarification on the crazy ways of white people, but she was silent, equally astonished at Deke's behavior. "Go ahead, Ridge," she finally said. "Just don't forget I need a ride home before you go back to Hugh's."

"Okay. Thank you." Ridge nodded at Deke, then hurried out the door.

"That was very generous of you, Deke," Mary said after the boy had gone.

"Hey, if I can't donate fifty bucks to young love, then I'd be pretty pathetic," he replied, perching on the corner of her desk. "Anyway, that poor girl needs all the help she can get."

"She seemed to have an odd reaction to your being here," Mary said. "How do you know her?"

"She used to play on my softball team—her dad, in fact, is my number-two man at Keener Construction, and still helps me coach. She was a great little girl when she was on the team, but once she hit high school, she went nuts. Sex, drugs, the works. Everybody in town thinks she's wonderful, but I get the real story from her mom and dad. She's one conniving little bitch."

Mary remembered the girl's wistful smile. "Has anybody tried to find out why?"

He shrugged. "I've tried to talk with her several times after church, but she just clams up. Her parents think this new boyfriend has made her worse. They wish he'd just go back to where he came from."

"Ridge seems okay to me." Mary defended the boy who'd so good-naturedly trucked her furniture in from the country.

"You know, he does. I was surprised when I met him. After listening to Glenn Daws, I didn't know what to expect." Deke shook his head. "Who knows with kids these days? I just hope she gets herself back on track."

"Me, too," said Mary, sorry to learn that she hadn't just imagined the sadness that flickered behind Bethany's eyes.

Deke checked his watch and stood up. "I've got to go. I'm meeting a man who wants me to build him a golf course on top of a mountain."

Mary smiled, brightening at the prospect of his imminent departure. Soon she would be able to draw an unchallenged breath peacefully, in her own office. She stuck out her hand. "Thanks for all your help, Deke. It was great seeing you again."

"My pleasure." He smiled. "Look, I wasn't kidding earlier. I'm working on a terrific new Cherokee project that you would be perfect for. How about I stop by later this afternoon and go over the specs with you?"

Mary didn't know what to say. Though her track record in real estate was abysmal and Deke Keener affected her like fingernails scraping a blackboard, she remembered Mr. Turnipseed, and his costly attempts at finding her a new well. Could she really afford to turn down a client who handed out fifty-dollar bills like they were shiny dimes? "Let me get myself a little more ready to do business," she hedged. "I've still got to get a phone line in and my computer hooked up. Why don't you come by first thing next week?"

"How about first thing tomorrow morning?" Deke countered. "If I don't move on this soon, I'm going to lose some favorable financing."

"Well, okay." Mary gave in. Suddenly she was too tired to joust with him any further. "Come on up about nine and I'll see what you've got."

"Great!" He grinned, then leaned over and kissed her cheek. "Welcome home. It's wonderful to see you again."

"Thanks, Deke. It's good to see you, too," she replied, hoping that her eyes did not reveal the enormity of her lie.

NINE

Mary closed the door. Immediately the tight knot at the back of her neck began to loosen. For the first moment since she'd gotten out of Hugh's truck, she was sans Keener. The silence in her office was delicious, and she stood there for a long moment, just breathing in the Deke-less air. When she walked over and looked out her windows, she saw that her one-man welcoming committee had just crossed the street and was now chatting with an overweight cop who was writing someone a parking ticket. Keener gave the cop's hand a hearty pump, then got back in his Lexus and pulled into the line of traffic heading west. She sighed. Deke Keener had not changed a bit since high school. He was just as annoying today as he had been on Miss Cooke's debate team, and she knew exactly why Bethany Daws had looked at him like he was Death himself.

"He probably harangued her into substance abuse," she said aloud. Though she knew she was making light of the girl's possibly serious problems, the idea of Deke Keener counseling troubled teenagers was laughable. No wonder the girl did drugs, thought Mary. I would too if I had to talk over my problems with someone who kept track of old forensics tournaments.

She turned from the windows and walked over to her desk, trying to picture herself meeting with clients. My God, she'd never had a client in her life. Yet tomorrow morning she was supposed to discuss real estate with a man who billed out sixty mil a year? Better get busy, she decided. At least try to look like you know what you're doing.

She got out her cell phone and made arrangements to have two land-lines installed. After she chose new numbers with lots of lucky fours and sevens, a nasal-voiced operator promised the installer would be there tomorrow, between eight A.M. and noon.

She switched off her phone and gazed at the blank plane of her desk-top. It looked so dismal with just Winona squatting on it that she took two pens from her purse and dropped them into a Styrofoam cup, and made a mental note to bring some photos from home. After that, she had nothing more to do. She'd forgotten to pack any of Irene's texts, so her bookcase stood empty. She wouldn't be able to start reading up on property law until she got home.

Anxious to get going, she rose and returned to the windows. Across the street, the Mercado Hispaño's red-and-yellow awning looked festive as a piñata. One bright-faced young Mexican man wearing a red bandanna was crossing the street, heading directly for her office. So were two older painters in white coveralls, and an overweight woman leading a tiny York-shire terrier on a rhinestone-studded leash. At first she wondered if word had gotten out that a new lawyer had opened up shop and these people needed legal advice, then she realized that they weren't coming to her office, they were going to the hardware store just below her.

"Maybe I should put a sign in Mr. Sutton's window," she told herself. "Legal help upstairs. Reasonable rates and *se hable español*." Chuckling at the idea of her taking on Mexican clients with her rudimentary knowl-edge of Peruvian Spanish, she leaned against the windowsill and kept watching for Ridge. As the same young bandannaed Mexican scurried back across the street, she saw a heavyset man with wild gray hair come barreling out of the newspaper office. He chugged across the street like a small locomotive, a smaller, brown-skinned man bobbing along in his wake.

"Oh, lord," she whispered. Sam Ravenel, her new next-door office neighbor, was coming to work.

Sighing, she opened her door. She'd at least try to get off on a better foot with him. Ravenel thundered up the stairs, apparently not caring if Dana was in the middle of a therapy session. When he reached the top of the steps, Mary thought he looked as if he'd been rolling around the Great Smoky Mountains instead of defending them. Bits of leaves and twigs clung to his wild gray locks and he was covered in mud, from the collar of his blue work shirt to the frayed hem of his jeans. He was whistling a jaunty little tune, and until he caught sight of her, he looked almost happy. His diminutive friend followed four steps behind him, wearing cream-colored pointy-toed cowboy boots and a shy grin on his obviously Cherokee face.

"Oh." Ravenel stopped his whistle when he caught sight of her. "You moved in."

"That generally follows when one signs a lease." Mary crossed her arms, her hopes for rapprochement fading. What was with this man? Did he hate her in particular, or just everyone in general?

Ravenel dug in his pocket for his keys. "One can always hope otherwise. I guess Dana needed the money. I understand she needs professional help with her tennis game."

Mary tried again. "Look, I'm sorry about yesterday. What kind of plans did you have for this space?"

He shrugged. "None in particular. But if I'd known Dana was going to rent it to you, I'd have paid her twice the price."

Mary's eyes narrowed as she noted Ravenel's barrel chest and ponderous belly. There was something more here, something beyond just losing a hundred square feet of office space and three nice windows on Main Street. "You're a Logan man, aren't you?"

"A what?" Ravenel scowled at her.

"A Logan man. You hate me because I killed the old sheriff, Stump Logan."

Ravenel opened his office door wide enough for Mary to see a stuffed raccoon perched on a desk and an old Cherokee fish basket overturned on the floor. "Ms. Crow, I don't know how many sheriffs you may have killed, but that is not the reason for my antipathy."

"Then what is?"

Ravenel swelled up like a bullfrog. "Because you are among the most despicable lot of vermin God ever put on the earth."

Mary was dumbfounded. She'd never seen this man before yesterday afternoon. What lot of vermin could he possibly be casting her in? "You mean because I'm Cherokee?"

"Because you're an attorney!" Ravenel looked as if someone had just fed him a spoonful of dog shit. "Now that perfectly nice little office will be turned into just another den of shystery. There are far too many lawyers in this town already, Ms. Crow. We do not need another one!"

With that, Ravenel opened his door wide enough for his copper-skinned friend to scamper through, then he stepped inside and slammed it shut so hard, the walls shuddered. Mary stood there stunned, wondering if the man wasn't one of Dana's ex-clients, on some kind of work-release program from the loony bin. Then she decided that Ravenel must be one of those men who'd gotten the short end of a divorce decree and now blamed the entire legal establishment for their loss. "Boy, I don't know how much Mrs. Ravenel came out with," she murmured. "But she deserved every penny she got."

She was about to go back in her own office when she heard the door from the street open. This time soft footsteps approached. Ridge appeared.

"Sorry I took so long," he said, out of breath. "I wanted to stop in the hardware store and see if they'd sold any of my masks. Are you ready to go?"

"More than ready," said Mary, glaring at Ravenel's door. She stepped into her office and scooped up her purse, happy to be leaving the confines of her new space, however charming it was. "How did it go with Bethany?"

Ridge shrugged. "I did what that man told me, but she's still upset."

"Did you ask her why?"

"She wouldn't talk about it. Said it was a secret."

"Then don't worry about it," Mary said, locking her door. "Just give her some time. She'll tell you if she wants to."

"I don't know." Ridge's voice was full of doubt. "She doesn't want to tell me a lot of things these days."

Mary paid Ridge twenty-five dollars, then bought him lunch at Hardee's. They drove home through land that looked like a page torn from a calendar—red barns dotting green fields; black and white cows grazing under a benevolent blue sky. Though much of it had remained as she remembered, she noticed a number of new housing developments sprawling over the mountainsides. Judaculla Close, Quallah Downs, Sequoia Ridge—all resembled the upscale, gated developments that surrounded Atlanta, but these bore the names of ancient, highly revered Cherokees. She winced when she passed a sign advertising "Tsali Trail," hoping it wasn't one of Deke's developments. It would be hard to work for someone who was so shamelessly cashing in on the names of her ancestors.

Before she got home, she took one further advantage of having Ridge Standingdeer and Hugh's truck. She had the boy stop at the grocery, where she bought a week's worth of water in ten-gallon jugs. Together they lugged it into the kitchen, then Ridge bade her good-bye.

"I should probably get back to Hugh's," the boy said, looking at her with that same frank, but not unfriendly, gaze. "Unless you need me for something else."

"No, Ridge. You've been more than helpful. Thank you so much. I hope I'll be seeing you soon."

He nodded and hurried back to the truck. Enjoying the embrace of the little house that still bore the stamp of its past owner, she leaned against the back door and watched as he drove down the drive. No ancestral names here, nor gates to keep visitors away. Irene's house was a haven of warm repose. Pale yellow rooms were decorated with brightly colored rugs, and books spilled from their shelves as profusely as Hugh's racing trophies did from his mahogany armoires. It's a satisfied house, Mary decided, smiling as a little glass vase above the sink refracted a small rainbow on the floor. A comfortable house. If only it had water! Ever hopeful, she stepped over to the sink and turned on the faucets, but nothing emerged from the pipes except a hacking choke that sounded like someone enduring the Heimlich maneuver.

Well, at least you've got a client coming, she reminded herself. Even if it meant putting up with Deke Keener, clients meant money. And money, in this case, translated directly into functional plumbing.

She grabbed a Coke from the refrigerator and padded into Irene's study, pulling Corbin's text on contracts from the bookshelf. It was just too pretty a day to read indoors, so she took an orange highlighter and went out on the porch, setting up shop in Irene's big wicker chair. Mr. Turnipseed had some kind of machine flailing away in one corner of the front pasture, but otherwise, all lay still. Monarch butterflies worked the orange daylilies that bloomed in the garden, and the blackberry bushes that grew along the creek bank were already drooping with the weight of dark, sweet berries that would ripen next month. The day, which for her had begun before dawn, had grown into a perfect example of summer in the Carolina mountains. The sun was warm, the breeze cool, the sky as blue as a bird's egg. This was what had drawn her back from Peru. This, and Jonathan Walkingstick.

Jonathan was a problem she would have to act on soon. She had a house, she had sort of a job. She was now going to have to muster her courage and make the trip to Little Jump Off. If she waited much longer, she could well just bump into him in Hartsville, as she might any other old acquaintance. As many things as Jonathan Walkingstick was to her, an old acquaintance was not one of them. She eyed the thick law book that lay like a stone on her lap and thought, Why not go see him right now?

Because you've got to read this book, she told herself sternly. Deke Keener's coming to see you, first thing tomorrow. You can't blow your first client.

She opened the book and started to read, but the impish part of her brain refused to be quiet. *You've just opened your office. You can put Keener off one more day. Be brave. Go see Walkingstick now. Before he sees you.*

She started the book over again, but after reading the first paragraph six times with no idea about what it said, she got up from the chair. Both her body and her brain were united in their opinion that she could put her reunion with Jonathan off no longer.

She went into the house, filled every pot and pan in Irene's kitchen with her store-bought water, and put them on the stove to heat. Keeping a whole bathtub full of water hot was impossible, but she'd learned that if she bathed by the sinkful, she could keep the water tolerably warm.

After fetching soap and towels from the linen closet, she transferred the hot stove water to the big kitchen sink, stripped off her clothes, and got to work.

Half an hour later, after a raft of contortions, one burned finger, and a badly stubbed toe, she stood there clean. With a towel wrapped around her, she hurried to her bedroom, where she dried her hair and pulled on jeans and a clean blouse. Humming as she donned a pair of small, intricately wrought earrings she'd bought in the Piura market, a memory of Gabe came rushing back to her.

"*Is this for me?*" he'd asked one day, peering into a paper sack she'd brought from Miraflores.

"*What?*"

"*This.*" He pulled a big straw jipijapa hat from the sack and put it on his head.

"*Oh, yes,*" she'd lied, not having the courage to admit that she hadn't bought it for him at all, but for Jonathan.

"*Thanks,*" he'd said, kissing her. "*It's terrific!*"

Thrilled with his gift, he'd worn it the rest of the evening, strutting around like a vaquero. They'd gone out to Barranco, gotten tipsy on margaritas, and kissed on the Bridge of Sighs. The next morning after he left for work, she'd gone out and bought another hat for Jonathan.

"Love is such a mean bitch," she whispered to her reflection in the mirror, ashamed that she'd treated such a good man so duplicitously. Suddenly she wondered if young Ridge had any idea of what he was getting into with Bethany. Probably not, she decided. If he did, he'd flee back into the mountains and resume conversing with bears.

She turned from the mirror and pulled a cardboard box from beneath her bed. Inside lay the hat for Jonathan, some toys for Lily, two ocarinas, and a rug that had been as skillfully woven as her mother's tapestry, except that the colors were the vibrant, tropical oranges and reds of Peru, instead of the cool blues of the Carolina mountains.

She looked at her Peruvian treasures. In Lima, their purchase had served to keep her connected to Jonathan, if only in her own mind. Now they seemed like sad, bright souvenirs of the year she'd spent in the arms of another man. She realized, as she carried the box out to her car, that Jonathan might not want either her or her gifts anymore.

With a deep breath, she started her little Miata, and headed out to test the waters at Little Jump Off.

The summer was lush, with tall, dark pines spangled with splotches of yellow light. Halfway up one mountain, she pulled over and put the top down on her car. She wanted to feel the breeze on her face, breathe in the sharp pungent air that had so disrupted her dreams in Peru. Jonathan notwithstanding, these mountains were a part of her. She could not deny their pull, any more than she could alter the color of her eyes or retool her own heart.

The road coiled down the mountain and began to parallel the Little Tennessee River, a bright ribbon of silver glittering beneath the blue sky. One curve, then a bend in the road, then her pulse quickened as she came to a wide spot in the river where Cherokees had swapped goods for the past five hundred years. Though greenbacks had long since replaced skins and wampum beads as legal tender, the mercantile tradition stretched back to the days when Hernando de Soto had tromped through these mountains seeking gold but winding up instead with a single buffalo skin.

Lots of history here, she thought, suddenly aware of the thousand silent voices raised at Little Jump Off, her mother's foremost among them.

She pulled into the parking lot. In the past year, she had not heard from Jonathan at all. Her postcards and letters had gone unanswered, and though none had been returned marked "addressee unknown," she did wonder if perhaps he'd married again. Jonathan never seemed to suffer from a lack of female companionship, and she knew Lena Owle had a long-standing case on him. What if she'd driven up here to find him once again involved with someone else? How humiliating would that be? Well, if it happened, it happened, she decided, grabbing her box of Peruvian treasures. She was the one who'd walked away this time. She had nobody to blame but herself.

Nervously she strode across the dusty parking lot, carrying the box as if it held diamonds. As she climbed up to the old plank porch, she looked around. The only thing that had changed was the mesh playpen that stood in one sunny corner underneath some wind chimes made of river cane. *Lily,* she thought with a smile. How good it would be to see her. She'd missed her dreadfully, too.

Finally she could put it off no longer. She took a deep, shaky breath and walked to the screen door. The inside was bathed in shadows, but she heard the sound of music playing, airy Indian flutes chanting a lullaby.

Softly she knocked on the door. "Jonathan?" she called, realizing that this was the first time in a year she'd called his name with any hope of a reply. "Anybody home?"

TEN

At that same moment, Deke Keener sat at his desk, indigestion glowing like a bright ember in the middle of his chest. It had started the moment he'd stepped out of Mary Crow's office and with each passing hour it had grown worse. Though he'd swallowed half a bottle of Tums and tried to concentrate on the plans for his new Bear Den development, his mind kept bouncing between Mary Crow and Bethany Daws. Yesterday Bethany had threatened him with tapes; today she'd shown up in Mary Crow's new office. The odd coincidence wasn't lost on him—the girl he'd sought to legally protect himself from had sought her own aid from the same attorney. And Mary Crow! As smart as she'd been in high school, Emory Law and being an Atlanta DA had only honed her intelligence further. Yesterday her smoky-quartz eyes had regarded him quite coolly, and it occurred to him, as they chatted, that having Mary Crow as his attorney might be like carrying a pet rattlesnake around in his pocket. With the first false move she'd no doubt sink her fangs into him as fast as she would any felon.

Trying to bring up a burp, he turned in his chair. Even Houdini, his chameleon, appeared testy. The lizard's eyes swiveled quickly, and he tested the air with quick darts of his tongue, his skin a splotchy, unsettled green.

"You in a bad place, too, buddy?" Deke tapped on Houdini's cage. As the creature scampered to another branch, he realized that the chameleon was mirroring his own mood—tense and edgy, sensing a serious threat yet unsure about how to deal with it. Though he couldn't imagine what information Houdini's tongue was sending up to his rather elemental neuron receptors, Deke knew quite well what alarm bells his own brain was ringing. *Bethany Daws means to bring you down. Better stop that girl before she stops you!*

Of course, Bethany was not the first to threaten him. There had been many, over the years. Most he'd easily scared into silence, reminding them of how hard their lies would be to prove, and what sorrows accusing a prominent man with well-placed friends would bring down upon their heads. That usually shut them up pretty fast, but a few had remained stubborn. Those he'd had to deal with differently. It hadn't been pretty or pleasant, but he'd taken care of them in such a way that they never bothered anybody again.

Deke shook out a couple of dried flies from a small box of food and dropped them in Houdini's cage. "So what would you do, buddy? If you were me?"

Almost faster than Deke could see, Houdini darted forward. He snapped up both flies in two quick gulps, the loose skin beneath his jaw waggling. The act of eating seemed to calm him and a moment later he climbed to a higher branch, and with half-closed eyes, began to ponder life in his oblong glass universe.

Deke smiled. "That's just what I thought you'd do." If Bethany had grown gutsy enough to visit a lawyer, he would have to do whatever it took. She was a beautiful girl and he loved her father like a brother, but she was, ultimately, just another fly in his cage. He would try to reason with her one last time. If that didn't work, he would take his next cue from Houdini. It was no less a law among humans than reptiles—eat or be eaten; at any cost, survive.

He turned back to his desk, where Linda had left three new employee files for him to read. He liked to know who was working for him, where and what they had done before. The first was the file of a frame carpenter from Mexico, Manuel Vasquez. The second was a Ukrainian plumber named Bazyli Chornyn. Jesus, Deke thought as he squinted at Chornyn's flowery, European hand. *My crews used to be just hillbilly farmers who'd lost their tobacco allotments. Now they eat tortillas for lunch and knock back shots of vodka at happy hour.* Oh well, he decided, as he finished checking Chornyn's papers. *Shit probably runs downhill just as fast in Russia as it does in Pisgah County.*

As he moved on to the next file, a little shiver of electricity shot through him. Earl Martin, Avis's father. Eagerly he opened the folder and read the questionnaire Martin had filled out. In plain American blackboard printing, Martin had written that he'd graduated high school in Pickens, South Carolina, and thereafter had operated bulldozers and backhoes all over the deep South. He'd never been charged with a felony and though he'd made an erasure when he filled out his Social Security number, he was quite clear about the number of his dependents—three.

"One for your wife, one for your baby, and one for your pretty little bookworm, Avis."

Deke felt a sudden tug of desire in the pit of his stomach. Maybe that's what he needed. Maybe another encounter with his new Tracy Foster would put his problem with Bethany Daws in a new perspective. Quickly he closed Earl Martin's file. He went into his private bathroom, stripped off his clothes, and took a scorching hot shower. After toweling himself dry, he donned the adult Keener Kat uniform that hung behind the door. Dressed for his role as coach, he grabbed a smaller, regulation uniform from a closet in his office, and strode toward the lobby, whistling.

"I'm outta here, Linda," he told his secretary, who was going through their daily stack of unsolicited employment applications. "I'll come in early tomorrow, so don't dock my pay."

Linda looked up from her work. "I take it you've got a game this afternoon?"

"At five-thirty. Keener Kats versus Northside Graphics." He stopped at the door long enough to give her a corny, leering wink. "Be there or be square!"

He pulled out of the parking lot and headed north. Ten minutes later, he was driving up the recently paved road that led to Tsali Trail test house number one. It stood alone on a freshly sodded acre of red clay bulldozed from a thick pine forest. A modified A-frame with a soaring front window to take advantage of the mountain view, the house was a design of his own making, built to suit his own special needs. If it functioned as well as he hoped, he would put a version of it in all his new developments, and sell them with special consideration to families with young, blond daughters with breasts the size of plums.

He turned into the drive. Just as he'd figured, the U-Haul was gone. The Martins had labored like beavers for the past several days, solidifying their claim on the sleek new house by filling it with their own battered beds and scratched-up coffee tables. He smiled as he got out of his car. Their behavior was so typical, you could almost set your watch by it. Every family in every test house dumped their crappy shit in as soon as possible, as if doing that might turn the place into their own.

Holding Avis's uniform behind him, he walked to the front door and rang the bell. He knew that either she or her mother would answer—work wouldn't stop on Earl's job for another hour and the battered old Ford that the Martins had towed up from Greenville sat glowering in the drive. After a moment, the lock turned. He smiled as Darlene Martin opened the door.

"Mr. Keener." She blinked, her fingers worrying the stretched-out neck of her orange Clemson sweatshirt. "Is something wrong?"

"No, no." He took a step back. God forbid she should think the least little thing was wrong. "I didn't mean to scare you. I just stopped by to see how everything was going. And to give you this." He held out the Kats uniform.

"Everything's fine." Darlene laughed nervously, embarrassed by her overreaction. "We've been working real hard. Avis and Chrissy, too," she added, as if to assure him that all of the Martins were striving to be good members of the Keener family. She took the uniform and opened the door wider. "Won't you come in?"

Deke entered the house to find that the Martins had crammed a bunch of cheap overstuffed chintz furniture into a living room of sharp angles and soaring lines. A worn green recliner hulked in one corner, pointed at a large-screen TV. He knew that soon toys would be scattered all over the pristine floors, family photographs would mar the spotless walls. The cloying tackiness of it made him want to puke. "This looks great," he said. "How did the other rooms turn out?"

Darlene Martin looked at him like a scared rabbit. "We're still setting up the dining room. We wanted to get the living room and den together first."

"Say, would you mind if I took a peek around?" Deke tried to appear as if the idea had just occurred to him. "I always like to see how people use space."

"Well, okay," Darlene Martin said, twisting the wedding ring on her finger. "Come on. I'll show you."

She took him on a brief tour of the downstairs. Though the kitchen and den both looked like they'd been furnished from a Sears catalog, circa 1985, Deke made the appropriately approving responses. Family living areas held no interest for him. It was where one particular eleven-year-old would sleep that he wanted to see.

They returned to the foyer. "How did you sort out the bedrooms?" he asked Darlene, knowing he could ask her anything from the length of her periods to what she and Earl did in bed at night and she would answer in that same slightly quivery voice. He was Earl's boss. He held their economic well-being in the palm of his hand.

"Earl and I took the big one, off the kitchen." She nodded up the staircase. "The kids are on the second floor. Chrissy's right above us. Avis took the room on the end."

"The one with the little balcony?" Deke had hoped that particular architectural detail might have special appeal for little girls.

Nodding, Darlene gave an apologetic shrug. "She said she was going out there and write mysteries."

"Mysteries!" Deke feigned amazement. "Most girls would work on their suntans. That child must have a great imagination!"

"Oh, she does." For the first time, Darlene smiled without reservation. "She's real smart. Reads all the time. I just hope she'll get out and make a few friends before school starts."

He grinned. He had Darlene Martin exactly where he wanted her—scared and eager to please. "It's funny you should mention that. What I really dropped by for was to remind you about the girls' softball game this afternoon. If Avis came, she could meet some of the girls on the team."

Mrs. Martin's eyes grew brighter. "What time does the game start?"

"Five-thirty, at Keener sports complex. Avis should get there early, if she wants to meet anybody."

Mrs. Martin frowned. Deke knew she was wondering several things—where the Keener sports complex was, if good ol' Earl was going to make it home in time to take them, and if he didn't, then if she'd be able to get that clunker of a car to start. God forbid they not show up at a ball game that Mr. Keener had taken the trouble to stop by and invite them to!

"We—we'll try to come," she stammered. "I'm not sure how late Earl will work and I'm afraid I don't know where anything is yet."

This was the opening he'd been angling for. He began barking out rapid-fire directions to the ball field—turn right at Hartsville Highway, go through the four-way stop, then turn down the gravel road just past the Methodist Church. Though they were absolutely correct, when he finished, Darlene Martin looked so confused that he thought she might cry.

"Does that help?" he asked, knowing with absolute certainty that it did not.

"I—I guess so."

"Look." He cranked up his most guileless smile. "Since you're still unpacking boxes, why don't you let Avis come with me? I don't usually pick up my players, but heck, y'all haven't been here but a couple of days. You and Earl can join us after he gets home from work."

Darlene Martin twisted her ring again, not knowing what to say. Deke waited, secretly enjoying her squirming on the horns of this most delicate dilemma. He knew everything she'd ever seen, read, or heard told her not to entrust her children to strangers; certainly not to adult men who showed up on her doorstep with neither wife nor child. Yet here he stood, a successful businessman, a pillar of the community, the man who'd plucked her husband from the unemployment line, just wanting to help her little girl make new friends. What to do?

"Look," he said, backing up another step. "I totally understand if you're not comfortable with that. For all you know, I could be some kind of child molester. Just bring her whenever Earl gets home. She'll have to sit in the stands instead of the dugout, but at least she'll get to see some of the game."

"No, no, it's all right," Mrs. Martin reacted so predictably that he could have mouthed her words. She shook her head. "Of course she can go with you. I don't know what I was thinking. . . ."

"You were thinking about how to keep your daughter safe," Deke commended her. "And I would do exactly the same thing. You can't be too careful with children, even up here in little Pisgah County."

"Thank you," Mrs. Martin said, her relief visible. "I'm so glad you understand. It's hard, when you've just moved in and don't know anybody. . . ."

He smiled. "No offense meant, and none taken. How about I wait outside in my car while you get her ready to go? I've got some paperwork to do, anyway."

"We won't be a minute," promised Darlene Martin, clutching Avis's uniform against her chest. "God bless you, Mr. Keener. You're a wonderful man."

It was amazing how easy it was, how easy it had always been. "Just give them the person they expect to see," he muttered as he settled down in his car to wait for the next young fresh-faced girl who would come running into his life on grasshopper legs, and make him feel, at least for a little while, just as good as he had that night with Tracy Foster.

ELEVEN

Jonathan Walkingstick yawned, fighting the rhythmic, sleep-inducing squeak of the old oak rocking chair. The late afternoons were killers. He'd tracked boar in Murphy, white-tail in Oklahoma, and a knife-wielding madman locally, and none of it compared to keeping up with Lily. Like him, his daughter was an early riser. Like her late mother, she had vast curiosity and even vaster energies, each day whirling through the store like a tiny cyclone, chattering to the babies pictured on the diaper display, building wobbly skyscrapers with cartons of cigarettes. Though they went into Hartsville for Mother's Day Out twice a week and Aunt Little Tom spelled him on Friday nights, the rest of the time it was just the two of them. By four P.M. she'd exhausted him, so he closed the store, darkened the bedroom, and put her down in her crib. For a blessed half hour she slept while he rocked, dozing off only to wake moments later, wondering what in the hell he was going to do.

They had run out of room six months ago. Her toys lay scattered all over their small apartment; each night they slept not ten feet apart. He could not turn around without stepping on one of Lily's stuffed animals or on one of Lily's shoes or sometimes even on Lily herself. More troubling was the fact that she was shy around strangers. When he left her at

Mother's Day Out she wept bitterly, reaching her little arms out for him as if he were abandoning her forever. Though she loved animals, and could name every forest creature in both English and Cherokee, Big Bird and Mickey Mouse troubled her. *"Hurt?"* she would ask when she saw them in her picture books, pointing at Big Bird's long neck or Mickey Mouse's monstrous ears.

"No, Lily," he would say, laughing heartily as if to cue her in on the appropriate response. "They're funny! Ha-ha. Cartoons!"

But she continued to stare at the images, distressed, sometimes kissing the page, as if to alleviate the pain Big Bird must feel at having a neck like a yardstick, eyes like hard-boiled eggs.

He knew that if he didn't get her more accustomed to modern American culture, she would be considered freakish when she started school—a six-year-old who could filet a trout but who wept at the sight of Ronald McDonald. He sighed. As much as he loved Little Jump Off, he'd almost reached the conclusion that it was simply not the best place for them to be. Lily needed more, and he was determined to see that she had it.

Now he sat, reading for the hundredth time the letter he'd gotten two weeks ago. Written on heavy letterhead stationery from a private bank in Atlanta, it was from a Mr. Edward Pomeroy, who, along with his three partners, was pleased to offer him a position at a private hunting reserve in Tennessee.

"We are quite impressed with your references," Jonathan softly read parts of the letter aloud, mimicking Edward Pomeroy's twangy Texas accent. "And would like to offer you the position of gamekeeper. In exchange for your management of the preserve, we can offer you housing, transportation, and a salary of twenty-five thousand dollars annually. As we are considering other candidates, we need your reply as soon as possible. Sincerely, E.P."

Again, Jonathan ran his fingers over the gold crest embossed at the top of the paper. It had become a kind of ritual. Every afternoon he would read the letter while Lily slept, finger the coat of arms, then sit and wonder what working for Pomeroy would be like. The man had seemed nice enough, when they'd met back in April. A florid, cigar-smoking, cowboy-booted Texan who'd just purchased six hundred acres of land in Monroe County, Tennessee. While the broad-bottomed Pomeroy had spoken dreamily of hunting feral hogs with spears, Jonathan had paid more attention to the perks the job offered. The transportation, a bottom-of-the-line Toyota truck, and the salary were nothing to get excited about, but the job included a nice house with a fenced yard, where Lily could have her own bedroom and neighborhood children to play with. It seemed the answer to his prayers; if he signed on with Pomeroy, he could give Lily everything she needed.

He looked at the letter again. He knew he need only scratch "Okay, Walkingstick" along the bottom and Pomeroy would not only consider it a binding contract, but would probably chuckle at its Cherokee terseness. Still, something stayed his hand. Maybe it was his own selfish reluctance to leave the blue mountains that surrounded them, and the silver river that flowed just beyond their door.

"Oh, to hell with it," he whispered. He'd decided to get up and look for a pen to sign the damn thing with when he heard the jingle of the bell over the door downstairs. Shit, he thought. I must have forgotten to lock up. Now somebody would come in wanting beer or fishing worms and wake Lily up. Rising quickly from the rocker, he stashed the letter in his shirt pocket and headed down the stairs.

He padded down the steps shoeless and silent. He'd just turned to quietly ask what his customer wanted when he felt a bolt of lightning shoot through him, making him hot and cold all at once. Mary Crow was standing there, outlined in the pale green afternoon light. Her eyes were the color of rocks in a riverbed, gold earrings winked through her shoulder-length hair, and her smile—that smile—promised a million things that even today took his breath away as profoundly as it had when he was twelve. He felt as if he'd gotten up too quickly from a dream and he closed his eyes, telling himself it was simply someone who looked like her. *Mary is gone. Mary chose Gabe. Mary sends you postcards of parrots and llamas. That is all you have of Mary.*

He opened his eyes. Still she stood there, her smile so radiant, it made him ache with desire. He wanted to touch her, wanted to kiss her, wanted to take her in his arms and never let her go. He realized, though, that first he needed to say something, lest she interpret his silence as hostility. The rift between them was of his own making; it was he who had succumbed to the charms of Ruth Moon, he who had chosen Ruth to be his wife.

At the time it seemed the right thing to do; only later did it turn ugly as Ruth's jealousy drove her to murder and madness. His bride had nearly cost them all their lives. He gulped. Though he did not trust his throat to make a sound, he attempted speech.

"*Sheoh,*" he said warily, still expecting her to morph into just another pretty tourist right before his eyes.

"*Douhdunay.*" Her voice was still slightly husky, with the barest trace of a southern accent.

"Long time, no see." Ridiculous, but the only thing he could think of to say. Though she was close enough for him to touch, they may as well have been standing on opposite ends of the solar system.

"I've been in Peru," she said quietly.

Did she think he hadn't read her postcards? He had, every one, many times over, both on and between the lines, finally taping them low on the refrigerator door, at Lily's eye level.

"But now I'm back."

He glanced past her, out the door. If Gabe Benge came sauntering up on the porch, he would take his knife Ribtickler and cut him to shreds.

"Just me." She answered the question implicit in his eyes. She lifted the brown packing box she held in her arms. "I brought presents. For you and Lily."

He felt both relieved and terrified. She was truly here, truly alone. What to say next, though, and not sound like a fool?

"Lily's taking a nap now," he said. "But she'll wake up soon. Would you like something to drink?"

"That would be nice."

He stumbled to the back of the store. What should he offer her? It was too hot for coffee and he hadn't brewed any fresh iced tea. Beer seemed too familiar, water too cheap. Finally he grabbed two cold Cokes from the cooler and a jar of roasted peanuts from the shelf. It had been their favorite snack when they were teenagers. As he uncapped the bottles, he watched her out of the corner of his eye. She gazed for a moment at the fireplace, then strolled around the store. Usually she avoided the front corner, the spot where she'd years ago found her mother so brutally murdered, but today she went over and gazed at the floor with her head bowed, as someone might visit a grave. By the time he'd poured the peanuts into a bowl, she was standing in front of the fireplace, smiling.

"What happened to your Ding-Dongs?"

"Got rid of 'em," he said, secretly pleased that she'd remembered his passion for the little chocolate cupcakes. "Got rid of all the sweets."

"All of them?" She looked shocked, as if unable to conceive of any Cherokee-owned store without an extensive selection of sugary treats.

He nodded. "Lily's only had sugar twice in her life—a candy cane last Christmas and chocolate cake at Michael Swimmer's birthday party. Aunt Little Tom has to give herself insulin shots four times a day now."

"I'm sorry to hear that. But it's good that you got rid of the candy. You can't miss what you've never had."

Yes, you can, he thought, looking at her mouth, wishing he had the guts to just walk over and kiss her. *You can shrivel up and die, missing what you never had.*

They clicked their Coke bottles together and sat in front of the cold fireplace. He tried to make small talk, dancing around the subject of Gabe, until she finally just said, flat out, "Gabe's fine. He's still in Peru."

"You two aren't together anymore?" He held his breath, terrified of everything that rode upon those five words.

She shook her head. "I got homesick," she said, her tone neutrally including him, the store, maybe the entire state of North Carolina, for all he could tell. "So I came back home."

"To stay?" The question fell out of his mouth before he could stop it.

"I hope so," she replied with a cryptic smile. Cleverly, she then turned the subject to him, asking how he'd been, what being a single parent was like.

"If I had it to do all over again, I'd make some different choices." He acknowledged the train wreck Ruth Moon had made of his life with a bitter smile.

Mary lifted a brow, but made no further comment. They talked on. He listened, astonished, when she told him that she'd moved back to

Irene Hannah's house and had just opened her own law office on Main Street.

"So how long have you been here?" He tried to keep the hurt from his voice. Why had she not called him immediately? Had he fallen so far in her esteem that she now regarded him as just an old friend to be caught up with when she wasn't busy doing something more important?

"About two weeks." She laughed, then offered a lame apology. "I had to get reacclimated. Hartsville's really changed."

"You think so?"

"Yes. The last time I was here, we didn't have a Mercado Hispaño on Main Street. And Hugh Kavanagh didn't have an Ani Zaguhi in his employ."

"An Ani Zaguhi?" Jonathan smiled, happy that she'd remembered one of the shared terrors from their childhood. "One of Aunt Little Tom's big medicine Ani Zaguhi?"

"None other." Mary laughed. "Hugh has no idea what-all Ridge Standingdeer can do."

"So what's this guy like?" he asked, loving to see her smile.

"He's a nice boy," she replied. "Strong. Polite. But I've seen no signs that he's big medicine."

As they laughed, a plaintive little cry floated down the stairs.

"Uh-oh," said Jonathan. "She who must be obeyed has woken up." He handed Mary the bowl of peanuts. "Sit tight. I'll be right back."

He hurried upstairs. Lily sat in her crib, her dark eyes wide and questioning, as if she sensed a stranger in their midst.

"We've got company, Lily Bird," he whispered, lifting her out of her crib and into the bathroom, hurrying to give her a quick once-over with a wash rag. "Important company. So you be good, okay?"

Lily just looked at him and chuckled.

He washed her off, changed her into the little pink jumpsuit he'd bought her in town, and carried her downstairs, again wondering if Mary was really going to still be there. She was—still sitting in front of the fireplace, though she stood up when he brought Lily into the room.

"*Sheoh,* darling girl!" she cried, now giving Lily that smile he'd feared he'd never see again. "You've grown up!"

"Look, Lily!" He said. "It's Mary! Meyli!"

To his great consternation, Lily clung to his neck like a monkey and refused to look at Mary at all. Only when Mary opened the box from Peru did Lily loosen her grasp and squirm to be released from his arms.

"Guess what, Lily?" Mary's eyes danced as she spoke to the child. "I brought you some presents! Look!"

She leaned over the box and pulled out a fuzzy stuffed llama. Instantly Lily grabbed it, crying, *"Waga!"*—the Cherokee word for cow.

They both laughed. "No, Lily," he said. "Not cow. *Llama.* Can you say llama?"

"Does she speak only Cherokee?" asked Mary as the little girl clutched the toy llama like a teddy bear.

"She goes back and forth," he replied. "Some days she speaks Cherokee, other days English." He looked at his daughter and smiled. "Other days it's Lily-ese. Only she understands that."

The gifts continued. Mary gave them both hats—for him, something she called a jipijapa, which looked like a white straw fedora out of an old Humphrey Bogart movie; for Lily, a pointed woolen cap that made her look like an elf. Mary added more Peruvian toys to Lily's collection, then for him, some small sharp arrows and a bright yellow rug for the floor. Finally the box was empty.

"You were nice to think of us." He was ashamed that he'd sat here with his thumb up his ass, never responding to any of her letters or postcards. What a jerk she must think him.

She looked up quickly, as if wanting to say something else, but Lily bonged her in the nose with her new llama. Again they laughed, and suddenly it all felt as if they'd done this forever. He longed to ask why she'd come up here but he was afraid to speak, lest his question spook her, like a deer in the woods. It was enough that she'd come at all; to ask for more would be greedy. Still, he couldn't just give her a Coke and some peanuts and send her on her way.

"Lily and I usually eat pretty early," he began apologetically. "But would you join us for dinner? I've got some fresh corn and I can go catch us a few trout."

She gathered Lily in her arms and smiled. "Thank you," she said softly. "I'd love to have dinner with you."

So he left the two of them playing with Lily's new toys while he grabbed his fishing pole and dropped a line in the Little Tee. Cicadas chirped a summertime rant and the late afternoon sun undulated like liquid fire on the water. Suddenly he felt dizzy, as if the world was spinning out of kilter. Mary Crow, the woman he'd always loved, the woman he'd thought he'd lost forever, had dropped back into his life like a comet falling from the sky. Now she was here, in his house, about to eat dinner with him and his little girl. Every night since she'd gone to Peru, he'd promised himself that if he ever got a second chance, he would rectify his error of letting her go. Apparently that was happening now. As he cast his line into the water he felt the crinkle of Pomeroy's letter in his shirt pocket. Was this what had kept him from signing it and sending it back? On some fundamental, subcellular level, had he been waiting for a second chance with Mary Crow?

"Don't screw it up this time," he told himself as he whipped his line beneath a moss-slickened rock where the trout liked to hide. "You may have gotten a second chance. You sure as hell won't get a third."

TWELVE

Gooooooooo, Kats! Yaaaaaaaay!"

The little girls huddled in the middle of the pizza parlor, each extending one arm into a larger circle of arms, then lifting them toward the ceiling at the end of the cheer. His little pink-and-black-clad players had beaten their archrivals, the Northside Graphics Bombers, and he had brought the whole team downtown to Mick and Mack's Pizza, to celebrate. Now as the little girls ate their way through a dozen jumbo pizzas, Deke sipped beer with their parents and relived the highlights of the game. The day that had gotten off to such a rocky start with Bethany in Mary Crow's office had smoothed out. His drive to the ball field with Avis Martin and the Kats' bottom-of-the-ninth victory over the Bombers made Bethany seem no more significant than a mouse squeaking over a bit of cheese. Hell, her own parents were here celebrating with everybody else. Bethany could march in here right now, put her fucking tapes on the sound system, and nobody would even look up.

"You did a heck of a job tonight, Coach!" Ray Medford came over and pumped his hand. His daughter Lisa, a pudgy freckle-face whose butt was already way too big, played a credible second base. "I thought we were going down for sure."

"It wasn't anything I did, Ray. The girls did it. Lisa played a terrific game." Deke always made it a point to compliment the fathers. He knew that though most wouldn't admit it, they were merely pretending to be excited for girls who couldn't run or throw or bat half as well as any boy their age. But God had sent them daughters instead of sons and the out-field errors, the dropped balls at first base, the crying over striking out were all just part of the deal. He tried to make the guys feel as good about it as he could, but he knew that however much he praised their daughters, in the playing fields of their fathers' hearts, they would always be second-rate.

"You think we'll make it to the state tourney this year?" Medford, a husky forklift operator, always dreamed big for his modestly talented child.

"They keep playing like this, we will," Deke said, moving away from Medford's sour beer-breath. He scanned the crowd of players and their parents, then smiled when he saw Earl and Darlene Martin, standing shyly in the corner nearest the door. "Let's talk later, Ray. There's some-body over there I need to speak to."

"Sure thing." Medford stepped back. Deke could tell he was disap-pointed. His audience with the Prince of Pisgah County hadn't lasted nearly as long as he'd hoped. But why should it? The man drove a truck and his daughter was shaped like a bowling pin. There was no reason to spend any more time with Ray Medford. No reason at all.

He plunged into the crowd, accepting congratulatory hugs and hand-shakes as he went. As he neared the Martins, he saw that Glenn and Paula Daws had just introduced themselves to the new couple.

"Hey, everybody." Deke inserted himself between the two couples. "I was just going to introduce these guys. I see you beat me to it." He looked down at Avis, who was sticking close to her mother. "Hey, short stuff. How'd you like the game?"

"It was okay," she replied noncommittally. Earlier he'd introduced her to the rest of the team, and though they'd greeted her politely, they hadn't exactly welcomed her with open arms. Girls this age could be such little bitches that he'd kept her close to him, lest they spoil her first taste of being a Keener Kat. They'd all taken note of her special treatment and unless they found her to be a hopeless loser, eventually they would accept her.

"Think you'd like to dress out for the next one? Maybe play third base?"

For a long moment Avis didn't respond. Inwardly, Deke cursed himself for taking her too soon, for not introducing her to Kayla Daws first. Then Darlene Martin piped up. "I'm sure she'd love to. I think she's just a bit overwhelmed tonight."

"I can sure understand that." Paula Daws smiled at Avis sympathetically. "Settling into a new place is hard on girls this age." She tilted her head against Deke's shoulder. "Let this guy help her out. He's got a real way with kids."

"Aw, you're making me blush." Laughing, Deke lowered his eyes modestly. Bless Paula's heart. She had no idea what she was saying. He turned back to Avis. "Our next practice is tomorrow at five. Would you like another lift, in case your dad isn't home from work?"

Again, Avis didn't respond, then her mother must have poked her in the back because suddenly the girl nodded. "Yes sir," she said softly. "I'd like that."

"Great!" Deke exclaimed. "Then you mark it down on your calendar and I'll mark it down on mine. Tomorrow, five o'clock. Avis and Coach Keener, to the ball field."

The party broke up an hour later. The Atlanta Braves had a real game that most of the fathers wanted to watch, and the little girls were eager to go home with their respective best friends. It was dark outside when Deke handed Mick his American Express card to settle his tab.

"You've got some cute kids there, Mr. Keener. Any of 'em go on to play in high school or college?"

He didn't know, he didn't care. The cutest ones spent a fair amount of time naked on his lap. Who gave a shit about the others? "A couple have played in college," he answered, thinking of the way Avis Martin's little bird legs had looked. "Most of them, though, wash out in high school."

"That's too bad," said Mick. "A lot of girls seem to grow up too fast around here."

You got that right, brother, thought Deke, Bethany's face flashing before his eyes. *One or two have gotten entirely too big for their britches.*

He signed his credit card slip, adding a generous gratuity. "See you next time we beat Northside." He waved at the barkeep. "I'm going home to bed."

Mick smiled. "Have a good night, Mr. Keener. Glad you guys won!"

Deke opened the door and stepped out into the June night. The mountain air felt cool but humid, and a fog wrapped all the streetlights in halos. He'd parked his car a block from the courthouse, at his usual place in front of the Baptist Church. Main Street stood empty, except for a single bright puddle of yellow light that spilled out from the Mercado Hispaño across the street. There a knot of short, dark-haired men stood laughing, drinking Tecate beer, listening to the bouncy Tejano music that poured from the speakers inside the store. It looked as if a small bit of Mexico City had come to life once all of Hartsville's Anglo businesses closed for the night. Curious about the music and laughter, he crossed the street. He had no fear of Mexicans. He owned most of the houses they lived in, paid them more money in wages than they had ever made in their lives before. He approached the store whistling, jingling his car keys inside his pocket.

The men outside paid him little notice, glancing at him with their frank macho stares, then turning back to their friends. One man was gnawing on a chicken leg, while the others were laughing at another man who was holding up a vicious-looking pair of tiny spurs, the kind meant for fighting cocks. Deke had heard that Tito, the proprietor, held cockfights in his basement, but he'd never bothered to check it out. As long as Jerry Cochran didn't care, Deke didn't care. Hell, what was one less chicken to him?

"*Buenas noches,*" he said to the men, enjoying their looks of surprise at his decent Spanish. "*Qué pasa?*"

The chicken eater shrugged. "*Aquí nomás.*"

"Those belong to your bird?" Deke asked the man who held up the spurs.

"They used to." The chicken eater laughed with his mouth full. "Now his bird belongs to me!" He patted his stomach. The other men roared, finally cajoling even the man with the tiny spurs into a grin. *"No sale,"* he said in Spanish, he waved the chicken leg and shook his head in mock sorrow. *"No vale."*

Deke laughed with the other men, then turned to peer inside the store. Tito had moved some of his tables to the back and several couples were dancing to the bright music. Sylvia Goins, the big girl he avoided at Sutton's Hardware, was bouncing around the floor with a Mexican man half her size while a man he recognized as one of his framing carpenters danced an amazingly intricate step with a beautiful girl who looked like Jennifer Lopez. He smiled as an older couple danced a kind of upbeat tango, but then his face froze. The dancers swirled around, revealing a lead-footed couple, limping to the music in the middle of the floor. His pulse started to race. It was Bethany Daws, tipsy, trying to dance with a skinny Mexican man who was dressed all in black.

Better get the fuck out of here, he thought. If she sees me here, God knows what she might do. He started to back away from the door, but the cockfighters had clustered behind him, looking at the dancers. He was trying to ease his way through them when suddenly, the music stopped. Bethany's partner grabbed her to keep her from falling down. Deke backpedaled faster. He didn't want a confrontation with her here. Drunk, she might say anything, and though the Mexicans weren't considered upstanding members of the community, he didn't want them repeating any barroom gossip on his work crews. His foremen would get wind of it, eventually, and slowly it would work its way up the chain of command. He could just picture Glenn Daws' face then.

"Con permiso, amigos," he said, pushing his way through the crowd. *"Tengo que irme."*

The cockfighters parted obediently, but he'd waited too long. Breathless and dizzy from the dance, Bethany turned her face toward the door for a gulp of cool air. She looked happy and laughing, her eyes sparkling at the pleasure of the music and the night. Then her gaze fell on him. Her face changed just as it had in Mary Crow's office, only this time it went from placid to furious instead of afraid. As soon as she saw him, her eyes narrowed, and her mouth curled down in a snarl.

"Hey, look everybody!" she called, slurring her words slightly. "Look who's joining the dance. Good old Coach Keener, still in his Kats uniform!" She held on to her partner and searched the dance crowd with great extravagance. "Gosh, Coach, I don't think we have anybody here young enough for you! All these girls have pubic hair and periods!"

A silence fell over the room. The dancers and the cockfighters turned to stare at him. They didn't seem to quite understand what was going on. *"Es su novia, patrón?"* asked the chicken eater sympathetically.

"No." Deke shook his head, trying to distance himself from Bethany and her goddamn mouth. He circled his left ear with one finger. *"Está loca."*

"Ay caray!" the man agreed. *"Sí."*

Deke kept backing out the door. Bethany, though, had pushed herself away from her partner, and was now swooning into the arms of another man, this one with a dark mustache. "Do you know the Mexican word for child molester?" she asked him, woozily pointing her finger at him. " 'Cause that's one right there, standing in the door. El child molester-o."

With that, Deke turned. He needed to get out of there, and get out now. He had no idea who was in there, or how much English any of them knew. With Bethany going off like that, this could get bad, fast.

He fled from the light of the bodega and into the shadows, his shoes beating out a rapid tattoo on the pavement. Though he heard no more shrieks about him being "el child molestero," when he passed the furniture store he broke into a jog. By the time he reached his car, the music had come back on, and the cockfighters were starting a dice game on the sidewalk. He punched his remote. The door unlocked and he hurried inside. The smell of the leather seats comforted him, and he felt as if he'd slipped back into a safe, dark cocoon.

"That little cunt!" he whispered, grasping the steering wheel, wishing it were her neck. The damage she could have done! The damage she might well have done! My God, he couldn't let this go on. He'd hoped maybe her insanity would pass and she would just quietly go off to college and forget the whole thing, but she was not going to let it rest. She was too much of a drunk, too much of a slut, too much of what he'd made her. He would go to her parents, tomorrow morning, first thing. He wasn't sure what he would say, but he had all night to come up with that. Right now, all he was sure of was that this would be the last time Bethany Daws would ever stand up in downtown Hartsville and accuse him of being a child molester to his face.

THIRTEEN

Paula Daws groaned, stretching for the OFF button of her clock radio. Always she woke seconds before the alarm, just as the green numerals of the clock changed from 5:29 to 5:30. She had awakened like this every day for the past twenty years. Early in her marriage, she had loved to be the first one up, loved the still, breath-holding silence of a house before its inhabitants awoke. For the last several years, though, she'd dragged out of bed like a half-drowned cat, her alarm clock serving as reveille for a brand-new skirmish in the Great War with her daughter Bethany.

She threw her covers back and sat up, already weary at the thought of the day. Last night she'd heard Bethany come in at 2:43. The girl had sneaked out, despite being grounded, and had come home drunk. Paula could always tell by the noisy way she opened the kitchen door and her stumbling footsteps down the hall. Last night she'd fallen on her way up the stairs, and though Paula's first reaction had been to hurry out to her child, she'd just pulled the covers over her head instead. Bethany was drunk. Bethany had fallen. So what else was new? For the past five years she'd nursed the girl's bruised legs and hangovers. Paula was tired, and besides, there were other people in this family besides Bethany.

She stumbled her way to the bathroom, smelling the coffee that had just begun brewing from the small automatic pot on Glenn's dresser. It had been a Christmas gift from Glenn, one her mother heartily disapproved of. *"A good wife would fix her husband a big pot of coffee, and a real breakfast for her children."* With her mother's harsh opinion echoing in her head, Paula poured herself a cup of the hot, black brew and sighed. Maybe that was why Bethany had turned into a drunk. Maybe it was because she'd given Glenn his coffee in small doses and served her children granola for breakfast.

"God knows nobody's come up with a better reason," she whispered as she ran a brush through her curly brown hair. Years earlier, when Bethany's bad behavior had grown outrageous, they'd fled the microcosm of Hartsville and sought counseling for their child in nearby Sylva and Waynesville. None of the experts could decide why Bethany had changed from a sweet, happy child into an angry teenager who secretly tippled vodka and wept for hours in her locked room, although one steely-eyed Waynesville shrink looked at them as if they were vermin and informed them that Bethany was being sexually molested. That had so infuriated Glenn that he'd driven home thirty miles an hour over the posted limit. When they pulled into the driveway, he turned to Paula and raged, "If that pile of shit's the best the experts can do, then we'll just deal with this ourselves."

Sighing again, Paula fixed Glenn his own cup of coffee. As she sat down on the bed beside him, she thought how much like a small boy he looked, his hair tousled from sleep.

"Wake up, honey." She kissed the top of his head. "It's almost six."

Glenn sat up. He took the coffee she offered, then ran an affectionate hand under her nightgown, fondling her breast. "Thanks, babe," he said, then looked at her warily, as if they'd slept on a fight. "You hear Bethany come in last night?"

She nodded.

"It was bad, wasn't it?"

"She fell down." Paula, who didn't drink at all, wondered how much alcohol it would take to make a healthy eighteen-year-old falling down drunk. A lot, she guessed.

"That little Indian fucker!"

"Oh, Glenn, he didn't pour it down her throat." Glenn always blamed whatever boy Bethany was involved with. Never could he see his daughter for what she truly was. Paula smoothed the wiry blond hair on the top of his head. "Be thankful she made it home okay. At least she's not lying in a ditch somewhere, dead in a car wreck."

"I suppose," he said, his voice bitter as the coffee he drank.

She took a quick shower, pulled on black yoga pants and a pink FIGHT BREAST CANCER T-shirt, then ceded the bathroom to Glenn. She had a busy morning ahead of her. Her new yoga class was starting at the Y, Bethany had the breakfast shift at the café, and Kayla was scheduled to go horseback riding with Jeannette Peacock early, before the sun got too hot. Quickly she walked to the foot of the stairs.

"Bethany? Kayla? Time to get up!" Though both girls had loud alarm clocks, she found a personal summons always got them moving faster. "Bethany? Kayla?"

"I'm up!" Kayla's voice came faintly from behind her bedroom door.

"Then make sure your sister's up," Paula called. "And let Darby out of your room. He needs to go outside."

"Okay."

As she waited for the dog to come downstairs, she gazed up at Bethany's closed door, trying to imagine what her life would be like after Bethany went to college. *No more slamming doors. No more tears. No more drunks stumbling up the stairs in the middle of the night, no more skinhead Cherokee boyfriends.* It'll be nice, she decided guiltily. Real nice. Calm. Happy. But calm and happy lay a good two months away. She still had the rest of July and half of August to get through.

"Come on, Darby," she said to the ever-cheerful old Lab, who stood gray-muzzled and grinning down at her from the top of the stairs. "Let's go outside."

Darby followed her stiffly to the kitchen, where she let him out the back door. She noticed that though the white truck that Bethany had sneaked out in was parked sideways in her rose bed, there were no dents on the thing that would indicate any wrecks.

"Thank God for small favors," she whispered. As she filled Darby's dish with crunchies, she thought again of her mother's snippy remark about her little coffeepot. Maybe she had been a crappy wife and mother. Maybe if she'd just gotten up early enough to fix everyone a real breakfast Bethany would have turned out okay.

"So give it a shot today," she told herself, letting Darby back inside. Though she knew that nothing she could scramble up on the stove would change Bethany at this late date, at least when her children were grown they would be able to say that their mother hadn't been a total flop, at least once she'd fixed them a decent breakfast, way back in June of 2004.

Marveling at her own insanity, she brewed coffee in her twelve-cup pot, then pulled out her cast-iron skillet to fry some bacon. As she mixed up a bowl of lumpy pancake batter, she heard the thump of Kayla's stereo, but still nothing from Bethany's room. Once again, she went to the bottom of the stairs.

"Kayla!" she called, knowing that Bethany was still passed out. "Don't forget to wake up your sister before you come downstairs."

"Okay!" came the faint reply.

She returned to the kitchen to find Glenn pouring himself some coffee from the big pot. Dressed in khaki pants and a sport shirt, he still had comb tracks visible in his newly washed hair. At forty-six, he had a bit of gray sprouting around his temples, but he still had a construction worker's physique—flat stomach, big hands, deeply tanned face and arms. For twenty years she'd followed him all over the South—building skyscrapers in Atlanta, condos in Chattanooga, beach houses along Florida's redneck riviera. Ten years ago, when he finished a shopping mall in Charlotte, they'd found themselves, for the first time, without a job. The great Dixie construction boom had faltered and men spent their days going from the employment office to the unemployment lines. Competition was fierce from the Mexicans, who would work cheaper and accept money under the table. They themselves had gotten down to their last hundred dollars when a man from western North Carolina called. "Saw your ad in the Builders' Association magazine," he told Glenn. "I'm looking for an experienced foreman, and I'd prefer an American, with a family."

That man had been Deke Keener, who'd brought them here and given them a house, a good job, and security like they'd never known before. He and Glenn had, over the years, become like brothers, and when Glenn had confided in Deke about their problems with Bethany, Deke had reassured them as none of their paid professionals could. "It'll pass," he said sympathetically. "I've seen a little of this behavior in some of my ball players. You just have to ride it out."

"Why are you cooking breakfast?" Glenn blinked at the frying bacon, accustomed, as they all were, to her usual menu of cereal, milk, and fruit.

"I don't know." She didn't want to admit to falling victim to her mother's criticism, or to the specious logic that a hearty breakfast might start Bethany on the road to sobriety. "I thought maybe it might get everything off on a better foot."

"Everything or everybody?" asked Glenn pointedly.

Paula shook her head. "Doesn't matter, does it?" She poured the first pancake in the skillet. That one, she remembered, you were supposed to cook and then throw away. "So what are you up to today?" she asked as he spooned sugar in his coffee.

"Deke wants to visit that Bear Den site," he replied. "Although I don't know why. He hasn't even gotten the right-of-way from that old Cherokee."

"Maybe he thinks two of you can be more persuasive than one."

Her husband gave her a dour look. "You ever see an Indian who could be persuaded into anything he didn't want to do?"

Though his words were about a construction project, she knew he was really talking about Ridge Standingdeer. "Let's not go there," she told him wearily, dumping the first pancake in the garbage and pouring three new ones into the skillet. "It's too early, and anyway, he doesn't come around here anymore. You scared him off."

Glenn snorted as he sat down at the table. A few moments later, she put a plate of pancakes and bacon in front of him.

"Oh, wow. These look great." He grinned at her as he reached for the maple syrup. "Are there seconds?"

"I made enough for a small army."

"So where's our army?"

"I don't know. I'll call them again." She started across the kitchen to rouse her children once more, when Kayla appeared in the doorway.

"Hi, honey," said Paula. "I was just about to call you. Did you wake up your sister?"

"I banged on her door," Kayla replied, plopping down in the chair beside her father.

"She'll be down in a few minutes, then." Paula went back to the stove, hoping that her firstborn was indeed up, hoping that this wasn't going to be one of *those* mornings.

Two more months. Paula stacked pancakes on Kayla's plate, now imagining breakfast in September. They would all be here at the table, at the same time, getting ready for their day, sleepy but not nervous; quiet perhaps, but not out of fear that the wrong word or glance might set off a maelstrom of abuse. The tight sick knot that this family had been coiled in would loosen. For the first time in years, they could just be themselves.

Suddenly she heard a knock at the kitchen door. She turned. Her husband's boss stood there, grinning. She hurried to let him in. "Deke!" she leaned over and kissed his cheek. "What a nice surprise!"

"Good morning, beautiful! Your worthless husband awake yet?"

"He sure is. Come on in and have some breakfast with us." She held the door open wide. "I've made pancakes."

"Pancakes?" Deke came in and gave Kayla a wink, Glenn a playful punch on his shoulder. "What did y'all do to deserve pancakes this morning?"

"Beats me," Glenn replied. "I just showed up and here they were. Want some?"

"Have you got any extra?" asked Deke.

"I've got plenty," said Paula, thinking that maybe for once her sour old mother had been right. This was fun, sitting around the breakfast table, eating pancakes. Paula stacked three on a plate for Deke, then fixed him a cup of coffee just the way he liked it—one sugar, plenty of cream.

She sat down finally, and began to eat a pancake of her own, listening as the men discussed the softball team, the upcoming Fourth of July picnic, the new attorney Deke had hired to help him with the Bear Den site.

"That's one of the reasons I stopped by," Deke told Glenn. "I thought I would take this Bear Den mess over to her and free you up for that Tsali Trail meeting."

"Suits me," said Glenn. "What did you say her name was?"

"Mary Crow. I went to high school with her. She's half Cherokee." Deke grinned. "The other half is pure Atlanta belle." He looked around the breakfast table. "Say, where is our own little belle? She's the other reason I stopped by here."

"Good lord!" cried Paula, glancing at the clock over the refrigerator. "She's still asleep. And she's got to be at work by nine. You guys help yourselves to more pancakes. I'll go drag her out of bed."

Paula hurried out of the kitchen and up the stairs. Bethany's door was still closed. She knocked once, for an instant wondering what she would do if Bethany wasn't there; if Bethany had just ditched her scholarship and her future and run off with that Cherokee boy. Hurriedly she opened the door. To her relief Bethany still lay in bed, the sheets pulled up around her ears.

"Bethany!" Paula called. "Bethany! It's time to get up! You're going to be late!"

The girl did not move; did not even twitch. Lord, thought Paula. She must have really tied one on.

"Bethany!" she called, louder. Still no response.

"Bethany!" Walking over to the bed, she shook her daughter's shoulder. Then she saw her head, bashed in like a melon. The tomahawk that Ridge Standingdeer had given her lay on the bed beside her. She realized then, as she screamed a scream that filled the room, the house, the whole rest of the world, that she was not going to have to wait until August to find out what life was like without Bethany; for her, life without Bethany was beginning right now.

FOURTEEN

Later that morning, Mary Crow sat in her new office, gazing at the buttery sunlight that slanted across her desk. Usually her work surface was cluttered with evidence files and coroners' reports and a hundred other documents peculiar to prosecutors. Today her desk held only a growing list of items she needed from the hardware store, and three thick legal texts she had not cracked since first-year law. Two empty armchairs faced her desk and behind them, on the wall, a battery-operated clock she'd found in Irene's guestroom, a curious thing that marked the hours with various bird calls. She'd been waiting for Deke Keener since the mockingbird trilled nine; now the tufted titmouse had just chirped eleven. Her nervousness at having her first client was rapidly growing into irritation at his lateness, and she wondered if she'd fallen victim to one of those notorious Southern hyperboles, like "Come on over anytime" or "I'll call you real soon." Natives knew those airy phrases meant nothing, but they aroused great confusion in more literal-minded New Yorkers and Californians, who either showed up on the doorstep at inopportune moments or waited hopefully for phone calls that never came.

Still, Deke said he'd be here first thing this morning, so she assumed that eventually he would show up. Anyway, it wasn't like she had any other clients lined up outside the door. Taking a sip of the coffee she'd brought up from Layla's, she tried to refocus on the one book she'd opened. Her mind balked. Property estate had been dull enough in law school; after ten years as a criminal prosecutor, reading about general warranty deeds, special warranty deeds, and mortgage deeds made her feel as if her brain was shutting down, neuron by neuron. As she looked at the two other texts she had yet to open, a wave of dread washed over her, and it was all she could do not to close the book and run shrieking out the door.

"You can do this," she scolded herself. "Once you get accustomed to it, it won't seem so bad. Just remember Jonathan."

Jonathan. Although last night had gone far better than she'd hoped, there had been a tentativeness about Jonathan she'd never seen before. She'd glimpsed it in his eyes the moment she walked in the store; she'd felt it much later in his kiss, after they'd put Lily to bed.

"I can't believe you're really here," he'd said as they sat on the porch, watching a huge yellow moon rise over the pine trees across the river. With one finger, he traced her cheek, all the way down to the tip of her chin.

"Actually, I can't either." She closed her eyes, his touch electric on her skin. She was amazed that no other woman had staked a claim on the single father with the beautiful brown-eyed baby girl.

"And you're really going to open your own practice?" He sounded so much like a little boy, she almost laughed.

"I've signed a six-month lease in town," she told him. "If I can't drum up some business by Christmas, I may have to rethink things."

"But you'll still just be a general lawyer?"

"I'll do everything except divorces," she answered, remembering her promise to Dana Shope.

"What about DUIs? Assault and battery? Murder?"

She smiled. In different guises, he'd asked the same question three times since supper. She knew exactly why. As much as he loved her, Jonathan had always hated what she did. Hated the evidence files she'd brought home in Atlanta, hated the look in her eyes when a case wasn't going well, hated the thought that at any time some vengeful scumbag might be waiting for her with a knife in a dark parking lot. Her career choice had been an issue between them for years. Now, with a daughter to raise, as much as he might love Mary, she knew he would not tolerate Lily being exposed to the risk and squalor of a prosecutorial career. She understood perfectly; in fact, she fully agreed.

"DUIs maybe. Murder—no. I might not be a prosecutor anymore, but I'm certainly not going to work the other side of the aisle."

"For real?" The moonlight glittered in his eyes, the sometimes hard curve of his mouth was soft, relaxed.

"Yes," she said. She was not, after a three-thousand-mile journey back from Peru, going to let her choice of legal specialty stand between them. She had avenged her mother's murder many times over. Now it was time to let younger, hungrier prosecutors take up the fight. She wanted other things from life.

Her promise seemed to quell the turmoil inside him. He put his arm around her and together they watched the moon rise, becoming a small bright circle of light shimmering over the dark waters of the Little Tee.

Now she sat back, reliving the feel of his lips, until her gaze fell on the book that lay open in front of her.

Come on, she told herself, forcing her attention back to the present. Deke Keener is coming to see you. You'd damn well better at least try to sound like you know something about property law.

For the fourth time, she began the chapter on the various types of deeds. Line after line of print darkened the page, with little white space in between. Though she tried to comprehend the meaning of the text, as she read, the letters seemed to blend together, making an unintelligible hash of words. Finally she started reading the sentences out loud, just to keep her eyelids from closing. By the time she'd read to the end of the first page, the mourning dove clock cooed noon.

"Good grief!" She slammed the book shut, angry. In no way could noon be considered first thing in the morning. Apparently, Keener had stood her up. She could have gone to the hardware store, bought all the items on her list during the time she'd spent here, poring over stupid real estate law. She was considering calling him on the new land line they'd installed this morning, when she heard a chirp of another sort— her cell phone beeping in her purse.

"Hello?" she answered quickly, thinking perhaps Jonathan had brought Lily to town and they could have lunch.

"Mary? Is that you?" Hugh Kavanagh's normally low-pitched voice sounded high and breathy, as if he were in pain.

"Hugh!" Mary sat up straighter in her chair. "What's going on?"

"You've got to get over here! The cops have Ridge cornered in my barn!"

"Ridge? What on earth for?"

"They want to arrest him." She heard Hugh choke back a sob.

"Arrest him? Why?"

"Sweet Jesus, they think he killed Bethany Daws." The old man broke down in tears.

Mary nearly dropped the phone. Bethany Daws? The girl who'd just yesterday brought them muffins for breakfast—dead?

"I don't understand, Hugh—"

"Neither do I. But the girl's dead and the bastards have Ridge trapped in my barn. Mary, girl, you've got to come. These bloody fools will shoot him!"

She remembered the pill bottles lined up across Hugh's windowsill. Nitroglycerin, Inderal. Heart medications. Whatever the problem was between the cops and Ridge Standingdeer, it was spiking Hugh Kavanagh's stress level up to Mars. "Take a deep breath, Hugh," she said. "Go in the kitchen and take one of your pills, then go back outside and tell the officer in charge that there is no need for violence, your attorney is on the way."

"Aye." Hugh gave a loud sniff.

Mary could picture the old man with his Irish up, hobbling out to bash some cop over the head with his cane. "I know you're angry, Hugh, but you've got to stay calm. You mustn't give the cops any reason to think you're out of control, too."

"I won't. Just hurry, girl. *Please!*"

Switching off her phone, she grabbed her purse. She should probably leave Keener a note, but since he was the one who'd not shown up at the appointed time, she was off the hook. Anyway, she really didn't have time to write any notes of apology. If she left right now, it would still take her half an hour to get to Hugh's. Grabbing her car keys, she opened her door. She jumped. Directly in front of her, with his hand poised to knock, stood Deke Keener. His complexion was ashen beneath his freckles, and his brown eyes darted as if they were hooked up to small wires.

"Hi, Mary. I'm so sorry I'm late. Something terrible has—"

"I can't meet with you now, Deke," she interrupted, practically running over him. "I've got to get over to Hugh Kavanagh's farm."

"Is it something to do with Ridge Standingdeer?"

She frowned. "How did you know?"

"I just left Glenn Daws' house. I heard Jerry Cochran put out the APB on the boy."

Mary's heart fell. "So it's true? That pretty young girl is dead?"

Deke nodded sadly. "I was there this morning, when Paula found her. Someone smashed her head open with a tomahawk."

"A tomahawk?" Mary echoed, incredulous.

Deke swallowed, as if trying not to weep. "Yeah, you know, they sell them all over town. A river rock the size of my fist, tied to a length of white oak."

Mary nodded. She'd grown up selling the things to tourists at Little Jump Off. They were primitive, but lethal, weapons that now sold for about four bucks a pop.

"It was awful, horrible," Deke moaned. "The worst thing I've ever seen . . ."

"Hugh just called me. He says cops have Ridge cornered in his barn. They think he killed the girl."

"They do have a history," said Deke. "But when I left Glenn's house, Cochran just wanted to bring the boy in for questioning."

"Well, according to Hugh they have a SWAT team with every gunsight trained on Ridge. I've got to get over there before Hugh drops dead from the stress!"

"How about I drive you?" suggested Deke. "I know a shortcut that'll get us there fast."

"We may have to stay there a while," Mary warned him. "I have no idea what's going on out there."

"I don't mind. You know, Mary, that boy's going to need a whole lot better place to hide than Kavanagh's barn. Glenn already wants to kill him. When the rest of the town finds out about this, they're gonna go just as nuts."

"Deke, the boy's innocent until he's found guilty."

"Of course he is." Deke seemed embarrassed. "It's just been a very hard morning. I want Bethany's killer found just as badly as Glenn does."

"I'm sure you do, Deke," said Mary. "But you've got to make sure you've got the right killer before you shove the needle in the guy's arm."

FIFTEEN

Police cars blocked both the front and rear entrances to Hugh's barn. Hugh stood holding Cushla McCree on a lead rope, waggling his cane at a plainclothes officer the size of a small tree. The horse's ears were slapped back and Hugh's face looked purple as he raged at the man, who was further fanning Hugh's wrath with his best I'm-a-cop-and-you're-not smirk.

Mary scrambled out of the car before Deke came to a full stop. She could tell that Hugh was about thirty seconds away from a coronary and that nothing would please the cop more than to have the old Irishman drop dead at his feet.

"Hugh!" she called. "Wait! What's going on?"

Both men turned. Then Hugh stormed out to meet her, pulling Cushla behind him. The cop pushed his sunglasses higher on his nose and stared at them, animated as a stump.

"Ridge and I were working Cushla when this sorry bastard came into the ring." Hugh pointed his cane at the cop. "He spooked the horse into next Tuesday. By the time Ridge got her calmed down, more cops had come, and they were aiming rifles at him!"

"Did you take your pills, Hugh?" asked Mary, noticing that his color had gone from purple to a strange mottled gray. His breath was coming in shallow gulps. Are you having chest pains?"

"Aye. That I am."

"Hugh—take your medicine. Take it now."

The old man obediently handed her the horse's lead and dug a small blue plastic bottle from his pocket. With shaking hands, he poured some tiny white pills into his palm.

"That bloody fat fool came into the paddock," he went on, dropping two of the pills under his tongue. "Walked right up to Ridge. Said he wanted to talk to him about Bethany Daws. When Ridge asked why, the bastard told him she was dead." Hugh pulled a bandanna from his pocket and wiped his forehead. "Sweet Jesus, the boy had no idea! You could tell that by the look on his face."

"What did Ridge do then?" asked Mary, eyeing the cop with the sunglasses.

"Knocked that bastard down, he did," the old man said proudly. "Then when he saw he was trapped in the paddock, he ran into the barn. He's been holed up in there ever since. For the love of God, Mary. Don't let them kill him!"

"Okay, okay." Mary wrapped her arms around the old man, who was trying desperately not to cry. Since the boy in the barn wasn't going anywhere, her first concern was easing the stress on Hugh's heart. "Go sit in Deke's car. I'll talk to the detective."

She felt his body stiffen in her embrace. "It's my barn and my boy, Mary Crow. If there's any talkin' going on, I want to be part of it."

She stepped back and spoke softly. "Okay, but I need you to be calm, Hugh. Waving that cane around won't help a thing."

Hugh muttered some Irish thing she couldn't understand, but he took Cushla's lead rope and meekly followed Mary back over to the detective, who was now leaning against a police cruiser. By the gold badge on his belt and the bullhorn beside him, she assumed he was the officer in charge. She stepped forward and matched his wooden cop expression with her best lawyerly glare.

"Detective? Would you apprise me of the situation?"

The man stared at her for so long that she wondered if he'd heard her. She started to repeat her question, then she realized that she wasn't in Deckard County anymore; cops no longer had to heave to just because she showed up on the scene. Okay, she thought, biting back her anger. Two can play this game.

She stared into the man's sunglasses for another beat, then she gave a tiny shrug of her shoulders and started walking toward the barn. She hadn't gone two steps before the officer snapped: "You can't go in there. There's an armed fugitive from justice in there."

"Has this so-called fugitive been charged with anything?" asked Mary.

The man smirked. "Not yet. But his girlfriend got her head bashed in last night."

"Have you questioned him yet, Detective?"

"No."

"Then if you haven't either questioned or charged him, how can he be a fugitive from justice? Justice implies judgment, and since no charges have been placed against him, judgment could not have been rendered. So that boy's really not a fugitive from anything, is he?"

The detective did not move.

Mary continued. "It looks to me that he's fleeing from what he perceives to be danger, which, I must say, I would too, if I had been peacefully doing my job and suddenly found myself surrounded by six men aiming rifles at me."

The man's mouth drew down in an even more sullen line. "Who the hell are you?"

Mary dug her wallet from her purse. None of her old Georgia IDs would cut any ice with this guy, so she handed him one of her homemade business cards. "My name is Mary Crow. I'm Mr. Kavanagh's attorney."

He studied her card with excruciating slowness, then gave her a sneering smile. "You're the one who whacked Logan, aren't you?"

Mary thought of half a dozen snappy comebacks, but decided to save them for another time. Instead, she turned to Hugh. "Have you got any guns in that barn, Hugh?"

"Aye. A pistol and a varmint gun."

"Any ammunition?"

"A box or two, likely."

She turned back to the officer. "Gosh, Detective, it looks like you've turned this into a real situation. You rush the barn, some of your men could get hurt. Or the boy could freak and kill himself." Mary shook her head. "I know you're not going to believe this, but not only did I whack your old boss Logan, but I went to high school with your new boss Cochran. And I know for a fact that he isn't going to like an apprehension of a suspect going down like this."

The man crossed his arms, now defensive. "I don't see as how that's your problem."

"Plus the boy's an Ani Zaguhi Cherokee. He doesn't speak English well and he's lived so far back in the mountains that he doesn't understand police procedure. You mess this up and you could have both the BIA and the ACLU on your back." This was utter nonsense, but this guy looked like he might have difficulty keeping up with anything beyond the latest NASCAR standings.

One corner of his mouth twitched with uncertainty; she knew she had him.

"And as I'm Mr. Kavanagh's attorney, and as this is Mr. Kavanagh's property and you don't, apparently, have any kind of warrant, how about I go in and talk to this young man? I get the boy to come out, drive downtown to answer your questions. You look good, I look good, nobody goes home wearing any bullet holes."

The detective puffed up. "What makes you think you can persuade him better than this?" He touched the butt of the pistol that peeked from his shoulder holster.

"*Ahya Tsalagi,*" Mary said curtly. "I speak his language." Without another glance at the detective, she headed toward the stable, her footsteps the only sound as the eyes and gun barrels of Pisgah County's finest stayed trained upon her.

Inside, the stable was a cool and dark refuge from the midday sun, sweetly aromatic with hay and horse feed. With all the horses grazing down by the creek, the structure stood empty, its silence broken only by the meowing of two calico cats. As her eyes adjusted to the dimness, she realized she should announce herself, lest Ridge mistake her for someone with a badge and a gun.

"*Sheeoh?* Ridge? This is Mary Crow. *Toe heju?*" In Cherokee, she asked how he was.

No response. Taking two steps forward, she tried again.

"Ridge?" She looked at the ladder that led up to the hayloft. That was the place he likely would have gone, she decided, though she still heard nothing. Frustrated with her limited Cherokee, and aware that the cops' patience would not last forever, she switched to English, and directed her words toward the loft above her head.

"Ridge, you don't need to be afraid of me. I can help you, but you've got to come out so we can talk."

Again, she heard nothing. She sighed. Ridge wasn't going to give up easily. Moving quickly, she walked over to the ladder and began climbing, purposefully making a lot of noise. Just as the top of her head poked through the hayloft door, something flashed inches from her face. Instinctively she blinked. When she opened her eyes again, she saw the glittering prongs of a pitchfork, inches away from the end of her nose. Ridge stood, shirtless and barefoot, holding the pitchfork on her, his eyes wild with fear.

"*Waynuh gooee!*" he growled, the thick muscles of his arms taut. "Go *away*!"

She held up her hands. "I've come here to help you, Ridge. We've got to talk!"

"I have nothing to say!" The lethal tines of the pitchfork trembled as he shook the thing at her.

"Those men outside need to ask you some questions, Ridge."

"They think I killed Bethany, don't they?"

"I don't know what they think. But they need to talk to you."

"Then why did they come with guns?" he asked bitterly. "Why do they try to scare an old man?"

"Because they're bullies," Mary replied. "But they still need to talk to you."

"Yeah. First they talk, then they kill me. For killing Bethany." The boy's voice cracked.

"That's not how it works, Ridge. Before they kill anybody, they have to bring a case against them in court. They have to have a trial. They have to prove that someone did it."

"But I didn't kill her! I loved her!"

"That's what you have to tell them, Ridge. And I'll go with you when you do it. If you stay here, it'll only get worse. They'll bring more cops, more guns. They'll be like dogs after a rabbit. Only you will be the rabbit."

He considered that in silence.

"And don't forget Hugh," she continued. "This is putting him under a terrible stress. If you stay in here much longer, his heart will give out. Already, he's sick and taking his medicine. Look outside, if you don't believe me."

The boy made no move toward the window. "Is she really dead?" he asked softly, his eyes glistening.

"I'm so sorry," Mary answered. "But I think she might be."

He stood there, pitchfork in hand, gazing at her but seeing some private thing, totally his own. Though he shed no tears, she watched as his heart broke by inches, his face revealing a sadness so raw that she had to turn her eyes away.

When she looked back up, the pitchfork was pointed no longer at her, but at a spot just beneath his chin. For a terrible instant, she thought he was going to plunge the thing into his neck. But instead, he slowly raked the pitchfork down his bare chest, opening four neat furrows that spurted bright red blood.

"Ridge!" she cried. "Stop!"

He said nothing, but threw the pitchfork in the corner of the loft. Then he lifted his hands and face upward, rivulets of blood turning the straw at his feet red. A sudden chill came over the barn. The warm summer breeze that had just jingled the wind chime turned brisk and strangely cold. Ridge lowered his face to gaze at her. Mary gasped. Where moments before he'd looked like a despairing young man, his face now bore the savage angles and hooded eyes of an angry beast, wounded and hurting.

"Ridge?" Her voice came out in a whisper. Never had she seen anything like this, and though she was a full-grown woman who did not believe in ghosts, she couldn't help but remember Aunt Little Tom's dark Ani Zaguhi stories. "Ridge, are you okay?"

He turned his face away from her and in a high, keening voice, chanted a song so old, she had no idea of its meaning. The words sounded like the weeping of the damned. She stood there on the ladder, the hair on the back of her neck lifting, until Ridge finished. When he looked at her again his features had softened back into their familiar lines. This time, his eyes recognized her, and when he spoke, he used the English she best understood.

"I have only one thing to say, Mary Crow."

"What's that?" she asked, clinging to the ladder.

"I did not kill Bethany Daws." He swept his right hand under his chin.

Mary recognized his gesture immediately. It meant that Ridge had just said all he was going to say about Bethany Daws, and for all intents and purposes the subject was forever closed.

"Okay." Mary nodded. "But the police will still want to talk to you. Will you come down now? For Hugh's sake?"

The boy looked around the hayloft as if considering his options, then his dark eyes met hers unflinchingly. "Only because of Hugh," he replied.

She backed down the ladder. A moment later he stood beside her, gazing out into the sunlit world beyond the stable door. Deke and Hugh and the lumpish detective huddled next to the police car while half a dozen men with rifles stood posted around the paddock. All stared intently at the stable door.

"Will they kill me?" Ridge's coppery skin glistened with sweat and blood.

"No. They'll take you downtown, where they'll ask you questions about Bethany." Mary told him the truth, but left out the fact that they would probably question him for hours and then throw him in a small windowless cell, only to question him more. She hated that for him, but they had the right to hold him for forty-eight hours. "Don't worry. I'll go with you."

"If I do as they want, will they leave Hugh alone?"

Mary nodded. "They have no need of Hugh."

Ridge turned, casting a longing glance out the back door, where hazy, violet mountains glimmered in the distance. Up there, in some Appalachian Xanadu, was his home. How he must long to go there now! For an instant she held her breath, wondering if he wasn't going to leap over the gate and just run like hell for home. But instead he turned and squared his shoulders. "Okay," he said. "I'm ready."

"I'll go first," said Mary. "You walk right behind me. Hold your hands up so they can see you don't have a gun."

"Like on TV?" He held his hands up shoulder-high, palms out, fingers spread wide.

She nodded. "That'll do."

She stepped out into the sunlight. "Detective, have your men shoulder their weapons. The boy's surrendering, unarmed."

The detective hesitated, then gave a nearly imperceptible nod. "Do it her way, boys," he called.

The men pointed their rifles into the air. Mary glanced once behind her, then said evenly, "Okay, Ridge. Just follow me. We're going to walk over to that police car."

He made no response, but she started walking anyway. She knew he would follow—it would dishonor Hugh if he didn't.

Midway across the paddock she looked back, half wondering whether a man or a beast was following her. To her relief she saw a handsome young man walking about six feet behind her, his hands raised. When they neared the police car, two uniformed cops came out and grabbed his arms.

"Get over here, you little bastard," said one, grabbing Ridge's ponytail and jerking his head back, hard. "Some big bad brave you are, walking out of there behind a woman."

Ridged stiffened his legs and balked, but it was too late. The officers hauled him over to the waiting squad car, throwing him in the back and slamming the door.

Before Mary could utter a word, the car started to pull away. Quickly she ran toward it. Ridge sat pressed against the window, his eyes pleading, reminding her of a dog she'd once seen being hauled to the pound.

"Don't say anything until I get there," she called, amazed at the words coming out of her mouth. What was she thinking? She was a prosecutor, not a defense attorney. "I'll be five minutes behind you!"

With that, Ridge's car sped off, followed by the rest of the policemen. White dust billowed behind them as they tore down Hugh's driveway.

She hurried over to the Deke's Lexus. He stood there, one hand supporting Hugh while he held the young mare by her lead rope. Though Keener looked bright-eyed as a squirrel, Hugh's face was ashen pale.

"Hugh, are you okay?" Mary asked.

"I think so," he said, breathing heavily. "At least they aren't going to kill the lad before my eyes."

"Come on." She grabbed the lead rope from Deke and tugged the horse toward the open fields. "Let's turn Cushla out to graze with her friends. We've got to get going."

"Where to?" Deke asked, trotting along beside her.

"Downtown to the Justice Center," said Mary, marveling both at the strange boy who changed at will from man to monster and the equally strange words issuing from her mouth. "It looks like I've just gotten my first client."

SIXTEEN

Deke sped them back to town. Mary had told him to hurry—she knew from her Atlanta days that suspects often arrived at the jail in considerably worse condition than when they'd been picked up, and she didn't trust that loutish detective not to pull off into some little mountain cove and give Ridge a taste of Pisgah County justice.

"What will they do to him?" Perched in the middle of the backseat, his gnarled fingers worrying the head of his cane, Hugh seemed to read her thoughts.

"They'll interrogate him," Mary answered bluntly. "To find out what he did last night."

"After they beat the shit out of him." Deke giggled.

"Not if you get us there in time," she snapped, irritated that he would laugh about such a thing in front of Hugh.

"Will they let him come home after they're done with him?" The old man's voice rose with hope.

"I don't know, Hugh." She told him the truth, but gently. "In the States they can hold you for forty-eight hours."

"That one won't stand bein' locked up," said Hugh, his tone ominous. "It'll kill him, as surely as a noose around his neck."

Pisgah County had acquired a new jail in her absence. The opening of the Cherokee casino had necessitated larger facilities, so the quaint old building with the potbellied stove had given way to a new low-slung, sprawling structure that reminded her of a bunker. Though the lobby was clean and painted a cheery banana yellow, Mary recognized the familiar stink of jail the instant she walked in the door. All of them smelled alike—a combination of disinfectant and failed deodorant, overlaid with notes of cigarette. Not that anybody was ever allowed to smoke—in jail, all your stored-up nicotine just oozed out your pores.

She left Hugh and Deke in the waiting area and walked to the desk, where a gum-chewing female officer with hair of indeterminate color sat behind a computer screen.

"I'm here for Ridge Standingdeer," said Mary. "I'm afraid I don't know his case number."

"He an inmate?"

"He was brought in just a few minutes ago."

The woman glanced at Mary's straight, raven hair. "DUI from the reservation?"

Mary gave the woman a frosty smile. Apparently some staff members here still assumed that Indians had trouble holding their firewater. "Actually, he's being questioned on a homicide," she replied, enjoying the little flicker of alarm in the woman's eyes. "Considerably off the reservation."

The clerk pursed her lips. "You the attorney of record?"

Mary hesitated. In her whole career she'd never defended as much as a jaywalker. Yet here was a young Cherokee, a boy Hugh clearly loved, in very deep trouble. Surely she could at least make sure his rights were protected until a real defense attorney took over.

"Yes," she told the woman steadily. "For now, I am."

"Are you on our register?"

Mary shook her head. "I've just recently moved back to town."

The woman handed Mary a long sheet of paper attached to a clipboard. "Fill this out, then you can go in."

Mary stood at the desk and hastily filled out a form that registered her as a bona fide attorney, licensed to practice in North Carolina. When she passed the clipboard back to the officer, the woman's mouth curled down.

"Mary Crow?"

Mary nodded. The woman's vaguely derogatory tone had said it all—she was a loyal Loganite: no doubt she expected the infamous Mary Crow to walk on cloven hooves, her pointed tail whipping behind her.

"Follow me," the woman said curtly. "Your client's this way."

The officer led her down another eye-poppingly yellow hall, where she surrendered her purse to be searched as she stepped through a metal detector. When everyone was satisfied that she had no contraband concealed upon her person, the desk clerk led her further down the hall, stopping at the last door on the right.

"In there," the woman said. "The detectives are talking to him now."

Mary took a deep breath and looked through the small window in the middle of the door. She knew what kind of operation Stump Logan had run, and she half expected to see a broken and bloody Ridge slumping in a chair, signing some manufactured confession. Though the same hulk of a detective was standing there scowling at the boy, Ridge himself sat at the table, stony-faced but looking no worse than when he'd walked out of the barn. Someone had given him a white T-shirt, which now had a line of four red bloodstains down the front. To Mary's great relief, his features looked normal—his high cheekbones and coppery skin had not remorphed into whatever Mary had glimpsed in that hayloft. A dark-haired man sat with his back toward her, and a video camera high in the corner was recording the proceedings. At first glance, the scene was a textbook example of a legal interrogation. Praying that was truly the case, she took a deep breath and opened the door, trying to affect the incredulous, you've-got-shit-for-a-case demeanor of her old courtroom rival, Virginia Fox.

"Hello, gentlemen," she said, smiling at the two-way mirror, behind which she knew several more cops and possibly George Turpin himself would be watching. "My name is Mary Crow. I'm representing Mr. Standingdeer."

The dark-haired man in the chair stood up and turned around. He was tall and thin, and dressed casually, in jeans with a plaid sport shirt. The moment he saw her, he grinned. "Mary? Is that really you?"

At first she didn't recognize him, then the curly black hair and the glasses and the dimpled chin all fell into place. Years ago this man had been a chubby little bookworm who sneaked Philip K. Dick novels in behind his biology book. "Jerry? Jerry Cochran?"

Awkwardly he wrapped his arms around her. Her former lab partner now towered over her by half a foot, and from the feel of his back, had turned his baby fat into solid muscle.

"I heard you'd moved back to town." He loosened his hold on her, no doubt aware that they were being watched by Ridge and the detective and God knew who else behind the mirror. "But I didn't know you were practicing criminal law."

"And I heard you'd been elected sheriff. But I didn't know you'd be involved in this case."

"We don't get many murders here," Jerry said, almost apologizing. "I wanted to make sure everything went okay."

Mary's heart sank. In Atlanta, that usually meant the cops didn't want to bungle a good-looking case. Here the subtext was harder to read, but it still seemed that Ridge must be their number-one suspect. She looked over at the video camera, which had just recorded their blissful reunion. "Pisgah County's really gone high-tech."

Jerry started to say something, but the detective loudly cleared his throat. "Sheriff, do you want to go on with this now?"

Ignoring the derision that dripped from the man's words, Jerry answered, "We'll go ahead, Driver. Roll that tape back and let Ms. Crow have a look. Then everybody will be on the same page."

Mary smiled. Jerry certainly didn't have to make their previous questions known to her, but he had. Detective Driver slid his toothpick over to the opposite corner of his mouth, then moved the tape from the camera to a video player hooked to a TV set. He rewound the tape to the beginning and punched the PLAY button. Mary watched the whole interview. Driver had brought Ridge into the room, Jerry had read him his rights again, the questioning had begun. They hadn't played good cop/bad cop. Jerry had asked simple, straightforward questions while Driver had stood glowering at Ridge like an underpaid bouncer in a backstreet bar. To her great relief, Ridge had answered every question with the same six words. "I did not kill Bethany Daws."

When the tape went blank, Mary looked at Cochran. "Okay. Shall we start over again?"

Driver reloaded the camera, Jerry set up a folding chair for Mary beside Ridge, and the interview resumed. Mary glanced at her client, alert for any sign of nervousness, but the boy sat motionless, his eyes straight ahead, Zen-like in his stillness. She wished she felt half as calm as he looked.

"Mr. Standingdeer, please state your full name and legal address," said Jerry.

"I did not kill Bethany Daws."

"Please tell us where you work."

"I did not kill Bethany Daws."

"Was Bethany Daws your girlfriend?"

"I did not kill Bethany Daws."

Mary allowed Ridge to go on like this—he was kind of cooperating, and he wasn't damaging his case. But after ten minutes and about fifty *I did not kill Bethany Daws,* Jerry turned to her. "Can you help us out here, Counselor? These questions are answerable by half a dozen people. We'd just like to hear what he says."

"According to that old Irish fart, he's one of them Assy Galoshes," said Driver. "He probably cain't speak no better English 'n that."

Mary leaned over and whispered in her client's ear. "It's okay to answer these questions, Ridge. If they ask anything that will hurt your case, I'll stop you from answering."

He turned to look at her with deep-set eyes so brown, they appeared black. "I did not kill Bethany Daws. *Shki di!*" Again he made that ancient scrape of his chin. She knew then that Jerry could question Ridge from now till Kingdom Come: he would still get the same six-word answer.

"What did he say?" asked Jerry. "Do we need to get an interpreter?"

"He speaks English," Mary told the sheriff. "He simply chose to speak in Cherokee."

"So what did he say?" Driver demanded. "What did that chin signal mean?"

"He said he didn't kill Bethany Daws," Mary replied. "His gesture meant that he has nothing more to say."

Driver snorted. Cochran tried a few more questions, but the boy would say nothing more. Frustrated, Jerry looked at his old classmate. "Does he know that if he doesn't answer my questions I'm going to have to lock him up?"

"Let me explain that to him." Once again, Mary turned to Ridge, paraphrasing Jerry's words in English, then repeating them in Cherokee. When she asked Ridge if he understood, he nodded.

"You'll be locked in a tiny room," she explained further. "Bars on the windows, bars on the door. The lights never go off. It's midday, even at midnight." She remembered what Hugh had predicted in Deke's car and added, in Cherokee, *"It'll be hard, Ridge. Like nothing you've ever known before."*

He shrugged. His world had turned to shit. Nothing made any difference to him.

Mary looked at the new sheriff and shook her head.

"Okay." Jerry turned to Driver. "Get Schultz and Brennan to escort Mr. Standingdeer to a cell."

"I can take him," Driver offered eagerly.

"No," said Jerry. "I want you to file this tape, and fill out the report."

"Yes, sir." Driver sighed in ill-concealed disgust.

As two uniforms moved to escort Ridge to jail, Mary leaned over and whispered in the boy's ear. "Do exactly what they tell you. Don't make any trouble. I'll see you later this afternoon." His eyes were expressionless as he got up to go with the officers, his head held high.

She watched him as he walked out of the room, then she followed Jerry back into the hall, leaving the sour detective to file his reports. Once the door closed behind her, she leaned against the wall, feeling as if she'd just avoided a fatal car crash by mere inches. She knew she'd been ridiculously ineffective in Ridge's defense, but she knew, too, that she'd done no harm. Turpin didn't have any more ammunition than he had before they brought the boy in.

"You want some coffee?" Cochran gave her a shy smile. "You look a little upset."

She shook her head and told a small lie. "It's just been a while since I've worked defense."

"Well, it's been a while since I've worked a homicide," he said evenly. "I guess that makes us even."

She looked up at Cochran and suddenly saw the irony of it all. She, newly reincarnated as a defense attorney, was chatting pleasantly with the enemy, her old lab partner, who was newly reincarnated as the sheriff. This was Pisgah County in a nutshell—a place where rebel statues faced east instead of north and the district attorney cared more about his barbecue recipe than his conviction rate. "I guess it does, Jerry," she said, chuckling. "At least it's good to know I've got an old friend running the jail."

❥

While Mary chatted with the new Sheriff Cochran, Deke Keener sat waiting with Hugh Kavanagh, trying hard to keep himself zipped inside his own skin. For the past two hours he'd endured the old Irishman's ranting about Ridge Standingdeer, all the while trying to figure out where in the hell Bethany could have stashed those goddamned tapes. He'd searched the most obvious places (dresser drawers, her student desk) after he'd sent Paula down to the kitchen, but the cops had come thundering up the stairs before he'd had a chance to delve into her closet or her bedside table. Now he was stuck here, with this querulous old mick, while God knew what all was going on at Glenn and Paula's. He glanced at his watch. Christ, what was keeping Mary Crow? He needed to get out of here. He needed to get back and find those tapes!

Suddenly a number of loud-talking people came into the lobby. Deke turned to see three men in ties and sport shirts, followed by one young woman with a camera. Reporters. Charlie Smith, from the *Pisgah County Times,* he knew. The others, he surmised, were stringers from the papers in Asheville and Charlotte.

Story's broken, he thought. Somebody's blabbed. Either Glenn or Paula or some cop. He shrank down in his seat. The prospect of Charlie Smith recognizing him here, baby-sitting this crazy old Irishman, spooked him. As fun as watching Mary Crow wrangle that crazy kid out of the barn had been, he couldn't allow himself to be identified further with this case. He was an ardent supporter of family values, law and order. He couldn't be seen here, cooling his heels among real criminals. He was considering a quiet retreat to the men's room when it suddenly occurred to him that he was missing the opportunity of a lifetime. Reporters were standing not ten feet away, ravenous for information. If he could spin this case toward a Cherokee witch-boy, then who would give a rat's ass if some goofy tapes showed up? Worst case, he could tell them it was a joke or they were practicing for some church skit about preventing sexual molestation. Quickly he rose from his chair and walked toward the information desk where Smith was badgering the same female officer who'd given Mary the fish eye. Ignoring some rancorous bleating from Kavanagh, he hurried over and put a hand on Smith's shoulder.

"Hey, buddy," he said softly. "How's it going?"

Smith turned. For an instant he stopped in mid-gum-chew, no doubt astonished to find the richest man in Pisgah County standing in the lobby of the jail. "Deke Keener! What the hell are you doing here?"

"Just waiting for my new lawyer to tie up some loose ends on another case," replied Deke. "What's up with you?"

"I'm trying to find out who they pulled in for the Daws murder." Smith spoke with irritation, then paused. "You did know that Glenn Daws' daughter was murdered last night, didn't you?"

Deke gave a sorrowful nod. "I was eating breakfast with them when they found her."

"Holy shit." Smith leaned close and whispered, "Do you know who they collared for this?"

Deke smiled. "Actually, I do."

"Jesus H. Christ—who?" Smith whipped out his notebook faster than a magician might pull a rabbit from his hat.

Deke lowered his voice. "Ridge Standingdeer. A Cherokee witch." He nodded at Hugh, seated by the window. "Works for that old guy, over there."

"A Cherokee witch? You mean like a satanic cult?" Smith's eyes popped.

Deke shrugged. "I wouldn't know. Go ask the old guy. Name's Kavanagh."

"Thanks, Deke, I will," Smith started over toward Hugh, then looked over his shoulder. "I owe you one, buddy!"

"I'll remember that." Chuckling, Deke leaned against the desk, watching as Charlie Smith walked over and sat down beside Kavanagh. For a moment, the old man looked happy to have someone to talk to, then his face turned that odd, vitriolic purple. Deke knew something was about to happen when the old man struggled to his feet and roared that Smith was "no better than the bloody cops." Smith shook his head as if to deny the charge, but Kavanagh was in full rant. When the old geezer started poking at the reporter's shins with his cane, Smith scrambled out of his seat and headed for the door.

"See ya, Deke," he said, on his way out. "This is great stuff. Check out the paper tomorrow!"

Realizing they'd been scooped, the other newsmen started to gather around Kavanagh. Though it would be fun to watch another of the old man's fits, Deke needed to stay on Mary Crow's good side, and he knew she would be furious if she returned from Standingdeer's interrogation to find her precious Kavanagh being hassled by the press.

Taking Hugh by the arm, he told the other reporters that Mr. Kavanagh had no further statements to make and that all questions should be directed to his attorney, Mary Crow. With Ms. Crow nowhere in sight, they quickly went back to badgering their usual jailhouse source, the clerk behind the desk.

Deke walked the old man outside, where several hollow-eyed women stood on the sidewalk, sucking in cigarette smoke as if it were manna from heaven.

"I don't understand any of this." Kavanagh walked with his cane tapping on the pavement.

"It's really pretty simple," Deke said brightly. "Somebody murdered Bethany Daws. The police want to nail your hired hand."

"But he didn't do it!" the old man insisted. "He fancied her. They were sweethearts!"

"That makes the cops all the more suspicious, Hugh. Most murder victims are killed by people they love."

"That's a load of rot!" Kavanagh fumed. "Mary Crow will straighten this all out. Irene always said she was the best."

"Best prosecutor, maybe." Deke shook his head. "I don't think she knows that much about defense."

"Ah, to hell with you!" Kavanagh turned and started walking back toward the jail. Suddenly he cried out. "Sweet Jesus! Here she comes!"

Deke looked over his shoulder to see Mary Crow hurrying toward them.

"What happened?" blubbered Kavanagh. "Where's Ridge?"

"He's okay," Mary said gently, taking the old man's hand. "But they're holding him. He wouldn't answer any of their questions."

"Holding him? In jail? I thought you were going to keep that from happening!" For a moment, Deke wondered if Kavanagh might crack Mary with his cane, just as he'd almost done to that cop.

"Hugh, I'm not a defense attorney. All I did was make sure Ridge didn't incriminate himself or confess to something he didn't do."

"So what do we do now?" demanded Kavanagh.

She looked deeply into the old man's eyes. "I think we should go back home, Hugh. Ridge will be okay here. I've explained his situation to the new sheriff. Nothing bad will happen to him."

Keener listened closely to Mary's last statement. She'd talked to that wimp Cochran. At first it made him angry, then he realized having his attorney on friendly terms with the sheriff would do him no harm. "Mary's right, Hugh," Deke chimed in agreeably.

Kavanagh frowned. "But is there no way we can get the lad home? Reporters are already calling him a witch-boy. I'll stand for his bail, gladly."

Deke sighed in exasperation as Mary further tried to explain the American court system to the petulant old coot. "Hugh, a judge will set Ridge's bail at a hearing, if he's charged with this murder. Right now, there's nothing more to do. We need to wait and see what happens."

Hugh slammed the end of his cane down on the sidewalk. "But you can get him out! Irene always said you were the best!"

"Hugh, I'm not that kind of attorney. . . ."

Deke was suddenly sick of all this. He'd hadn't gotten more than an hour of sleep since the afternoon he'd driven Bethany and Kayla home. He needed to get quiet in his own head; he needed to figure out exactly who he needed to be next. "Mary's right, Hugh. Let's go back to your house now. Mary can explain on the way why she's not the attorney for Standingdeer."

The old man glared at them both with eyes like ice. "Boyo, she's explained all she needs to," he growled. "I'm just glad Irene Hannah isn't here to see what her precious Mary has become."

SEVENTEEN

"Hello?" Jonathan squeezed the telephone receiver between his left shoulder and ear, trying to answer the phone while scrubbing the dirt from between Lily's toes. Though all day he'd been thinking about Mary, the actual sound of her voice on the phone surprised him. She was truly here. Last night had not been a dream.

"I've got some bad news," she said.

His heart clenched, instinctive as a knee jerk. She was leaving, he knew it. She'd gotten her old job back in Atlanta or some new job somewhere else or maybe even Gabe Benge had wooed her back to Peru. "What is it?" He immediately adopted his Aunt Little Tom's superstitious habit of holding the phone away from his ear, so bad news couldn't touch him quite so closely.

"They nabbed Hugh's Ani Zaguhi for murder."

"Murder? Good grief!"

He listened as she related the whole saga of Hugh, Ridge Standingdeer, and Bethany Daws. Despite the seriousness of her words, he felt like smiling. Mary was not leaving. Nothing had happened to burst the charmed bubble that had surrounded them since the night before. He rinsed Lily off as Mary went on about the reporter who'd called Ridge a "witch-boy" and Hugh Kavanagh's cane-waving tantrums.

"So how do you figure into all this?" he asked when she came to the end of her story. *No criminals, she'd promised last night. No rapists, child molesters, kidnappers, or murderers.*

"I'm not figuring into any of it, but I don't think I'd better come over tonight, Jonathan."

"Why not? Isn't the kid already in jail?"

"Yes. That's just the problem. I'm afraid to leave Hugh here by himself."

"Oh." He tried to mask his disappointment. It was only one night she was talking about, not the rest of their lives. Still, he hadn't seen her in so long. His skin still tingled from her touch, and all day he'd kept looking out the window, listening for the high-pitched hum of her little black convertible, pulling into the parking lot. He'd replayed yesterday a thousand times in his head, recalling her voice at the door: "Hello? Anybody home?"

"I'm sorry," she continued. "But he's already had to take a handful of heart medications. He's hurt and confused and he's got no one here to help him with these horses."

"Okay." Jonathan was unpleasantly surprised by the petulance in his voice. Christ, he sounded like some horny housewife whose husband had gotten stuck working late at the office. "Maybe you can come tomorrow night."

He heard some static on the line, then she spoke again. "Why don't you and Lily come over here? I'll fix supper and she can see the horses. She would love it."

"Oh, I don't know." He liked Kavanagh well enough, but he didn't want to intrude upon the old man's distress, especially with a toddler in arms.

"Please come, Jonathan. It'll do Hugh good to see Lily. He had to spend most of the afternoon with Deke Keener."

Jonathan considered their redheaded classmate. He'd regarded Keener as an asshole ever since ninth-grade gym, and the ensuing twenty years had not changed his opinion. "Pisgah County's answer to Donald Trump? Why was he there?"

"He wants me to do some real estate work for him," Mary replied. "Please say you'll come."

Jonathan glanced at Lily, who was intent on rubbing her plastic yellow duck with a bar of Ivory soap. Wild, woodsy creatures she knew; she'd never seen a horse up close. It might be a good experience for her. Seeing Mary again would certainly be a good experience for him. "Okay. Let me get Lily dressed and we'll drive on over."

"Great!" said Mary. "Come on up to the main house. I'll be watching for you."

He packed up Lily and her diaper bag, closed the store, and headed for Hugh's. As he drove down the twisting mountain roads, he thought of what Mary had said. Hugh Kavanagh's employee had been arrested, on suspicion of murder. Naturally the old man would have called Mary, and of course Mary would have responded. But what next? Could she really not get further involved? Hunting was in her blood, no less than in his. Was extracting her promise not to do criminal law akin to asking a deer not to run? He couldn't say. All he knew was that ever since her phone call, the great joy that had exploded through him yesterday now felt tentative, held in check by the specter of her past vocation.

Forty minutes later, they reached Kavanagh's farm. As they rode down a long drive that bisected verdant pastures, Lily pointed one tiny finger at the horses that grazed along the fence, gurgling a word of her own invention.

"That's a horse, Lily," Jonathan told her, thinking he should probably start teaching more in English than in Cherokee.

"Hoss," Lily echoed, looking so solemn that he couldn't help but laugh.

When they pulled up in front of Kavanagh's low-slung ranch house, Mary came out to greet them. Even wearing an apron with her shirt-sleeves rolled up to the elbow, she looked like something from a dream. What a fool he'd been! He should have done anything to have kept her from going to Peru.

"Meyliii!" Lily squealed as Mary hurried up to the truck.

"Lily Bird!" Mary leaned in the open window and kissed him, a quick but sincere buss on the lips. "I'm so glad you could come." Once more she smiled the smile that somehow always reached down and caught his very soul.

Lily kept up her squealing, so he unbuckled her from her car seat, whereupon she crawled over him and into Mary's arms. He got out of the truck as Kavanagh came out on the porch. Lily took one look at the wild-haired old coot and lunged for her father, burying her head against his neck.

"Its okay, Lily," Jonathan told her softly. "He's *ehdudu*. Grandfather."

"She thinks I'm a fright, likely," Hugh said, his thick, bristly brows making him look like a porcupine. "And God knows, today she wouldn't be wrong."

"Mary told me what happened." Jonathan tried to loosen his daughter's stranglehold from his neck. "I'm sorry to hear things have gone so badly."

Hugh nodded, morose. "I'm not having half the bad time of poor Ridge."

Mary glanced at him and tried to lighten the subject. "Hugh, our roast should be done in about an hour. I thought we might show Lily around till then. Are you still going to take a nap?"

"I reckon." Hugh smiled sadly at Lily, then turned his gaze toward the barn. "You two mind that goose. A mean one, she is."

With that, Kavanagh went back into the house, the screen door slapping shut behind him. Jonathan looked at Mary, surprised by the old Irishman's brusqueness. "I see the troubles have come to County Pisgah," he said, affecting a brogue.

"The troubles arrived this morning with badges and guns." Mary sighed. "Come on. Let's give Lily the ten-cent tour."

They fell into step together. Away from Hugh, Lily squirmed out of Jonathan's arms and toddled a few steps ahead of them. As they made their way to the barn, his hand brushed against Mary's. Nervous as a schoolboy, he intertwined his fingers with hers. She smiled, and suddenly the only thing he could think of was what it would be like to take her up to the hayloft and remove her apron and that blouse and make love to her until the hot gold sun shrank to just a small white light in the darkness. Though the thought of it made him weak with desire, that could not happen now. Now he had Lily to take care of.

Mary introduced them to Fireball and Geezer, the barn cats, who curled their tails around Lily's short little legs. Napoleon, the aging German shepherd, greeted her with his own tail-wag while Lucy, the goose Hugh had adopted when Irene Hannah died, waddled up and regarded Lily with a beady blue eye. Dropping Mary's hand, Jonathan scooped the child up into his arms before the bird could strike.

"Guess what lives in here, Lily?" Mary crooned as they neared the barn. "Horses!"

"Hosses?" Lily repeated, her little voice piping like a flute. She looked at him, her brown eyes wide. "Hosses?"

Mary led them into the cool, sweet-smelling shadows. Though most of the horses were still out grazing, one small dun-colored mare stood waiting for dinner, her head poked over the back gate. As they walked toward her, Mary stepped over to a small door next to the tack room that had been left ajar. She stepped over to close it, then jumped, startled. "Good grief!" she cried. "Come look at this!"

He walked over, Lily in his arms, then gave a low whistle. Staring down from the walls of the room were a dozen different masks. Birds, snakes, medicine men—all were carved in the starkly primitive style of the ancient Cherokees. All glared down from the wall with hollow, eerie eyes.

Mary opened the door wider. A cot was positioned beneath the window, next to a bookcase that held a small CD player, a pouch of pipe tobacco, a minuscule TV set, and a flute fashioned from river cane.

"This must be Ridge's room," she said, studying the boy's strange conglomeration of the very old and the very new.

"Not much into housekeeping, is he?" He pointed to the other end of the room, where a closet full of discarded blue jeans mingled with the spill from an overturned workbench—wood shavings, glue, some small knives, an upended cane basket.

"That's cop mess," Mary replied, disgusted. "They must have searched this room while Hugh and I were downtown."

"Don't they need a warrant to do that?" He remembered all the warrants she'd stewed over when he'd lived with her in Atlanta.

"Yep." She leaned over and pulled a crumpled sheet of paper from beneath an old T-shirt. "And here it is. Signed by Turpin and some magistrate." She read the sheet, then began folding Ridge's jeans into an orderly pile. "There's no point to leaving all this stuff out on the floor."

"Here." Jonathan put Lily on the cot and knelt beside her. "I'll help."

They worked cleaning up the mess in Ridge's room. Lily played with two feathers from a blue jay while her father was happy to be close enough to breathe in the slightly spicy smell of Mary's hair, and to watch the ever changing shadows of her eyes. When he managed to focus on something other than his amazement that she was indeed here, he realized that most of the boy's carving implements were simply razor-sharp pieces of dark flint, and much of his clothing was deerskin, decorated with intricate beadwork.

"Look at these." He fished out a pair of moccasins from under the cot, and ran his finger down row after row of tiny red, white, and black beads. "These look like they belong in a museum."

Mary turned the moccasins over. The soles were buttery-soft deerskin, but obviously worn, stained with grass and dirt. "Hugh said Ridge came from way up in the mountains. I guess these are just sneakers, to him."

Grinning, Jonathan leaned close. "Wooooooooooooooo," he moaned softly in her ear, much to Lily's delight. "Better not mess with those! They're Ani Zaguhi witch moccasins!"

"Oh, Jonathan." Mary wiggled away, laughing, then she turned to him, her eyes serious. "You know, he did do something weird today."

"What?" He'd always loved it when she confided in him, when she told him things she would tell no other. He regarded them as little gifts, things of importance to her.

"We were up here, in the hayloft. I was trying to convince him to turn himself in. Ridge looked at me and changed his face."

Jonathan watched the steady throb of her pulse in her neck. How soft her skin looked. How he longed to touch her! "What did he change his face into?"

Mary stared at the masks. "I don't know. His mouth got feral-looking, and his eyes sort of glittered. . . ." Her voice faded and she shook her head, embarrassed. "I'm sure I imagined it. Haylofts are spooky and it was a pretty stressful situation."

Suddenly Lily pointed up at one owl mask that hung over the window. *"Ugugu?"*

"That's right, Lily," Jonathan said. "Owl." He pointed at the mask next to it. "What's that one?"

"Guhli." Lily answered, catching on to the game.

"Good! Raccoon. And that one?"

Jonathan laughed as Lily started naming all the masks, shifting between Cherokee and English. Squirrel. Fox. Crow. As they went around the room, he tried to catch Mary's eye, hoping she would join in their game, but she was staring at a medicine man mask, which hung just above the door.

"What are you thinking about?" he asked, disappointed that she hadn't paid the slightest attention to Lily's latest accomplishment.

"I was just wondering why he hasn't carved any bear masks. If the Ani Zaguhi are the Bear people, you'd think they'd carve bear masks."

Jonathan hoisted Lily to his shoulders. "He can't. It's forbidden."

"Forbidden? What do you mean?"

"Don't you remember what Aunt Little Tom told us? Bear masks are such big medicine that Bear people don't like to carve them."

"But I see lots of them every time I go to Cherokee."

"They aren't carved by the Ani Zaguhi." Jonathan widened his eyes and mimicked his aunt's breathy speech. "If Ani Zaguhi ever carves a *yonah ahgudulo,* run. That's such big medicine, the moon will chase the sun from the sky and possums will feast on foxes."

Mary studied him a moment, then she started laughing. "And possums will feast on foxes?"

He shrugged. "I'm just telling you what Aunt Little Tom says. You're the one who thinks this kid's an Ani Zaguhi."

"I know. I'm sorry." Chuckling, Mary pushed the moccasins back under the cot. "It's been a very strange day."

"So do you think he killed this girl?" he asked, abruptly serious.

Mary sighed. "I'm not as convinced of his innocence as Hugh."

"How come?"

"Young love is strong stuff." He noticed that Mary's cheeks had grown pink: was she remembering their own manic, teenage passion for each other? "Ridge seems like a nice kid, but I've seen nothing in him that would convince me he's incapable of murder."

With a deep sigh, Jonathan finally drummed up the courage to ask the question that had gnawed at him since she'd called. "So you really aren't going to get involved in this?"

She shook her head. "Today, I was the emergency room attorney. Tomorrow, I'm turning Ridge over to Timothy Brendle."

"Who's Timothy Brendle?"

"Ben Bryson's criminal defense guy. You'll be happy to know Tim was the third person I called when we got back from the jail."

He frowned. "Who were numbers one and two?"

"Number two was Turnipseed, my well digger. He mentioned last week that his son needed work, so I arranged for him to come out here tomorrow and take over for Ridge."

He gave a low whistle. "You're pretty damn efficient. Who'd you call first?"

A twinkle came into Mary's eye. "Gosh, I can't think of his name. Tall, good-looking guy. Lives out by the Little Tee with the cutest baby girl you've ever seen. I practically had to *beg* him to come have dinner with me."

Jonathan looked at her. "So you weren't kidding last night? You meant what you said?"

Mary scooped Lily up in her arms. "Tonight, I'm going to fix us a nice dinner and help Hugh with his horses. Tomorrow, I'm going to introduce Ridge to his new attorney."

She reached up and pulled him toward her. "After that, I'm going back to my office and hang out my shingle. Hopefully, some new non-lethal clients will find their way to my door."

Jonathan leaned over and kissed her. "Sounds like a plan to me," he said. Once again joy swept over him. Mary was not leaving, nor was she returning to criminal law. More than that, he dared not hope for.

EIGHTEEN

The next morning, Jonathan drove her downtown, dropping her off in front of the frilly mustard-colored Victorian that housed Bryson & Finch. As she got out of the truck, he asked when he would see her again.

"I've got an appointment with Deke Keener this afternoon," she replied, leaning in to kiss Lily good-bye. "How about I call you after that?"

He chuckled knowingly as he pulled away from the curb. "Talk to you later, then. Have fun with the Deke."

The prospect of spending the afternoon discussing real estate with Keener held about as much excitement as trudging up a hill through wet cement, but Mary pushed that feeling aside. For Jonathan and Lily, she had committed to a noncriminal law practice. If that meant brain-numbing afternoons with a self-righteous chatterbox who owned half the town, then so be it.

She walked into Bryson & Finch and announced herself to the secretary, who promptly led her into Timothy Brendle's office. Brendle was a small, slender young man who looked as if he'd slid off the pages of *GQ*. Dressed in a perfectly tailored blue suit that matched his eyes, he kept his dark blond hair moussed back from his face, and took notes with a thick Mont Blanc fountain pen that looked far too heavy for his slender, manicured fingers. "I read a terribly lurid account of the murder in the paper," he said, his accent tinged with a faintly British inflection.

"They charged Ridge early this morning," said Mary. "I think way prematurely."

"Tell me everything you know." Brendle's pen was poised over his legal pad.

She sat down and turned her case over to him with just a twinge of wistfulness, telling him everything she knew, noting with relief that he asked for clarification at exactly the same points she would have. "Okay." He capped his fountain pen when she finished. "Let's go see Mr. Standingdeer. I can't say I've ever defended an Arty Galoshi."

Mary smiled as she stood up. "Ani Zaguhi," she corrected him softly.

Half an hour later, they sat around a Formica-topped table in one of the jail's interview rooms. It smelled of pine disinfectant and the pizza that the kitchen was apparently readying for lunch. Ridge sat across from them, his shoulders straining against his too-small orange jumpsuit, the tattoos that decorated his arms looking like dark bruises on his skin. His eyes had the same look Mary often saw in Jonathan's—a wary watchfulness that white people read as hostile, but for Cherokees simply meant *I am here, I am listening, what do you want of me?* She herself loved that look; often searched for it in her own reflection, but her face had too much of her father in it. His fair Anglo-Saxon-ness softened her Cherokee features like cream in strong coffee.

Although Mary hoped that Hugh's dire prediction about imprisoning Ridge would prove false, he already seemed somehow *less* than he had just yesterday. Less muscular, less bright-eyed. Less Ani Zaguhi. "Ridge, how are you? How are they treating you?" She would not have this boy beaten; she would take it up with Jerry Cochran again, if she had to.

"Ostah," he replied, speaking in Cherokee. "I'm okay. How is Hugh?"

Mary replied in kind, trying to pull up words she seldom used. *"Azkahi."*

"What are you saying?" Brendle clucked like a hen. "Are you speaking Ani Galoshi?"

"Ani Zaguhi." Again, Mary corrected him. "And no, we were speaking Cherokee. He asked how Hugh was. I told him he was scared."

"Well, you'll have to speak in English if you want any help from me," Brendle sniffed.

In Cherokee, Mary told Ridge that they would have to speak English from here on out, then she explained why Brendle was there. "Ridge, this is Timothy Brendle. He's going to help you. He's a lawyer, like me, but he'll be better for you. He specializes in cases like yours."

Brendle stuck out his small white hand. Next to Ridge, the lawyer had the physical presence of an unbaked pretzel. Ridge did not move to shake his hand, but instead stared at him so intently that Brendle squirmed in his chair. Mary finally felt compelled to ease the impasse between the two.

"Ridge, Tim and I need to talk to you about Bethany."

Ridge turned his eyes away from Brendle and focused on her. For a moment, his deep, dark gaze caught her like a fly in a spiderweb. She felt sweat begin to trickle between her breasts.

"I did not kill Bethany Daws," he said.

"We know that, Ridge," Mary replied. "And we believe you. But we need to know a little bit more."

"I did not kill Bethany Daws," he repeated flatly.

Brendle leaned forward. "Mr. Standingdeer, I don't particularly want to know what happened the night your girl was killed. But I do need to know about you. What you did before she died, what you'd like to do after we get you out of jail."

Ridge gave Brendle a hard stare, then he rose from his chair, walked over beneath the room's single, high window, and sat down cross-legged on the floor, in a little patch of sunlight. He turned his face to the window and closed his eyes, like someone meditating. That, apparently, was what Ridge wanted to do. Go back to the sun and the air from which he'd come. Mary and Brendle sat there watching him in helpless silence until, a few moments later, the deputy came and took Ridge away.

Mary slumped back in her chair, disappointed. She had been hoping the boy might display the innocent charm that he had when they'd had dinner at Hugh's. Instead, he'd come across as a hostile mute. Brendle was making notes on his legal pad, the scratch of his pen audible in the small room. When he came to the end of the page, he dotted a large exclamation point.

"So what do you think?" she asked.

Brendle capped his fountain pen. "He's weird as hell, is what I think."

"I mean what do you think about his case?"

"That ponytail will have to go. It makes him look like he eats children for breakfast. And he's going to have to wear something to cover those tattoos."

"I'll get him a nice suit. I'll make sure he looks good."

"It wouldn't hurt for his hair to grow beyond skinhead length. And what was that creepy evil eye thing he had going on? He certainly can't look at a jury like that."

"I know, I know." Mary was growing impatient with Brendle's lectures on the obvious. "Do you think you can work with him?"

Frowning, Brendle tapped his pen on the table, then he said, "I think so. Turpin probably has a circumstantial case. If we mainstream this kid's appearance, put him in Armani and load the jury with youngish women, then he'll probably have a fair chance." He smiled, as if envisioning Ridge transformed for the courtroom. "Hell, dressed right, he might come out of this with a movie deal. A high-concept Hiawatha."

Mary smiled, too, but remembered the gaunt look in Ridge's face, the dejected slope of his shoulders. He'd clearly faded, just overnight. "Refresh my memory about North Carolina criminal statutes. Is this a right-to-speedy-trial state?"

Brendle laughed. "Hardly. Here, the average time from charges to disposition is three hundred and seventy-two days. One poor bastard in Durham spent four and a half years just waiting to go to trial."

"Didn't he appeal? On due process? Sixth amendment?"

Brendle shrugged. "Of course he did. Our Tarheel justices said it was his tough luck. The docket was backed up."

Mary felt sick inside. However tough Ridge Standingdeer was, he would not survive three hundred and seventy-two days in a jail cell. He was a young man of the forest and sky. Concrete walls and barred windows would kill him as surely as that crude tomahawk killed Bethany Daws.

Brendle must have noticed her distress. When he spoke next, his tone was more upbeat. "Look, the DA's up for reelection in November. A lot of people are tired of his stupid barbecue obsession. Turpin needs a conviction, fresh in the voters' minds. I imagine he'll go to trial pretty fast with this."

Mary stared at the swatch of sunlight where Ridge had sat. "I don't know whether that makes me feel better or worse."

"It's a toss-up," Brendle said. "Turpin won't have any extra time to build his case, but we won't have the advantage of memories growing foggy, should he scare up any eyewitnesses." Brendle snapped his briefcase shut. "Can I take you to lunch?"

"Thanks, but I've got a pretty busy afternoon. I'd love a lift to my office, however."

"Sure thing." As Brendle rose, he smiled. "Hey, I really appreciate your calling me in on this. It'll be my first defense of an Ani Galoshi."

"Ani Zaguhi," Mary corrected him for the third time as they headed for the door.

A few minutes later, she was about to start the climb to her office, in hopes of cramming a few more property statutes into her head, when she impulsively put that chore off again and headed into Sutton's Hardware. She wanted to display her diplomas on her walls. For that, she needed picture hangers. As she walked into the store directly beneath her own office, she felt the same sense of déjà vu that she had when she'd stopped to visit with Johnny Reb, two weeks ago. Though the interior had been repainted and dirt-hiding commercial grade carpeting now covered the old plank floors, the store still functioned for urban Pisgah Countians as Little Jump Off did for their mountain-bound cousins—a one-stop-shopping place where money, tall tales, and town gossip were exchanged in nearly equal parts. Sutton's stocked birdseed for the local Audubon society, rifles for deer hunters, surge protectors for cyber Hartsville. They even popped popcorn for the children; Mary smelled the salty aroma as soon as she entered the store.

"Can I help you?" a tall, buxom girl called from behind the counter.

"Picture hangers?" Mary was certain they had them, she just couldn't imagine where.

"Midway down the back wall. You need me to get them for you?"

Mary smiled. "No thanks. I can find them myself." She passed old-fashioned washboards stacked below microwave ovens, butter churns beneath electric ice cream freezers. Picture hangers were displayed next to school supplies. She grabbed two packages and headed back to the counter.

"Is that all today?" Up close, Mary saw that the clerk was more than just buxom. The girl was, in fact, quite obese. Though her mouth was a beestung pout and her blue eyes were astonishingly beautiful, both were lost in the soft, doughy expanse of her face.

"That's it for now." Mary fished her wallet from her purse as the girl rang up her tab.

"That'll be two dollars and sixty-seven cents. You're Mary Crow, the lawyer, aren't you?"

"Yes," Mary replied. She mentally prepared herself for the usual *you're the one who killed Stump Logan* routine, but mercifully, the girl didn't go there. "Have we met before?"

"No." The girl giggled. "Ridge told me you'd moved in upstairs. I sweep the landing up there and deliver y'all's mail."

"Then it's nice to meet you." Mary handed the girl a five-dollar bill. "Are you friends with Ridge?"

"Mr. Sutton lets me run the gift shop for the tourists," she said proudly. "I've sold a bunch of masks for Ridge." The girl pointed again, this time to the front corner of the store. There, among dreamcatchers and baskets and a couple of pint-sized bows and arrows, hung three of Ridge's masks—a raccoon, a fox, and a scary-looking medicine man. Again, Mary noted, no bears.

"He's a very talented young man," said Mary as the girl handed her the change.

Unexpectedly, the girl leaned closer. She whispered, "Is it true that they arrested him yesterday? For killing Bethany?"

"Unfortunately, they did," Mary said truthfully, astonished at the alacrity of small-town gossip.

"I'm so sorry," said the girl. "I like Ridge a lot. I liked Bethany a lot, too. I don't think he killed her."

"Oh? Who do think did?" Too late, Mary realized that she'd pounced as if she had this poor fat girl sweating on the witness stand.

"I don't know." Flustered, the girl's pudgy cheeks grew crimson. "I just work this register all day and listen to all the crazy things people come up with."

"I guess you do hear it all," Mary said, more kindly. "What's your name?"

"Sylvia," said the big girl. "Sylvia Goins."

Mary held out her hand. "Nice to meet you, Sylvia."

Sylvia shook Mary's hand with obvious relief. Are you taking Ridge's case?" Her blue eyes widened in her sea of flesh.

"No. I'm not doing criminal work anymore." Mary wondered how long it would take that little tidbit to race through town. Suddenly Sylvia Goins' face cracked, Humpty Dumpty–like, into a smile. Mary turned to see the bandanna-wearing young man from the Mexican market across the street hurry into the store, his own wide face shyly reflecting the joy of his girlfriend's.

"Sylvia, it's been a pleasure meeting you," Mary said, excusing herself quickly in the face of young love. "I'm sure I'll be back soon. There's always a lot to buy when you set up an office."

"Welcome to our block, Ms. Crow." Sylvia's smile revealed deep dimples in both cheeks. "Anything you need that we don't have, I'll be happy to order for you."

Mary nodded to the girl's Mexican beau, then left the oddly matched pair to commune among the butter churns, undisturbed. As she stepped back into the bright morning light, she gazed up the street toward the courthouse, wondering what kind of case George Turpin was cooking up against Ridge.

It's not your problem, she reminded herself. You got the boy a good attorney, you got Hugh new help with his farm. Now you need to keep your promise to Jonathan. You need to become the very best real estate attorney in all of Pisgah County. With a final, lingering glance at Johnny Reb and the courthouse that towered behind him, she turned toward her office, and her brand-new career as Deke Keener's dirt lawyer.

NINETEEN

Six Weeks Later

Thwack! The ball banged against the garage door. *Thwack! Thwack!* Kayla Daws played a mindless game of catch with herself. For the past month she'd passed the slow, hot afternoons in this way, first throwing soccer balls, then basketballs, then tennis balls at the wide door directly beneath her mother's bedroom. Now she was using a half-chewed rubber ball that had belonged to Darby when he was a puppy.

Thwack! This time the ball bounced high. She caught it in her right hand, then turned and threw it at Darby, who lay sleeping on the cool flagstone patio. The old Lab yelped as the ball struck his hip. Then he struggled stiffly to his feet, tail wagging but confused, as if his mistress had invented some new game he hadn't quite caught on to.

Stupid dog, thought Kayla. You were upstairs that night. You were sleeping in my bedroom. Why didn't you bark? Why couldn't you have at least whimpered?

Because Darby is thirteen, she told herself for the thousandth time. Darby is mostly deaf. And even though he would have defended any of them to the death, Darby had not heard whoever came to kill Bethany.

Remorse swept over her as quickly as her anger had lashed out, and she ran over to the old dog, her eyes filling with tears. "I'm sorry, Darb," she cried, kneeling to throw her arms around his bony shoulders. "I didn't mean to do that." She held the dog tight, as if he were the last soft, kind thing left of her family.

Suddenly she heard a scraping sound, just above her head. She looked up. Her mother had opened her bedroom window and was leaning out, squinting into the bright July afternoon. Paula Daws still wore the same lacy pink nightgown that she'd worn for the past week, the black mascara streaking down her cheeks making her look like a mournful raccoon. "What's going on down there?" she demanded, lurching so far forward that she almost tumbled out the window.

"Nothing, Mama," Kayla replied.

"Why are you crying?"

"I'm not crying."

"Then go back to bed."

Before Kayla could explain that it wasn't bedtime, that it was just the middle of an endless afternoon that had seemingly begun several years ago, her mother slammed the window shut. Kayla knew, then, her mother would spend this day like all the others—lying in a darkened bedroom, staring at the home makeover channel, trying to find her way through the next nineteen million minutes of her life. She might get up when her father came home or it could just as easily be her and her dad sitting at the kitchen table together—Kayla eating canned soup, her father starting on the first of his evening six-packs. When he only drank it was tolerable—he slowly got drunk in front of whatever baseball game was on TV and fell asleep in the recliner. The nights she truly hated were the nights Glenn Daws brought home a newspaper. Then he would crack open a tall boy and make her sit down and listen while he read aloud every word devoted to Ridge Standingdeer. He'd started weeks ago, when Ridge had been charged with Bethany's murder, and he hadn't lost interest since. The more he drank the angrier he grew, calling Ridge and his lawyer terrible names, finally crushing the beer cans as if they were mere paper cups. She'd complained about it once, at the grief therapy sessions that Coach Keener arranged for everybody, but it hadn't done any good. Her father had come home the next night and made her listen while he read the whole paper, just to spite her.

She sighed. The sky was a sullen, dull white and the blacktop drive-way radiated heat like a stove, but she had no desire to go inside. Not that she was scared, though sometimes it did make her shiver to think that whoever killed Bethany could have just as easily killed any or all of the rest of them. What really creeped her out was the smell of the place. Coach Keener had special teams of men clean the whole house immedi-ately after the police finished in Bethany's room, even helping out in the attic and garage himself. Though it was good to have all the blood and police crap cleared away, the house now had a weird new disinfectant smell. Despite the fact that Coach Keener had fancy alarm systems put in every room and floodlights now covered the yard, once you went in-side, the smell always there; always reminding you that somebody had sneaked in and murdered Bethany.

As bad as that was, the silence was worse. It had settled on the house a week after the funeral. Up to then, everything had seemed as festive as Christmas. People had dropped by to "keep them company"; sent them tuna casseroles and blackberry pies. Women came over to meditate with her mother every morning, and all the girls on the softball team had sat right behind her at the funeral, crying softly into wadded-up tissues as Coach Keener gave the eulogy. Many had sent cards, and Jeannette Peacock had even sent her daisies from the florist, Lauren Reynolds a Ludacris CD.

All that, however, had ended. As the weeks passed the phone grew silent, the casseroles stopped coming, and the softball team greeted her with an increasingly awkward silence. Jeannette and Lauren just looked at her with shy, stunned eyes, and although they always made room for her on the bench, Kayla could tell that none of the girls really wanted to sit beside her. In one day she'd gone from being someone with a lot of friends to someone whose phone rang only with calls from tele-marketers. Two months ago, she had been looking forward to starting junior high school. Now she dreaded it. Nobody would want to sit with someone whose sister got murdered.

"I miss my family," she said, rubbing Darby's velvety ears. "I wish I could put us all back together again." That, she knew, was impossible. Not only could she not bring Bethany back to life, but she couldn't even join in her father's utter conviction that Ridge Standingdeer had killed her. However much he ranted and raved, she just couldn't believe that Ridge had done it. He was too good, too kind. He'd been nice even to her, and not just because she was Bethany's kid sister. He always included her when they went out together; always talked to her seriously, as if she were someone who mattered.

She heard a car pulling in the driveway. She turned, hoping maybe it was Jeannette, out joyriding with her big sister Dot, or even Coach Keener on one of his goodwill missions, but her father's white truck pulled up, dusted pale orange with construction-site clay. Kayla stood still, holding Darby by his collar. She used to like it when her father came home. He'd play a game of catch or shoot baskets with her. Now he just got out of his truck and hurried inside, glaring at her as if she were some weed growing in an otherwise pristine garden.

"Hi, Dad," she called, wondering if today could be the day they might start to knit themselves back together. They weren't scheduled for therapy this afternoon, but she had a softball practice later on. Sometimes going to the ball field helped to take his mind off things.

"Hi." He replied with the briefest of nods as he headed inside, his shoulders slumped, a brown grocery sack in his hand. As the door slammed behind him with a resounding *shunnnnt,* she knew it was unlikely that anything was going to get knitted back together today.

Still, Dr. Shope had told her not to give up, and she wasn't going to. Maybe she could persuade her mother to join them for ball practice and they could go get ice cream afterward. Anything to leave this land of the living dead.

Buoyed by that hope, she took Darby and walked the perimeter of the backyard. The wet, rainy spring had dried into a month-long drought, leaving their usually luxuriant green lawn yellow and brittle as glass. She walked with her head down, always searching for the odd footprint or scrap of a clue the cops might have missed—the one that would clear Ridge and convict the real murderer. Though all she ever found were mole tunnels and Darby's dried-up turds, she never quit looking. She was watching Darby nose around a chipmunk burrow when the back door opened like a shot.

"Kayla!" her father yelled. "Get in here!"

He sounded as if she'd done something awful, but then, he always sounded like that these days. Though mostly she knew that it had nothing to do with her, a small part of her wondered if her father wasn't most furious that his pretty blond daughter had been killed, and his chunky, brown-haired one had been left alive.

She ran inside, Darby close on her heels. Her heart rose as she saw that for the first time in weeks, both her parents sat at the kitchen table. Her mother, still in her pink nightgown, was watching her father dish something up from the stove.

"Sit down," he said. "Eat."

She sat down in her usual place, across from the now empty chair that had once been Bethany's. Darby lay down on the floor at her feet. Her father passed a plate to her mother, then one to her—two bright red hot dogs on a bed of slimy-looking sauerkraut. She could tell by the way he slapped the plates on the table that he was well into his first six-pack, and she noticed with dread that the day's paper lay open beside his plate. Maybe, she thought, if she started talking about something else, she could distract him from his usual tirade about how if they'd only let him in Standingdeer's cell for just three minutes he could save the taxpayers a lot of trouble and energy.

"Did you know there's a softball practice tonight?" She made her voice small, so as not to attract the wrong kind of attention.

Neither of her parents responded.

"We're playing the McDougal Dolls on Thursday."

Her father chewed a mouthful of sauerkraut; her mother just stared at her plate.

"Coach Keener said he might let me pitch."

Her words fell on a room so quiet, she could hear Darby panting under the table. Still, she refused to give up.

"Are you coming tonight, too, Dad?"

He made a noise—something between a grunt and a question. She took it as a yes.

"Mom, why don't you come with us? You could sit in the stands and watch and maybe we could get ice cream later . . ."

Her father's fist came down on the table so hard, the hot dogs on her plate jumped. "For Christ's sake, Kayla! Shut up! Nobody's going to take you for ice cream after softball practice. We've got things to do here!"

Kayla turned to her mother, who had not blinked an eye since she sat down. "We do?"

"Yes we do!" her father stormed. "We've got to read the paper. The trial starts tomorrow!"

"So?"

"So?" He lowered his head and glared at her. "Don't you want to be ready? Don't you want to see that little bastard pay for what he did?"

"But what if he didn't do it?" The words flew out of her mouth like birds scattering into the sky, gone before she could stop them. For an instant her eyes locked with her father's, then the left side of her face exploded in pain and she felt herself falling. When she opened her eyes again, her head was ringing like a buzzer and she was nose to nose with Darby, on the floor.

"What do you mean if he didn't do it? Who the fuck's side are you on, you little shit?"

She watched her father's mud-encrusted boot kick back his chair while her mother began to wail loud, gulping sobs that sounded like some animal. Pulling Darby close, Kayla began to scoot along the floor toward the door. If she could just get to the garage, she could grab her glove and ride to the ball field on her bike. Forget about them being a family or eating ice cream, ever again. All she wanted to do was get out of this house with her head still attached to her shoulders.

"Where are you going?" her father bellowed. "Get back in here, young lady! I'm not done with you!"

"Yes, you are!" she screamed as she flung herself out the door, her cheek stinging where he'd struck it, as if stung by a hundred bees. "Ridge is innocent! He didn't kill Bethany and I'm going to prove it!"

TWENTY

Two subdivisions away, another Keener Kat was getting ready for softball practice.

"Avis?" Her mother was calling from the foot of the stairs, but her voice sounded as if she stood out in the front yard. "Are you getting ready to go?"

As much as Avis Martin longed to return to her balcony and the refuge of her Nero Wolfe novel, she finished tying her sneakers and opened her door. "Yes, Mama," she called loudly, her own voice dying in the carpeted, soundproofed hall. "I'll be down in a minute."

"Well, hurry up. Coach Keener will be here soon."

"Lucky me," she muttered, going into her bathroom and plunking down on the toilet. Leaning forward, she felt the stubble on her legs. Until three days ago, she hadn't shaved her legs—her hair was short, and blond to the point of invisibility. But last Monday, at a softball game, she'd looked down the bench to find three girls pointing at her legs and snickering. When Coach Keener had subbed her in, she'd heard Regina Drake say, "Go, Apegirl!" The whole bench roared. Though she'd pulled her cap down low and trotted out to the field pretending she hadn't heard, inside she wanted to die. Later, after she got home, she stole one of her mother's disposable razors. She'd turned her shower on hot and soaped up mightily, but the little razor was slippery in her hand. She thought she'd gotten all the hair but the next day, at practice, she looked down to see that she had long scratches running up both legs, and she'd missed at least three patches of hair. Though Regina Drake hadn't called her Apegirl again, everyone had looked as if they might burst with laughter, and at practice yesterday, someone had left a jar of Nair in her glove while she'd been in the bathroom.

"Stupid geeks," she whispered. Back in Greenville, they wouldn't have treated her like this. Back in Greenville, she had *friends*.

She brushed her teeth, swiped extra deodorant under her arms, then headed downstairs. Her footsteps were soundless on the thickly carpeted hall, and as she hurried she wondered if this was the way the Cherokee witch had sneaked in to kill Kayla Daws' sister—sneaking up stairs so cushy with carpeting that nobody heard him coming. She'd heard on the bench that he was about to rape and kill Kayla, too, when the dog finally woke up and scared him away.

She walked into the den. Her mother sat on the couch snapping beans while her sister napped beside her.

"Hey, Scooter." Her mother smiled, greeting her with the nickname they'd called her since she was a baby. She didn't much like it, but it was better than Apegirl. "You ready to go?"

"I guess." She slumped down on the floor at her mother's feet, dreading the coming afternoon, wondering if Regina Drake was going to leave another little personal grooming aid in her glove. What would it be this time? Mouthwash? Deodorant? *Tampax?* Oh, God, please not that. If Coach Keener saw her with a box of tampons in her glove, she would die, right there, on the spot.

Her mother stopped her bean-snapping. "What's the matter, Avis? You look like such a crosspatch."

Without warning, the tears Avis had been fighting all afternoon began to flow. "They don't like me, Mama," she sobbed, humiliated to be crying to her mother. "I try to fit in, but they all think I'm weird."

"Oh honey, sometimes it just takes a while to make new friends." Darlene Martin put her beans aside and sat down on the floor beside her daughter. "We moved around a lot when I was little, and I remember how hard it was. Every time you drive off to practice with Coach Keener, I think how proud I am of you."

"Oh, Mama!" The idea of her mother being proud of her for riding with Coach Keener made Avis cry even harder. "I don't want to play softball anymore. Please just let me stay home till school starts. I'll just read and baby-sit Chrissy."

"Avis, that doesn't sound like much of a summer." Her mother stroked her hair. "Let's try and think what we can do to make this better."

Avis wept, wishing she were anywhere else on the planet. She was eleven, old enough to manage her own social affairs, yet here she sat, bawling like a baby in front of her mother. Small wonder no one on the team liked her. She didn't even like herself.

"Scooter?" She heard her mother's voice somewhere over her head. "I've got an idea."

Oh, God, thought Avis ungenerously. Now she's going to embarrass me even more. "What?" she asked, cringing as she waited for the answer.

"We've got the house looking pretty good these days. Why don't you invite some of your teammates to spend the night?"

"Because they all hate me."

"They don't all hate you, Avis," her mother insisted. "They don't even know you. You had lots of friends in Greenville."

"The kids were nicer in Greenville." She looked up at her mother. "These girls are all snobs. None of them would come over here and they'd laugh at me for inviting them."

"Well, they certainly won't come if you don't ask. Why don't you ask just one, if you don't want to invite a bunch?"

"I don't know who I'd ask," said Avis miserably. "None of them like me."

Her mother gently rubbed her back. "What about that little Daws girl?"

"The one whose sister got killed? Oh, Mama. She'd never want to come and spend the night with me."

"I bet she would. She's had an awful summer. She might love to get away from things for a while."

Avis had to admit that Kayla Daws might possibly find spending the night with her preferable to sleeping in the house where her sister was murdered, but still. Kayla Daws? She was one of the most popular girls on the team. Kayla probably wouldn't be caught dead even talking to her. "I don't think so, Mama. Anyway, I wouldn't know what to say to somebody whose sister's just been killed."

"All you have to say is how sorry you are, Avis. Come on. Be brave. Act like some of those detectives you're always reading about. Ask Kayla tonight, at practice. Any time she wants to come is fine with me."

Avis doubted that Kayla Daws would do anything but look at her as if she were crazy, but she knew she had to do something. If she started seventh grade with no friends at all, she would be a social outcast for the rest of the year. Not even the geeks would sit with her at lunch.

"Won't you give it a try, honey? Just for me?"

"I don't know, Mama," Avis said, drying her eyes as she heard Coach Keener honking from the driveway. "I'll see how things go."

Half an hour later, after a long detour along a woodsy road where Coach Keener felt her arm muscle and then told her about all these fabulous trips to Disney World he took his special girls on, they arrived at the ball field. As if aware of her mother's suggestions on how to make friends, Coach Keener paired her with Kayla Daws, and told them to warm each other up by playing catch. Avis knew immediately that something was wrong with Kayla. One whole side of her face was red and swollen, and she held her head like it ached, tilting it to one side. Avis decided to say nothing and concentrate hard on throwing straight and accurately. Kayla, though, had difficulty with her pitches.

"Are you okay?" Avis asked after the normally athletic girl flubbed two easy catches.

Kayla shrugged off her errors. "Just a little tired."

"I'm sorry about your sister," Avis ventured as Kayla stooped to pick up a low one.

"I know," the other girl replied coldly. "I got your card."

"No, really. I *am* sorry." Avis didn't know what else to say; no one in her acquaintance had ever died before.

"I know." Kayla's tone softened. "Thanks."

The ball went back and forth. Though its slap-pop rhythm was the only sound breaking the silence between them, it was, at least, a comfortable silence. Avis didn't get the feeling that Kayla was merely biding her time, waiting for the moment when she could join back up with Jeannette and Lauren. Buoyed by her small success, Avis began to wonder if she dared risk an invitation. Back in Greenville, she knew the lingo: *Hey, wanna come spend the night with me?* Here, they talked differently. Slumber parties were sleepovers, and when one wretched girl who played right field messed up and asked Jeanette Peacock to "spend the night," the whole team had called her "Lesbo" for days afterward. Lord, Avis thought. That would be the end of me here; if everyone started thinking I was queer, I might as well go home and spend the rest of my life reading on the balcony. She continued to stew about the proper phrasing of her invitation until she saw that Coach Keener was about to whistle them into the dugout. Then, all at once, she blurted the words out.

"Would you like to come over to my house tonight after the game? For a sleepover?" Heart hammering, she braced herself for Kayla's fake smile and flimsy excuse, but instead she just blinked at her, as if Avis were speaking Swahili.

"Me and who else?" Kayla finally asked.

Avis shrugged. "Just you. My mom said it was okay."

For a horrible moment Kayla's eyes teared up. Avis held her breath, terrified that the team would blame her for making the poor beleaguered girl cry, but Kayla blinked back her tears and gave the barest of smiles. "Yeah," she said. "I'd like to."

They played on the same scrimmage team; then, after practice, the rest of the Keener Kats watched, stunned, as Kayla got into the Martins' car. The Martins stopped by Kayla's house to let her get her pajamas, and now she stood, overnight bag in hand, in the middle of Avis's fancy new bedroom. Avis could hardly believe her good luck. For once, her mother had been right.

"Is this a test house?" Kayla surveyed the room, noting Avis's mystery-filled bookcases.

"Yes." Avis waited for the girl to sneer, but instead, Kayla give three little hops on the balls of her feet.

"Ours is, too. You can always tell by the carpeting. It's really thick and bouncy."

"This is made from recycled Coke bottles," said Avis. "It kind of freaks me out. You can't ever hear anybody coming until they're right there, standing in the middle of your room."

"I know what you mean." Kayla set her blue overnight bag down in the middle of the floor. "But at least you can play music as loud as you want."

Avis took that as a cue to get some music going, so she went over and turned on the small CD player beside her bed. Ringo Starr's voice soon filled the room, singing about how he got by with a little help from his friends. Inwardly Avis groaned, thinking that Kayla would surely find her hopeless, playing such old music, but again the girl surprised her.

"Ooh, that's a good one." She sang along with Ringo, smiling. "I love the Beatles."

"Me, too," said Avis.

Soundlessly, Avis's mother appeared in the doorway with a tray of warm cookies. "You girls doing okay?" she asked, smiling.

"Yes, ma'am." Kayla answered politely, but Avis noticed that when her mother put the cookies down on her bed, Kayla teared up, just as abruptly as she had at ball practice.

"There's more downstairs, when you want them. Pizza and Coke, too." She winked at Avis as she closed their door. "Dad and I are going to bed. You can watch TV in the den, if you want."

"Thanks, Mom," said Avis, humbled. Frozen pizza and real Coca-Cola had not been on their grocery list in months. Her mother must have gone to the store and splurged while they were at practice.

They sat on the floor, eating their cookies and listening to the Beatles. Kayla graciously admired Avis's two puny softball trophies, then began rummaging through her books.

"You sure do read a lot of mysteries," she said, leafing through Josephine Tey's *Daughter of Time*.

"My third grade teacher gave me a Nancy Drew book. I read all of them, then the Hardy Boys. Then I moved on to Agatha Christie and Edgar Allan Poe." She grabbed her throat and bugged out her eyes. "Murder most foul!"

Instantly, she realized her faux pas. Crimson-faced, she dropped her hands and stammered, "I—I'm so sorry. I didn't mean . . ."

"It's okay." Kayla said as she stared at the last cookie on the plate. "Don't worry about it." For what seemed like hours, neither of them spoke. Avis was desperate to think of something to mop up the awkward silence with, when Kayla turned and looked at the sliding door in the corner of the room.

"What's out there?" she asked.

"My balcony." Avis jumped up, so eager to remove her foot from her mouth that she turned the cookie plate over. "Come see."

Avis slid the door open, and the two stepped out into a cool night thunderous with crickets.

"Wow!" said Kayla. "This is awesome! Our house doesn't have one of these."

"Coach Keener said it was a new design," Avis explained. "Hey, would you like to sleep out here tonight? We could bring up two sleeping bags from the basement."

Kayla gazed at the wide expanse of empty backyard and the dark leafy pines that whispered beyond it. "No," she said, stepping back into Avis's bedroom. "I don't want to."

"It's okay," Avis reassured her. "Nothing's out there but a bunch of pine trees."

"No." Kayla rubbed her arms as if she were cold. "Something bad's out there. Whoever killed my sister's out there."

Avis followed Kayla back inside, stunned by what the girl had just said. "I thought they caught the man who killed your sister. He's a Cherokee witch."

"They put her boyfriend in jail," replied Kayla bitterly. "But he's not a witch. And he's *not* the one who killed her."

"How do you know?" Avis's pulse quickened. She felt like Josephine Tey had picked her up and plunked her down in the middle of her own mystery.

"Because I just know. Ridge Standingdeer loved Bethany. He would never have done anything to her."

"So who do you think did it?"

Kayla fingered the red mark on her cheek. "I don't know. But somehow I'm going to find out."

Suddenly a bright new world of possibility opened for Avis. In her books, ordinary people solved mysteries all the time. Nancy Drew, Frank Hardy, even dotty old Miss Marple. Why could the name Avis Martin not be added to their number? If she solved the mystery of Bethany Daws' murder, then Kayla would be her friend for life. She could start school eating lunch with one of the most popular girls in town!

"You know, we could work on that together if you wanted to," Avis said, locking the balcony door behind her.

"Work on what?" asked Kayla.

"Finding out who killed your sister. I've read enough mysteries to know that sometimes ordinary people can figure out things when the cops can't. They know the victim so well that they can find clues that policemen overlook."

"Really?"

"Absolutely," said Avis, brimming with confidence. "We'll go over to your house first thing in the morning. I bet we can find a bunch of stuff the cops missed."

For a moment Kayla looked at her as if she were crazy, then, for the first time ever, Avis saw her truly smile. "Okay. We'll have to work fast, though. Ridge's trial begins tomorrow."

TWENTY-ONE

"So are we still on for Aunt Little Tom's birthday?" Jonathan's voice sounded tinny through the phone lines.

"Absolutely. I'm just going with Deke out to Bear Den. I told him I needed to be back by five."

"Bear Den, the luxurious gated mountain community?" Mary could hear his derision as he parodied the billboards that advertised Keener's newest development.

"That's the one," she answered sharply. "It pays my rent and keeps Mr. Turnipseed on his quixotic quest for water on my farm."

"I just can't help but wonder who Keener's gating out at thirty-eight hundred feet," said Jonathan. "Larcenous gangs of mountain goats?"

Mary had to laugh. Jonathan had a valid point. At that elevation, B&Es would be the last thing the residents of Bear Den would need to worry about, yet Deke proudly touted his manned guardhouse as if home invaders roamed the mountains like bushwhackers, sniffing out relocated New Yorkers to pillage and plunder. Jonathan had teased her about it ever since the first ads went up. "Since I'm now running a non-criminal practice, I have to represent my clients in their legal matters, regardless of how I feel about it," she said. In truth, she hated Bear Den, hated real estate work, hated driving all over creation with Deke Keener, listening to his CD of music that had been hot when they were in high school—INXS, U2, the Georgia Satellites. Still, she'd promised Jonathan no criminals, and she intended to keep her word.

"Okay, okay," he said as if realizing he'd jabbed too hard. "So, it's Bear Den this afternoon, Aunt Little Tom's tonight. What are you up to this morning?"

"I'm going to the courthouse. Ridge's trial starts today." She wondered if, after his Bear Den comment, he would have the nerve to object.

"Oh, really?" His tone revealed nothing.

"Yes. I want to speak to Hugh, wish Brendle good luck. I'll leave at the first recess."

"Say hello to Hugh for me, then," he said. "Tell him I hope the boy gets off."

"Thanks." Her smile returned as their relationship recovered from its brief wobble. "I'll meet you at Aunt Little Tom's around six. Okay?"

"Lily and I will be waiting."

She hung up the phone and returned to the window. For the past hour she'd watched a procession of people making their way to the courthouse, ambling in the way of Southerners on a hot summer morning, yet proceeding with a kind of grim purpose as well. Bethany Daws' murder had not slipped from Hartsville's collective consciousness. Though the downtown merchants had weeks ago replaced their black window drapes and somber floral displays, a heaviness still hung in the air, as if a massive thunderstorm was rumbling around the mountains that encircled the town. Every morning Mary read the day's paper while eating breakfast at Layla's, and every day both the editorial page and her fellow diners were of the same opinion—that Ridge Standingdeer, the Cherokee witch, deserved a fair trial, but when they found him guilty, they should slide the needle in his arm, pronto.

"You'd better get going," she told herself. Slipping on the jacket of her beige linen suit, she grabbed her purse and opened her office door. As she headed for the stairs, she heard airy flute music coming from Dana's office, while the Smoky Mountain Defenders' stood locked and silent, mail stacked up against the door. Ravenel and his little Cherokee sidekick must be out on some expedition, she decided, then hoped, uncharitably, that maybe it would be one from which they didn't return.

She stepped out into the already hot morning. All of Hartsville seemed to be heading for the courthouse, scurrying like ants up the steps toward Johnny Reb. As she joined them, she was reminded of a short story she'd read in high school, where every June 27 the ordinary residents of an ordinary town drew lots and stoned one of their neighbors to death. Once again, she thought of Ridge. Though the young man's stoic demeanor had not cracked for the past six weeks, she wondered if he regretted ever laying eyes on the beautiful Bethany Daws.

She fell into step behind Carl Matheny, the pastor of the Baptist Church, and old Abe Sutton, hardware magnate. The two men trudged up the hundred-and-five-step climb just ahead of her, leaving a wake of Aramis cologne and civic chitchat behind them.

"I've never seen the town quite like this," Brother Matheny was saying. "After church, all anybody talks about is Indian witchcraft and satanic rituals. It's got everybody spooked."

"I've sold more deadbolt locks and bedside pistols in the past two months than I have in the past two years." Sutton wiped the back of his neck with a white handkerchief. "I hate to say it, but this little gal's murder's been mighty good for business."

"I know what you mean," enthused the preacher. "Attendance in church is up like crazy, too."

Mary passed the pair as soon as they reached the top of the steps. No point in going into the courtroom behind them, she decided, uncomfortable with the avarice she'd heard in their voices. She already knew what Hartsville thought of Ridge Standingdeer. She didn't need to have it reconfirmed just moments before his trial began. She entered the courthouse and, bypassing the crowd waiting for the elevator, headed for the stairs. Pisgah County's single criminal courtroom was on the third floor, a beautiful old room wainscoted in preblight chestnut, with twelve-foot ceilings and a portrait of Thomas Jefferson behind the bench. Soon the Honorable Barbara W. Wood, one of Irene's old tennis partners, would take that bench. Soon the case of North Carolina v. Ridge Standingdeer would begin.

Her heart thudding, she reached the third floor and stepped into a noisy hall packed with people. A news crew from the TV station in Asheville was filming; a pretty, diminutive reporter was already taping her intro in one corner of the hall. Mary skirted them and started to worm her way through the crowd, toward the courtroom. When she finally reached the entrance, she pulled open one of the heavy oak doors and squeezed inside. Though the big, square room felt like an oven and one deputy accidentally jabbed her with his sidearm, an electric pretrial tingle zinged up her spine. She grinned. For the first time since she'd moved back here, she felt as if she'd come home.

"I'm afraid this courtroom's full, ma'am," one of deputies whispered.

"I'm assisting defense counsel," she informed him, fudging just a bit with the truth. She wanted to wish Ridge and Brendle good luck, then she would try to squeeze in beside Hugh.

"Go ahead, then."

She hurried down the long center aisle of the courtroom. Hugh and young Turnipseed were sitting together on the left, while on the right, Deke sat beside Glenn and Paula Daws. As Mary passed, she noticed that the people behind her began to stir, and a murmur of whispers followed her wave-like to the front of the room. Loganites, she told herself. No doubt appalled that the half-breed lawyer who'd ended the career—and the life—of their beloved Stump was now cozying up to the Cherokee bastard who'd smashed Bethany Daws' skull with a tomahawk. She squared her shoulders and walked with her head held high. She had nothing to be ashamed of with regard to either Stump Logan or Ridge Standingdeer.

She'd planned to give all her good wishes before everything got started, but Judge Wood entered the courtroom just as she slipped through the gate. Quickly, Mary went over to stand beside Ridge. He was wearing the Armani suit she'd bought him with Hugh's credit card and the bewildered look of some beautiful, wild creature captured by dwarves. Timothy Brendle's chair was empty.

"Ridge?" she asked, stunned. "Where's Brendle?"

The boy started to answer when suddenly someone tapped her on the shoulder. Assuming it was Brendle scooting in just as the bailiff called the court to order, she turned to wish her colleague good luck. Her jaw dropped. Timothy Brendle wasn't arriving late to defend Ridge Standingdeer. It was the Great Smoky Mountain jackass, Sam Ravenel!

"Good morning, Miss Crow," Ravenel greeted her acidly.

"What are you doing here?" she demanded in a savage whisper. "Where's Timothy Brendle?"

"His father died last night." Ravenel dropped a battered briefcase on the table. "I'm filling in."

"Filling in?" Mary couldn't believe her eyes. "Are you even a lawyer?"

"I'm a member of the Western North Carolina Defense Bar," he replied huffily. "Which leads me to ask why you are here? I thought you were Deke Keener's dirt lawyer!"

Mary was about to tell him why she was there when she suddenly grew aware of a silence in the courtroom. She looked up. Judge Wood, George Turpin, and no doubt everyone else in the courtroom were staring at her and Ravenel.

"Well?" Judge Wood asked, puzzled about which of them to address. "I repeat my question. Which one of you is representing the defendant?"

"I am, Your Honor." Mary answered in exact unison with Ravenel, her voice back to its old courtroom strength.

"Ms. Crow, I'm confused," Barbara Wood said. "I know you were co-counsel at Mr. Standingdeer's arraignment, but I thought you'd turned this case over to Mr. Brendle. Now you're back. Will you or will you not be part of this case?"

Before Mary could reply Ridge touched her arm. Though he said not a word, he gazed deep into her eyes with a look of such despair that her heart broke.

"*Hawazah,*" he whispered. "Please help me."

"Well, Ms. Crow?" Judge Wood impatiently fingered the dozen small gold bracelets she wore on her left wrist.

Mary paused. An invisible road seemed to fork ahead of her. Going one way would mean dull days with Deke, but amazing nights with Jonathan. Going the other way could mean the loss of both and even more enmity from the town that she longed to call home. She considered her answer for as long as she dared, then she chose the road from which she knew there would be no return.

"I'm co-counsel, Your Honor. For Mr. Standingdeer's defense."

For an instant, Deke Keener wanted to leap from his seat and rip the chestnut paneling from the courtroom walls. What did Mary Crow mean, she was co-counsel for Mr. Standingdeer's defense? Hell, he'd intentionally hired her *away* from this case. They were supposed to confer about Bear Den at one o'clock this afternoon, yet here she stood, striding into the courtroom as if she were God's own lawyer, come to save Ridge Standingdeer from death row. Jesus Christ, she'd flummoxed him again, just like she had in high school! He looked over at Glenn. He was clenching his fists so hard his knuckles had gone white.

"What the hell is going on?" Glenn glared at Deke with angry eyes. "I thought she was your real estate girl."

Deke shrugged to let Glenn know he was equally at sea. "I thought she was, too."

He sat back, watching as Mary Crow talked first with Standingdeer, then with that fool, Ravenel. Goddamn, he raged. Would this mess never be over? The day had started out so well—Standingdeer was going to trial, almost certain to be convicted of the murder of Bethany Daws. They would sentence the Indian to either death or life in prison and after that, everything would start getting back to normal. People would stop obsessing about this case, asking all too many questions that had no real good answers. But no! His asshole classmate Mary Crow had to barge in at the last fucking goddamned minute! Now she would turn that great brain of hers loose on this case and God knows what she would come up with. Christ, he thought, sinking in his seat. Too bad his wasn't one of the companies rebuilding Iraq. He could have sent Mary Crow to look at property in Baghdad.

Sick inside, he returned his attention to the front of the courtroom. Now Sam Ravenel, whom Deke had never known to do anything beyond carp about environmental rapists and file nuisance suits against Keener Construction, was standing up, yammering something about bail.

"Your Honor, could we discuss bail again? My client is a lifelong resident of North Carolina with no criminal record whatsoever. He works for and lives with Mr. Hugh Kavanagh, as his farm hand. I ask that the court take pity on this young man, and at least set some figure for bail."

"Your Honor . . ." Turpin leapt up as if he'd been stuck with a pin. "The accused was remanded to custody six weeks ago. . . ."

"Calm down, Mr. Turpin," said Judge Wood. "Sorry, Mr. Ravenel. I'm not going to set bail now. Your client is still remanded."

"Then I need to ask for a continuance, Your Honor. I got the call to take this case only three hours ago. I haven't had time to go through any of Mr. Brendle's notes."

The judge peered at Mary. "What about you, Ms. Crow? Are you up to speed here?"

"No, Your Honor," she answered. "I'm sorry."

Judge Wood cast a slightly disgusted look at the spectators cramming her courtroom. "Okay. As ready as everybody else seems to be for this trial to begin, two of the most important participants are not. Since this is due to circumstances beyond their control, I'm setting the trial date for one month from today. That should give Mr. Ravenel and Ms. Crow ample time to prepare." She looked at the three attorneys standing before her. "Anything else?"

"No, Your Honor," all three answered at the same time.

"Then we'll try this again Monday, August 27. Court stands adjourned." Judge Wood gave a swift tap with her gavel, then disappeared through the door behind her chair. For an instant the courtroom was silent, then like children released from the charge of a stern teacher, everyone stood up and started talking at once.

"Goddamn Cherokee bitch!" Glenn Daws looked at Deke. "Did you see Turpin's face when she came in? He looked like he pissed himself."

"Oh, Turpin's not scared of her, Glenn," Deke lied, craning to catch a glimpse of Mary through the crowd.

"The hell he's not! You can smell it from here!" Daws ran a hand through his sun-bleached hair. "Man, I don't get it. My little girl gets murdered in her bed and the bastard who did it gets Mary Crow for his lawyer."

"Come on, y'all." Deke put his arms around Glenn and Paula, lest the DA himself hear the criticism. "Let's get out of here. Let's go get some lunch."

"I don't want any fucking lunch." Glenn's voice cracked. "I want my daughter back."

"I do, too," Deke said softly. "But let's go, just the same."

He steered Glenn and Paula toward the door, sweat suddenly pouring off his forehead. Never would he have dreamed of Mary Crow's abrupt about-face, or that she would form some kind of dream team with Ravenel. Though the guy acted like a deep-fried version of Paul Bunyan, Deke knew he was plenty smart and came from some big-time Charleston family. Once again he looked back over his shoulder, toward the front of the courtroom. Mary had disappeared, he guessed to talk with her new client. That left him alone, with land still to acquire for Bear Den, the grieving Daws to attend to, and Bethany's murder to firmly affix upon Standingdeer before somebody found those goddamn tapes.

TWENTY-TWO

"Mom, can you drive us over to Kayla's house?"

"Kayla's house?" Darlene Martin looked up from the kitchen sink. Avis and her new friend had been so quiet while she'd gone about her morning chores that she'd almost forgotten they were upstairs. Now her daughter was standing in front of her, asking to visit a house where a girl's head had been cracked open while the poor thing slept.

"I don't know, honey. The Daws have had a lot of trouble, I wouldn't want you to disturb them."

"I wouldn't disturb them, Mama. I'd be real quiet. And Kayla wants me to come."

As if on cue, Kayla appeared in the doorway, as eager to go as Avis. "I called my mom, Mrs. Martin. She said it's okay."

Still, Darlene Martin was reluctant. "Can't you two find something to do here?"

Avis shook her head. "Please, Mom. We really want to go."

Mrs. Martin glanced around the kitchen. She'd gotten most of her morning's work done. She supposed she could take the girls over to the Daws' house, although the prospect sent a chill down her spine. Her child, so close to where all that horror had taken place. Yet, what was there to fear now? The police had caught the young man responsible. He now sat in jail, his trial, she thought, scheduled to start any day now. Plus, Avis had been through a hard time of her own this summer. The child deserved to have some fun, to make a new friend. Why should she stand in her daughter's way, just because the Daws' tragedy gave her the willies?

"You're sure it's okay with your mom?" she asked Kayla.

"Yes, ma'am." The girl nodded briskly. "She won't even know we're there."

"Well, okay." Smiling, Mrs. Martin wiped her hands on a dish towel. "Let me gather Chrissy up and I'll drive you over there."

Avis noticed that her mother turned off the radio as soon as she turned in Kayla's driveway and slowed the car to a crawl, as if they were driving into a funeral parlor instead of a two-story brick home with an American flag proudly flapping in the front yard. When she let them out of the car, she again asked Kayla if she was positive her mother had agreed to her having company.

"Yes, ma'am, it's fine," Kayla assured her. "I called her twice, early this morning."

"Well, Avis, you call me when you get ready to come home," her mother said, eyeing the house as if she expected to see another bloody tomahawk dangling from the upstairs window.

"I will, Mom." Embarrassed by her mother's protectiveness, Avis scrambled out of the car at Kayla's heels. When the old blue Ford finally started backing out the driveway, she felt a great wave of relief.

"Sorry," she said to Kayla as an elderly Lab hobbled up to greet them, his tail wagging with joy. "I don't know why she's treating me like such a baby."

"Probably because she's never left you at a house where someone's been murdered," Kayla said matter-of-factly as she gave the dog a pat, then unlocked the front door.

As Kayla began disarming the complicated alarm pad by the front door, Avis realized she was way out of her league. This was *real*. A living, breathing person had been killed here, not some character in a paperback book. Although the house looked normal, with the distinctive Keener noise-deadening carpet throughout, a heavy disinfectant odor permeated the air, along with a silence that she found more disturbing than a scream.

"Where's your mom?" whispered Avis, not wishing to bother whatever lived here, unseen.

"Downtown, in court." Kayla gave a sheepish grin. "So's my dad. I told your mom a fib. I knew she wouldn't let you come over with nobody home, so I just pretended to call. I was really listening to the answering machine." Oblivious to the silence, she walked down a hall decorated with old school pictures and family photographs. "You want something to eat before we get started?"

"Sure." Avis was too scared to be hungry, but she dutifully followed her hostess to the kitchen. Although it boasted the latest stainless steel appliances, the sink was full of dirty dishes, and someone had left a chair upended at the table. Kayla hurried over to straighten it. "My mom's been pretty busy lately," she said apologetically. She ran hot water over the dishes and squirted in some liquid detergent, then opened the refrigerator. Apparently the Daws lived on Budweiser beer and foil-covered casseroles. Avis saw no milk, no eggs, no butter, not even one of the liter-sized Cokes that her mother sometimes bought as a treat for her and Chrissy.

"Sorry there's not much to choose from," Kayla said. "I don't guess Mom's had a chance to go to the store."

"That's okay," Avis replied hastily, although she wondered how busy you had to be to forget things like milk and eggs. "I'm not all that hungry."

"Wait." Kayla reached back in the cavernous refrigerator and pulled out a carton of orange juice and a mound of something wrapped in tin foil. "Mrs. Follis made us one of her coconut cakes. They're real good."

The two girls sat at the table and ate coconut cake and orange juice. Avis found the combination disgusting, but she ate without comment. It was the best Kayla had to offer; to refuse it would be rude, and she didn't want to rock the boat of their tenuous new relationship. They ate without talking, the blossoming camaraderie they'd enjoyed in Avis's room quashed by the house's oppressive atmosphere. Though the mournful silence thundered in Avis's head, Kayla seemed not to hear it at all. Avis was dying to know if the house had ghosts, but figured that now was probably not the best time to ask. When they finished their cake, Kayla said, "Come on, let's get out of here."

Avis followed Kayla upstairs to a corner bedroom that was obviously the abode of a young athlete. A poster of the entire Tennessee women's basketball team hung on the wall, and an array of basketball trophies glittered from a shelf above Kayla's bed.

"Wow." Avis blinked at all of Kayla's gold-plated booty. "You're really into basketball."

"I just play softball for fun," Kayla told her. When I graduate from high school, I'm going to play basketball at UT."

"You must be pretty good." Avis said it wistfully, keenly aware that she was not any better at basketball than she was at softball.

"I'm okay. I used to practice a lot with my dad."

"Don't you still?"

"Nah. He doesn't do stuff like that anymore." Kayla sat down on her bed and studied Avis with expectant eyes. "I'm not sure when my parents will get home, so let's get busy looking for clues. What do we do first?"

Suddenly Avis went blank. Nancy Drew would have done things one way, Hercule Poirot another. Avis Martin had never done any real detecting in her life. "Let's go to your sister's room," she suggested desperately, grasping at the first thing that popped in her head. "And look around."

"The police already did that," said Kayla. "They stayed over here the whole day it happened, taking pictures and bagging up stuff."

"But they might have missed something. They didn't know her like you did."

"Okay." Kayla shrugged agreeably. "Come on."

They went back out into the hall. Kayla led her past one closed door, then stopped at the next. Avis's stomach clenched as she realized how close they'd been sitting to the actual murder scene. She held her breath, steeling herself for her first glimpse of where Bethany Daws' life had so violently ended, but when Kayla opened the door, Avis felt a deep pang of disappointment. She'd expected something—a ghostly shape hovering over the bed or blood sprays on the wall. Instead, she saw just a tidy bedroom of a once popular teenage girl—purple-and-gold pom-poms over a mirror, a little stuffed teddy bear on the bed, a CD player on a bookshelf with some CDs stacked next to it.

"Did the police dust the room for prints?" she asked in a whisper.

"Yeah, but Coach Keener had all that cleaned up."

"Coach Keener?" asked Avis, frowning.

"Yeah. He's been great. Sent us to my grandmother's house for a week after the funeral. He had the whole house cleaned, special, while we were gone. The basement and attic, too."

Avis's stomach gave a violent wrench. What had made her think she knew anything about investigating a murder? Right now Kayla was expecting her to find some clue that would nail the killer, and she didn't even have the slightest idea about what to look for. She was a fraud of the most awful kind; in just a few moments Kayla would realize that, and the one new friend she'd managed to make would be gone forever. She would have to start the seventh grade totally alone.

"Okay," said Kayla cheerfully. "Where do we begin?"

"We look at stuff," Avis answered with authority, trying to sound as if she combed through murder scenes every day.

"What stuff?"

"All of her stuff. Anything could be a clue. You take her desk. I'll go through her closet. You look at every shred of paper, I'll search the pockets of her clothes. If anything looks unusual, call me."

"Okay."

Praying that they would find *something,* Avis opened the closet door. All of Bethany Daws' clothes hung neatly on hangers, her shoes lined up on the floor. As Kayla began to sort through the items on the desk, Avis started rummaging through the dead girl's clothes. She went carefully through every pocket, but when she finished, she'd found only a wadded up tissue, an old ticket stub from the movie *Cold Mountain,* and twelve cents in change. No clues in the closet.

"Find anything?" she asked hopefully as Kayla rummaged through the desk's bottom drawer.

"Nothing special. A hall pass from school. Her work schedule at the café." She closed the drawer. "What do we do next?"

"Look through the books in her bookcase," said Avis promptly. "Flip through the pages to see if she hid any notes. I'll look through the CDs. You can hide a lot of stuff inside a CD box."

While Kayla rifled through Bethany's books, Avis opened each of her CDs, prying up the plastic inserts, peering behind the thin paper labels. Though she worked her way from Norah Jones to Matchbox Twenty, she found nothing. Again, her stomach clenched. Kayla was expecting results and she was coming up empty. This was growing worse by the minute.

She looked up to see Kayla re-shelving the last book. "Any luck?" she asked hopefully.

"Just this picture of Ridge," said Kayla.

"Let's see." Avis got up from the floor to look at the picture Kayla held. Apparently it had been taken just weeks before. Bethany and her boyfriend sat beside a swimming pool. Bethany had worn a huge Carolina T-shirt over her bathing suit while her boyfriend wore cutoff jeans. Avis blinked at the image. Although Ridge Standingdeer wore his hair like a skinhead, he looked like a movie star and gazed at Bethany in a way that made Avis feel funny inside.

"Golly," she whispered, wondering if any boy would ever look at her like that. "He's really cute."

"He's also really nice," Kayla added. "And he really loved Bethany. He'd never have killed her."

The ardent tone in Kayla's voice again reminded Avis of her sorry detective charade, only this time she felt a wave of true nausea. Whether it was her deception or the lethal combination of orange juice and coconut cake, she suddenly knew she needed to get to a bathroom, and fast.

She gave the picture back to Kayla. "I need to use the bathroom," she said, trying to keep her voice from wobbling.

"Come on," said Kayla. "You can use mine and Bethany's."

Kayla led her back out into the hall. She opened the next door on the left and turned on the light. "Come on back to my room when you're done."

"Thanks." Avis closed the door behind her and raced for the commode. She reached it about two seconds before a cascade of undigested coconut cake erupted from her mouth. Sinking to her knees, she clasped the toilet with both hands, clumsily knocking over a basket of magazines in the process. As she vomited, she squeezed her eyes shut, knowing that every heave of her stomach was making her friendship with Kayla Daws a thing of the past. Absolutely nobody would ever invite anyone back to their house who started hurling their food in midvisit.

Minutes later, she felt weak and drained, and the only thing she wanted was to call her mother and go home. This detective visit had been an utter disaster. The best she could hope for now was that Kayla would have mercy and not tell everyone on the softball team that nerdy Avis Martin had come over promising to find clues to a murder and had wound up puking in her toilet.

With a deep, humiliated sigh, she began to gather up the magazines that had spilled from the basket. As she scooped up old issues of *Glamour* and *Mademoiselle,* something sharp dug underneath her thumbnail.

"Ouch!" She lifted the magazines to see what had punctured her finger. Stuffed in between the pages of an old *Elle* she found a small, blue spiral notebook. Not fat, like the ones they used in the sixth grade, but the thin-ruled, high school kind. Opening it, she found an uncapped pen stuck between two pages. On the last page, the round cursive writing stopped in midparagraph, as if the writer had been suddenly interrupted. Then Avis's heart stopped: Nearly every page had a doodle on it, and every doodle included the initials "RS", or "RS + BD," or "Mrs. Ridge Standingdeer."

"Oh, my gosh!" she whispered, her fingers trembling. She'd just found Bethany Daws' diary.

TWENTY-THREE

"What the hell do you think you're doing?"

Ravenel slammed his office door so hard that the stuffed owl suspended from his ceiling dropped one of its tail feathers. Mary had walked back from the courthouse with him, both of them tight-lipped and furious, keeping a reluctant lid on their anger while on the streets of Hartsville. Now, alone in Ravenel's office, their hostilities bubbled over like milk left on too hot a flame.

"I just stopped in to wish Ridge and Brendle good luck," said Mary, dodging the swaying owl. "I wouldn't have bothered if I'd known you were going to be there."

"I got the call from Barb Wood at six A.M. this morning, Ms. Crow." Ravenel tore off his elegant jacket and tossed it over the one chair that didn't have books piled on it. "Brendle's father dropped dead on a business trip to Tokyo. The judge didn't want to postpone everything, so she asked me to step in."

Mary looked at her next-door neighbor's wild assortment of stuffed birds and raccoon skulls. His office looked like a broom closet in the Smithsonian Institution. "I still can't believe you're really an attorney."

"Well, gosh. Let me prove it." Ravenel turned and flipped through some dry-mounted maps behind his desk, then pulled up something in a battered picture frame. He held it out. Through a layer of thick dust she could see that it was a cum laude JD from the University of Virginia. She didn't know what to say. Virginia was one of the best law schools in the country. She couldn't fathom that this bombastic misogynist had actually sat through classes there.

He blew the dust away from the diploma and peered at the lettering. "Yup. This here says I did purty good at lawyerin'. I reckon Judge Wood knew what she was a-doin'."

"I beg your pardon," Mary snapped. "Virginia just seems a bit too genteel for the likes of you."

Ravenel gave her a dark look. "Where did you go to school, Ms. Crow? Cherokee Tech?"

"Emory," Mary countered proudly.

He laughed. "Ah, the college that Coke built. You ever litigate a trial before?"

"Many times. For the past ten years, I was ADA for Deckard County, Georgia."

"What's your conviction rate?"

"A hundred percent."

Ravenel snorted. "Out of how many cases? Three?"

"Twelve capital murders. I lose count of the lesser charges."

"Then what the hell are you doing here in Pisgah County?" demanded Ravenel. "Working the other side of the aisle?"

Right now, Mary was wondering that herself. After nearly two months, she still had no water, at least half the county hated her for killing Stump Logan, and she would be in deep, deep shit with Jonathan as soon as she told him what she'd done today. "I grew up here," she finally told Ravenel. "I wanted to come back home."

"You wanted to come back home?" He mimicked her as he sat down behind his desk. "Jesus Christ, a homecoming! Now, there's a concept I've found to be highly overrated."

He didn't ask her to sit, so she emptied one chair of its collection of U.S. Geological Survey papers and plopped down in it. Ravenel sat with his eyes closed as if the air was too highly charged for his delicate sensibilities. When the silence grew unendurable, Mary said, "You know, I could ask the same of you."

"What?" He peered at her through half-opened eyes.

"What are *you* doing here?"

A delicate chambered nautilus shell sat perched on one corner of his desk. For a long moment he stared at it, then he spoke with what sounded almost like regret. "I used to be the criminal litigator for the biggest firm in Charleston, South Carolina. My honorable, oh-so-proper partners sold me out, so I came up here."

Mary wondered how a criminal defense attorney could screw up that badly, then she decided spitefully that Ravenel had probably gotten someone so egregiously guilty off the hook that his partners had forced him out, for the good of the firm. Usually, that was when defense lawyers struck out on their own, writing their own tickets with high-profile clients. Ravenel, though, had chosen another path. "Why did you come here?" she pressed him. "Why the mountains?"

"My family has property here. And I personally have become very concerned with the recent dismantling of our environmental statutes. The Smoky Mountain Defenders files suits to at least slow that dismantling down, since no one in either Washington or Raleigh seems to give a shit about stopping it altogether."

"So you started a snail-darter practice." Mary remembered the famous little endangered fish that had tied up the Tennessee courts for years.

"Yes, I did," Ravenel answered evenly. "Which brings us back to my original question. Why is a sleek little ex-prosecutor like you taking such an interest in this case? It has to be more than the fact you're both Cherokee."

Mary thought of the look in Ridge's dark eyes, his whispered *hawazah*—please.

"The boy's employer is a dear friend of mine," said Mary. "Hugh Kavanagh asked me to take the case, originally. And I think that Turpin's trying to push this through."

Ravenel hooted. "Boy, nothing gets by you, Counselor. Of course Turpin's pushing this through. He couldn't get to Raleigh on his barbecue laurels, so he's decided that putting someone on death row might help his chances."

"So what are we going to do?" Mary shot back.

"Well, since I would like to stay in Barbara Wood's good graces, I'm going to defend him. You can do what you please. Go back to playing mountain monopoly with that moron Keener. I understand Bear Den and the Saunooke Hills are enviable properties to acquire."

Inwardly, Mary winced. Twice in two days she'd been characterized as being Deke Keener's girl. She did not like the way it made her feel inside. Still, Ravenel had the law on his side. Judge Wood had appointed him, and unless Ridge himself officially fired Ravenel and hired her, she could not just invite herself to join his defense. However pleadingly the boy might look at her, she was trapped.

"Okay, Ravenel. I guess you must know a little bit about a courtroom. Just tell me—lawyer to lawyer—have you met with Standingdeer privately?"

"I have. At eight o'clock this morning."

"Then what's his version of the story?"

"I don't know."

"You don't know?"

"I don't need to know. No defense counsel wants to know that."

"Well, what does your client think of jail?"

"What would you think of jail, Ms. Crow? I assume he finds it somewhat less appealing than the Plaza Hotel."

"But does he ask for different food? For a book to read? To be kept away from people who want to fuck him in the mouth?" It was only part of the litany of complaints she'd heard from Atlanta inmates.

Ravenel shrugged. "We haven't had that discussion."

Mary leaned forward. "I know you haven't had it. And you haven't had it because Ridge Standingdeer has told you exactly what he's told everybody else, which is nothing!"

She knew she'd struck pay dirt. Ravenel's face grew so red that she expected steam to start spewing from his ears. "Like I said before." He slammed his fist down on the desk. "I don't need to know that!"

"But how can you defend him if you don't know how much he

comprehends of your defense? That compromises you, right there. You don't even know how much English your client understands!"

"What do you suggest I do, Ms. Crow?" Ravenel spoke through gritted teeth. "Learn Kituwah Cherokee in the next month?"

"Let me be co-counsel. Ridge knows me, I think he trusts me. And I speak Cherokee."

"Fluently?" asked Ravenel with a sneer.

"Better than you do."

Ravenel glared at her, furious. She glared right back. They looked like two dogs about to square off over a bone, then a slow smile spread across Ravenel's face.

"Okay, Ms. Crow," he said. "If you're itching to work this case so badly, then I won't stand in your way. I will, however, maintain my position as lead counsel."

"All right," said Mary, amazed at the fragility of the male ego. She could stay on the case as long as she wanted, if she let Ravenel go first and ride in the front seat and have the biggest slice of pie. Fine. She didn't care. All she wanted to do was keep Ridge Standingdeer from being railroaded into prison by dopey George Turpin.

"And I will present the case in court."

"Okay."

"And since you speak Cherokee, you can be in charge of explaining everything to our client."

"Fine," said Mary. "When would you like me to start?"

"Right now," replied Ravenel. "Go over to the jail and see if you can get him to say anything more than the six words he keeps repeating to me."

"And they are?"

"I did not kill Bethany Daws."

Miles away, at the scene of Ridge's alleged crime, Avis Martin looked up, terrified. For a moment, all she could do was stare at the pages of Bethany's diary, the girl's words looking like script written in a foreign language. Finally she realized that she couldn't just stay crouching in front of the Daws' toilet, holding what could be the clue of a lifetime.

Quickly she shoved the other magazines back in the basket and rose, clutching the small notebook to her chest. She opened the bathroom door, turned out the light, and hurried into Kayla's room. Kayla was sitting on the floor, with Darby sprawled across her lap. Both of them looked up when Avis entered.

"Are you okay?" Kayla asked, as if puzzled by Avis's lengthy sojourn in the bathroom.

Avis held up the spiral notebook. "Look what I found."

Kayla frowned. "What is it?"

"I think it's your sister's diary."

Pushing Darby off her lap, Kayla jumped to her feet. "Where did you find it?"

"In the bathroom. I accidentally knocked over that basket with all the magazines," admitted Avis. "This was stuffed in the Christmas issue of *Elle*." She held up the page where Bethany had stopped writing. "It looks like she got interrupted, and hid it, fast."

"Holy shit!" said Kayla, rifling through the pages. "Let's see what it says."

Kayla shut her door, then the two girls huddled close together on the bed. With the notebook spread across Kayla's lap, they switched on the bedside lamp and started at page one.

Avis held her breath, hoping for revelations that might immediately exonerate the handsome Cherokee boy, but Kayla read nothing more than page after page of complaints. Bethany griped about her mother *(Why can't she remember what it was like to be young?)*, her father *(All he cares about is his job. I hate him—he doesn't believe a thing I say.)*, and Mr. Rogers, her algebra teacher *(He's so mean, particularly if you aren't good in math.)*. She had kinder words for her French teacher, Madame Bailey *(elle est tres drole)*, her friend Chloe Smith, and even her sister Kayla *(she's so much smarter than me, she'll probably get a full ride at Tennessee)*. The two girls read all the way to page eight when suddenly, their eyes caught on one line: *I wish D would get cancer and die.*

"Whoa!" Avis perked up, noting that Bethany had underlined the whole sentence, and even circled the word "die" twice. She looked at Kayla. "Who is D?"

"I don't know." Kayla frowned, mystified. "She was friends with

Diane Merritt and she dated David Lawrence. But she didn't want them to die. I don't think either of them would have sneaked up here and bashed her head in."

"How about Darby?"

Kayla shook her head without hesitation. "Bethany raised Darby from a puppy. That can't be it."

They continued to read. As they turned the pages, although Bethany began to talk about Ridge Standingdeer in wildly glowing terms, she also continued an accompanying recitative about the mysterious D: *Saw D early—wanted to vomit. D's jokes are so lame.* With every line, her hatred of the mysterious D grew right along with her deep love of Ridge. She devoted pages to the boy—how sweet he was, what a wonderful lover, how they were going to marry as soon as she got settled at college.

"Wow," said Kayla. "My folks sure didn't know about that."

"Let's read this next page real carefully," said Avis. "It's the last one she wrote."

The first paragraphs were nothing more than a lengthy complaint about some customer at the café, then Kayla read the last words Bethany ever wrote out loud: *"Ridge hid my insurance policy last night. D is really fucked now. Hooray!"*

"Gosh," said Avis, reassuming her role of lead detective. "Don't you have any idea what she could have meant?"

Kayla shook her head. "She had her own money. Maybe she bought an insurance policy."

"But that's just a paper you keep in a drawer," said Avis. "Why would Ridge need to hide that?"

"Maybe D wanted it." Kayla frowned.

"But why did she hate D so? Was D a girl or a boy?"

"I don't know." Kayla's voice cracked. She dropped down to the floor and again cradled Darby in her arms. "This is terrible. Now we know all this new stuff about somebody named D, but it still won't help get Ridge out of jail!"

For a moment Avis gazed out the window, panicked, thinking both her investigation and her budding friendship with Kayla were stymied.

Then a new idea occurred to her. "Not right now it won't," she said, trying to sound as confident as Nancy Drew. "But we're not finished yet."

"What do you mean?" Kayla looked at her through her tears. "How can we find out about all this now?"

"We need to get to the jail," said Avis. "We need to ask Ridge Standingdeer who D was."

TWENTY-FOUR

Mary's decision to rejoin Ridge's defense team pleased only Hugh. Deke Keener whined for days, calling her every morning to beg her to drive out to the Bear Den property or look at some other mountain he wanted to carve up for new homes.

"Aw, come on, Mary," he'd plead, his voice bright as new money. "I really need you on my team."

"Thanks for calling, Deke," she replied firmly. "But you'll have to consider me benched until after the Standingdeer case." This would continue, like Ping-Pong, for another round or two, then he would say good-bye only to call again the next morning. Though she always refused Deke politely, every day she didn't spend working for him felt like a day she'd been sprung from jail. Only when she avoided all her Keener Construction duties did she realize how much she detested them.

Jonathan, on the other hand, neither whined nor wheedled. He accepted her decision quietly, only once revealing his sorrow late one night, as they sat beside the river, watching the moon rise. "Lily and I aren't going to be enough, are we?"

"What do you mean?" Mary asked, stalling, knowing exactly what he meant.

"I've watched you these past two weeks. You walk like a panther when you leave to work for Standingdeer."

She laughed, though the sting of truth lay just beneath the surface of his words. "And how do I walk when I leave to work for Keener?"

"Like someone headed for a long stretch in jail."

Ravenel, at least, remained consistent. After the lawyer's first appearance in court, he'd immediately reverted to his mud-caked jeans and musky shirt, burrowing back into some environmental case he called "the road to nowhere." Though he did hire a sad looking PI named Elmo McGruder and a team of forensic defense experts, neither came up with anything new. McGruder had found Bethany to be a typical teenager. The murdered girl had no police record, though she had once been driven home when officers broke up a keg party after a football game. She'd made excellent grades in both junior and senior high, and was popular with her classmates and teachers. She went to the Baptist Church and had been awarded a Keener Construction scholarship that she planned to use at Chapel Hill, where she'd planned to study nursing. According to Elmo McGruder's expert opinion, the girl had just pissed off the wrong boyfriend.

Ravenel's forensic experts fared no better. When they turned their own microscopes on the case, they came up with exactly the same results as the state. Bethany's time of death was around four A.M.; the cause of death was head trauma from a blunt instrument, wounds consistent with the primitive tomahawk found beside her pillow. The house had no signs of forced entry, no defensive wounds marred her body; no skin or hair was trapped beneath her nails. Her blood alcohol level was 1.7, Ridge's semen was in her vagina, Ridge's fingerprints were in her room, on the tomahawk; Ridge's footprints were all over the muddy path behind her house that led into the woods. To Mary, the case felt as oppressive as the heat that bore down from the August sun. Every day she drove over to the Justice Center to meet with Ridge. Every day the same thing happened. The boy would come in, bid her a polite *"sheoh,"* then sit like a stump while she attempted to cajole words out of him. She'd begged, she'd demanded, she'd tried to reason with him in every language she knew. The only thing he ever said beyond "hello" was "I did not kill Bethany Daws." Mary wanted to scream. In two weeks they would go to trial, and she knew nothing more about what happened the night Bethany was murdered than she did that first day in Hugh's barn.

"How's it going, Ms. Crow?" Ravenel asked her one day as she was about to make her umpteenth trip to jail. He was sitting with his office door open, plotting some course on one of his topo maps. "Hiawatha talking yet?"

"Not yet," she replied with an acid smile. "But at least I'm working on it."

He looked up, feigning hurt. "You think I'm not working?"

She leaned against the doorjamb, almost knocking over his stick with its bear bell. "Not unless you're mapping out his escape route to Canada."

Ravenel snorted. "I'm doing something a little more important than that, Ms. Crow. These acres within the lines of my pencil will be an inviolate ecological preserve, much like the Kilmer Forest."

"The Kilmer Forest?" Mary was tempted to crack Ravenel over the head with his own stick. "Are you aware that you're only two weeks away from a murder trial? Has it dawned on you, Mr. I'm-the Attorney-of-Record, that you need to prepare a defense?"

"Ms. Crow, I've saved as many people from death row as you've sent there. I don't need you to tell me how to plan a defense, but since you're so concerned about how I spend my time, let me assure you that when we next appear in court together, I, at least, will have made a contribution to this case."

She wanted to kill him; instead she slammed his door so hard that she heard his stick crash to the floor. She stormed down the steps, ignoring Dana's house rule of quiet. Ravenel was the most infuriating man she'd ever met. If he was half as good a defense attorney as he was a jackass, then Ridge had nothing to worry about.

She got in her car and sped to the Justice Center. The afternoon was sultry and sullen, and as soon as she walked into the lobby, she saw her nemesis, Officer Jane, the Loganite clerk who commanded the front desk. When the cop caught sight of Mary, her thin lips tightened sourly and she immediately turned her attention to her computer screen. At that moment Mary realized that the number of townspeople who truly hated her had not diminished in the past eight weeks; if anything, their number had grown. Not only had she killed Stump Logan, but now she was helping the Cherokee witch who had bludgeoned the town sweetheart to death. A headache began to throb at her temples as she scrawled her name on Officer Jane's register, only to receive her snippy instructions to "go down the hall to room three."

Gritting her teeth, she passed through security, and took her usual place in room three. Moments later, Ridge sat in the chair opposite hers.

"*Sheoh,*" he greeted her, polite as ever, calmly content to let her make all the effort.

Suddenly he enraged her as much as Ravenel and Officer Jane. How dare this boy take such a cavalier attitude toward his own life? Did he think she found this fun? Did he not realize that there were other, equally innocent men sitting in jail who would salivate at having an attorney beg them for their story? And not just once, but every frigging day of the week? She snapped her still-blank notebook shut.

"Okay, Ridge," she seethed. "You need to ditch this noble savage routine. If you don't start talking right now, you're going to spend what life you have left in prison, and then they're going to execute you."

His dark eyes regarded her curiously, as if she were a monkey in a zoo.

She repeated her words in Cherokee. Still, the boy made no response.

"Do you understand *execute?*" She wanted to shake him. "It means kill, Ridge. *Atsidihi. Atsidihi* until you're dead!"

He sat motionless.

The headache that had flirted around her temples now clamped down across the base of Mary's skull. All at once she realized she'd been suckered into the most foolish of undertakings, that of trying to force somebody to do what they were determined not to. She might as well have spent the past two weeks of her life trying to alter the orbit of Mars.

"Okay, Ridge," she said, taking a deep breath. "I'm going to ask you one last time, then I'm not going to bother you anymore. Tell me what you did the night Bethany was murdered."

His dark eyes flickered. For a moment she thought she'd gotten through to him, but when he opened his mouth to speak, he said only: "I did not kill Bethany Daws."

At that instant, her head flooded with such a rage that she feared she might have a stroke. Then the hot, squeezing pressure dissipated as swiftly as it had come, leaving her strangely calm, as if she were looking down on this mess from a great height.

"All right," she said, giving him a bright smile as she rose to her feet. "Since you won't explain your innocence, I can only assume you're guilty. I wish you all the luck in court. Except for one thing, you've been the perfect Cherokee."

He raised his brows, as if to ask, "What?"

"You forgot that it's no disgrace to take help when it's offered."

With that she turned, and for the first time, left the interview room first, leaving Ridge to the care of the Pisgah County jail. She gave Officer Jane a jaunty wave as she walked through the lobby and out the door. She was crazy to have thought she could practice law in Hartsville. Most of the town hated her on sight, and those who didn't wanted her to be something she was not.

"So be it," she muttered as she unlocked her car. "I'll sell Irene's farm and go back to Atlanta. I can start a practice with Alex and Joan, buy a little house in Virginia Highlands. Lily could have her own bedroom, Jonathan could still hire out as a guide. I could make it work!" Suddenly everything seemed so clear that she thought if she looked up at the sky, she would see clouds spelling out "Come back, Mary" and a finger pointing toward Georgia.

"Okay," she said as she pulled up in front of Sutton's Hardware. "Sounds good to me."

Feeling lighter than she had in weeks, she skipped up her stairs. Ravenel's door was locked, so she went into her office and scribbled him a note: *Standingdeer still won't talk, so I feel that my usefulness to this case has come to an end. Best of luck on August 27.* She pondered a moment about whether to add that it had been a pleasure working with him, but since it had truly been about as much fun as a root canal, she simply signed her name.

Grabbing her checkbook, she slipped the note under Ravenel's door and headed for Dana's office. Since it was exactly four o'clock, she doubted she was disrupting a therapy session, but she tapped softly on the door just in case. Seconds later, Dana opened it, looking as if she'd just awakened.

"Hi," she said, blinking.

"Are you okay?" asked Mary.

"Yeah." Dana yawned. "I was just cleaning out my files. Work like that makes me drowsy. What's up?"

Mary gave her a regretful smile. "I've come to pay next month's rent and to tell you that I'm moving out."

"Moving out? But you haven't even been here two months! Is something wrong with your space?"

"Oh, no. The space is fine. It's everything else. I don't think Harstville and I were meant to be together."

"But you seemed to be going great guns." Dana glanced at Ravenel's door. "Did Sam say something to offend you?"

"Ravenel hasn't said much that didn't offend me," replied Mary. "But that's not why I'm leaving." She knew she should explain further, but she didn't wish to dredge up the Logan saga or the Standingdeer fiasco or the grimmer prospect of an endless career brokering land deals for Deke Keener. "Some people can come back home, and some people can't. I guess I'm one of the latter."

"Gosh," said Dana sadly. "We haven't even gotten to play tennis. . . ."

"I'm not all that good," Mary admitted. "You'd probably have been bored."

"So what are you going to do?"

"I'm going back to Atlanta."

The next person she needed to tell was Hugh Kavanagh. Mary pulled up in front of his barn and found him standing by the paddock fence, directing young Turnipseed as to the proper way of longeing a horse.

"I've got some bad news," she said as she walked up beside him.

"Oh, God, is it Ridge?" The color drained from the old man's face.

"No. Ridge is fine. It's me."

She told him; he teared up, then swiped at his eyes with a blue bandanna. "Please don't go, girl."

"Hugh, if I thought I was doing a damn bit of good, I would stay. But I'm not. Ridge won't talk to anybody and I'm just in Ravenel's way."

"I'll go get in Ravenel's way myself, then," Hugh threatened, balling his thick-veined hands into fists.

"You don't have to, Hugh." She wrapped her arms around the old man. "Ravenel will do a good job. He's got excellent credentials."

"Is he going to get the boy off?"

"I don't know," Mary answered truthfully. "I don't think anyone can answer that."

~ ~

After that, she headed to Irene's farm. She drove the half mile to the turnoff and rolled down the driveway. Parking beside the rickety footbridge that spanned the trickle of a creek, she got out of the car and gazed at her inheritance. The little yellow house sat under the trees as warm and inviting as the woman who'd been Mary's friend. Mary sighed. How she wished things had worked out! How she wished she could have practiced law here and carried Irene's legacy forward.

"It just wasn't meant to be, kiddo," she told herself as she started across the jouncing footbridge, fighting the world-atilt sensation it always left in the pit of her stomach. "Not in this lifetime, anyway."

Inside, she threw some clean clothes in a suitcase. Tomorrow she would call off Turnipseed and his well-drilling. Right now, she wanted nothing more than to return to Little Jump Off and the man who ran it. Moving to Atlanta might be a hard sell as far as Jonathan was concerned, but she would give it her best shot. She glanced once more around her bedroom, then headed toward the front door, stopping in front of the portrait over the fireplace.

"I tried my best, Irene," she said, her apologetic words ringing in the house. "But I just don't fit in here anymore."

TWENTY-FIVE

She told him she'd quit the moment she stepped inside the store. He raised an eyebrow, but otherwise accepted the news with the same equanimity with which he'd greeted her decision to help in Standingdeer's defense. They grilled hamburgers on the porch for supper, helped Lily catch fireflies in a mayonnaise jar, then released them later, over the river. The tiny flickering dots of light reflected in the dark water as Lily squealed with delight. Later, after they'd put her to bed, Mary told him the rest of her plan as they sat on the porch steps, sharing a glass of Jonathan's homemade wine.

"All night I've been thinking about what we should do," she began.

"You haven't changed your mind, have you?" He looked at her, alarmed. "You're not going to rejoin this case?"

"No, no. I was just thinking that we might do something totally different."

"Like what?"

"How about we move back to Atlanta?" She said it flat-out and open. Beating around the bush with Jonathan was pointless.

"Atlanta?" He took a sip of the deep red wine and frowned. "Why?"

"It would answer all our needs, Jonathan. I could start some kind of general practice with Alex Carter. We could buy a little house in Decatur. Lily could have playmates, good schools. There, they would consider her being Cherokee something special."

Jonathan passed the wine to her and, for a long moment, pondered the stars. "What would I do? Go back to selling fishing tackle?"

Mary had known that was coming. When he'd lived with her before, he'd worked the hunting-and-fishing aisle of a sporting goods store, and had hated every minute of it. "No," she said, giving him a quick kiss. "You do what you love to do here. You hire out as a guide. Nobody knows the Southeastern forests like you do. There are a thousand rich Atlanta businessmen who would love to take advantage of your expertise."

"Think so?"

"I know so," she assured him, encouraged that he hadn't said an immediate no. "You could go and not have to worry about Lily. I would stay and take care of her."

"And no criminals?"

"No criminals, sweetheart," she said, putting the wine down and kissing him for real. "I promise."

❥

The next morning Mary awoke to the sound of a flute, playing amazingly close to her left ear. She opened her eyes to see a red plastic cassette player on her pillow and a little face beaming bright-eyed above it.

"Mey-liii!" Laughing, Lily clapped her hands.

"Is she awake, Lily?" Mary heard Jonathan's voice somewhere above her head.

With deep seriousness, Lily looked at Mary's open eyes. "Unh-huh," she told her father, nodding.

"Then tell her you brought her some coffee. Just the way she likes it."

For a moment Lily looked at her father, as if trying to translate his words, then she grinned down at Mary again. "Kawfee, Meyli! Kawfee!"

"Thank you, darling girl." Mary sat up and pulled Lily into her lap. She smelled of soap and powder and was already dressed in a pink playsuit, her little sneakers tied securely on her feet. Jonathan stood by the bed holding a cup of coffee. He too was dressed for an outing, wearing khaki trousers and a blue dress shirt.

"Did I miss something?" Mary asked sleepily as she took the coffee he offered. "Are we supposed to go somewhere?"

"Maamaadowwww!" said Lily, punching the fast-forward button on her tape player. Suddenly the languid flute music sped to a manic tempo, as Lily waved her arms in frantic accompaniment.

Jonathan laughed at Mary's befuddled stare. "We're going to Mother's Day Out. I think Lily wants you to get up and come with us."

"Okay, Lily Bird," said Mary, laughing at the child's antics. "Give me five minutes in the bathroom, and I'll be ready to go!"

Mary brushed her teeth and pulled on a pair of jeans, and taking her coffee with her, rode with Jonathan and Lily to Hartsville's First Methodist Church. She waited in the truck while Jonathan, along with several other parents, walked their children into a playground that opened off the Sunday school building. Despite Jonathan's misgivings about her isolated upbringing, Lily did not act shy at all, but immediately ran over to join two other little girls playing in the sandbox. Jonathan was greeted warmly as well, with a hug from one of the staff workers, a dimpled, beaming brunette. Mary watched, amused. There was nothing quite as appealing as a handsome man who was totally unaware of his own good looks.

"That went well," she observed as he climbed back into the truck after conferring with Lily's teacher. "Lily seems to fit in here just fine."

"She didn't always," Jonathan said, backing out of the parking space. "When I first started bringing her here, she would cry so hard that they would call me to come get her as soon as I got back to the store. Claudia took a special interest in her, though."

"Claudia the brunette?"

"Yeah. She has a degree from Western in early childhood education. Said she wanted to try some new techniques out on Lily."

"Looks like Claudia's had quite a bit of success." Mary tried to squelch the smile that played at the corners of her mouth.

Jonathan shrugged. "Lily likes to go there now. She doesn't cry anymore and I get a few hours to get my own chores done."

They drove over to Nero's, a diner on the highway between Hartsville and Cherokee. Mary was glad to be out of the gossipy atmosphere of the restaurants in town and into the more straightforward service that Nero Greenwalt had dished out for the past forty years. The bandy-legged little man waved at Jonathan as they walked in the door and told him his table was waiting. Mary followed him out to a small deck that overlooked Tuckaseegee Creek. A waitress brought them coffee and a basket of hot biscuits, then took their breakfast orders back to the kitchen.

Mary sipped her coffee, watching the water curling white on the creek rocks below. Though the sun warmed her shoulders and the caffeine eased her reentry into humanity, she did not feel one bit different about remaining in Hartsville. She'd opted out for good, and was ready to face whatever future she had with Jonathan. As she watched him turn a practiced gaze on the creek below, she suddenly realized that their conversation of the night before had not yet ended. She knew his face almost as well as she knew her own; it was clear he had something to say.

"What's up?" she asked, praying that he hadn't soured on the Atlanta plan.

Sheepishly he pulled a letter from his back pocket and gave it to her. "I guess I should have mentioned this last night. I got this job offer back in March. I was about to take it, when you came back from Peru, then I held off, waiting to see how things would go between us. I guess if you're really serious about leaving Carolina, then we should consider this, too."

"What is it?"

"A private game preserve over in Tennessee. The owner wants me to be the warden. The money's nothing to write home about, but the benefits are great, and there's free housing. Lily would have other kids to play with."

"Jonathan, that sounds wonderful!"

He shrugged. "I don't know what you could do there, though. Chattanooga's the closest town, and it's thirty miles away."

"I could open a practice there. It would probably take me less time to drive thirty miles in Tennessee than it would to go ten blocks in Atlanta."

She studied the raised crest on the stationery. She had no particular desire to practice law in Chattanooga, Tennessee, but maybe it would be better for Jonathan to have the full-time job and her to be the family freelancer.

"So you would consider doing that?"

"Jonathan, all I want to do is live a normal life, preferably with you. Why don't we eat breakfast, then go down and start cleaning out my office? We can talk about both our options."

"So you're truly serious? No more Hartsville? No more law office? A brand-new life with no more criminals?"

She thought of Officer Jane's supercilious stare, the whispers that followed her each time she went to the jail, Deke Keener's mania to fill her every waking minute with real estate maneuverings. Truly, she was deeply tired of it all. "A brand-new life, Jonathan. With no more killers or cops or land barons."

He leaned over and kissed her as a cool, damp breeze gusted up from the creek below. "This is more than I ever hoped for, *Koga*. I promise you will not be sorry."

They lingered at Nero's, as if unwilling to leave the charmed circle that their agreement had cast around them. Jonathan bought a newspaper. Mary drank a second cup of coffee while he worked the crossword puzzle. For the first time in what seemed like years she was content; she even dared, at one point, to project herself into the future. Lily would be a teenager, maybe driving a younger sister or brother to school. She and Jonathan would be middle-aged—heavier and perhaps beginning to gray, but he would still be able to read the woods as no other, and she would—what? Conduct house closings? Write wills? *It doesn't matter,* she told herself. *You'll have Jonathan and Lily. You'll have a good life with the man you've always loved.*

By the time she finished her coffee, Jonathan had filled in the last word of his puzzle. "Well," he said, tossing the paper onto the vacant table next to them. "Are you done? Shall we go get your stuff?"

"I'm ready when you are."

They paid their bill and drove into town. Nothing had changed, although she didn't know what kind of change she'd expected in the course of a night. *Good-bye Mary* banners might have been appropriate, she thought. *Farewell to the killer of our beloved Stump.* She sighed as Jonathan pulled up in front of her office. Though something deep inside her balked at the idea of giving up, she ignored it. She should have taken the hint when she'd first trudged up all those steps to Turpin's office. A law career for her in Pisgah County wasn't meant to happen.

"How much stuff have you got up there?" Jonathan asked, rolling up his shirtsleeves.

"A small desk, a couple of chairs. One of Mama's tapestries. We should be able to get all of it in the back of your truck."

"Then we'd better get moving. It's only going to get hotter, and we've got to pick Lily up at three."

They walked up the stairs hand in hand, just barely fitting on the narrow staircase. She pressed her finger to her lips to warn him to be quiet, but when they reached the top of the stairs she was the one who broke the silence as she saw Sylvia Goins, the girl from the hardware store, standing next to Sam Ravenel and his little Cherokee cohort. All three of them were gaping at her office door.

"Hi, everybody," she said, oozing cheer at Ravenel's broad back. "What's up?"

They turned. Nobody said a word. Everyone just looked at her with expressions of awe and surprise.

"What's going on?" Growing alarmed, she moved closer, tugging Jonathan with her.

The threesome stepped back, giving her the same kind of berth they might give someone with an active case of tuberculosis. Sylvia finally broke the awkward silence.

"You've had some visitors up here, Ms. Crow."

Mary hurried to see what they were staring at, then she gasped. Hanging from her door knob was the one thing that Aunt Little Tom had terrified them with when they were children and that even today gave her pause. On her door, someone had hung the most honored and horrific thing an Ani Zaguhi could send—the *yonuh ahgudulo,* the mask of the bear with bleeding eyes.

TWENTY-SIX

The mailman just left!" Avis Martin leaned over her balcony, craning her neck to catch a glimpse of the rural delivery Jeep as it roared back to the main road.

"Let's go see what came," said Kayla.

Leaving their game of Clue spread out on Avis's deck, the two girls raced through her bedroom, down the stairs, and out the front door. Kayla, the more athletic, easily reached the mailbox several strides ahead of Avis, but deferentially allowed her to retrieve her own family's mail. She waited with increasing impatience as Avis first managed to spill all the mail on the ground, then scooped it up to flip through a Sears bill, four credit card applications, complementary address labels from the Defenders of Wildlife, and a Lands' End catalog.

"Anything from Ridge?" asked Kayla.

Avis went through the stack of mail again, then shook her head. "No." She looked over at the suntanned girl who, in the course of the past two weeks, had become her dearest and only friend. "Are you sure he can read?"

"You saw that letter he wrote Bethany," Kayla reminded her. "If he can write, he must be able to read."

"Maybe he got somebody to write that letter for him," said Avis.

"The only other person he knows is that crazy old Irish guy he lives with. Anyway, I've seen him read before. The menu at Bayberry's, and once, the movie listings in the paper. We all went to see *Troy* together."

Avis tucked the mail under her arm and started walking back to the house. "Then I don't know what's wrong. He's had lots of time to answer our letter."

"Maybe they won't let him have any mail," said Kayla. "Or maybe he didn't understand that he was supposed to write back."

"But we worked so hard on that letter. We made sure he would be the only one who would know what we were talking about."

Kayla thought of the letter they'd labored for hours over—a rambling, two-page epistle in which Avis had underlined certain key words *(hide, insurance policy, where)* for emphasis. A week ago she'd thought it brilliant; now it seemed idiotic. "Maybe we made it too hard," she said miserably. "Maybe he couldn't read it. Maybe he just threw it away."

"All I know is that until we hear from Ridge, we're stuck," Avis said.

For the past week, Kayla had spent most of her time at Avis's. They kept real food in the refrigerator here, and Mrs. Martin actually got out of bed and got dressed, unlike her own mother, who, after rousing herself for the one day of Ridge's trial, had since disappeared back into her darkened bedroom. Though Kayla still found Avis weird, with her mystery books and peanut butter-and-Cheeto sandwiches, she was beginning to like her a lot. Avis wasn't nearly as cool as Jeannette Peacock or Lauren Reynolds, but at least she treated her like a regular person and not the poor pitiful Paulette that everybody else on the softball team did.

Mrs. Martin had taken Chrissy to a swimming lesson at the Y, so they dumped the mail in the kitchen, got two Cokes from the refrigerator, and retreated to the larger deck that sprawled out from the den. Above them, the white sky hung so hot and still that the earth seemed stalled in its rotation. The usually percussive cicadas managed only an occasional chirp, and even flight was apparently too much effort for the crows, which perched listlessly in the pine trees. The two girls collapsed in the big hammock that Mr. Martin had suspended on one end of the deck and

sat together, drinking their Cokes and staring into the woods that surrounded the backyard.

"I just can't figure out what kind of insurance policy she would have
gotten." Once again Avis pondered the question that had plagued them
ever since that first afternoon at Kayla's house.

"Jeez, Avis, I don't know. We won't know until Ridge writes us," said
Kayla testily. As much as she wanted to exonerate Ridge, Avis's endless
discussing of Bethany's insurance policy was driving her crazy. If this was
what real detective work was like, then she wanted none of it. Leave it
to brains like Avis, who liked nothing better than to sit around and read
creepy poems by some guy named Poe.

"But he's not going to write to us." Avis pushed off against the wall
with her bare feet and started the hammock swinging.

"Then let's ask your mom to take us to see him. 'Mrs. Martin, would
you drive Avis and me down to the jail? We need to talk to Ridge
Standingdeer. Who? Oh, you know. He's the Cherokee witch accused of
murdering my sister.' " Kayla hated it when Avis acted so stubborn.

Avis sighed. "Look, even if we could persuade somebody to take us to
the jail, they wouldn't let us in. You have to be related to somebody in
jail, and you have to go at special times, and you have to stay with an
adult."

Kayla shot her friend a curious look. "How do you know?"

"I called the jail," replied Avis. "While my mom was taking a nap. I
tried to sound older. I don't think they believed me, but they answered
my questions." She took a swig of Coke. "We're not going to get to go
see Ridge, so you'd better start trying to figure out why your sister
would buy an insurance policy."

Irritated, Kayla jumped out of the hammock. She walked over to the
deck railing, her throat constricted with tears. It all seemed so stupid
and hopeless. Bethany was dead. Her mother spent her days in bed like a
zombie while her father relieved his frustrations with Budweiser beer
and an occasional right cross to her jaw. All while a boy she knew was innocent rotted in jail and she sat in Avis Martin's hammock, with Avis
pretending to be Nancy Drew or Miss Marple or whoever the hell else
she babbled about. She ought to just leave now. Walk back to her house,
get on her bike, and pedal down to the jail herself. Maybe she could

throw rocks at Ridge's window, or demand to see him, as her right as an American citizen. Or maybe she could say she was Ridge's long-lost sister and talk her way inside. He had called her that one time, when she was out with him and Bethany. "Little sister," he'd said, laughing. "Lie in the backseat and sleep. . . ."

"Holy shit!" she cried, as a sudden memory flashed through her brain.

"What's the matter?" asked Avis, alarmed. "Did you get stung by a sweat bee?"

"I think I know what Bethany meant by an insurance policy! I think I know where she buried it!"

Avis was so stunned, she slipped out of the hammock, landing with a thud on the deck. "What are you talking about?"

"It was back in the spring, after Jeannette Peacock had a sleepover for her birthday party. Ridge and Bethany picked me up. We got hamburgers and drove around. I was really tired, since we hadn't slept much, so I curled up in the backseat. They went up to Laurel Overlook," said Kayla. "It's where everybody goes to park."

Avis scrunched up her nose. "Ugh! Did they make out and stuff, with you right there?"

"No. They just parked and talked. I did see them kiss a couple of times, though. They thought I was asleep."

"What did they talk about?"

"I don't know. Nothing much. She wanted him to take her to the prom. He didn't know what a prom was."

"What's this got to do with him hiding her insurance policy?"

"I'm coming to that." Kayla took a quick gulp of Coke. "I was half-asleep in the backseat, when all of a sudden they got out of the car. That woke me up, so I watched them. I thought they were going to have sex."

"Did they?" Avis asked, bright-eyed and breathless.

"No. They didn't hug or kiss or anything. They walked over and knelt down underneath a tree."

"Maybe Ridge believes in tree gods, like the Druids."

"They weren't kneeling to pray. They were crouching down. They looked like they were burying something."

Avis rolled her eyes. "Kayla, why didn't you think of this before?"

"I forgot about it. It was months ago and I wasn't really sure it happened. When I asked Bethany about it the next day, she just said I'd dreamed it."

"Okay, okay," said Avis. "What did they do after that?"

"Nothing." Kayla shrugged. "They came back to the truck, holding hands. I must have gone to sleep for real then, because the next thing I knew, Ridge was carrying me to my front door."

Avis got to her feet and began to pace, her bare feet slapping softly on the wooden deck. "How did you see all that stuff at night?"

"The moon was full. That's why they went up there in the first place."

Avis frowned. "Do you know the way to this Laurel Overlook?"

"Kind of."

"How far away is it?"

"I don't know."

"Could we walk there?"

"No, it's too far. We'd never get back in time." Kayla sighed. Ever since her sister's murder, everyone's parents had tightened their curfews. This summer, no one in Hartsville was playing outside after dark.

"My mother might drive us there," said Avis. "At least it's not a jail."

"Yeah, and what do we say when we get up there? 'Excuse us, Mrs. Martin, but we have to go look for a hole in the ground where Ridge Standingdeer might have buried my dead sister's insurance policy'? That's crazier than asking her to take us to the jail," Kayla said, evening the conversational score between them.

Avis didn't give up. "Okay, okay. You've lived here all your life. Surely you must know somebody else who would take us up there."

For a long moment, Kayla stared at the hammock. When she turned back to Avis, she blinked back tears. "Before, any of Bethany's friends would have taken me. Now, nobody calls us anymore. It's like we've all gotten contagious with something."

"Don't worry about it." Avis said softly. "People are jerks. We'll think of some way to get there."

Just then, Mrs. Martin pulled around to the back of the driveway, the brakes on the blue Ford squealing. Chrissy scrambled out of the car still in her pink bathing suit, looking like some small animal, recently drowned.

"I've got it," Kayla said quietly, waving at the little girl who danced around the driveway, the blacktop singeing the soles of her bare feet. "I know how we can get there."

"How?" asked Avis.

"We can ride our bikes."

"I don't have a bike."

"What do you mean you don't have a bike? Everybody has a bike!"

"Well, I don't," snapped Avis. "I've never had one," she added proudly, relegating bikes to the same inferior category as pimples on her chin or Ds in school.

Kayla started to say something else, then she realized that Avis had probably never had a bike because her parents hadn't been able to afford one. The Martins didn't have a computer or a DVD player or a lot of stuff her family did. "Can you ride one?" she asked tactfully.

"I don't know." Avis shrugged. "I rode my cousin's bike, two years ago."

"Okay. Then you get your mom to let you come over and spend the night at my house. My dad'll tap out halfway through the late news. After that, we'll sneak out. I'll ride Bethany's bike and you can ride mine. We ought to be able to get to Laurel Overlook and back before morning."

"I don't know, Kayla." Avis frowned.

"We can take some candy bars from your house, and a shovel and flashlights from my garage," said Kayla. After all of Avis's yammering about being a detective and solving crimes, she wasn't about to let her chicken out over a stupid bike ride. "Put up or shut up, Avis," she said sharply. "It's the only way we're going to find that policy in time to save Ridge."

Avis stared out at the dark green pines that surrounded her backyard. Her chin wobbled so that Kayla thought she might start crying, but then she seemed to resolve some conflict inside herself. "Okay," she said, swallowing hard. "If my mom'll let me sleep over at your house, then we'll ride our bikes and we'll find out what Ridge buried on that hill."

TWENTY-SEVEN

The ancient mask possessed an awful beauty. Carved of pale white beech, it was stained from eye sockets to jowls with bloodroot, giving the impression that the bear was weeping blood, howling in mute outrage centuries old. To Mary, it seemed to wail for those who had no recourse, while demanding vengeance from those who could act in their behalf. She could feel those deep, unseeing eyes working on all of them, and for once not even Ravenel dared break the silence of the room.

"Do you know what that is?" Ravenel's sidekick finally asked, speaking surprisingly fluent Cherokee.

"A bear mask." Mary replied in English, reluctant to say the thing's true name.

"It's big medicine," the man replied ominously, eyeing the mask as if it might be radioactive. "Holy as a drum. Now you have to do what it wants."

Mary frowned. "How did it get here?"

"The Ani Zaguhi. They turned themselves into smoke and brought it under the door!"

"Would somebody please explain what the hell you two are talking about?" Ravenel interrupted. "I mean, should I alert the media or just call the local ghost-buster franchise?"

"The Ani Zaguhi send them," said Sylvia Goins. "Ridge said those masks are like a curse."

"The only Ani Zaguhi I know is sitting in jail right now," Ravenel sneered. "In no position to curse anything other than his own rotten luck."

Ravenel's friend looked at Mary and started to giggle. "That just shows how much he knows, eh?" He turned to Ravenel and held his thumb and index finger an inch apart. "You white people know that much." He winked at Mary. "All the rest, we keep secret."

Ravenel snorted. "Did you two work this out earlier or are you just making it up as you go along?"

Jonathan stepped forward, looking down at the shorter Ravenel as if he were a mealworm. "The Ani Zaguhi send the bear mask when they need help. Whoever gets it is honor-bound to respond."

Mary carefully unhooked the mask from the doorknob. Ravenel's friend gasped as she touched it, as if it might turn her to dust. The mask was old and exquisitely beautiful, and attached to the back by a strip of deerskin was a single eagle feather.

"Aiiiieee!" Ravenel's friend jumped back. "They sent an eagle feather! To a woman!"

Mary's hands trembled. Even with her sketchy knowledge of Cherokee lore, she knew that an eagle feather was an honor of the high-est order, a gift signifying huge respect. Seldom were they given to men, almost never to women.

"So what does all this mean?" asked Ravenel.

I don't know," Mary replied, impatient with his skeptical carping.

"Maybe that you're canceling your rather terse note of yesterday?"

She looked at Jonathan, knowing that the mask could totally derail all the plans they'd discussed this morning. Although she did not for one moment believe that the Ani Zaguhi turned themselves into bears and cursed people who refused to help them, she did believe there could be people who lived so deep in the woods that they'd become rents in the fabric of time. If that were true, then one of those people might certainly want to save someone they loved; one of them might be begging her for help.

"I can't say what it means yet, Ravenel," she said, holding the mask tightly. "I'll have to get back to you on that."

She and Jonathan walked into her office, closing the door on the three people who still stood gaping on the landing. Laying the mask down on her desk, she went over and wrapped her arms around him.

"I don't know what's going on," she said, burying herself in his sweet, warm smell, the feel of his arms around her. "I don't know what to do."

"What do you want to do?" His voice was tender.

"I want to have a life with you and Lily."

"Then what's stopping you?"

She opened her eyes and saw the mask, with its eagle feather, glowing like bleached bone in the sunlight. "The same thing that would stop you, I imagine."

"Do you believe in the Ani Zaguhi?"

She struggled to give voice to her feelings. "Do I believe there could be an old tribe of Tsalagi, deep in the mountains? Yes. Do I think they're going to put a curse on my head if I ignore that mask? No."

"There are more ways to be cursed than by the Ani Zaguhi." His smile was ironic.

"What do you mean?"

"You are cursed by your own blood, Koga. You won't turn the mask down because you won't dishonor your mother's memory." He held her close. "I knew it the moment I saw it hanging on your door."

She closed her eyes, his shirt soft against her cheek. How well he knew her troubled heart! "What do you think we should do?"

"What we both have to do."

She knew without asking what that was. She would go back and work with Ravenel, for Ridge. Jonathan would go to the job in Tennessee, for Lily. She looked up at him, terrified at the thought of losing him all over again, after having come so far to find him. "Can't we talk about this? Ridge's trial won't last forever."

"Neither will Pomeroy's job offer," said Jonathan. He shook his head. "Let me go home and give him a call. Maybe he can hold it for me a little while longer."

She stepped back and looked up into his eyes. "I love you. I still want to be with you."

"I know you do." He smiled down at her. "We can talk about it tonight. Right now, I think you'd better get busy."

With a sorrowful glance at the bear mask, he turned and walked out of her office.

She fought back a moment of panic, when she was tempted to run after him. Let's just pack up my stuff and pretend this never happened, she'd say. . . . But the mask with its request for succor kept her in her office. Jonathan was right about one thing: As much as she wanted to make her life with him, she could not make a happy life until she saw this through. She watched out her window as he got in his truck and drove away, then she strode over to Ravenel's office, entering without bothering to knock.

"Yes?" He looked up from behind his desk, startled. He was alone, with a shot glass and a bottle of Jack Daniel's whiskey in front of him. Carefully, Mary picked the brimming glass up and moved it to the corner of his desk, beyond his reach.

"Okay, Ravenel, since happy hour doesn't officially start for another seven hours, why don't you tell me where we are in this case."

"Exactly the same place as yesterday," Ravenel announced snidely. "My experts still haven't found any leaks in the state's case."

"Any offers on the table?"

"With the forensics and all that circumstantial evidence and the whole town cheering him on, Turpin's in the driver's seat."

"Have you considered asking for a change of venue?"

"So moved and subsequently denied. Wood wants to get this over with." Ravenel shrugged. "I figure it's one thing we can use on appeal."

"So what's your game plan?"

"Kick as much dirt on their evidence as we can. The boy has maintained his silence, so I can argue anything." Ravenel glanced at the whiskey; a sheen of sweat began to glisten on his forehead.

"And you think that's the way to go?" Mary had never been able to tolerate the willful ignorance that defense attorneys thrived on. Though she knew they considered it the best way to mount a defense, it felt to her like going to the doctor and then ignoring your own pathology report.

Ravenel nodded. "I know it flies in the face of your prosecutorial modus operandi, but for us, sometimes what actually happened is the last thing we want to know."

She noted with pleasure that sweat had begun to drip from Ravenel's face. He must want that drink pretty bad, she thought, making no move to give it to him. She reveled in his discomfort for a moment, then asked him her final question.

"Okay, Ravenel. I'm back on board. Tell me how I can help."

"You could return my whiskey. That would be a good start."

"Sorry. I've got to do more than that."

"How about returning my whiskey and going away?"

She lifted the glass. "Point me in the right direction, and it's yours to enjoy."

Ravenel gave a quick little grunt, as if she'd poked him in the stomach, but he must have realized that she meant business. When next he spoke, it was with resignation.

"Okay, Ms. Crow, do as your mask commands. I don't, though, have the time to get you up to speed on defense strategies, so why don't you just play investigator and leave the courtroom stuff to me. Frankly, I think the only way this boy will get off is if somebody else nails the killer."

"So that's my job?" asked Mary. "Find the murderer of Bethany Daws?"

"You're the one who got the eagle feather, Ms. Crow." Ravenel looked at the whiskey as a dying man might eye water. "Not me."

She returned to her office. As soon as she closed the door, the mask began exerting a strange power on her, relegating to Ravenel and all his pontificating no more importance than a fly buzzing against a screen. She wondered, as she looked into the shadowy holes of its eyes, how old the thing was, if the Ani Zaguhi had sent it as far back as when de Soto tromped through looking for gold. She felt its worn smoothness in her hand. Who knew how many lives this mask might have touched?

"Okay, *yonah ahgudulo,*" she said, tracing the bloodroot-stained tears. "Let's see what you can do."

She went back to Ravenel's office, wrapped the mask in one of his camping blankets, and asked for the keys to his car. "Just for a little while," she explained. "My car's still at home."

He tossed his keys in her direction. Minutes later she was heading toward the Justice Center, driving a battered Subaru that smelled like a mixture of whiskey and Sterno. She pulled into the lot and parked in the sunniest spot she could find, hoping the heat of the day might burn the stink out of Ravenel's car.

She insisted that Officer Jane bring Ridge up from his cell. In the interview room, she watched the boy walk toward her, his expression unchanged from her last, farewell visit. He at least ought to look glad to see me, she thought with some irritation.

"*Sheoh,*" she greeted him.

"*Sheoh,*" he answered back.

"I have something for you," she said, watching his eyes. "I believe someone is trying to send you a message."

Without another word, she lifted the mask from the blanket. Ridge's eyes widened.

"Do you know what this is?"

He nodded.

"An hour ago I had quit this case. But then I found this hanging on my office door, eagle feather and all. Someone wants me to help you, Ridge."

He pinched his lips together as if what he had to say might be painful, but he nodded in agreement.

"Will you do what I ask you to do?" Mary asked.

"Yes."

She pulled out a legal pad and leaned back in her chair. "Then tell me what happened the night Bethany died."

TWENTY-EIGHT

Over the past month Ridge's English had grown rusty with disuse and often he reverted to Cherokee. Still, Mary sat taking careful notes as he talked.

"She picked me up at Hugh's after her parents took her little sister to a ball game. She seemed angry."

"What about?" asked Mary.

Ridge shrugged. "I don't know. She said she'd had a fight with her mother."

"Did she say what they'd fought about?"

"No. Only that both her parents hated her."

Mary frowned. "Where did you go after she picked you up?"

"We went to Smitty's tavern and got beer and hamburgers." He spoke more softly. "Then we drove up to a place we go to."

"What place?"

"A cliff place," he said, his eyes faraway. "She calls it Laurel Overlook."

"What did you do there?"

He stiffened in his chair, unwilling to speak.

"Ridge?"

Again, nothing.

Mary remembered years ago when Stump Logan had asked Jonathan the same questions. Apparently Cherokee males were still loath to reveal their sexual partners. "Ridge, it's okay to tell. We know you two made love. The police did a DNA test. They found your semen inside her."

He looked mortified, as if she'd seen him naked, then his gaze fell on the mask, and he nodded.

"Yes," he admitted. "We made love."

"And then what?" asked Mary.

"Then she dropped me off at Hugh's. I thought she went home."

Mary sat up straighter. This was the first curve Ridge's version of the story had thrown her. "You're saying that you weren't in her room that night at all?"

"I've been in her room other nights," Ridge admitted. "I go along that path, through the woods behind her house. But not that night. We both had to get up early the next morning. She had the breakfast shift at the café, and I had to help the farrier with Hugh's horses."

"Ridge, you know that you must tell me the truth—*zeeyuck?*"

"*Zeeyuck gunohezay.*"

"What did you do when she dropped you off at Hugh's?"

"I went inside to check on him. He was cleaning a bridle in the kitchen. I helped him put it back together—his fingers are old and he can't do the buckles. Then I went out to the barn and went to bed."

"And what time was that?"

The boy frowned, trying to remember. "It was before eleven o'clock. Hugh was waiting for the late news to come on television."

A red light flashed inside Mary's head. She knew absolutely that Ridge had not communicated with Hugh since before his arrest, yet he'd just corroborated the story that Hugh himself had told her. Plus, Ridge had revealed a big gap in the time line of Bethany's death. According to the police report, Paula Daws heard her daughter stumble in drunk at 2:43. The ME put her death at approximately 4 A.M., yet Ridge had bid her good night before eleven. What had Bethany done between 11:00 and 2:43?

Mary looked over her notes. She tapped her pen on the paper, then asked a question she'd wondered about ever since Ravenel had showed her the evidence Turpin had shared with them.

"When Bethany dropped you off, what kind of mood was she in?"

Ridge frowned as if he didn't understand the question. "Mood?"

"Was she happy? Sad? Angry? Excited?"

"She was mad at her parents," he replied. "She stayed mad at her parents."

"Did she ever say why?"

He shook his head. "She said they were both cowards. Sometimes she said her father was just like Lot."

"Lot?" Mary knew that was a character from somewhere in the Bible, but she couldn't remember what he was supposed to have done. "Did she ever talk about her father hitting her? Abusing her?"

"Mostly, she just talked about leaving. She always said once we got to Chapel Hill, we would never come back here."

Mary sighed at the fragility of Bethany's dream, shattered now as tragically as the young woman who'd dreamed it. "What were you going to do in Chapel Hill while she went to college?"

"I don't know," he said, morose. "Get another job, I guess."

Mary studied her notes for a moment, then she leaned forward. "Ridge, we haven't got much time before your trial starts. Is there anything else you can think of to tell me? Any little detail about you and Bethany at all?"

For a moment his eyes glittered, and she thought he was going to say something else. But then the moment passed. He retreated into the same bewildering stoicism of the last two months. "No," he said with finality. "Nothing more."

"Okay," she said, wondering if he was lying, if those dark Ani Zaguhi eyes were hiding something. "Then I'll get to work. If you think of anything else, tell the deputy that you need to see your lawyer. They'll make sure I get the message."

"*Sheoh.*" He stood up and smiled.

"*Sheoh,* Ridge," she replied. "Think about what I said."

She watched him stride out of the interview room, then she wrapped the mask back in the blanket and headed for the door. Though Ridge had still not uttered all that many words, he had readily backed up Hugh Kavanagh's version of the night of the murder and he had confirmed the strained relationship between Bethany Daws and her parents.

Driving quickly back to town, she found a parking space in front of her building and was about to head up the stairs when she saw Deke, sauntering down the other side of the street. Though her immediate reaction was to duck up the stairs and avoid him, she realized that for the first time in her life, she actually had something she wanted to ask him.

"Deke!" she called, waving.

"Hey, Mary! I was just coming to see you."

"What a coincidence. Have you got a moment to chat?"

"All the time in the world for you, sweetheart. Come on. Let me buy you a drink at Layla's!"

Before she could steer him upstairs to her office he'd swooped her two doors down the street, into the icy dark coolness of Layla's, and his usual booth in the corner. After ordering two gin-and-tonics, he loosened his tie and sank back in the seat. She had not seen him in a few days and he looked worn around the edges, as if he hadn't been sleeping well.

"Are you okay?" she asked.

"Sure. Why? Do I look sick?" He sat up straighter, immediately at attention.

"No. Just not quite yourself."

"Honestly, I am so ready for fall to come. This has been one shitty summer." He blew out a long breath as the waitress brought their drinks. "I can't get the financing worked out on that golf course deal, the Bear Den specs aren't ready, hell, I can't even get my softball team to bat over two-thirty."

"I guess that could happen when one of your players loses her sister." Mary gently reminded him of the summer's true tragedy.

"Oh, and Bethany Daws!" He picked up on the cue at once. "That's the worst of all. That poor girl. I don't think Glenn and Paula are ever going to get over it."

"I see them going to their therapy sessions every week," said Mary. "Dana must be doing them some good."

"I don't know." Deke's brows wrinkled above his nose. "Glenn's still a basket case. He never used to miss a ball game—hell, he was my assistant coach. Now he hardly ever shows up at all."

Mary watched a droplet of water make its way down her icy glass. This was going to be easier than she'd thought. Deke himself had opened the door, now all she had to do was step in. "Did Glenn and Bethany have a good relationship?"

Deke shrugged. "Not particularly. Why?"

"You mentioned once what a troubled girl she was. I just wondered if anyone had ever figured out why. The papers haven't made any mention of that."

For an instant he looked puzzled, then he leaned forward. "I wouldn't want this to get back to Glenn or Paula," he confided. "But Bethany slept around."

Mary stifled a laugh at his small-town naiveté. "Deke, by our eighty-seven standards, almost all teenage girls sleep around."

"No, I mean pathologically." He tapped his red swizzle stick on the side of his glass. "She tried to hook up with everybody. Old men, married men, tourists stopping at the café . . . Hell, she used to come on to me after our softball games."

Mary blinked. "You're kidding."

"No. I tried to josh her out of it, you know? Keep things light, but it got ugly at the end."

"How do you mean?"

He spread his hands, helpless. "I finally had to tell her that I was a grown man. I liked women, not little girls. Bethany got real mad after that. Starting spreading all sorts of rumors about me."

"Rumors?" Mary frowned, trying to square this girl with the one Ridge Standingdeer regarded as an angel from heaven.

"That I'd tried to rape her, that I'd been having sex with her for years." Deke looked pale beneath his freckles and took another swallow of his drink. "When that didn't work, she started telling everyone that I was gay, that I'd fucked boys in the church basement."

"That's interesting." Mary sat back, trying to fit this piece of the Bethany puzzle together with the others. Today alone, the girl had been described as an angel, a drunk, and now a rumor-mongering nympho-maniac. "How exactly did it end?"

"Excuse me?"

"You said it got ugly at the end. How did it end?"

He blew out another stream of gin-enhanced breath. "I hate to admit this, but I told her that if she ever came on to me again, I would take away her scholarship."

"So you thought taking away the one thing she truly wanted would make her quit her bad behavior?"

"Worked for my parents when I was a kid," he replied, as if proud of the scars of his childhood. "I screwed up, and I didn't get the new base-ball glove, or the trip to the movies."

"Sounds like her problems might have been a bit different from yours, Deke."

For an instant, a look of utter rage flickered across his face, then, just as suddenly, it vanished, replaced by his familiar, broad smile and a help-less shake of his head. "Look, maybe I didn't handle it as well as I could have, Mary, but that girl was trouble. All I knew was that I was going to be mighty glad when she took off for college, if only for her parents' sake."

Mary took a sip of gin. "That's a sad story."

"I know. And please keep it to yourself. I'd rather cut off my arm than cause Glenn or Paula any more pain."

"Oh, absolutely."

They sat in silence until Deke motioned for the waitress to bring them menus. "So, Miss Keener Construction Counsel, since I've finally got you here, how about I buy you an early dinner? I can show you the changes to Bear Den."

Quickly she swallowed the last of her drink. Bear Den was the last thing she wanted to talk about. "Some other time, Deke. I have some things I really need to catch up on."

"Are you sure? The lamb chops are wonderful here."

"Let's both take a rain check," she said, scooting out of the booth.

"Tonight, I need to get back to Little Jump Off. And I need you to give me a lift out there."

"If I do, can we talk about Bear Den first thing in the morning?" he asked, never one to give away a simple favor.

"For sure, Deke," she lied, flat-out and unrepentant. "There's nothing I'd like better."

TWENTY-NINE

After a long and tedious drive to Little Jump Off, Deke dropped Mary off at the front steps. "I'll call you first thing in the morning," he said, opting not to stay and chat with Jonathan. "We can talk about Bear Den."

"Thanks for the lift, Deke," she replied, happy to leave Deke's car and Deke's music and Deke's maniacal plans for developing Pisgah County. "I really appreciate it!"

She watched, with relief, as his sleek Lexus pulled around the curve, then she headed inside the store. There she found Lily napping in her playpen in front of the fireplace while Jonathan was filling two big plastic laundry baskets with toys and diapers.

"What's going on?" she asked, noticing three suitcases standing by the front door.

"I called Pomeroy," explained Jonathan. "He's kept that Tennessee job open for me, but he wants me to start immediately."

"So you're leaving right now?" she asked. If she'd come back half an hour later, would she have found the place empty?

"Tomorrow. For a trial run," he replied. "I've already given Bill Welch the keys to the store. He'll come open up in the morning."

She sat down in the rocking chair, stunned. He smiled at her but worked perfunctorily, making trip after trip upstairs and back. Finally, when she could stand it no longer, she followed him up to the bedroom.

"Jonathan, weren't we going to talk about this? When you left my office, we hadn't decided what to do."

"I hadn't talked to Pomeroy then," he replied helplessly. "If I didn't commit to something today, he was going to give the position to another guy."

"Look, I know this isn't what we planned, but what am I supposed to do? What would you do?"

He looked at her for a moment, then took her in his arms. "I don't know what I would do."

"I know what you wouldn't do," she told him. "You wouldn't ignore that mask. You certainly wouldn't ignore eagle feathers."

He was silent.

"I only broke my promise because of that mask." She reached up and turned his face toward hers. "It doesn't change my feelings toward you and Lily at all."

"It doesn't change mine, either, Mary. But what about the next mask? The next eagle feather? I thought about this all afternoon. You're a born hunter, just like me. Your quarry's different, but the chase is still the same."

"But I was willing to stop. I want to live with you and Lily."

"I know you do," he whispered, gently tracing the line of her jaw. "But I don't think you can stop, any more than I can." He gave a deep sigh. "I love you more than anything, but I can't live wondering when the next mask will show up, and how far away it will take you."

"Oh, Jonathan." She fought back tears. Eagle feather be damned, she wished she'd brought that mask to hurl in the river and bring its five hundred years of misery to an end.

"Look, let's just enjoy being together tonight. Lily and I will head over to Tennessee tomorrow and check things out. I'll call you from there. Who knows? The job might suck, you might get Standingdeer off immediately. It's not the end of the world."

She felt like a fool; felt even worse than she had the night Jonathan told her he was marrying Ruth Moon. She should never have come back here. She should have just stayed in Peru, with sweet, good-hearted

Gabe. Still, she wasn't going to beg Jonathan to give her another chance, and she certainly wasn't going to let him see her cry. "I think that's a good idea," she said, lifting her head to smile. "Living together is a pretty big step. Maybe we should both give it a second thought."

He started to say something else, then Lily wailed. Mary gave her a bath while Jonathan caught trout for supper. They had as festive an evening as they could, drinking beer and shooting fireworks over the river, much to Lily's delight. After they put her to bed they made love. Long acquainted with the curves and angles of her body, he touched her with a surety that was his alone. She responded in kind, hungry for the hardness of his body, the smell of his skin as she tried to embed the taste of him firmly in her brain. When they finally finished they lay in each other's arms, listening to the croak of a bullfrog, lost in their own thoughts. Though they tried to sleep, neither of them could, and finally they got up. Mary made a pot of coffee and they drank it, watching the sun rise over the river. Then Lily was awake and it was time for diapers and breakfast and all the other chores that toddlers entail. Soon Bill Welch came to open the store, and they had to go. Jonathan buckled Lily in her car seat and once again took Mary in his arms.

"I love you," he whispered. "I'll talk to you soon."

"I love you, too," she replied. "Take care of Lily."

She stood and watched as they drove off. Jonathan beeped his horn twice, Lily waved a small, star-shaped hand, then they were gone. Through the mountains, to Tennessee, to a life that once again did not include her. For a moment, she thought her heart was going to shatter, right there on the porch of Little Jump Off. Then she got in her own car and headed to town. Desperately she longed to follow them, but she'd promised to help Ridge. So with aching familiarity, she once again worked on packing away her feelings for Jonathan Walkingstick.

By the time she pulled up in front of her office, she was ready to share with Ravenel all she'd learned about Bethany. She was halfway up the stairs when she remembered that she needed an answering machine for her office—if she was truly going to practice law and play detective, she had to do more than just catch phone calls on the fly. Also, she would hate to miss a call from Jonathan, should he ring her office number. Shouldering her purse, she turned and headed back down to Sutton's Hardware.

She went inside the store, interrupting a passionate embrace between Sylvia Goins and her sweetheart, Ruben Morales, from the Mercado Hispaño across the street. As soon as she walked in, Ruben jumped back from Sylvia and scurried for the door, red-faced.

"*Buenos días,* Ruben," Mary said as the little man beat a hasty retreat. "*Como esta?*"

"*Buenos días, Señorita,*" he replied, his voice a horrified whisper.

"Sorry to interrupt, Sylvia," said Mary, walking up to the counter.

"Oh, don't worry about it, Ms. Crow," Sylvia said airily, as if pleased to be caught necking. "Ruben's Mexican. The men are prudish that way. How's it going? You get any more bear masks?"

"Not so far." Mary smiled at the rotund girl who had, over the past two months, sold her everything from lightbulbs to picture hangers. Though the heavy jowls of flesh on her face made her look thirty, she probably wasn't out of her teens. "How are you?"

"I'm okay. Can I help you find something?"

"I need an answering machine for my office phone. Do you carry those?"

"Right back here." Sylvia started waddling down one aisle, her wide hips swaying from side to side. "You working on Ridge's case?"

"Sort of." Mary followed Sylvia through the bird seed display and on into sporting goods. They were headed toward school supplies when she noticed an array of photographs hanging on the wall. Several years' worth of Keener Kats softball teams beamed down at her. In every one Deke Keener stood behind two rows of little girls, all dressed in pink-and-black uniforms. Glenn Daws also grinned from the photos, a big, beefy blond who looked as if he might have once played football.

"Oh," said Mary, surprised. "The Keener Kats. There's Deke, and there's Glenn Daws."

"Yes ma'am," Sylvia said somberly. "That's both of 'em."

Mary frowned at the photos. "Which one is Bethany?"

Sylvia pointed a chubby finger at a beautiful little heart-shaped face smiling from a photo in the top left corner. "That's her." She moved her finger down a row, to a slightly chubbier face. "And that's me."

"You two played on the same team?"

Sylvia nodded. "We were in the same grade in school, till I quit." She looked down at her protruding stomach and gave an embarrassed laugh. "Though I don't guess anybody could tell that now."

"Sure they could," Mary lied, wanting to lift the girl's sub-basement opinion of herself. "You've got the same terrific hair and that killer smile."

"Well, I don't know about that." Sylvia blushed at Mary's compliment. "But that's us. Bethany was left-handed, so she played first base. I played center field."

"What did you think of her?" asked Mary.

"She was okay back then."

"Back then?"

"She changed, later on." Sylvia shrugged, as if not wanting to speak ill of the dead. "But a lot of us did."

"Changed like how?"

"Well, everybody liked her and everything, but she did some really crazy stuff."

"What do you mean?"

A sour look crossed Sylvia's face. "Bethany slept with everybody in town. Most girls would get into big trouble, doing what she did, but not Bethany. She gets a scholarship to college and a handsome Indian boyfriend."

"Don't forget Bethany's dead, Sylvia," Mary reminded her. "And Ridge is in jail for her murder."

The girl shrugged. "There are more people than Ridge Standingdeer with good reason to kill Bethany Daws." She lowered her voice to a whisper. "And most of 'em have 'Mrs.' in front of their names. Bethany used to trade old Maynard Locust blow jobs for vodka, back behind the liquor store when his wife was working the counter. I saw her do that with my own two eyes!"

Mary feigned shock. "You don't mean it! She seemed like such a nice girl."

"She was nice," Sylvia said with finality. "But she was crazy, too."

Mary checked out Sutton's modest selection of answering machines, chose the least expensive one, and headed toward the checkout counter. After Sylvia rang up her purchase, Mary wrote out a check. "Thanks, Sylvia. It's always interesting to hear another side of the story."

"It's God's own truth!" Sylvia said defiantly, closing her cash drawer.

"If you want my opinion, I don't think Ridge Standingdeer killed her at all. I think Bethany Daws just pissed off the wrong wife!"

Mary walked back to her office, mulling over what Sylvia had just told her. It echoed what Deke had revealed last night, although he had not hinted at the extent of Bethany's sexual exploits. If that was indeed the case, maybe some aggrieved wife had killed the girl. It would take no huge amount of strength to crack her skull open with a four-dollar tomahawk. But how would someone sneak into her room at night? Mary shook her head. Unless some angry wife was running around Pisgah County with the skills of a cat burglar, Bethany's killer was someone the girl had known well.

She reached her office door and paused, trying to decide whether to go over and confer with Ravenel. Though tempted to fill him in on all the things his man McGruder had apparently overlooked, at the last minute she changed her mind. She wanted to pay a visit to the one man Sylvia had mentioned by name, liquor clerk Maynard Locust.

She got in her car and made a U-turn on Main Street, driving over to the local ABC store. Like every other state-run liquor outlet, it was puritanical in its approach to vending hooch—no flashing signs, no giant plastic Tennessee Walking Horses in the parking lot, just a nondescript brick building with a sign that warned you'd damn well better be twenty-one years old before you set foot inside the door.

Mary went inside, jingling a small bell over the transom. She hadn't planned on buying anything, but when she remembered that she was going to be spending her foreseeable future all alone, she walked over and picked up a bottle of Sapphire gin. She took her purchase to the checkout counter, where an oily-skinned man wearing a bright Hawaiian shirt sat reading the sports page of the paper. Mary charged her gin to her Visa card, then asked, "Is Maynard here today?"

"Nah, him and his wife went to Myrtle Beach." The man smirked, flirting. "Why? You a friend of his?"

"Actually, I work for the paper," Mary lied, officially kicking off her career as a private detective. She fished a newspaper photo of Bethany from her purse. "Someone told me Maynard knew this girl."

The man took the clipping. Though he tried to seem uninterested, the look on his face confirmed what Sylvia Goins had just told her. Bethany Daws had apparently been generous with her charms at the ABC store.

The man shook his head. "I've never seen her."

"Really? I heard she came in a lot, but I guess you get a lot of minors in here."

He shrugged. "We sell liquor. Kids want to get drunk. We get our share of fake IDs."

"But you never sold this girl any?"

"Not me," the man assured her. "The new sheriff's a real nutcase about that. He'd bust my ass in a heartbeat."

Yeah, right, thought Mary. Provided your ass wasn't in the back room, getting serviced by Bethany Daws. She put the clipping back in her purse and smiled. "Well, thanks. Maybe I'll come back later and talk to Maynard."

"He'll be back next week," the man said, his interest fast returning to the sports page. "But I can tell you right now that he never sold her any whiskey, either."

Mary picked up her gin and headed for the door. She had no doubt that the man was telling the truth. Why sell a pretty girl whiskey when you could just barter for it, off the books?

As she waited at a traffic light, she considered everything she'd learned about Bethany Daws. Outwardly, the girl led an enviable existence—popular at school, high-performing academically. Secretly though, she'd led a shadow life, filled with alcoholism and promiscuous sex—the classic behaviors of a victim of sexual abuse. Usually that meant the father, and Deke had admitted last night that Glenn Daws and his older daughter had a difficult relationship. Mary wondered—could Daws have killed her? He had access, maybe motive. No, she thought, discarding the idea. Jerry Cochran was a bright guy. He would have put Glenn Daws at the top of his suspect list. But what about the mother? And didn't Bethany also have a little sister?

"Something was making that girl see Ridge as her savior," Mary said aloud. "He was an outsider, with no knowledge of her past. Nobody here knew him, so no one could tell him her dirty little secrets." Before, Mary hadn't understood why a girl with a full ride to Chapel Hill would want to run off with a boy of primitive upbringing in backcountry Appalachia, but now she saw it clearly. Bethany could mold Ridge into anything she wanted. Bethany could use Ridge as a wedge against her family. And finally, running away with a boy with no family nearby meant you never had to come home again.

"Wow," Mary whispered, pulling up across the street from her office. Trying to figure out Bethany Daws was like peeling an onion—lots of layers had to be discarded before you got to the core of everything.

She got out of the car and hurried up the stairs. Just as she was about to unlock her office door, she saw Dana coming out of the small rest room all the tenants shared.

"Mary! Is it true you're not moving?"

"Well, not anytime in the immediate future."

"All right!" Dana lifted her fist in triumph. "I'm so happy to hear that!"

Mary gave an embarrassed shrug at her own indecision, but then she grew serious. "Dana, do you have a professional moment? I'd like to run something by you."

Dana glanced at her watch. "I've got a client coming at noon. But I can give you my undivided attention for the next ten minutes."

"Thanks." Mary followed her into her office. "How would you diagnose this? A bright, attractive teenage girl is everyone's sweetheart in public, but is wildly abusive and promiscuous on the sly."

Dana sat down behind her desk. "Abusive of what?"

"Alcohol for sure. Maybe street drugs as well."

"Any friends?"

Mary remembered Sylvia Goins' sullen disapproval of Bethany. "Popular at school, but I'm guessing nobody really close."

"Two-parent family?"

Mary nodded.

"Daddy's word law?"

"Possibly. Certainly there's a troubled relationship with the father."

"Sexual abuse," Dana said perfunctorily.

"That's what I guessed." Mary sighed. For some reason, she'd clung to the naïve hope that she'd left all that behind in Atlanta.

Dana gave a grim nod. "Statistically, we lead the region."

"You're kidding!"

"Nope. I live with a woman named Genevieve Lyles. She's a psychologist with the state board of education. She thinks we have a serial child rapist."

Mary was taken aback. "Excuse me?"

Dana's eyes flashed with anger. "Jen's convinced that someone out there is fucking Pisgah County kids. She says she can prove it. She just can't get anybody to believe her, except me."

"Try me," said Mary.

"Are you serious?"

"As a heart attack."

"Then come over for dinner tonight," said Dana. "I'll have Jen prove it to you."

THIRTY

Dana had invited her for dinner at seven, so at six-thirty Mary drove over to a street that wound up the hill behind the bookstore. It was an older residential neighborhood, shaded with tall oaks and sycamores, where people sat on their front porches and children played outside after dark, squeezing out every drop of summer before school and homework and the sorrows of growing up started over again. A multivoiced choir of katydids chirped a contrapuntal rhythm and though the breeze was still warm, it carried the first bittersweet notes of fall. With the exception of the late-model cars parked in the driveways and a dish antenna that sprouted from one house, the neighborhood seemed timeless; it could have been August in the 1940s as easily as August in the new millennium.

Mary pulled up in front of a small red-brick bungalow that sat amid carefully tended flower beds. White impatiens and colorful snapdragons spread out in profusion, guarded by a scruffy black-and-white dog that wagged his tail at the sight of her.

"Hey, fella." Mary smiled, approaching the little beast cautiously.

He gave a halfhearted woof, as if fulfilling his watchdog duties, then trotted down the steps and started licking her hand.

The screen door opened with a squeak as a woman came out on the porch. She wore jeans and had brown hair, cut like a cap on her head.

"Don't be afraid," the woman called. "Bobby will lick to you death long before he'll bite."

"So I see," Mary replied, rubbing the dog's soft fur.

"Are you Mary?" The woman came down the steps. Up close, Mary could see that she was around forty, with deep blue eyes and a sprinkling of freckles over her nose.

Nodding, Mary extended her hand. "Are you Dana's partner?"

The woman laughed. "I'm Genevieve Lyles. Jen for short. Come on in. Dana's fixing the salad."

Mary gave the dog a final pat and followed Jen into a living room where overstuffed bookshelves surrounded a small stone hearth. Candles of varying heights glowed from the fireplace as bouncy Latin jazz played softly from a CD player. Dana had stashed her tennis racquets behind the front door, and Bobby had littered a bright red rug with an array of well-chewed dog toys. Mary smiled. It looked very much like the home of any other American couple. Nothing about it would indicate that both partners wore bras and likely kept the toilet seat down.

"Come on back," said Jen, leading Mary through a small dining room, into a much larger kitchen. "Like I said, Dana's doing the salad. May I pour you a glass of wine?"

"Sure," said Mary. "Sounds wonderful."

"Hi, Mary!" Dana looked up from the sink, where she was rinsing mushrooms in a cascade of running water. "I see you met my two running buddies."

"Yes, I did." Mary looked enviously at Dana's plumbing, then took the glass of wine Jen offered. "A formidable pair. Who's the gardener in the family?"

The two women looked at each other in the way of longtime couples, as if trying to remember who exactly did what. "Jen plants the annuals every spring. I do bulbs in the fall." Dana laughed. "I guess I want more long-term bang for my buck."

"Actually, she'd rather just be on the tennis court," Jen teased with a wink. "Plus she's afraid of breaking a nail."

Dana shook her head. "Such a fibber! I'll have you know I almost broke *two* nails uncorking that wine!"

Laughing, Mary touched her glass to Jen's. "Well, whatever you broke was worth it. This wine is wonderful."

Dana turned to join in the toast. "We pulled out all the stops tonight, Mary. We intend to keep you from ever leaving Hartsville!"

They ate on a deck that opened off the back of the house. Dana grilled shish kebabs while Jen picked fresh corn and tomatoes from their garden. Dinner was just as delicious as the wine, and Mary learned that the two women had met in graduate school, at Duke. Both were psychologists; while Dana had a private practice, Jen taught at nearby Western Carolina and collected statistics for the state board of education.

"Statistics on what?" Mary asked as Dana plopped a scoop of vanilla ice cream on some warm peach cobbler.

"Pretty much anything the state dreams up," said Jen. "Plus, I do some contract work for the BIA, and the Department of Human Services."

Mary didn't quite know how to broach the subject that had, in fact, precipitated her coming. Jen, however, was not as shy.

"Dana tells me you suspect some of the same things I do about Pisgah County."

A moment of silence arose as Mary struggled to voice her wild suspicions. Finally she simply said, "I think someone was molesting Bethany Daws. And I think someone killed her to shut her up."

Jen glanced at Dana, then drained her glass of wine. "You have all but one thing right, Mary."

"What's that?"

"Someone has been molesting a lot more than just one child."

Dana reached over and squeezed her partner's arm. "Why don't you show Mary your files? I'll clean up out here and make us some coffee."

Reluctantly leaving the dinner dishes to Dana, Mary followed Jen back into a small bedroom that doubled as a home office. She sat down on a futon while Jen rummaged through a file cabinet in the closet, finally emerging with two thick manila folders.

"Okay," she said, glancing quickly through all the pages, then dividing them into four piles. "This is a statistical study I've kept current for the past ten years. It covers all the kids enrolled in the school systems of Graham, Haywood, Jackson, Pisgah, and Swain Counties."

"What exactly are you studying?" Mary asked.

"Originally, Raleigh wanted to know why Pisgah County dropout numbers were so high. I interviewed everybody who would talk to me. The boys gave pretty typical reasons, but almost all the girls had stonewalling honed to a fine art. It niggled at me, so I started gathering data on behavioral reactions to sexual abuse. That's when things got interesting."

She handed Mary a stack of bar graphs printed on old-fashioned sheet-fed computer paper. "The five counties are on the left. Each page represents a different year and a different behavior. I've measured suicides, attempted suicides, illegal drug arrests, dropout rates, illegitimate pregnancies, and treatment for STDs. As you can see, Pisgah County, which is the lowest in population, nonetheless leads the pack, and leads by a significant margin."

Mary flipped through the pages, noting the strange little marks that meant so much to statisticians. "Couldn't the Cherokees be skewing the numbers?" She felt disloyal, asking the question, but she knew that Indian kids fell victim to self-destructive behaviors far more readily than their white peers. That, she'd seen up close.

"I thought that, too, at first." Jen pulled another sheet from her folder. "So I did a separate subgroup study. The Cherokee numbers held steady until the late nineties, then they actually began to improve. The money that the casino is generating for them is really pumping up their self-esteem."

Imagine that, thought Mary dryly. Give poor people a little money and they turn out to be just regular folks!

"And look at this," Jen picked up another pile of papers. "Look at these numbers on the kids who've disappeared and never been heard from again. In the past decade you've got one in Haywood County, one in Swain, and five in Pisgah!"

"And they're all white?" Mary ruefully thought of Jonathan and the

Cherokee proclivity to strike out for greener pastures when things weren't working out.

Jen said, "Every one was white, female, and under eighteen years old. Kids run away all the time, but most are heard from again. These are still on the police books as unsolved disappearances. Cold cases, I suppose."

"So what's your theory?" asked Mary.

"We think someone in Pisgah County is preying on little girls," Dana said from the doorway.

Jen nodded. "Somebody able to intimidate most into silence, and able to get rid of the ones who threaten to talk."

"What about their fathers? Sexual molestation is a family crime."

Jen shrugged. "Unless Pisgah County has become the dysfunctional-family capital of North Carolina, the reported incidences should reflect that of the general population. We're spiking these graphs to high heaven."

Mary took the cup of coffee Dana offered. "Have you told the police your suspicions?"

"We told Stump Logan." Jen's voice was bitter. "He got a good laugh out of it. He said we were just . . ."

"Two frustrated dykes trying to stir up trouble," Dana finished her partner's sentence. "He was of the old 'all lesbians need is a good fuck from a real man' school."

Mary shook her head. She could just picture Logan leaning back in his chair, smug in his possession of a dick and a badge. "Have you tried Jerry Cochran?"

Jen nodded. "He was a huge improvement on Logan, but he said he couldn't act without harder evidence. Names, dates, places."

"Do you have any names? Of the ones who disappeared?"

"I do." Jen reached for another folder, this one full of newspaper clippings. "I've got six, dating back a decade. If you add Bethany Daws to this list, in Pisgah County, a girl winds up missing every seventeen months. You want them all?"

"Yes," said Mary. "I do."

Jen thumbed through her papers and handed Mary a sheet that listed the names of the vanished. "That's all the ones I've come up with. There are probably more we'll never know about." Sighing, she looked at her partner. "Dana and I don't have a child, but I can't imagine a worse hell than having one walk out the door and never be heard from again."

"Neither can I," said Mary, remembering her own personal hell when Lily Walkingstick went missing at the tender age of three months old, another bit of Stump Logan's handiwork. "Can I take these files with me?"

"If you think they might help find out what happened to these poor girls," said Jen.

"I do." Mary gave a sad nod. "Though I'm officially working on the Bethany Daws case, I have the feeling that whatever happened to these girls, happened to her as well."

Not far away, Bethany Daws had been the topic of conversation among another group of people. Three men had been discussing the young woman for the better part of the evening and were now bidding each other good night.

"It's a wonderful thing to do, Deke." Reverend Carl Matheny stood on the steps of the First Baptist Church and gave Deke Keener's hand a sincere shake. "Our denomination has taken a lot of heat over our attitude toward women. This will let everybody know that here, at First Baptist, we consider our sisters important members of Christ's flock."

"I totally agree, Deke." Bob Forsythe awaited his turn to pump Keener's hand. "The Bethany Daws Camp for Girls will be a wonderful ministry. What a great way to remember that poor little girl."

Every day of my life I remember that poor little girl, Keener thought bitterly as he accepted the thanks of the two men. "It's the least I can do for Glenn," he said, faking a humble smile. "He's like my own brother."

"He and Paula will be thrilled," said Reverend Matheny. "How about I set up a ground-breaking in the next few days? Get a photographer out from the paper?"

"Just let me know when to show up." Deke headed down the church steps. "I've got to be at a job site tomorrow morning, so I need to run. It's been a pleasure, though."

"Thanks again, Deke!" called Bob Forsythe. "We'll see you real soon."

Deke hurried across the street to his car. Dear Christ! Usually he loved doling out little gifts to the Baptist Church—playground equipment here, a church van there. Tonight, in that meeting, he felt as if fire ants were crawling just beneath his skin. He did not need to be sitting there planning a camp in memory of Bethany Daws. He needed to be out looking for those tapes that Bethany had waved in his face the day before she died. Every day that passed with Standingdeer still awaiting trial was a day that his own life could be ended by a cassette played for the wrong set of ears. He had to laugh at the irony of it all—a sword did not hang over his head—just a few bits of shiny brown tape encased in some small plastic boxes.

As he punched the keyless remote that Kayla Daws had once played with, a Pisgah County police cruiser slowly approached. Deke's stomach clenched. Had they found them? Were they coming to arrest him, right here, in the shadow of the church? Suddenly he saw the rest of his life spooling out like a bad TV movie. *Mr. Keener?* The cop would say. *I need to take you over to the Justice Center. Some tapes have surfaced that Sheriff Cochran would like to talk to you about.* It would be civilized, as arrests go; after all, he was the Prince of Pisgah County. But eventually Cockroach would cuff him; George Turpin would read a laundry list of his perversions in court while all his fat Rotary friends would sit punching each other and laughing. He would spend the succulent years of his life in prison and when he got out they would tag him like a dog, make him report in to the cops, and list his address on every pedophile website in the world. There would be no place he could go where people wouldn't try to root him out like vermin.

Near panic, he was about to get in his car and tear down the alley when the cop car rolled on by, serenely patrolling the soft summer night. He watched, breathing hard, slowly realizing that they weren't after him. *It's okay. You might not have found the tapes, but neither have they.*

He got into his car, sweat stinging his eyes. He needed to formulate some kind of new plan. It was just a matter of time before those tapes surfaced and someone with a badge and a gun showed up at his door.

If I only knew what they said, he thought as he eased the Lexus down Main Street, waving at Bob and Carl. If I only knew what she had on me. Maybe nothing, he told himself, as he drove out Hiawassee Road. Maybe it was all a trick, just to keep me away from Kayla. He smiled at the irony of that. Here he was, driving himself crazy to find something meant to prevent him from doing something he had no intention of doing at all. He stopped at an intersection, then the car turned almost by itself, down Glenn and Paula's street. Suddenly he was passing their house, 1 Audrey Drive. The tapes had to be there, somewhere, he decided. Bethany didn't go all that many places. She'd just put them someplace he'd yet to find.

He drove to the corner, then turned right, pulling off the street at the service road that ran behind all his houses. Set fifty feet back from the plot lines, it gave repairmen access to the properties without cluttering up the look of the neighborhoods. Though dressed in a sport coat and tie, he got out of his car and started down the dark service road toward Glenn's house. When Bethany was little, she'd played for hours in her backyard. Maybe she had some secret hiding place there he'd overlooked.

The pungent aroma of pine mingled with the sweet smell of new-mown grass. A few late-summer fireflies dotted the night and he could hear the gurgle of the small creek that meandered through the woods. Though creeping toward a murder scene in the dark might give people like Cochran pause, to Deke it felt like coming home. He was still just as comfortable in the woods as he had been that long-ago night with Tracy Foster.

When he reached the low bushes that bordered Glenn's property, he stopped. The backyard looked just as he'd remembered—Kayla's basketball goal hung over the garage, Darby's never-used doghouse sat beside the patio, an old tire swing swayed gently from the big oak in the middle of the yard. How Bethany had loved that swing when she was little! Often he'd seen her whirling like a dervish in the thing, only to get up and stagger away, dizzy and giggling. He squinted at the tree in the dark. Wonder if she had any hidey-holes there? A knot, widened by an owl or a squirrel, big enough to stash some tapes? He was just wondering if he dared creep across the backyard and check it out when he heard something over his shoulder. He turned. A soft growl rumbled from the trees behind him. It sounded much bigger than a dog, and the low, throaty snarl evoked warning; something was protecting its territory.

"Scat!" he whispered, knowing that most animals could be spooked by a single word. He listened for the sound of something retreating through the woods, but heard nothing except the gurgle of the creek. Satisfied that he'd scared whatever had growled into submission, he returned his attention to Bethany's tree. He'd just decided that a visit to the old tire swing might be a good idea when a breeze gusted from the trees behind him. Suddenly the sharp tang of bear replaced the aroma of pine, and an odd coldness seemed to envelop him. Deke tried to turn, to look back, but his neck felt as if it were bolted, rigid and immovable, to his body. His heart started to race as his tongue thickened in his mouth, useless as an old sock. He tried to loosen his tie, but his fingers would not move and he knew then that he must be having some kind of fit, no doubt brought on by the stress of those goddamned tapes! Then he heard that growl again. It seemed to come from everywhere and nowhere at once, closer and far more ominous than before.

Forget the tree, he told himself. You're having a stroke. If you don't get out of here now, tomorrow they're going to find you dead in the middle of your own service road!

Again, that deep growl rumbled, so close now that he could almost feel whatever-it-was's breath on the back of his neck. All at once his paralysis lifted, and without thinking of Glenn or Paula or any of the neighbors, he sprinted along the road, his tie flying out behind him, his legs pumping as if something with teeth and claws snapped at his heels. He knew he looked ridiculous, *he felt ridiculous,* yet he knew, too, that going one step slower would cost him his life. When he came to the end of the service road he skidded around the corner, unlocking the Lexus with his remote, diving into the driver's seat and locking the doors behind him. Gasping for breath, he turned on headlights, fog lights, every light he had, waiting to see a bear or a coyote or perhaps some huge feral dog. Instead, he felt a thud against his door that lifted the car on its springs, as if some large, ferocious beast had missed killing him by mere inches. Yet as hard as he peered into the bright field of light that now surrounded his car, he saw nothing but heavy brush and tall pines; heard nothing but the frantic beating of his own heart.

"Jesus," he whispered, gripping the steering wheel with trembling hands, suddenly realizing that he'd just felt the spectral tap of Bethany Daws upon his shoulder and that from here on out, he had far more than just some lost cassettes to worry about.

THIRTY-ONE

A few hours later that night, Avis Martin sat pressing one ear between the banisters of Kayla Daws' staircase. "So when's he going to pass out?" she asked in a whisper.

"I don't know," Kayla whispered back, unnerved by the sounds of the baseball game issuing from the television in the den. Her father's nights usually traveled a predictable course—he pulled his recliner in clear view of the kitchen door, turned on the TV, and then sat cleaning his deer rifles, as if preparing to blow away any new intruder who might venture into their house. As the national news came on, he would start the first of his dozen nightly tall boys, and for the next four hours he would alternately drink and weep or drink and curse his way through prime time TV. By the time Jay Leno concluded his monologue, Glenn Daws usually sat unconscious in his recliner, his last can of beer fallen to the floor.

Tonight, of all nights, however, had been different. While he'd still sat with his rifle across his lap, on this night he'd stayed relatively sober, caught up in watching the Braves battle Chicago. Every time Kayla had tiptoed past the den she'd found him staring at the TV screen, frowning in concentration. The one night she and Avis had plans that depended upon his passing out on schedule, he'd stayed awake! All afternoon they'd gathered their supplies, made sure they had enough to eat, enough air in the tires of their bikes. Now if her stupid father would just get the hell to sleep, they could get their mission under way. It was nearly midnight now. If they didn't leave soon, they wouldn't be able to make it back before daylight.

Avis started to say something else, but Kayla shushed her. "Wait!" she cautioned. "I hear something."

She listened, then crept halfway down the stairs and listened again. Underneath the muffled roar from Wrigley Field she was certain she now heard the rhythmic *yawp* of her father's snoring. She looked up at Avis, pointed to the den, and sneaked down into the hall. Then she stopped. Before they went any further, she needed to be absolutely certain that her father was asleep. If he awoke bleary-eyed and saw two figures lurking near the door, he might very well put a bullet through both of them.

She peeked around the corner. Though the room was dark, she could see her father splayed out in the recliner, rifle across his lap, snoring with one arm slung over his face. Quickly she counted the beer cans around his chair. Just nine—down three from his nightly dozen. That might be enough to keep him asleep long enough for them to leave, but would it be enough to keep him sleeping through their return? She sighed, not knowing what to do. If they left right this minute, they had a pretty good chance of getting back in time, despite Avis's total lack of talent at pedaling a bicycle. If they waited, who knew if they would ever have the opportunity to go again? Kayla knew how badly Mrs. Martin hated to let Avis come over here, and next week, school would start.

Taking a deep breath, she tiptoed back to the bottom of the steps and motioned to Avis to come on down. Tonight was the night. She had to try to lift this curse that had afflicted what was left of her family. She was going to prove Ridge Standingdeer innocent, even if her father shot her dead in the process.

Avis crept down the steps at Kayla's beckoning, relieved to finally be doing something other than waiting for Mr. Daws to tap out. This was undoubtedly the creepiest house she'd ever set foot in, with Mrs. Daws holed up in her bedroom while Mr. Daws drank himself stupid in front of the TV. As hopelessly dull as her own parents were, at least they kept normal hours and had decent food to eat. Every time she looked in Kayla's fridge, all she saw was beer and little half-empty cartons of take-out Chinese food. She didn't really care, though. After she'd discovered Bethany's diary, Kayla had decided she was a genius, and was happy to do her bidding in their detective endeavors. For the first time in her life, Avis felt important.

"Is he asleep?" She reached the bottom step and nearly tripped over her own feet.

"Yes." Kayla grabbed her before she fell. "We'll have to pass the den door to get to the garage, so be careful. You can't make any noise!"

"Where's Darby?"

"In my mom's bedroom. Anyway, he's too deaf to hear anything."

Avis followed Kayla through the dark house, her mouth dry with fear. Keeping to the wall like mice, they edged along the foyer until they came to the doorway of the den. Mr. Daws sprawled with his rifle in front the TV, his mouth wide and snoring, oblivious to the fact that the Braves had scored a run. Again, Avis thought of her own family. Her dad sometimes fell asleep in front of the TV, but he usually had his banjo in his lap, his rifle locked far away, in a trunk in the basement. She watched as Kayla tiptoed silently across the doorway, then motioned for her to join her.

Now came the tricky part. Avis knew they had to get out of the house without waking Mr. Daws. Willing her usual clumsiness away, she started across the doorway on tiptoe, every nerve in her body attuned to Mr. Daws' snoring. *Braaaaaaack, sooooooo. Braaaaaaack, soooooooo.* Halfway to the door, a nervous giggle escaped her throat as she seemed to see everything as if from a great distance—Mr. Daws sounding like a buzz saw, Kayla looking like a scared rabbit. She clamped her jaws together, trying hard not to burst out laughing, when suddenly the snoring stopped. She froze, staring into Kayla's eyes. Had Mr. Daws woken up? Was he now aiming his gun at her head?

With her gaze locked on Kayla's, she stood like a statue. For what seemed an eternity, all she heard was the ball game, then Mr. Daws gave a strangled little *snerk* and resumed his snoring. Once again, she began to breathe. For now, they were still okay.

● ◄ ►

They sneaked into the garage, rolled their bikes into the driveway and pedaled off into the night, Kayla riding smoothly while Avis followed behind, awkwardly trying to shift the gears. She managed to keep up with Kayla on the level stretches, but when the road went uphill, she fell behind, often just pedaling after the distant red dot of Kayla's rear reflector. They met no traffic, so they rode down the center of the pavement, their tires hissing like snakes in the darkness. Halfway to Laurel Overlook they stopped for water and a candy bar.

"How much farther is it?" gasped Avis, her thighs feeling as if someone was toasting them with a blow torch.

"Not much." Kayla took a long drink of water. "But it's all uphill. Through really thick woods."

"Will we see any bears?" Avis's heart fluttered as she envisioned wolves and wildcats.

"I didn't the last time I was up there, but then I wasn't really looking for them."

Avis knew that to question Kayla further would brand her a chicken, so she stuffed the rest of her candy bar in her mouth and kept quiet. With her tailbone aching, she climbed back on the bike. This time they pushed along a rougher road that twisted upward through a black lacework of pine trees. As her leaden feet pumped the pedals, a screech owl swooped so close to her head that she had to duck, its eerie trill raising the hairs on the back of her neck. They rounded another tight curve and a possum scuttled in front of the them, its bare pink tail whipping behind it.

She pedaled faster, trying to close the distance to Kayla before anything else leapt out at them. The climb grew steeper, and she pushed the pedals with all her strength, barely able to keep the bike upright and moving. Just when she thought her lungs might explode, the road ended in a small clearing. Kayla stopped, got off her bike, and walked to the edge. There, spread out like diamonds on dark velvet, were the lights of Hartsville, twinkling in the distance. Realizing that she'd just ridden to the top of a mountain, Avis dismounted her bike and on legs trembling with fatigue, walked over to stand beside her friend.

"Wow!" For a moment she forgot her burning lungs and aching tailbone as she stared at the glittering earth below. "No wonder they came up here."

Kayla took off the backpack that held their digging equipment. "Come on. We need to get busy. The trip took a lot longer than I thought.

"I think we parked here," she said, trying to retrace her sister's steps. "Then they got out of the truck and went over there." She walked toward a grassy area where low-growing cacti covered the rocky ground. Avis followed, keeping a wary eye out for more possums.

"Then they turned this way," Kayla said almost to herself, playing her flashlight along the ground beneath the trees. Avis searched for any place that looked dug-up, but she saw nothing but scrubby grass and fallen pine needles. As Kayla began to walk deeper into the surrounding woods, making wide sweeps with her flashlight, something caught Avis's eye.

"Shine the flashlight over there!" she cried. "I thought I saw something!"

Kayla pointed the light where Avis directed. A twig protruded upward from the ground at an odd angle. Stripped of its outer bark, it glowed like a skeletal finger in Kayla's light.

"Maybe that's it," said Avis. "Maybe Ridge marked the place with that stick."

Kayla looked doubtful. "I remember it as being more over that way, but I guess we could dig a little bit and see."

They hurried over to the twig. Kayla laid the flashlight on the ground and gave Avis one of the two camp shovels she'd brought. Kneeling down, the girls started to dig. They could tell immediately that the earth was different from the hard clay soil around it—loosely packed and interspersed with what smelled to Avis like some kind of animal dung. She was wondering why Ridge would have buried shit in his hole when suddenly the blade of her shovel scraped against something hard.

"Get the light!" she cried. "I found something!"

Kayla grabbed the flashlight as Avis uncovered a piece of flat shale, the kind of rock normally found at a creek.

"This is it!" Kayla said, elated. "I saw them with a big rock that night! Here." She handed Avis the flashlight. "Give me some light while I pry this up."

Using the other end of her shovel, she tried to pry the stone up, but the dirt around it was too hard. She tried a stick, then the blade of her Swiss Army knife, but nothing would budge the rock.

"What can we do?" Avis cried as Kayla began to sweat from her efforts.

"Loosen the dirt around it with your shovel," ordered Kayla. "I'll try to wedge my fingers underneath it."

Avis dropped the flashlight and did as Kayla ordered. She loosened the sticky clay soil from one edge of the rock until Kayla was able to get her fingers beneath it.

"Okay," she said. "Here goes nothing."

She lifted, straining. The rock moved, but not nearly enough. "Help me," said Kayla.

Avis joined her, now wedging her fingers beneath the stone. Together, they pulled with all their strength. At first the rock only moved an inch or two, then suddenly it flipped on its edge, throwing dirt into their faces.

"Quick!" said Kayla. "Shine the light down there."

Avis did as she was told. The flashlight revealed a foot-deep hole in the ground that wiggled with earthworms and pill bugs. At the very bottom lay a tanned deerskin pouch.

"Golly!" Avis was so surprised, she almost dropped the flashlight. "We found it!"

Kayla reached down and retrieved the pouch. It was soft and supple, and wrapped with a leather thong. Quickly she untied it and dumped the contents on the ground between them. Out tumbled two Sacagawea gold dollars, a small knife, a picture strip of Ridge and Bethany at the mall, and three Altoid mint boxes bound with rubber bands.

"Shine the light down there again," said Kayla. "There must be something else."

Avis poked the flashlight down the hole. It revealed nothing more than a few more wiggling earthworms.

"There's no insurance policy here." Kayla's voice broke. "They must have dug another hole somewhere else!"

For a moment Avis stared, heartbroken, at the odd collection of junk, then her gaze fell on the mint boxes, wrapped in rubber bands. "Hold the light a minute."

Kayla took the flashlight. With shaky fingers, Avis picked up one of the Altoid tins. Though the lid had warped, she tore off the rubber band and pried it open. When the flashlight beam fell on the contents, she gasped. Inside lay not breath mints, but two tiny tape cassettes, labeled the "personal private property of Bethany Ann Daws." Hurriedly the girls opened the other two small boxes. They held similar contents—cassette tapes, bound and labeled the private property of Bethany Daws.

"What on earth?" The glow from the flashlight made Kayla's face look round and moon-like. "Why would she bury six minicassettes?"

"I don't know." Avis cupped the little tapes in her hand. "But I bet something important must be on them."

"Probably her stupid love poetry," said Kayla, disgusted.

"No," Avis replied urgently. "You wouldn't tape love poetry. You'd write it in your diary. Read it to your boyfriend, if you were really brave. You bury stuff you don't want anybody else to find. Something's on these tapes, Kayla. Something that Bethany didn't want anybody else to hear!"

Kayla stared at the tapes. "My dad's got one of those little recorders. He keeps it in his desk, at home."

"Then we need to take these back to your house and listen to them," said Avis, trying to sound like an expert. "And if anything is on them, we'll take them to the cops."

Kayla shrugged, acquiescing to her friend's vaster investigative experience, then she looked up at the sky. The eastern horizon was growing light. "Come on! We've got to get back home. If my dad finds out what we've done, he'll kill me!"

"He might be mad, Kayla," corrected Avis. "But he won't kill you."

Kayla shook her head. "No, Avis. You don't understand. If my dad finds out about this, he'll kill me."

THIRTY-TWO

The next morning, the deep jangle of Irene's old-fashioned telephone roused Mary from a dream about driving Lily around one of Deke Keener's housing developments in a golf cart. Opening one eye to the dim morning light, she groped for the heavy receiver of the phone beside her bed.

"Hello?" she croaked, wondering if Jen had remembered any more vanished girls.

"Mary?" A deep, familiar voice broke through the muzziness in her head. "Are you awake?"

"Jonathan?" She sat up in bed. He sounded so close. "Where are you?"

"Polk County, Tennessee."

"Where's that?"

"Just across the mountains. I can see North Carolina from my living room."

She shut her eyes, feeling queasy inside. His living room. His house. His whole new life with Lily, without her.

"It's not that far away," he continued. "We're no more than an inch apart, on my map."

An inch, she thought. Nothing to a cartographer. In real terms, if she got in her car, it would take her hours to reach him, and then only by driving along twisting mountain two-lanes. And how far apart their hearts were, she couldn't begin to fathom.

"So what's your house like?" she asked, determined to sound upbeat and cheerful. "How's Lily?"

"We have a kitchen with a dishwasher. And a clothes washer and dryer. And our own bedrooms, although Lily didn't sleep in hers last night."

"Where did she sleep?"

"In my room." He laughed. "I guess it all just seems too strange to her."

I know exactly how she feels, thought Mary. Still, she tried to keep her voice light. "I bet she'll be fine by tonight. Kids adjust quickly."

There was an awkward pause, then he said, "So how are you doing?"

"I'm okay."

"Anything new with Standingdeer?"

"I'm working on a few things." She glanced at the thick stack of papers she'd brought back from Dana's. "I might have something in a day or two."

"Any more masks hanging on your door?"

"Not so far, but I haven't been in to work this morning."

Another pause, as if he wanted to say something further, but had no idea of how to begin. "Well," he finally said. "I guess I'd better go. Pomeroy's coming over and I have to give Lily her breakfast."

"Give her a kiss for me, will you, Jonathan?" She was fighting tears. How had they come to this? How had this happened?

"I will. I'll call you in a couple of days, okay?"

"Okay." She held the phone tightly, as if that might keep him close. "You be careful!"

He said good-bye, and suddenly she was sitting alone in bed, the dial tone ringing in her ears. For a moment she considered calling him back and telling him that she was driving on over, right now. Then she thought of the mask and all of Jen's meticulously gathered data.

"Just find these girls first," she told herself as she threw off her covers and headed for the kitchen to heat water for a sponge bath. "Then you can find Jonathan."

She hurried down to her office. She'd hoped to catch Dana before she started her morning's work, but her DO NOT DISTURB sign was hanging on her door. Instead she ran into Ravenel, banging up the stairs with a seedy-looking briefcase. He frowned when he saw her.

"Any new leads, Detective Crow?" he asked, his voice dripping with sarcasm. "Any more masks from the Ani Zaguhi?"

"Possibly," she called airily as she walked past him. "I'll let you know. Just don't take any deals, Ravenel. And for God's sake, don't plead out."

His brows lifted in surprise. "Have you got something to tell me?"

"Don't know yet," she answered, not wanting to get his hopes up. "But I think you could have seriously overpaid your man McGruder."

"I rather doubt that," Ravenel replied with an arrogant chuckle.

She went into her office and closed the door behind her. The bear mask stared at her intently from her desk, its dark eye holes pinioning her with a look of fierce entreaty.

"Okay, okay," she whispered, as if the thing had been awaiting her return all night, impatient for her to get to work. She grabbed her phone book and began looking up the numbers of the families whose daughters had disappeared. Out of the six names Jen had given her, three still apparently lived in the area. The Chester Flemings at 1 Acquoni Road, the Dawson Rankins at 1 Swannanoa Lane, and the J. C. Hendersons at 1 Cullasaja Crescent. Odd, she thought as she jotted down the addresses. They all lived at the same street number, but she didn't recognize any of the streets.

She put down the phone book, puzzled. Had the town grown so large in her absence that she now only knew half the streets? Frowning, she stared vacantly at the map of the Keener empire Deke had left propped against one wall, then she realized what it was. Acquoni Road, Swannanoa Lane, Cullasaja Crescent were all Keener streets, running through new Keener developments. Each of these girls had lived in a house built by Deke Keener and Glenn Daws.

"Wahdo, yonuh ahgudulo," she murmured to the mask as she grabbed her car keys. "If it hadn't been for you, I might not have figured that out."

Twenty minutes later she stood at the door of 1 Acquoni Road, a sprawling red-brick rancher that stood at the entrance of Acquoni Acres.

According to the phone book, Chester and Lurlene Fleming lived here, as once had their daughter, Valerie.

As she let the door knocker fall, Mary realized that she had not thought of what she was going to ask these people, provided they would even talk to her. Dredging up memories of a long-lost child wasn't anything distraught parents particularly enjoyed. Still, she badly needed some answers to her questions. She decided she would simply tell the truth, as much as she could, and be very careful not to raise any false hopes.

She'd just lifted her hand to knock again when the door opened. A woman with skin like parchment stood before her. Though it was easily ninety degrees outside, she clutched a pink chenille bathrobe as if she were freezing. Her lips were thin and pinched and she wore thick glasses that magnified pale, red-rimmed eyes. Somewhere deep in the house, Mary could hear the melodramatic dialog of a television soap opera. "Yes?" the woman said, her voice as anemic as her complexion. "Can I help you?"

Mary had seen people like this before; people whose lives had stopped forever on the day their loved one had disappeared. Although their hearts still pumped blood and their lungs still moved air, they were, for all intents and purposes, dead. Mostly they were women; mostly it was a child they mourned. "Are you Valerie Fleming's mother?"

"Yes." The woman's eyes brightened. After all these years, she still longed for some word of her girl. How Mary wished she could oblige her.

"My name is Mary Crow. I'm an attorney. I was wondering if I might ask you a few questions."

"Do you know something about Valerie?" The woman's hands fluttered to her throat.

"No, ma'am. I'm sorry. I'm just trying to see if some pieces of information fit together." Mary watched the hope in the woman's eyes die. *No news of Valerie. This day would be just like all the other days, just like all the other days to come until the end of her life.* "May I come in for a few moments? I won't take much of your time."

"All right." Mrs. Fleming stepped away from the door.

Mary entered a living room that was a small shrine to the girl who'd disappeared. Photos were displayed on every flat surface available, from the top of the spinet piano to the china cabinet in the corner. Skinny, blond, and pretty in the gawky way of young teenagers, Valerie appeared in every photo. Mrs. Fleming then confirmed that she'd disappeared on September 29, just weeks after she started the ninth grade.

"She went to school one morning and just never came home." Mrs. Fleming nervously rubbed her cheek. "Everybody saw her in sixth period study hall. Then they didn't see her anymore—not in the parking lot or on the bus or anywhere." The woman clutched at her bathrobe again. "She was always trying to run away. I guess she finally succeeded."

"Why did she want to run away?" asked Mary gently.

"We moved here when Val was ten. She was fine at first, then she changed." The frail little woman leaned closer. "She got so moody—laughing one minute, crying the next. She would say awful things to her father and me, then cry. Or run away. We tried to control her, but nothing worked."

"Did she play sports? Have any hobbies?"

"She loved to play that piano," Mrs. Fleming nodded at the instrument across the room. "And she played softball. My husband's company had a team."

"Your husband's company?"

"Keener Construction. Chester was a carpenter."

"Mr. Fleming *was* a carpenter?" Mary wondered why Mrs. Fleming was speaking of her husband in the past tense.

"He was framing a house over in Swannanoa Downs and took a wrong step backwards. The fall broke his neck."

"I'm so sorry, Mrs. Fleming."

"I am, too. Sometimes I think it would've been better if we'd just stayed in Alabama. We might have been poor, but at least we'd still be together. . . ."

❧

Mary thanked the grieving woman for her time and assured her that she would be in touch, if she found anything that might pertain to Valerie.

The second house on her list was a modern version of a clapboard cottage, listed as the home of Hope Henderson, but it was locked up tight, with a Hartsville Realty sign in the front yard. "Not much hope for Hope," Mary said, checking off the girl's name. "Now on to Suzanne Rankin."

Swannanoa Downs was not far from Acquoni Acres. Like Mrs. Fleming, the Rankins lived just inside the entrance to the subdivision, at the very first street number. This house had a bit more Arts and Crafts look to it, with clean, squared-off lines. Mary had to admit that however much Ravenel railed against Deke's subdivisions, they looked classier than most, and appeared to be constructed with a great deal of care.

She rang the doorbell. A man dressed in the brown uniform of a UPS driver jerked open the door immediately, as if he'd been tapping his foot, waiting for her to come.

"Yeah?" The man's jaws worked overtime, chewing gum.

"Are you Suzanne Rankin's father?"

"Yep."

"I'd like to talk to you about your daughter."

Mary asked him the same questions as Mrs. Fleming. After some initial reluctance, he told her a similar tale. His daughter had been the joy of his life until junior high school, when she'd taken up with a bad crowd of kids. After getting a "smart mouth and a bad attitude" Suzanne had disappeared one Saturday night, after her mother had dropped her off at the skating rink. Nobody had seen her since.

"Was she athletic?" Mary asked, remembering something Mrs. Fleming had said.

"Yeah. Skating, bowling. Won a softball trophy one summer. She was real proud of that."

"Did you work for Keener Construction?"

"Drove dozers for 'em for five years. Keener himself put me up in this house."

Mary frowned. "In this house?"

"Yeah. You know, one of their test houses. They let new employees move in and test 'em out for a year." He gave a bitter laugh. "That's why I'm number one, Swannanoa Lane. All the test houses are number ones."

Mary blinked. So the Hendersons and the Flemings had all lived in test houses. She was so excited, she could barely ask the next question. "Do you still work for Keener?"

Mr. Rankin shook his head. "I couldn't take it anymore after Suzie. You know, seein' kids she'd known grow up, get married and all. I quit and started driving for UPS. Keener understood. He was great about the whole thing."

"What about Mrs. Rankin?"

He took a long swig of beer. "She moved back to her people in New Jersey." He shrugged. "She never liked the South much, anyway. With Suzie gone, she had no reason to like it at all."

THIRTY-THREE

K ayla? Are you awake?" Avis Martin lay still, even the minimal effort of a whisper almost too much for her to undertake.

"Yes."

"Has your dad gone to work yet?"

"I don't know. I think I drifted off to sleep."

"What should we do?"

"Just lie still. Keep listening."

Avis had no difficulty lying still. Every muscle in her body throbbed with pain, and when she did muster the strength to move, agonizing prickles of fire raced all over her. Their bike trip had left no part of her unaffected. Her thighs burned from pumping the pedals, her hands ached from squeezing the brakes, and the hard, unforgiving bicycle seat had turned her bottom into a pulsating boil. She was pretty sure she was going to die. Right this very minute she ought to be calling her mother, telling her that she loved her, that she was sorry she'd been such a hopeless screw-up. Then she realized that was ridiculous. Nobody *died* of a bicycle trip, unless you fell off and broke your neck or got eaten by a mountain lion. She was just profoundly, amazingly exhausted. Don't be such a nelly, she told herself. Kayla's right beside you. At least pretend to be brave.

Wincing, she reached down and felt beneath the bed. Her fingers curled around the treasure that they'd struggled so to retrieve. Bethany's tapes. Bethany's *insurance policy*. What could be on them? Some secret about the mysterious D? Some sex scandal at school? God, I hope so, she thought. She prayed it wasn't some sappy love tape, with Bethany cooing about how much she loved Ridge Standingdeer.

She pushed the tapes further under the bed, then massaged her left shoulder. She and Kayla had managed to get home just as the sun was cresting the mountains. They had ridden like fiends all the way, terrified that Kayla's father would be awake and waiting for them, but when they tiptoed back inside the house, the only sign of him was a cluster of beer cans around the recliner in the den. Darby was nowhere to be seen; the television had been turned off, the rifle put back wherever it belonged. Still, they'd crept up the stairs like burglars, too scared to breathe until they reached the sanctuary of Kayla's room. Once they'd gotten there, Kayla closed the door and they fell on the bed together. "We'll wait until he leaves for work," Kayla had whispered. "Then we'll go down and get his tape recorder."

That, however, had been hours ago. Now, according to Kayla's swiveling Elvis Presley clock, it was nearing ten A.M., and the only sound she'd heard was an occasional *woof* from Darby, who'd somehow gotten into the kitchen.

Suddenly she jumped. Downstairs, a door was closing.

"Kayla!" She punched her friend. "Do you hear that?"

Kayla's eyelids flew open. She gazed at the ceiling, listening as heavy footsteps drew closer to the bottom of the stairs.

"It's him," she whispered.

"Is he going to work now?"

Kayla shook her head. "It sounds like he's coming up here."

Avis listened as the man who'd last night passed out with a deer rifle across his lap started walking up the stairs. Her heart began beating so fast that she thought it might jump out of her chest. Closer the footsteps came, angry and urgent. Mr. Daws must have woken up and found them gone; now he was coming to have it out with them. She clenched her aching fists, waiting for the door to burst open, when, abruptly, the footsteps stopped. For a long moment she and Kayla froze, suspended in a fearsome silence, then they heard the footsteps again. Only this time, they were going down the stairs. Too scared to move, the girls listened as the kitchen door opened, then shut. They heard sharper footsteps of someone walking on concrete, Darby barking for real, then the roar of a truck engine. Kayla leapt from the bed and peeked out her window.

"It's him," she whispered, watching as the truck pulled out of the driveway. "He's going to work."

"Finally!" said Avis, willing her battered body into a sitting position.

"I'll go check and see if Mom's asleep," Kayla told her. "She probably is, but we still need to hurry. These days my dad could come back any minute."

Avis waited as Kayla scurried down the stairs to check on Mrs. Daws. Moments later she was back, standing in the doorway, motioning her to come on.

"We'll have to hurry," she whispered. "Mom's in the shower. Darby's outside."

With her heart pounding, Avis hobbled after Kayla. Down the stairs they crept. They crossed the kitchen again, then tiptoed down the back hall to a bedroom that Mr. Daws used as his office.

"Stand at the door and keep watch," said Kayla. "I don't know where he keeps that recorder."

Avis did what Kayla asked, gazing down the empty hall while Kayla rifled through Mr. Daws' desk. What they would say if Mrs. Daws caught them, she had no idea. She just crossed her fingers and hoped her shower would take a long time.

"Hurry up!" she urged Kayla, who was rummaging in the desk. "Can't you find it?"

"Not yet," Kayla replied.

"Try the file drawer. Look under T or R." Avis bounced nervously on the balls of her feet.

"Not in there," reported Kayla, pulling one drawer open as she closed another. "Or in here. Shit. Where could it be?"

"Could Bethany have taken it?"

"I don't know." Kayla frowned, thinking. "Wait a minute! Maybe he keeps it with all his dopey old self-improvement tapes."

She opened a closet in the corner of the room. Reaching to a high shelf, she pulled down an old shoe box. Hurriedly, she brought it over to the desk.

Avis glanced over from her sentry post. "What's in there?"

"Inspirational tapes," Kayla replied drearily. "My father used to make us listen to them on the way to school. 'The Power of Faith.' 'Believing in Yourself.' 'Listening to Your Inner Fear.' Crap like that."

"I am listening to my inner fear," Avis muttered as Kayla rummaged through the box. "And it's saying to get out of here."

"Bingo!" Kayla cried suddenly. "Look!"

Avis turned. Kayla held up a tape recorder, not much bigger than a pack of cigarettes. "Great," said Avis. "Now just hurry and put everything back like you found it!"

Avis kept watch while Kayla restored the room, then they both crept back to the kitchen. Avis was starving, but she knew that Kayla had nothing to offer but old Chinese take-out, so she ignored the rumbling of her stomach and followed her friend upstairs. Once inside her bedroom, Kayla closed the door and this time pushed her desk chair against it, just in case.

"Get the tapes," she commanded.

Avis limped over to the stash beneath the bed, sick with dread. What if they'd gone to all this trouble only to hear Bethany pouring out her love for Ridge? How stupid would they feel then? Just examine the evidence, she told herself, trying to be as dispassionate as Sherlock Holmes. Let it speak for itself.

Kayla inserted the first tape into the machine and turned the volume all the way up. The two girls stared at the small turning wheels, listening intently. At first they heard only silence, then Kayla opened the little machine to find the tape twisted up like a streamer, the wheels of the recorder unable to move.

"Damn!" she said, gently uncoiling a length of shiny brown tape. "We'll have to rewind this by hand."

"Go on to the next one, then." Avis looked at the rusty orange dirt the tape had left on her hand. "This one must have gotten damaged underground."

Kayla snapped in the second tape. Once more, they listened. This time they heard a girl's voice, coming on sporadically, between long gaps of silence.

"Is that your sister?" asked Avis.

Kayla nodded. "She sounds a lot younger, but I think it's her."

The tape continued. They heard rustling over some old eighties music, then Bethany, angrily crying, "I hate you!" With every moment Avis grew increasingly disturbed. It sounded like something awful was happening to Bethany on the tape. Sitting here listening to it made her feel sick to her stomach.

For the rest of the second tape, though occasional phrases were audible, they still couldn't figure out exactly what was going on. The third and fourth tapes coiled up as badly as the first had, and the fifth was nothing but static. Finally, Kayla put the last tape in the machine.

"Listen as hard as you can," said Avis. "Unless this tape is a hundred times better than the others, it's not going to do us a bit of good."

Kayla punched the PLAY button. Avis held her breath as the little wheels began to turn, again feeling awful at having to listen to a crying girl who was now dead. *Please,* she prayed silently. *Let something be on here.*

Her prayer was answered so suddenly, she jumped. All at once the same eighties music they'd heard on the other tape blared forth, so loud that Kayla had to turn the volume down. "What is all this old stuff?" Kayla whispered.

Avis shook her head. "Listen."

Over the music, they heard a car door slam. "Hey," a man's voice said, clear as a bell. "How's it going?" A long silence, then, "Aren't you even going to talk to me?"

"Let's just get it over with." This time it was clearly Bethany, only older. Sounding now more like sixteen than twelve.

"You want to go in the front or the back?" the man asked, still pleasant.

"I don't care."

"Then let's do it right up here, in the driver's seat."

Avis looked at Kayla, feeling like she might vomit. She wasn't sure what was going on, but she could tell Bethany wanted no part of it.

The music continued. For a while no one spoke and they heard a shuffling noise, then Bethany came back on.

"Ouch," she cried. "That hurts."

"Stick your bottom out more," said the man. "Then sit down." He moaned as if someone was giving him a massage. "That's it. Slow and easy, just like our old merry-go-round game."

For a long moment they heard nothing, then the man gave a long, expulsive cry. "You're so good, baby," he told her. "So very, very good."

"Can I get dressed now?" asked Bethany.

They listened, their eyes wide as the tape went on. Though there were gaps when the recorder had apparently been turned off, the rest of it was more of the same. The same old music always played, the same man always asked her how she was doing, then proceeded to make her play the merry-go-round game or touch something "right there" or "lick something hard." As they listened, tears began to stream down Kayla's cheeks.

"That must be D," Avis told Kayla. "Do you recognize his voice?"

Kayla shook her head. "All I know is that it's not my dad," she said, wiping her eyes, answering the question that Avis had been too chicken to ask.

The tape ended; they flipped it over. Though neither wanted to listen further, they knew it was the only way they were ever going to find out who D was. The B side consisted of more music, more groaning. Then, halfway through, both their hearts stopped. At the end of a long rapturous moan, the man said, quite clearly, "Way to go, Bethany girl! You've just made your old Coach Keener a very happy man!"

Avis looked at Kayla, stricken. The man on the tape was the same man who drove her to softball practice three times a week. Her father's boss, the one who'd plucked them off the unemployment rolls of Greenville, South Carolina.

"D didn't stand for Dad at all," said Kayla, her voice an odd mixture of bitterness and triumph. "D stood for Deke. D was Coach Keener, all along."

THIRTY-FOUR

Miles away, Coach Keener was driving to the First Baptist Men's Club meeting. They'd scheduled a box lunch and groundbreaking for Camp Bethany Daws—a retreat, Reverend Matheny had decided, "where poor city kids could come for a week, enjoy the woods, and deepen their relationship with Jesus Christ."

Deke snorted as he drove out to the hundred acres of scrub pine that his Mexican carpenters and Ukrainian plumbers would turn into a memorial for Bethany. He hoped the kids who came out here would leave with a deeper relationship with Jesus Christ than he ever had. Maybe it depended on the setting. Maybe Jesus responded to prayers sent up from kids around campfires more readily than He did from scared little boys who scrubbed themselves raw in the shower.

As he turned off the wide highway and onto the narrow, tree-draped road that led to the camp property, he felt a sour nervousness in the pit of his stomach. He was still puzzling about what exactly had happened last night as he reconnoitered Glenn's backyard. The moment he'd started looking at that tree with the tire swing, the temperature had plummeted. Then that growl. So close, so deep, so fucking angry. Jesus, he'd never heard anything like it. For the first time in his life he'd run away from something—flat-out and farting, as big a chicken as Jerry Cochran had been, back when they wore lanyards and worked on merit badges. Forget finding Bethany's tapes—all he'd wanted to do was put a significant distance between him and whatever it was in those bushes. Although in the morning light his cowardice embarrassed him, the foot-wide dent in the door of his car reaffirmed his decision to run the hell away from whatever had been out there.

"It must have been a bear," he told himself for the hundredth time. "Coming down from the mountains to fatten up at people's garbage cans."

He knew about bears. He'd grown up in western North Carolina, had even studied them in Scouts. But he'd also spent enough time in the woods to know he was kidding himself. Ursus americanus did not lower the temperature and T-bone a Lexus like a small truck.

He pulled into the wide, flat field that his bulldozers would soon grade into a parking lot. Matheny and a number of deacons were already there, hammering a sign into place. CAMP BETHANY DAWS—OPENING NEXT SUMMER, it said in cheerful red letters. A JOINT PROJECT OF HARTSVILLE'S FIRST BAPTIST CHURCH AND KEENER CONSTRUCTION. Yeah, right, thought Deke, getting out of his car. Keener supplies the architects and site plans and construction crews and First Baptist supplies what? Campers, he thought with a smile. Every summer, a new little girl, just for me. What a fitting tribute to Bethany!

"Come on, Deke!" Reverend Matheny called jovially, one arm around a somber-faced Glenn Daws. "The photographer from the paper'll be here any minute!"

"Hang on, Carl." Deke waved at the men, then turned. His ghost bear apparently had a bad effect on his bladder. He walked a few feet into the woods for some privacy, unzipped his pants, and aimed a stream of urine at the base of a tree. Freeing his penis brought Avis Martin to mind, and he remembered that lately she'd seemed less skittish when he ran his hand up her leg. Maybe tomorrow night, after the game, he could go a bit farther—maybe give those little breasts a squeeze. Smiling, he started imagining how that might feel, when suddenly the temperature began to drop. All at once he was standing in late November instead of mid-August, in cold air that smelled like dry dead leaves and deer musk. His dick shrank even as he peed, and once more he heard that same low, savage growl that had last night sent him running. He looked around wildly, wondering if he'd run into yet another bear, but in front of him he saw nothing beyond thick pine trees; behind him, seven paunchy, middle-aged men hammering a sign into the ground. None of them were shivering from the cold or standing huddled against a growl that seemed to come from the air itself. Hell, they were telling jokes and passing out lunches, happy as schoolboys at recess.

"It's all in your head," he told himself, his voice cracking. He hoped to take comfort in those words, then he realized, horribly, their truth. *It was all in his head. This was his legacy from Bethany Daws. A monster that plagued only him, who lurked only at the edges of his own consciousness.*

Gulping, he zipped his pants and hurried toward the men, trying to put a lid on his panic, doing everything he could to keep from screaming, *"Don't you hear it? Can't you smell the fucker?"*

But no, they didn't; they never would. God had blessed Daws and Matheny and the others with simple normalcy. He was a twisted thing upon whom God had visited the worst of curses. A plague of frogs would be a welcome respite from the ache in his gut for young girls.

"Deke?" Carl Matheny's wide grin shrank into a frown of concern. "Are you okay, buddy? You look like something's after you!"

"Oh, no," Deke gasped, trying to breathe. Why would that stink not go away? Didn't any of them smell it? "I'm fine. Just don't want to miss lunch."

"Well, here." Matheny unfolded the lawn chair he'd brought with him. "Sit down. Have some lemonade. It's good and cold."

Deke took the paper cup the preacher offered. The lemonade tasted both sweet and sour. It helped to clear the bear smell from his head and cool his overheated brain. Someone handed him lunch—a ham sandwich, potato chips, and a chocolate cookie, neatly packed in a white box. He unwrapped the sandwich and concentrated on eating, hoping the salty ham would reanchor him in reality. By the time he finished the photographer had arrived; everyone was waiting for him to step into the celebratory picture that would appear in Sunday's paper.

"Coming," he said as they called to him. He dragged himself to his feet, walked over to stand beside Glenn Daws, moving in slow motion. Though he now smelled nothing but the sun-warmed pines, and heard nothing but the good-natured joking of the Baptist men, he still trembled inside. He had to do something before whatever was either in his head or out there in those woods turned and ripped out his heart.

After pasting a sick grin on his face, Deke left the ground-breaking immediately after the photographer freed them from their pose. "I'll talk to you later, buddy," he told Glenn Daws. "I've got to go see about some things downtown." He avoided mentioning Mary Crow's name to Glenn—Daws had hated her since the moment she stood up in court on behalf of Ridge Standingdeer. That didn't stop Deke, however, from actively seeking her professional advice. In legal matters both personal and professional, he intended to keep that woman on his side, Glenn Daws be damned.

He got in his Lexus and roared back to town. His sweaty hands were slick on the wheel, and he tried to focus his attention on other, more pleasant things. Just remember that soon Standingdeer will be convicted, he told himself. Soon, too, you'll be back on track with Avis. Though the girl had been more squirmy and distractible than most her age, soon he would have her just where he wanted her. He smiled at the thought of all that soft young skin beneath his fingers.

He drove on, turning down Main Street. The afternoon sun glistened off the cars parked along the curb. He looked for the black Miata that still bore Georgia plates, but did not see it. She's gone, he decided, his panic sharp and immediate. She's stayed at home today, or worse, she's out with that loser Walkingstick.

Or maybe she rode into town with Walkingstick, he thought, forcing himself to remain calm. Maybe right now she's upstairs in her office, going over the plans for Bear Den. Suddenly the name of the property sent a wave of nausea through him. He would have to call it something else. He no longer wanted anything to do with bears. He parked his Lexus in front of the Mercado Hispaño and hurried across the street, bounding up the stairs like a fireman rushing into a burning building. His heart sank when he saw Sylvia Goins shoving mail under Sam Ravenel's door.

"Coach Keener!" She brushed a greasy lock of hair back from her face. "What are you doing up here?"

"I've got some business with Mary Crow," he said. "Have you seen her?"

"Not this morning," Sylvia replied. *Lord,* he thought, *she always speaks so slowly, it makes me tired just to say hello to her.* "I can give her a message, though, if you like."

Yeah, right, Sylvia. Tell her that an invisible bear has twice lowered the temperature of my personal environment by thirty degrees, and has trashed one side of my car while growling like he wants to eat me alive. Just tell her that and see what she says.

"No," Deke said, loosening his tie. "I'll check back with her later."

"I'll tell her you came by!" he heard the big girl call as he hurried back down the stairs.

He walked out of the cool building and into the bright afternoon. Again he looked for Mary's Miata but saw only trucks and low-riding Fords parked in front of the Mercado Hispaño. A cluster of Mexicans stood by the side of his Lexus, pointing at the huge dent in the driver's door. *Oh, shit,* he thought. *What now?*

He crossed the street. Tito, the owner of the market, was standing there jabbering in Spanish to another man who wore cowboy boots and a pie-eyed boy he thought was Sylvia Goins' boyfriend. He wondered, for a moment, if one of them hadn't dented his poor car further, then as he drew closer, he saw what they were looking at. Now not only was his door smashed, but four long, deep scratches traveled down the side of the vehicle, from the edge of the window almost to the rear bumper. He gulped. It must have happened while he was having his picture taken, and he'd been too upset to notice before he took off for town.

"*Buenos días, Señor Keener.*" Tito nodded, the gold tooth in the front of his mouth glinting in the sun. "We were just looking at your car."

He walked to examine them closer. He was speechless. They went all the way through the finish on the car, down to the bare metal.

"Did you hit some kind of animal?" Tito's tone was respectful, but his bright, dark eyes reminded Deke of the roosters that supposedly fought in his basement—sharp and clever, keen to find any weakness in the opposing bird.

"I—I don't know," Deke replied, not knowing what else to say.

The man with the cowboy boots began to snicker, rattling off something in Spanish.

"*Sí, sí.*" Laughing, Tito turned to his friend, as if he, Deke Keener, the Prince of Pisgah County, was no more important than a fly. "*Qué le espera un tipo que lo hace con niñitas?*"

The two Mexicans laughed as if at some private joke, then turned to stroll back in the store. Deke was left staring at his dented, scratched-up Lexus with Sylvia Goins' Mexican boyfriend.

"Well?" he said, furious at Tito's arrogance. "What are you staring at?"

"Your car, *señor*. It was once very beautiful. I can fix it back if you like." The little man twisted the red bandanna he always wore around his neck.

Deke's first impulse was to laugh—the idea of a bunch of Mexicans working on his Lexus was ludicrous, but then he realized that if he took the car to his usual mechanic, everyone in town would soon know that he'd hit something with teeth and claws. Normally, that wouldn't bother him, but with everything like it was now, it would probably serve him best not to attract any kind of attention at all. Zero. *Nada,* as his little Mexican friend would say.

"How much?" he asked the little man.

"Two hundred dollars." He blinked, his eyes hopeful and wide.

"Could you do it quickly? *Pronto?*"

"*Claro que sí.*" He nodded, grinning. "You take me and the car to the house of my cousin, Luis. It will be finished tomorrow, in the morning."

He considered the Mexican's proposition. After he dropped him and the car off, he could call Linda to pick him up. He could get a loaner from Bradley for the rest of the day, then get his Lexus back tomorrow. If José here fucked up, it would give him an excuse to come after Tito. If

José did a good job, all traces of the bear would be gone without Randy Bradley or any other of those idiots knowing, and he would only be out two hundred bucks.

"Okay, amigo," he said, slapping the little man on the back. "Climb in. You just got yourself a job."

THIRTY-FIVE

I can't believe it." Kayla lifted her face, looking as if she'd broken out in hives. "Coach Keener's like our uncle. He's been my father's *best* friend, like forever."

Avis gulped as she thought of her own parents' total adoration of the coach. How could the man who took her to ball practice and had given them a brand-new house be the same man on that tape? Yet they'd both heard him clearly, moaning with pleasure, telling Bethany how to do things Avis had never even dreamed people did. "I know what you mean," she whispered. "My parents like him, too."

"But you don't understand!" cried Kayla. "He's always been there for us! Bethany acted really rude to him before she died, but he was the first one over here the morning Mom found her. Helping the cops, trying to calm everybody down. He took me out for doughnuts, just to get me away from everything."

Avis stared at her friend, wondering if she realized what she'd just said, but Kayla sat unaware, staring at the tape recorder, tears streaking her face.

"How did Bethany act rude?" asked Avis.

"Coach Keener gave us a ride home, after Bethany got off work. She acted like such a bitch! I called shotgun, but she made me sit in the backseat. She acted pissy all the way home and after I got out of his brand-new car, she slammed the door and started yelling at him! My mom had to come out and apologize!"

"Didn't you wonder why?" asked Avis.

"Bethany was mean to everybody. My dad had made her quit seeing Ridge, and she took it out on all of us." Suddenly Kayla started sobbing anew. "But she wasn't really being mean at all! She just hated Coach Keener!"

Avis put an arm around Kayla's shoulder. "Let's put the tape recorder back in your dad's office and go for a walk. Sometimes it's easier to think when you're moving." Avis didn't know if this was true or not, but she really needed to get out of this house. The enormity of what she'd just begun to suspect about Coach Keener was too big for Kayla's room. She needed to consider it outside, where the big blue bowl of a sky might dilute its awfulness.

"Okay." Kayla sniffed as she removed the last tape from the machine and handed it to Avis. "But be sure and hide these again. I don't want my dad to find them."

While Kayla went downstairs to return the tape player, Avis hid the tapes in the bottom drawer of Kayla's dresser, beneath her underpants. Moments later they stood outside, hoping the hot sun would toast away the icy, chill fear inside them. With Darby huffing along behind, they crossed Kayla's backyard and retreated to the woods just beyond the service road. Walking in silence, each pondered the magnitude of what they'd just learned. The most powerful man in Pisgah County; the man responsible for the quality of their lives and their families' fortunes, had molested Kayla's sister. Who and whatever else he might have done was still too frightening for Avis to give voice to, so she just followed Kayla along the creek, wondering sickly what Coach Keener might have in mind for her.

"I just can't believe it," Kayla repeated for the hundredth time, plopping down on a log that had fallen over the small stream. "I mean, he's been so good to us. All of us. Even the stupid softball team." She looked up at Avis. "I wonder how many of them he's fucked?"

Avis lowered her eyes. She knew, of course, what *fuck* meant, but she'd never once spoken the word aloud.

"You ride to the games with him," Kayla said accusingly. "Is he putting it to you, too?"

"No!" Avis said quickly. "But sometimes I think he'd like to. . . ."

"What do you mean?" Kayla's face twisted in new horror.

"Every time he gives me a ride to the game he always touches me," Avis admitted, her pale face growing red with shame.

"Touches you where?"

"So far, just my legs and arms. He jokes around. Says he's checking to make sure I have enough muscles to play softball." She swallowed hard. "But the way he does it really creeps me out."

"And that didn't clue you in to something, Miss Private Detective?"

Avis shook her head, humiliated. She didn't know why she'd ignored her own revulsion. She just thought that was the way it was here, that was the way the coach treated all the girls on his team. She'd only wanted to fit in. Now she'd be a pariah for the rest of her life. Nobody would want to be friends with a girl who had allowed herself to be touched by a middle-aged pervert.

"I just can't believe any of this," Kayla cried. "First he fucks Bethany, now he's about to fuck you!"

Avis looked at her new friend, then squared her shoulders, preparing to share what had become clear to her in Kayla's bedroom. "Kayla, I think he did a lot worse than fuck Bethany," she said, the word *fuck* feeling deliciously mature on her tongue. "I think he killed her."

"You what?" Kayla said, her voice high and breathy.

"You said it up in your room," explained Avis. "Bethany was rude to him. They argued about something after you went inside your house. She probably told him that she was going to take her tapes to the police. That's why she had Ridge bury them, for safekeeping."

Kayla didn't speak for so long, Avis wondered if she'd heard her, then she started shaking her head. "You actually think Coach Keener killed Bethany?"

"Think about it, Kayla! It all adds up! Coach Keener is like the king of Hartsville. Nobody in the world would suspect him. But we have his voice on tape. We know that he and Bethany argued just before she was killed, and you said he was at your house when they found her body. You said he even helped the police." Avis paused to let her theory sink in, then spoke again. "He probably put the cops on to Ridge!"

Frowning, Kayla tried to see the logic of Avis's reasoning. For a long moment she just sat there, squinting at the sunlight dancing upon the water, then she turned and looked at her newest friend. "If that's true, then we've got to stop him. Before he kills some other girl."

"I know," said Avis. "First, though, we've got to figure out how."

For a long time they sat on the log that spanned the creek, watching the water rush below them, each lost in her own thoughts. Everywhere they looked they saw Deke Keener—from the service road that bordered the subdivision, to the new sneakers on Avis's feet, purchased at a real shoe store instead of the Goodwill, with money her father had earned building yet another Keener development.

"So what are you thinking?" Avis spoke after what felt like a lifetime of silence, desperate to reestablish a connection with Kayla. Already she'd felt a cooling in their friendship. She was marked, damaged. She had been fondled by Coach Keener: Kayla had not.

"I don't know what I'm thinking," Kayla replied miserably. "I wish I didn't have to think at all."

"Then I'll think for both of us," said Avis. "I think we should take those tapes to the police. They can do voice prints on them, just like they do fingerprints in a crime lab. That'll definitely prove it's his voice."

"Coach Keener's friends with the new sheriff," said Kayla. "He's not going to rush out and arrest his pal for murdering my sister."

Avis started to protest, believing that most cops were honest fighters of crime. Then she remembered a mystery she'd read last winter, where a DA had intentionally destroyed important evidence because he'd fallen in love with a girl who'd poisoned the mayor of the town. Coach Keener owned their town. Who's to say that evidence against him wouldn't get "accidentally" lost?

"Okay," she said, scrambling to come up with an alternative plan. "Then we'll go play the tapes for our parents. They can figure out what to do."

Kayla regarded her with utter scorn. "Avis, my dad would beat the shit out of me if I showed him those tapes."

"Then we'll take them to my dad. Or my mom."

"And just how long do you think Coach Keener would let you live in that brand-new house of yours?"

Avis gulped. Of course Kayla was right. She knew her parents would go to the police with these tapes. And then her father would be out of a job, all of them out of a home. They would have to load up another rented truck and go back to Greenville. There, she would again have to share a room with her grandmother and listen not to Ringo Starr, but to all her grandmother's hellfire-and-brimstone preachers on the radio. Even with Coach Keener, here was better than back in Greenville. She looked over at Kayla. Though she was sitting on the log right beside her, Avis knew in reality she was far away, and growing more distant every second. If Avis didn't come up with something fast, she was going to lose her one friend forever. The thought of life without Kayla made her heartsick. She was gazing down, growing slightly hypnotized by the sunlight on the water, when suddenly she had an idea. Though it made her tremble inside, she knew it was the one foolproof way to nail Coach Keener.

"Why don't we set a trap for him?" she said, her voice breathy with fear. "And use me for bait."

Kayla turned to her, her eyes wide. "What are you talking about?"

"I'll take your dad's tape recorder. I'll hide it. Then when Coach Keener starts rubbing my leg, I'll—I'll . . ." Avis gulped. "I'll make him start saying those same things he said to Bethany." Though Avis had no idea how she was going to manage that, she went on. "Once we have two tapes where he's doing things to girls, and me as a victim who's willing to press charges, we can go to the cops. We'll have proof."

When Kayla finally spoke, her voice was like stone. "You're so full of shit, Avis. Nobody does stuff like that, except in your stupid books."

"So? That doesn't mean it can't be done!" Avis knew this was her last chance with Kayla. If she couldn't convince her of this, she might as well plan on staying in her room, friendless, until she graduated from high school.

"Then how are you going to do it? Where can you possibly hide that tape recorder so he won't see it?"

Avis thought. As tiny as the recorder was, it was still too bulky to hide anywhere on her toothpick of a body. She could, she supposed, stash it in her gear bag, but Coach Keener would find it odd if she kept shoving that big thing in his face every time he talked. She racked her brain, desperate, then suddenly she had it. "I'll wear a cap! One of my father's big ones. I'll tape the recorder to the inside with duct tape, then tape the microphone to one of the air holes."

Kayla gave her a cold blue stare.

"I can do it tomorrow night. He's picking me up and bringing me back from the game—my parents are going to Greenville after my dad gets off work, to buy a new car."

"How are you going to get Coach Keener to do anything?" Kayla asked sullenly. "I mean, nobody's going to send him to prison just for rubbing your stupid leg."

"I'll pretend I really like what he's doing," Avis said wildly. "When he rubs my leg, I'll groan."

"You'll groan?"

"Yeah. You know, like they do on TV. Unnnhhhhh." Avis tried to replicate the orgasmic groans she'd heard on her mother's soap operas.

Kayla tilted her head, marginally impressed. "What if he goes crazy? What if he like puts his hand down your pants or tries to take off your bra?"

Avis couldn't answer. She felt a million different things, all at once. Disgust at the idea of an old man slobbering over her; embarrassment that Coach Keener might touch her in places that had heretofore been solely her own; a worse fear that he would laugh at what he discovered—breasts the size of peas, a crotch that was still as bald as a baby's. What would she do if he laughed at her? What would she do if the other girls on the team found out?

She looked at Kayla. "I'll vomit," she decided. "Then I'll scream."

A fish leapt suddenly from the water, snapping up an iridescent dragonfly. It happened so quickly that before Kayla knew what had happened, the only thing left was small, concentric waves rippling outward through the water. She watched until they disappeared, then she looked back at Avis.

"You would really do that?"

Avis gave a solemn nod, silently ecstatic at being readmitted into the charmed circle of Kayla's affection. "It's the only way we'll ever prove who killed your sister."

THIRTY-SIX

Mary could not sleep. At six A.M., she finally arose from bed, brewed a pot of strong coffee, and padded into Irene's study. Bethany's calling her father "Lot" kept ringing in her head. Convinced that the term was biblical, she plucked Irene's family Bible from the shelf and began thumbing through it. The pages were wafer-thin, covered in minuscule text, and heavily footnoted. This is as bad as Corbin's text on contracts, she decided. It'll take me days to find out who Lot was. She flipped through both the Old and New Testaments, then she had an idea. She reached over to turn on Irene's computer, and a few moments later she was online. She punched in the URL for Google, then she typed in "Lot." Several hundred thousand hits came up, but none were about anybody in the Bible. She tried again, typing in "biblical characters." A moment later, Lot popped up as the hero of Sodom and Gomorrah, as written in Genesis eighteen and nineteen.

"Okay," she muttered, turning to the first book of the Bible. "Let's see just what our friend Lot did."

She read the story. Lot was the only righteous man in Sodom, who gave shelter to two undercover angels. When all the men of the town demanded that Lot turn over his angelic guests for them to have sex with,

Lot refused. What caught Mary's eye was Lot's alternative plan—*Behold I have two daughters which have not known men; let me, I pray you, bring them out unto you and do ye to them as is good in your eyes.*

She stopped reading, appalled. Lot was apparently a man who had no compunction about handing his virginal daughters over to a crowd of men. By calling her own father Lot, had Bethany meant that Glenn was complicitous in her sexual abuse? Was he letting other men fuck his daughter?

Good God, she thought, signing off the Internet. This just stinks worse with every passing day.

She dressed quickly and hurried to her office. On her answering machine Ravenel had left a barely audible message for her to stop in and see him, but she ignored it. She would talk to him later, after she reexamined the files spread out on her desk. She didn't want to meet with Ravenel until she could give him a solid alternative scenario with which he could counter Turpin's version of the murder.

Two hours later, she had a pattern. Using the copies of the school records that Jen had pirated, she pieced together a basic profile of all the victims. Each girl had been new to the area. Their families had relocated here to work for Keener Construction, moving into houses that Keener supplied. All were blond and slender, and looked younger than their peers, with nearly flat chests and clear skin. Their various test scores indicated that all were brighter than average, but tended to be introverts; little girls who did not run with the crowd.

They moved here with parents who were desperate for work, no doubt as grateful as Mr. Rankin for the good life in a Keener test house. In school they'd started off as strong B students, with As in conduct and regular in attendance. Soon, though, their school lives disintegrated. Hope Henderson was noted as having a "suspected drinking problem," while an English teacher wrote that she'd caught Valerie Fleming having sex with a boy behind a door in the cafeteria. There were no farewell notes or exit interviews when any of these girls disappeared. Their teachers' comments simply stopped; their final legacy was nothing more than an empty page. Mary sighed. She despised cases that dealt with children. Prosecution or defense, it was the saddest legal work imaginable.

She opened the last file. Bethany was the anomaly, the one who didn't fit the pattern. At her death, she was five years older than the others, brighter by a full grade point average; on paper, a popular, successful young woman. Yet Ridge and Sylvia Goins told another story of a girl who drank and kept dark secrets, and her school records revealed the concern of several teachers. "Bethany is a joy, but sometimes seems sad," wrote her algebra teacher. "Bethany's participation in gym is sporadic," scrawled a male PE coach, attributing the behavior to "female problems."

"Yeah, I'd say she had some female problems," Mary muttered as she read his scribbled remarks. "You would too if you had Lot for a father."

She finished the file and tossed it on the desk with the others. Bethany, she decided, was different because she'd been Glenn Daws' daughter. As big a monster as he might be, Glenn would surely be reluctant to kill his own child. Maybe he thought she would never tell, or that she would go off to college and just forget about everything. Maybe he hadn't meant to kill her at all, but teach her some kind of lesson. Then, when he realized she meant business, he couldn't risk being exposed to the world. He had to stop her before she caused him to lose everything—his job, his family, his precious Keener career. Firstborn daughter or not, Bethany had to be silenced. Mary looked over at the bear mask.

"So he silenced her. And hung it on your boy."

She waited for the familiar hum deep inside her when she knew she'd gotten a case dead-to-right. It wasn't quite there, but it was close. Close enough, she decided, to go see Ravenel.

She gathered up her papers and stepped over to his office.

"Yes?" answered a voice so sonorous that she almost laughed. Sober, Ravenel sounded like an old-time radio announcer.

She opened his door. For the first time, he looked halfway like a practicing attorney. He was pecking on a laptop computer, a legal pad lay on his desk, and the stuffed owl that usually dangled from his ceiling now held a law book open to a particular page.

"Ms. Crow!" He looked up and frowned. "How delightful of you to stop by! Only hours after I asked you to come over."

"You didn't specify any time, Ravenel," she shot back. "Next time tell me when my audience starts. I'll try my best to be prompt."

"An oversight on my part," he apologized. "I forgot how time-consuming second-guessing a PI can be."

His last remark carried the sting of truth, so she ignored it and moved a cardboard box full of what looked like ginseng from a chair, and sat down. "Well? Why did you want to see me?"

"Turpin would be willing to lower the charge for a guilty plea."

Mary was stunned. "Why? This is Hartsville's trial of the century, and Turpin's holding all the aces."

Ravenel sat back in his chair. "I think he must've gotten wind of your mask. According to my associate, Mr. Henchy, it's quite the topic in the Qualla Boundary."

Oh, great, thought Mary. Now I'll be persona non grata on the reservation as well as in town. "Why would my mask bother Turpin? He's not Cherokee."

"No, but he has lots of Cherokee voters that he doesn't want to offend. A plea serves both constituencies—the whites get their conviction, the Indians are spared the humiliation of seeing one of their big medicine Ani Zaguhi sent to death row."

"Who says anybody's going to put Ridge on death row?"

"Oh, come on, Ms. Crow! You've been sherlocking around here for weeks. What have you come up with that McGruder didn't? And don't waste my time with the fact that Bethany Daws was living a secret life of sex, drugs, and rock 'n' roll. That I already know."

"Do you know about Glenn Daws?"

"Glenn Daws, father of the murdered Bethany?"

Mary nodded.

Ravenel chuckled. "If you're offering Mr. Daws as a suspect, he checked out."

"Who checked him out?"

"The state did, right off the bat. Sheriff Cochran isn't a total idiot. But my man McGruder did his own investigation. Daws' hair and fingerprints were in the room, but he'd lived in the house for nearly ten years. And no, he didn't have a witness to swear he'd been asleep when she was killed, but who does? At night, your witness is usually snoring beside you."

"What did McGruder find out about him personally?" asked Mary.

Ravenel shrugged. "That's a bit dicier. He had a couple of drunk-and-disorderlies a few years back, plus one arrest for assault. Can't hold his whiskey, apparently. Last time the judge said either jail or AA, and he chose the latter. He's stayed sober, or at least not drunk enough to get into trouble, ever since."

"A lesson for us all," Mary said pointedly, her reference to Ravenel's bottle of whiskey unmistakable. "Did McGruder find any bad blood between Daws and his daughter?"

"No more than the usual teenage stuff. The parents didn't like her dating Standingdeer. Thought he was a bum, wanted her to go to college and make something of herself." Ravenel sniffed. "I would want much the same for my kids, if I were unlucky enough to have any."

"Me, too." Mary thought of Jonathan and his dreams for Lily.

Ravenel leaned forward. "Well, Ms. Crow? Do you still think I overpaid McGruder? Can you and your bear mask add anything more to this grim little saga?"

"Only that Bethany referred to her father as 'Lot' and she isn't the only girl to have come to a mysteriously bad end in this county."

Ravenel frowned. "Lot, as in Sodom and Gomorrah?"

"Yes," said Mary. "The man who staffed rent-a-date with his own maiden daughters."

"Okay," said Ravenel. "Who else met the same fate as the Daws girl?"

"I got the names of six. Two of their families still live in the area. The similarity between them and Bethany Daws is remarkable. Their fathers worked for Keener Construction, they lived in Keener test houses, and they played on the Keener softball team."

"Keener's the second-biggest employer in the county, Ms. Crow. Were these girls found dead in their beds?"

"No. They all just went to school one day and never came home. Vanished."

Ravenel looked at her as if she were crazy. "And that's all you've got?"

"I've seen statistics from the surrounding counties, Ravenel. Pisgah beats them all as far as dropout rates, teen pregnancy rates, attempts at suicide. All those are behaviors indicative of sexual molestation."

"So on the basis of that, you're saying that Daws molests every kid in

Pisgah County, farms his daughters out to other men, and then kills the ones who threaten to spill the beans?"

Her theory sounded ridiculous in Ravenel's dulcet tones, but she stuck to her guns. "Look at how well Daws fits. He's built their homes, he coaches their children, everybody loves him. That's SOP for a child molester." An odd thought struck her as she spoke, but Ravenel shot another question.

"If he's such a monster, why haven't any of these molested girls come forward?"

"And accuse a popular guy who's the number-two man at your father's job as well as your softball coach? I've put kids on the stand before, Ravenel. They are absolutely terrified of taking on adults."

Ravenel scowled. "So you're saying Glenn's killed only the brave ones—the ones he was afraid would speak out."

Mary nodded.

"Then why didn't he make Bethany just disappear like the others? To kill his own daughter and then leave her in her own bed makes no sense. He'd be the first one the cops looked at."

"Because he knew he could blame it on Standingdeer! He found out they were having secret trysts in her bedroom, so he knew the cops would find all sorts of evidence that would implicate the boy."

Ravenel stared at his stuffed owl for a moment, then he shook his head. "Nice try, Ms. Crow. But I still don't think I overpaid McGruder."

She sat back in her chair. She realized that, out loud, her theory about Glenn Daws had holes big enough to drive a truck through. Insert Deke Keener, however, and it tightened considerably. Suddenly, her throat felt dry and sticky. She needed to go back to her own office and think this through. "So when are you going to meet with Turpin?" she asked Ravenel.

"Actually, I'm not."

"Then why did you call me in here?"

"Because right now I need you to go talk to Hugh Kavanagh. Tell the old guy that I'm going to call him as a character witness and I don't want any displays of Irish temper on the stand."

"I don't think that's possible," said Mary. "Hugh and his temper come as a package deal."

"Then put it to him this way, Ms. Crow. Explain that the prospects for Standingdeer are looking pretty grim. If Kavanagh can't come across as a sweet old man who depended on and trusted the boy with his very life, then I may as well call Turpin and accept his offer."

Mary rose from her chair. "That's a pretty tall order, Ravenel."

Ravenel laughed. "I hear tall orders are your specialty, Ms. Crow.

THIRTY-SEVEN

Kayla Daws lay in bed, watching late morning shadows dance on the ceiling of her room. All night she'd lain awake, fingering the strawberry necklace that she'd put on just before she'd gone to bed. Ridge had carved it for Bethany, and though her father had thrown it in the kitchen garbage before they took Bethany's body away, Kayla had impulsively plucked it out, and hidden it in her dresser drawer for safekeeping. Last night she'd hoped it would keep away bad dreams and evil spirits, but every time she closed her eyes all she could see was Coach Keener. Could he truly have done what Avis suggested? Molested Bethany and then smashed her head in with that tomahawk? She'd tried to wrap her mind around that ever since Avis went home, and she still couldn't do it. Now Avis had this crackpot scheme to trap Coach Keener. It was all so nuts, it made her feel like her skin was on fire.

She'd gotten up a dozen times during the night, trying to read, then listening to her radio, trying to put everything out of her head. Suddenly, at 2:53 A.M., she had bolted upright in bed. She and her parents had a therapy session with Dr. Shope this afternoon! Dr. Shope's office was right across the hall from that woman her father despised so much—Mary Crow. She was Ridge's lawyer, so why not give the tapes to her? Kayla could write her a letter, explaining everything, and put the tapes inside. Mary Crow would listen and then decide what to do. Excited, Kayla had given up sleep altogether, and propped herself up in bed to write the letter.

Now, with the sun climbing toward noon, she reached under her pillow to read what she'd written. It had sounded pretty good in the middle of the night. She only hoped it still made sense now. Unfolding the sheet of notebook paper, she read aloud, in a whisper.

Dear Ms. Crow,

Please listen to these tapes (particularly the one with the red label). They prove that Ridge Standingdeer did not kill my sister. Avis Martin and I think that Coach Keener did. He was molesting her. We are going to try and trap him. Please call me at 555-9782, but don't tell my dad who you are.

Yours truly,

Kayla Elizabeth Daws

Though Avis could have made it sound much more adult and official, she'd said what she'd wanted to say. If this Mary Crow was half the lawyer her father said she was, then she'd get to work on this immediately. Maybe she could even get Ridge out of jail today and have the cops arrest Coach Keener before the ball game. Then Avis wouldn't have to go through with plan B.

For an instant Kayla's heart soared, then she realized that she wouldn't even be able to get the tape to Mary Crow until three, and Coach Keener usually picked Avis up at four. However wonderful Ms. Crow might be, Kayla knew nobody could get Ridge out of jail and Coach Keener arrested in less than an hour.

She folded the letter up and placed it, along with the three best tapes, in a long white envelope she'd filched from her dad's office. She hid it in the bottom of her purse, then picked up the phone to call Avis. As she waited for someone to answer, her mouth went chalky with fear. Last night, she'd come up with about a million things that could go wrong with Avis's plan—from Coach Keener discovering the tape recorder to him driving Avis off in the woods somewhere to have sex. As smart and brave as Avis was, Kayla figured that listening to that tape must have driven her temporarily insane yesterday. That was the only reason for her to have dreamed up such a crazy scheme.

"Avis?" She recognized her friend's slightly adenoidal *hello*. "What are you doing?"

"Testing the cap," Avis whispered. "It works pretty good. I wore it at breakfast and taped an entire conversation with my mother, until she made me take it off."

Kayla began to sweat, feeling as if the first domino in some monstrous chain reaction had just begun to topple. "Look, Avis, I don't think you ought to do this. It's too dangerous and I've got a better idea, anyway."

"What?"

"This afternoon we have our therapy session right across the hall from Ridge's lawyer. I'll put the tapes inside a letter and give it to her. Mary Crow can listen to them and call the cops on Coach Keener."

"But she won't recognize his voice," said Avis.

"Sure she will," Kayla insisted. "He says his own name twice."

"She'll think it's just some stupid trick."

"No, she won't." Kayla twisted the telephone cord. "I'll give her the tapes today, then tomorrow we can call her and tell her what we know."

"But how would you give them to her? You can't just get up from the therapy session and say, 'Excuse me, but I've got to go give Ridge's lawyer some tapes.' Your father hates her guts!"

"I know," said Kayla, morose. "That's the hard part."

"I think we'd better just go ahead with my plan," Avis said. "I don't think giving Mary Crow those tapes will work, and we need every shred of evidence we can get."

Kayla envisioned Coach Keener sticking his tongue in Avis's mouth and shuddered. "But what if he tries, you know, to do something to you?"

"If he does, I'll scream. Or throw up. Rapists hate it when you throw up on them," Avis said knowledgeably.

Kayla closed her eyes. All night she'd worried about this and despite Avis's assurances, she still had a terrible feeling about the plan. "Avis, please just forget about this. It's too dangerous."

"Don't you want to catch the man who murdered Bethany?"

"You know I do," Kayla whispered, feeling like she'd just swallowed sand.

"Then this is the only way we can do it," said Avis. "It'll be okay. I won't be with him long enough for much to happen. He's got to show up at ball practice, then he'll take me home. My parents will be back by then. If I'm gone too long they'll get suspicious, and he won't want that."

Kayla sank down on her bed. Avis did have a point. Coach Keener wouldn't have more than about ten minutes to mess around with her, coming to and from the ball field.

"Look, Kayla, I've got to go—my mom wants me to help sort out some clothes we're giving to Goodwill."

"Will you call me the second you get home?"

"I will." She heard the smile in Avis's voice. "I promise."

Kayla fingered Bethany's strawberry necklace that now hung around her neck, trying to send Avis all the good luck that had eluded her sister. "Just be careful, Avis. I don't want anything to happen to you."

❤

After that, Kayla had nothing left to do but wait. Usually, on grief-counseling days, her mother managed to rouse herself at noon, showering and dressing in time to appear downstairs to wait for her father's arrival at two-fifteen. He'd pick them up in his Keener car. They always saw Dr. Shope as a family, though her father did most of the talking, telling the therapist how "they felt this" or "they were angry about that." Today was no exception. As her mother sat dressed in jeans and a cotton sweater, picking at a plate of cottage cheese, her father roared up the driveway, blowing his horn.

"Oh." Her mother looked up stunned, as if she never heard of Bethany or Kayla or Pisgah County or for that matter, planet Earth.

"Come on, Mom." Kayla shouldered her all-important purse. "Hurry. He'll get mad if we're late."

Her mother, who'd just six months ago run a five-kilometer race, now shuffled to the car with tentative, old lady steps. Her father revved the engine while Kayla hopped in the backseat, hoping to avoid his notice. He drove them to town angrily, going too fast along the twisting roads, squealing to a stop at the intersections. Twenty minutes after their trip began, they sat in Dana Shope's office, her father telling Dana that he thought they all might be feeling "a little better these days." Kayla had to bite her lip to keep from laughing.

"Really?" Dr. Shope raised a dubious brow and looked directly at her. "How about you, Kayla? How are you feeling today?"

She clutched her purse. Ever since she'd said good-bye to Avis, she'd racked her brain for a way to get the letter to Mary Crow. She thought she'd come up with something that might work, provided her father wouldn't act like the asshole he truly was.

"I'm feeling okay," she finally replied. She wanted to say she was feeling like shit, like she wanted to scream, like she wished Coach Keener had killed her father instead of her sister, but she knew better than to tell the truth. Today she needed to keep Dr. Shope's therapeutic spotlight focused on some other member of her fucked-up family. "I'm getting worried about my mom," she said, oozing concern. "All she does is sleep."

Kayla held her breath as both Dana Shope and her father turned on her mother. Paula Daws looked as if they'd all caught her picking her nose in public.

"How about that, Paula?" asked Dr. Shope kindly. "Have you been sleeping a lot?"

Her mother fumbled for an answer, saying well, yes, maybe she had been spending a lot of time in the bedroom. Dr. Shope asked her another question, then her father chimed in. Kayla smiled. So far, the first part of her plan was working like a charm. Now safely out of the therapeutical loop, she turned her attention to the next step.

She looked at Dana's closed door. Outside, just across the landing not fifteen feet away, stood Mary Crow's office. She just had to figure out how to leave Dr. Shope's, and press her letter into the lawyer's hand without her father catching on. Mary Crow would probably think she was crazy until she read the letter and listened to the tapes. All hell would break loose then. Who knew what her father would do if Avis was right about Coach Keener? With her fingers nervously working the strap of her purse, she waited for a pause in the conversation, then she stood up.

"I'm sorry." She clutched her purse as everyone looked at her in surprise. "I need to use the rest room."

"The rest room?" Her father scowled, as if *rest room* was some new word he'd never heard before.

"It's right outside the door, honey," Dr. Shope smiled. "On the landing."

Her father stood up and opened the door. "Hurry up," he growled, glaring at her. "This therapy is costing Coach Keener a lot of money."

"I'll be right back," she said as she trotted past him, her voice squeaky as a mouse.

She hurried into the bathroom and locked the door behind her. She was so nervous that she went ahead and peed, even though she'd been unaware that she had to. As she sat on the toilet she dug the letter from the bottom of her purse. *Just get up, cross the hall, tap on Mary Crow's door, and get back to Dr. Shope's. It won't take you thirty seconds, tops.*

She breathed deeply, filling her lungs with air as if she were about to swim an underwater race. She stood up to flush the toilet, but stopped just as she was about to press the small lever. If her father heard the flush, he would expect her back immediately. If he didn't hear it, she would have more time. Though it was gross to leave a commode un- flushed, that's exactly what she did. Holding the letter tightly in her hand, she cracked open the bathroom door. Her father had left Dr. Shope's door slightly ajar. She could see him sitting beside her mother, his arm around her.

Damn, she thought. He changed seats! He's now facing this direction. She would have to wait, and dart across the landing when he wasn't looking. With her heart beating a million miles an hour, she watched and waited. Suddenly he pulled out his handkerchief and covered his nose to sneeze. Now, she told herself. *Go now!*

Slipping from the bathroom door, she strode quickly across the land- ing. When she reached Mary Crow's office she tapped softly on the door. Seconds ticked by as she waited for an answer, but no one came. Nervously, she tapped again, but again, nothing. Desperate, she tried the knob, but it did not turn.

Shit! She thought. I can't come this far and fail. Ridge's trial begins in just a few days and I won't be up here again for another week. Quickly she dropped to her knees. Though the envelope was thick with the tapes, if she pushed hard, she could just work it underneath Mary

Crow's door. *Hurry,* she told herself as she wiggled the flimsy paper forward. *Hurry, hurry, hurry!*

"Kayla!" Her father's voice scared her so badly, she jumped. "What the hell are you doing?"

She gave the envelope a final push. "I—I dropped a quarter," she lied, scrambling to her feet. "It rolled under this door."

He looked at her with eyes that seemed to bore down into her core. She could tell he thought she was lying, and he would make her pay for it later.

"Since when have you ever cared about a quarter?"

She shook her head. Her tongue felt stuck to the roof of her mouth. "It was a North Carolina quarter," she blurted. "I dropped it when I came out of the bathroom. It rolled all the way across the floor, under this door."

For a long moment he just looked at her, but questioned her no further. "Get back in here," he finally said, jerking his head toward Dr. Shope's door. "And stay away from that office. I'd hate for you to disturb Ms. Crow."

I just disturbed Ms. Crow more than you'll ever know, Daddy, she thought as she walked past him, back into where Dr. Shope was telling her mother that she really should make an effort to get out of bed and help Kayla's life get back to normal.

THIRTY-EIGHT

"Avis? We're leaving for Greenville now. We'll see you later!"

Avis rushed from her bedroom to the staircase to catch her mother and little sister before they walked out the door. "What time will you be back?"

Darlene Martin looked up at her daughter, who hung over the banister, an oversized Panthers cap on her head. "Around nine, probably. It's two hours there and back, plus Dad says we can stop for supper. You sure you don't want to skip softball and come with us?"

Yes, thought Avis. The prospect of sitting around a dopey old truck showroom suddenly seemed infinitely preferable to secretly taping Coach Keener. *Yes, yes, yes. A million times yes.* What had she been thinking when she dreamed this up? She sighed wistfully. "I guess I'd better stay here."

"Well, there's lots to eat in the fridge, if you get hungry. And don't forget to thank Coach Keener for bringing you home."

"I won't," Avis answered, feeling as if her voice belonged to somebody else.

"Then we'll see you in a few hours," her mother called, tugging Chrissy along behind her.

"Bye." Avis gave a dejected wave. "Have a good time." She almost added *I love you,* but stopped herself. Her mother would think it odd for her to bid them such a profound farewell for a trip to buy a Dodge.

The house was still, silent except for the muffled hum of the central air. Her stomach was churning. As she sat down on the toilet for the umpteenth time that day, she wondered why none of her favorite fictional detectives ever felt the physical manifestations of fear. Sherlock Holmes never had diarrhea; Hercule Poirot never had to *cherche une toilette.* Why her?

"Because you're not a detective at all," she reminded herself bitterly. "You're just a fake. A pathetic fake who couldn't stand the thought of losing your one friend."

Her words echoed in the tiled bathroom as their truth made her eyes sting. She knew nothing about solving crimes. She was just a loser who preferred the worlds that books offered—where clever detectives could sniff clues from a handkerchief and discern motive by the glint in someone's eyes. She herself could barely figure out whether to bat or bunt. Now here she was, about to lure creepy Coach Keener into feeling her up? And then taping him? Had she lost her mind?

"Just call Kayla," she told herself reasonably. "Call her and tell her that you can't get the tape recorder to work. Or that your mother is making you go to pick up the truck with them." She looked at herself unsparingly in the bathroom mirror. "Or tell her that you're just too chicken. It'll be okay. Kayla will understand."

Yes, she thought as she leaned over to wash her hands. Kayla would understand. Kayla would probably even forgive her. But Kayla would also never again talk to her in quite the same way, her eyes sparkling with plans, her voice intimate with secrets and confidences. She would continue to call for the rest of the summer, then their friendship would fade. When school started they might chat briefly between classes, but by Christmas they would pass each other in the hall like strangers. People would forget the bad things that had happened to Kayla, and welcome her back into the tribe. Avis, on the other hand, would sink back to being that loser from South Carolina, who, for two bizarre months last summer, had been best friends with Kayla Daws.

"No," she whispered, tearing up as she imagined her life reverted to its former friendless state. "You've got to go through with it."

Wiping her eyes, she studied herself in the mirror. She'd widened the adjustable band of her father's cap—a necessity with the minirecorder taped inside. Though it had, just as she'd told Kayla, clearly recorded her mother's voice, the thing was so heavy that at first it sat on her head like a bowl, not moving at all when she turned her head to either side. She'd fixed that with four of Chrissy's bobby pins, anchoring the hat with two on each side of her head, just behind her ears. Though she knew the cap looked odd and would only further deepen her teammates' already low opinion of her fashion sense, it concealed the tape recorder perfectly. She couldn't even hear the whirring of its tiny wheels when it was on her head.

"Okay," she nervously told her reflection. "Show time!"

She grabbed her softball glove and ran downstairs to the kitchen, her legs as rubbery as if she'd just gotten off a boat. It was 4:22. Coach Keener would be here in eight minutes. He was always on time. She opened the refrigerator, wondering if she dared eat. She didn't want to risk having an upset stomach when Coach Keener showed up. She was trying to decide what to do when she heard two beeps from a familiar horn. She looked out the kitchen window. Coach Keener's black SUV sat waiting, sleek as a beetle in the late afternoon sun. She glanced at the clock again: 4:28. For some reason, he'd come early.

"Okay," she said, her fingers like ice. "This is it." Just as she'd practiced, she reached up to punch the RECORD button of the tape machine through the wool of her cap. When she heard the barest hiss of the recorder, she knew she was ready to go. Scooping her glove from the kitchen table, she glanced one final time at their wonderful test house, then she went outside to greet the man who'd given it to them.

❦

"Hey, good-looking!" He called her that every time he saw her—his voice upbeat and happy, but something else, as well. Until she'd listened to those tapes, she hadn't known he'd been coming on to her, in a joking kind of way. "What's up?"

"Nothing." She climbed into his car, the leather seats cold against her bare legs.

"You expecting rain?" Laughing, he tugged at the bill of her cap. Involuntarily she shrank back in the seat and gave a small yip of alarm.

"No," she replied sharply, her voice thready with fear. She hadn't been in his car ten seconds and already she'd almost blown everything. "Why?"

He grinned. "I just never have seen you in such a big cap."

"Jeannette Peacock wore one this big last week," she huffed, defensive. "A Dodgers cap, too."

"Okay, okay. I know how you girls are. Far be it from me to buck a fashion trend."

He backed out of her driveway. She knew from experience that for the first few blocks he would say either nothing or ask how her family was doing. Then, five minutes into the trip, he would turn on his CD player and start firing little jokes at her. Just like clockwork, as soon as he turned on Cowee Road, he started asking if her mother was excited about getting a new truck, and if her little sister played softball, too. When he punched in one of his CD's, her heart gave a little jerk—it was the same music she'd heard on Bethany's tape! Old rock 'n' roll—the kind of stuff her parents liked. Closing her eyes, she tried to force air deep into her lungs. Act nice. Cute. Sexy. Get him to do something, but don't let him see the inside of that cap!

She rearranged herself on the seat, curling up in what she considered an alluring pose, and forced her trembling lips up in a smile. He asked about the books she was reading, whether or not she was looking forward to school. She answered his questions coyly, just like some of the girls she'd seen on television. At first he kept grabbing quick little glances at her—one minute he'd pay attention to the road, then he'd look at her, the smile on his face growing. Finally he made a sharp turn onto a winding road that twisted through some woodsy picnic grounds. Her hands grew clammy with fear. He'd never driven her this way before.

"How're those puny little muscles of yours today?" He reached over and ran his hand up her leg from midcalf to midthigh.

"Fine," she replied, trying hard to keep her voice from wobbling as the same hands that had smashed Bethany Daws' skull now caressed her leg.

"What happened there?" He pointed to a red scratch across her kneecap.

"I cut myself shaving."

"Shaving?" He widened his eyes in mock alarm. "You shave your legs? You actually have enough hair on your legs to shave it off?"

She nodded, remembering the early summer taunts of "Apegirl" and the jar of Nair someone had left in her baseball glove.

"Well, gosh, I didn't know you were that old. How about there? You shave there yet?" He grabbed her left shoulder with one hand and slipped his thumb under her sleeve, tickling the bare skin of her armpit.

"Yes," she whispered, instinctively squirming away.

"Son of a gun!" He whistled. "You're not getting bikini waxes yet, are you?"

She couldn't speak; her face felt so hot, she feared it might melt. As she shook her head in answer to his question, he turned the car off the road into a shabby little picnic shelter half-hidden by straggly laurel. He parked his car behind some pine trees, then reached over and unbuckled her seat belt. Up close, she could smell his cologne; she could also smell the odor of her own fear.

"Avis, have you ever met somebody and just known right off the bat that they were going to be special in your life?"

She nodded, struggling to turn her head so the microphone would be closer to his mouth.

"Well, that's exactly what I felt about you, that first day I saw you. You reminded me of a little girl I knew a long time ago. A sweet, beautiful little girl."

Her blood turned to ice as he reached over and hoisted her into his lap.

"We haven't known each other very long, but I bet as time goes by, you and I will become real close friends." She felt his breath, hot and moist on her neck. "The kind of friends that do each other favors. Would you like that?"

She sat, rigid with fear, unable to reply. She gave the merest nod of her head as she grew increasingly aware of the tape recorder, hard and heavy as it dug into her scalp.

"I'd like that, too. Of course, we'll have to keep it our own little secret. Your mom and dad wouldn't understand. The other girls on the team would be jealous."

"Okay," she mouthed the words, or at least she tried to.

"Good. Then from here on out, Avis, you'll be my special friend. We'll have lots of fun. I guarantee it."

She couldn't remember what she said. Suddenly she didn't care who had killed Bethany Daws; she didn't even care about being Kayla's friend. All she wanted was to get away from this man's hands and voice and hot, damp breath. She sat as still as she could, desperately hoping he would just put her back in her own seat, then she felt his hands slip under her T-shirt. At that moment, she panicked. Struggling to free herself from his embrace, she sprawled between both seats, trying to reach for the door when she felt the baseball cap topple off her head.

"Oh!" she cried. "I need that!" Frantically she made a grab for the cap. She couldn't let him see it; if he did, he would certainly kill her just as he'd killed Bethany.

He groaned, surprised, as her elbow dug into the top of his shoulder. "What the hell?" she heard him say as he shifted in the driver's seat. "Here, I can help——" he began.

"That's okay," she said, too loudly. "I've got it."

The cap lay upside down on the backseat, the tape recorder wheels still spinning. As she felt him turning, she made a desperate grab for it. Her fingers curled around the brim and she planted it back on her head, keeping one hand on it as she plopped down in the passenger seat.

"There," she said, gasping as if she'd caught a line drive at third base. "I got it."

For a long moment, he just looked at her. "I had no idea you were such a Panthers fan," he finally said as he rebuckled his seat belt.

"It's my dad's cap," she explained, breathless. "I promised I'd take good care of it."

He gave her a tight smile. "You're taking care of a lot of things this summer, aren't you?"

She didn't know what to say, so she just sat back in the seat. He reached over and gave her thigh a promissory squeeze, but he did not touch her anywhere else. Already she felt sullied and ashamed. She wanted nothing more than to go home and wash his slobber from her neck, the feel of his hands from her skin. He started the car and they drove on to practice in a tense bubble of silence, Avis saying a silent prayer of thanks that Coach Keener had not seen what her father's cap concealed.

THIRTY-NINE

K eener drove to the softball field in a hot delirium. *Avis was taping him! With a minicassette taped inside her damn cap!* While he'd been holding her on his lap, his fingers just inches from her sweet little breasts, hidden wheels had been turning his words into magnetic signals that could end his life as profoundly as a bullet to his brain. And for what reason? Until today he'd never touched her with anything other than coach-like concern. He even thought she liked him—certainly she liked riding in his Lexus, and being driven to the games as if she were an important member of the team.

Kayla Daws! She must have put her up to it! He'd noticed that the other girls had been giving Kayla a wide berth since Bethany's murder, so she'd hooked up with this little hayseed from Greenville. But why had they set him up? Had Bethany hidden her tapes with Kayla? If so, then why hadn't Kayla given them to the cops? Or handed them over them to her father? He'd seen Glenn just this morning. The man had greeted him warmly and thanked him for the grief therapy for him and his family. If Daws suspected a tenth of what had gone on between him and Bethany, he would have curled his big ham hands into fists and beat him to death on the spot.

He sneaked a glance at Avis. She sat small on the seat, her knees tight together, one hand trying to casually hold that ridiculous cap on her head. So much for his new Tracy Foster. The kid was scared shitless. Her skin looked like waxed paper, and he could see a blue vein in her neck, quivering with her pulse. Suddenly he remembered something her father had said. *She keeps her nose buried in a book—mysteries, mostly.* With Kayla as her new pal, Avis must have decided to impress the girl by turning real life into a game of Clue. Instead of Colonel Mustard in the kitchen with a knife, it was Coach Keener, in the bedroom, with a fucking tomahawk. Nonsense, of course. *But why were they trying to set him up with tapes?*

The answer smacked Deke like a jolt of electricity. Bethany must have given Kayla the tapes, but they must not have quite enough to hang him with, yet. That was it! They needed more proof. A good tape of him and Avis would make a poor tape of him and Bethany infinitely more believable, so the two girls had set out to trap him. Avis had been the point man because she'd been clever enough to recognize that he was interested in her in a very different way from the others on the team. *Jesus! Little hayseed is smarter than she looks!*

Now he had to figure out what to do. He could, of course, just reach over, swipe the cap off her head, and be done with it. But that would tip his hand, and either drive the two of them underground to think up worse mischief or send them immediately to the cops with what tapes they had. No, better to cut off the lead runner first. If he could neutralize Avis right now, he could take care of Kayla later. It would, of course, be tragic to lose two members of the Keener family in such quick succession but, hey, shit happens.

He drove on, concentrating on slowing his breathing, trying to mute the thudding in his ears and return the world back to its normal colors. By the time he'd turned the trees from a sick red-gray into a marginal green, he had a plan. And a good one, too. He would have to be careful, but the most incriminating tape would be gone forever. Of course, Avis would die, but maybe she deserved to die. Little girls shouldn't snoop, particularly on people to whom they owed so much.

Whistling, he pulled off the road and into the parking lot of a convenience store, taking the first step in what was going to be the rest of Avis Martin's extremely brief life.

"You want anything?" he asked her cheerfully, breaking the thick silence that had enveloped the car. "I'm going to get some chewing gum."

"No, thanks. I brought some water." She held up a clear purple water
bottle. He noticed that her hand was trembling.

He eased back into his old smile. "You sure? My treat?"

"I'm sure." She kept her eyes straight ahead, apparently afraid to even
look at him.

"Then I'll be right back." He walked into the store, bought a pack of
gum, then stood a moment at the magazine racks. He wanted to let her
calm down, alone. He needed her to be off guard, to think he hadn't
seen the tape. His little red meltdown notwithstanding, if he could just
play dumb and convince her that this was just another ball practice,
everything would be okay.

He left the store, stuffed a stick of gum in his mouth, and got back in
the car. "Here." He offered her some, his own hand no steadier than
hers. "This keeps your mouth from getting dry when you're on the
field."

By the time they reached the park, the rest of the team was warming
up. Glenn Daws was shagging pop flies to right field. Kayla stood at first
base, looking not at the ball but at the parking lot, watching to see who
was coming in. Deke saw her face brighten when Avis got out of his car,
and he realized that whatever else he did during practice, he must keep
those two apart. If Avis got the chance to slip Kayla that tape, his game
would be over forever.

"Hotshot, you're already such a good player, how about you help me
today?" he suggested as he pulled a clipboard from the backseat. "I need
to turn in some paperwork to the league office. Maybe you could stay
here and help me fill out all these forms."

Avis looked longingly at the ball field, but said nothing.

"I promise I'll make it up to you." He grinned. *If you only knew how.*

She shrugged, still holding the cap on her head, apparently catching
on that she had no choice but to continue her charade of dutiful player.
"What do you want me to do?"

"Just sit here with me. And double-check these forms as I fill them
out."

They sat side by side in the dugout while Glenn Daws ran the practice.

Deke filled out ridiculous forms that listed the name, address, and position played by each girl, then Avis scanned names she barely knew and addresses she didn't recognize to make sure they were correct. He drew the process out as long as he could. Fielding practice was over long before they finished.

"Gosh," he said as the team lined up for a water break. "I thought we'd be through by now. I'll try and work faster."

She squirmed beside him, but made no protest. He watched from beneath his brows as Kayla came up to the water cooler, then tiptoed over to where they sat, shy as a deer.

"Hi, Avis, hi, Coach Keener," she said hesitantly. "Aren't you two going to play tonight?"

"We will in a little while." He smiled up at her. "I had to fill out these forms. Avis volunteered to help."

He watched Kayla as she looked at her friend, desperate to glean answers to questions she could not ask. *Did he make the same moves on you that he did on my sister? Did you tape him while he did it?* Avis looked up at her, but before she could communicate anything back, Deke tossed his clipboard on the bench and stood.

"Okay, Avis. We can finish this later. Let's go play ball." Grinning, he put his arms around both their shoulders and walked onto the field. The other little girls swarmed around him like an army of termites attending their queen.

"All right," he said, still keeping Kayla and Avis on either side of him. "You guys got in some pretty good fielding practice, so let's divide into teams and have a little scrimmage. Number off. Kayla and Avis are going to be captains. Evens are on Kayla's team, odds on Avis's."

He smiled as the girls counted off. As opposing captains, Kayla and Avis would still not get a chance to talk, and since Avis usually played third base, he could station himself behind her, as third-base coach. It would be interesting to see if the little twit could play third base and still keep that cap on her head.

For an hour he watched them play, carefully reviewing the rest of his plan. Though he cheered at their hits and groaned at their errors, he

couldn't have said what the score was or even who was at bat. Avis
held his full attention. She was all he could see; her death was all he
could envision. As their scrimmage ended in a tie, he was sweating as if
he'd just coached the Yankees through the seventh game of the World
Series.

"Okay," he said, out of breath as his team once again gathered around
him. "That was pretty good. Now I want all of you to go home, get some
rest, and come back tomorrow night ready to play the Thompson
Tigers."

"If we win will you take us out for pizza?" asked Jeanette Peacock as
the others giggled.

He gave her a solemn nod, although he knew that would not happen.
They were going to have to forfeit tomorrow's game. Amazingly, the
Keener Kats would suffer another tragic loss. The girls would, of
course, be too heartbroken to play, but he was the only one who knew
that now. "Absolutely, Jeannette." He grinned as he put his arm lightly
around Avis's shoulders. "You guys win, and we'll party all night."

They leaned in close, gave their traditional Keener Kat war whoop,
then scattered back to their waiting parents. Only Avis and Kayla stayed
behind, Kayla reluctantly helping her father gather up the bats, while
Avis was stuck with Deke for her ride home.

"Coach Keener, if you've got stuff to do, I could ride home with
Kayla. I'm sure my mother wouldn't mind." Her voice was piping as a
bird's.

"Why, Avis, you aren't telling me that you don't want to ride with me
anymore, are you?" He looked at her, feigning hurt. "I thought you and I
were pals."

"Oh, no," she said, again lifting one hand to keep the cap on her head.
"I just thought it might save you some time."

"I've got all the time in the world for you, honey," he said, waving at
Glenn Daws as he gently guided the girl back to his car. "You want to go
get something to eat?" he asked brightly. He needed to get her away
from Kayla, fast. "A burger and some fries?"

"No, thanks," she said. "I'm not hungry."

"Suit yourself, then." He clicked his remote. The car unlocked its
doors, turned on its running lights. He held his breath. He knew that

any moment she could change her mind and bolt toward Kayla, but she kept walking toward his car. When she climbed into the passenger seat and buckled her seatbelt, he knew he was home free.

Quickly, he climbed in beside her and locked the door. "Okay," he said, still working hard at being good old Coach Keener. "I've just got one little errand to run, then I'll have you home before you know it."

"What kind of errand?" She turned and looked at him with wide eyes.

"No big deal. I've just got to run over to my house and pick up some blueprints." She fingered the door handle. "It won't take a minute," he assured her. "Here." He flipped out his cell phone. "Call your folks. Tell them where we're going, and that you'll be just a little bit later than you expected. We wouldn't want them to worry, would we?"

She looked at him a moment, then punched in her own number. As he steered the car out of the parking lot, he listened to the message she left on her parents' answering machine.

"Mom, this is Avis. I'm going with Coach Keener to run an errand at his house, but he's going to bring me home right after that." She hesitated a moment, as if trying to decide what to say next, but as he pulled out onto the highway, he heard her opt for the noncommittal, "I'll talk to you later, then. Bye."

She handed the phone back to him. He smiled. *So sorry, Mr. and Mrs. Martin. It's going to be a bit of a while before you talk to your Avis again. A bit of a while, for sure.*

FORTY

Mary put the top down on her convertible and drove back to town fast, letting the evening breeze ripple through her hair. She'd had a long visit with Hugh that had ended in him fixing her an early dinner of corned beef sandwiches and cold potato salad. Though the old man teared up when she told him, gently, that Ravenel had some fairly serious doubts about Ridge's case, he eagerly agreed to testify on Ridge's behalf, promising he would leave his infamous temper behind when he took the stand.

"Fer luck," Hugh said, handing Mary a silver Celtic cross and a plaid woolen tie as she got in her car. "Ridge doesn't know anything about the Church or tartan plaids, but maybe Patrick and Bridget will protect him, just the same."

"Patrick and Bridget?" asked Mary, confused.

"The holy saints of Ireland, girl," replied Hugh. "Don't you know that?"

"I just forgot." Mary gave an ironic smile, thinking that Patrick and Bridget had better protect Ridge, because Mary and Sam weren't doing such a bang-up job. After all her legwork, she'd come to two conclusions: first, that whoever had molested all those girls had killed Bethany Daws; second, that the murderer was either Glenn Daws or someone closely connected to Keener Construction. She knew that the killer was still out there. Had her job with Turpin worked out, she could have brought him to justice with a phalanx of judges and detectives and cops. As it stood now, she could do nothing except help Ravenel get Ridge off a murder rap. And even if they did luck out and get the boy life instead of the needle, the end result would be the same: Ridge Standingdeer would wither behind bars. It would be a less cruel and unusual punishment just to hang him on the courthouse lawn.

She pushed the little car up to eighty as she sped back to town. She hadn't heard from Jonathan in what seemed like forever. When last they talked, he'd met with his boss and Lily had finally spent a night in her own room. Though he said he missed her, he sounded excited about his work, happy that Lily had already joined a daily play group. Guess it's working out, she thought wistfully. Too bad it couldn't have worked out on this side of the mountains, with me.

With the light fading fast, she pulled up in front of her office. A group of men were spilling out of the Baptist Church while Sylvia Goins was hurrying to get in her Jeep, for once without her beloved Ruben.

Maybe those two have broken up, too, thought Mary, sighing. Maybe August is just hard on couples here in Pisgah County.

She went up to her office to find the message light blinking on her answering machine. Hoping that it might be Jonathan, she hurried over to it without bothering to turn on the light. After she punched the PLAY button, a thunderous voice blasted out. She'd turned the thing up after Ravenel's whisper of a message and had apparently gone overboard. Wincing, she turned down the volume, and sat on the edge of her desk to listen.

"This is Kayla Daws again. You've got to help us. Coach Keener has taken Avis to his house. I think he might be going to kill her. Please call me as soon as you get this."

"Huh?" Frowning, Mary pressed the REPLAY button. The same high breathy voice repeated the message. It was a girl, presumably Bethany Daws' little sister, either playing a monstrous phone prank or truly in trouble. But who was Avis? And how did Deke figure into everything?

She walked over and turned on the overhead light. On the floor lay a thick white envelope.

She leaned over, wondering if this was some stupid missive from Ravenel, but someone had addressed the bulging envelope in round, almost childish printing: "To Mary Crow, Ridge Standingdeer's Lawyer." Inside she found three tiny cassette tapes and a letter written in the same schoolgirl hand.

Dear Ms, Crow,

Please listen to these tapes (particularly the one with the red label.) They prove that Ridge Standingdeer did not kill my sister. Avis Martin and I think that Coach Keener did. He was molesting her. We are going to try and trap him. Please call me at 555-9782, but don't tell my dad who you are.

Yours truly,

Kayla Elizabeth Daws

Mary stood there, astonished. Bethany Daws' sister was accusing Deke Keener of her murder? She and somebody named Avis Martin were going to trap him? She turned the letter over, hoping for further explanation, but the page was blank.

"Oh, Jesus," she whispered. Had she been right about Keener, days ago in Ravenel's office?

Quickly, she punched in the girl's number. She got a busy signal, then tried twice more. Deciding that someone must be surfing the Net with a dial-up modem, she dug her old personal tape recorder out of her drawer and plugged it in. She read the letter again, inserted the tape marked with a red label, and leaned close to listen.

For the first few moments, she heard nothing but tape hiss, then INXS's "Need You Tonight" came on. She groaned; she'd heard that song at least a dozen times this summer while driving around in Deke's car. As the music grew louder, she heard voices begin to speak.

"Just get it over with," a girl was saying.

"*You want to go in the front or the back?*" asked a man.

"*I don't care.*"

"*Then let's do it here, in the driver's seat.*"

Though the man could have been any adult male anywhere, Mary's hands grew cold as the music went on. U2 followed INXS, with "I Still Haven't Found What I'm Looking For." Then "Keep Your Hands to Yourself" by the Georgia Satellites. Soon Peter Gabriel's "Big Time" would start. All hits from her senior year in high school, played in exactly the same order as the CD in Deke Keener's car.

"Oh, my God," she whispered as the man told the girl to "stick her bottom out." She flipped the tape over, hoping the B side offered something different, but it continued on with the Beastie Boys, now accompanied by male groaning. She sat, horrified, listening with the ears of both prosecution and defense. So far, she'd heard nothing on the tape that positively identified either the molester or his victim. And though the background music was definitely the same as Deke's, who could prove that it belonged to him? He might have copied it from somebody else, or even loaned it to one of his child-molester pals. She'd just pulled out a legal pad to make notes when, at the end of one long, climactic groan, the molester nailed his own coffin shut. "Oh, Bethany! You've just made your old Coach Keener a very happy man!"

Shaking, she rewound the tape and listened again. Her intuition had been right, but she had ignored it. Deke had played her for a fool since day one. How he must have enjoyed these past weeks, secretly laughing while she struggled with Ridge's defense!

"You bastard!" she cried. She picked up her phone to call Jerry Cochran. If indeed those little girls were out trying to trap this man, God knows what kind of trouble they could be getting into. She had to get them away from Keener right now. *You can't turn him in,* a small smug voice seemed to taunt inside her head. *Deke's your client. It would break attorney/client privilege.* She stopped, paralyzed, halfway through Jerry's number. Keener had set her up even worse than she'd imagined. Though she'd never represented him in anything other than real estate matters, she was nonetheless his counsel. If she turned over criminal evidence against him, it could conceivably end her practicing any kind of law, prosecution or defense.

"Damn!" She sat down, staring at the mask in the corner, then she picked up the phone and frantically redialed Kayla Daws' number.

Some miles away, Kayla Daws was sitting on her bed, watching her little Elvis Presley wall clock hip-swivel the seconds away. She'd stared at it ever since she'd gotten home from ball practice, a sick feeling of dread growing as she waited for Avis to call. Something had gone wrong. Though Avis and Coach Keener had showed up at the ball field, Coach Keener had made Avis sit right beside him for most of the practice. She'd desperately tried to make eye contact with her friend, but the bill of Avis's huge Panthers cap covered her eyes, making it impossible to read her expression. Kayla had no idea what had transpired between Avis and Coach Keener, and whether Avis was happy, sad, triumphant, or terrified. Then, when she'd called Avis twenty minutes ago, Mrs. Martin had just gotten back from getting their new truck and told her that Avis had gone home with Coach Keener. After that she'd gotten really scared, and she called Mary Crow. Now, every second that the phone sat silent made her feel sicker inside.

"Come on, Avis!" She lifted her telephone receiver to make sure that neither of her parents were on the line. A few minutes ago her father had received a long, involved call from somebody on a roofing crew, but now, blessedly, she heard nothing but the buzz of the dial tone. "Two more minutes," Kayla vowed. "Then I'll call her again."

She returned her gaze to Elvis Presley, wishing she and Avis had never dreamed this up. This was real, not some stupid novel, and Avis was no more a detective than Darby was. Coach Keener had killed her sister. Was he about to kill her best friend as well?

"Please not," she whispered, fighting back tears. "Please let Avis be all right."

She watched Elvis Presley swivel for another ten seconds, then she picked up the phone. Maybe Avis was back by now. Maybe she was just getting ready to call her. The phone rang once, twice, then Mrs. Martin said, "Hello?"

Kayla's heart leapt. Please, please, *please* let Avis be home! "May I speak to Avis please?"

"Kayla? Is that you again?"

Kayla sucked in her breath. Mrs. Martin sounded like a normal mother on a normal night—certainly not like someone whose daughter had just been kidnapped by her murderous softball coach.

"Yes, ma'am."

"I'm afraid Avis is still not back from softball practice," said Mrs. Martin. "But I promise I'll have her call you when she gets in."

"Don't forget, okay?" Kayla begged, knowing Avis would never get back, that this would be the last time she would ever again have a regular conversation with anyone. "It doesn't matter how late."

She hung up the phone. She felt frozen in place, like a stupid cartoon character, too scared to move. What should she do? She'd already called Mary Crow. She supposed now she could try to tell her father, but he was back with his six-packs and her mother had locked herself in her room with the home makeover channel. She could call Mrs. Martin back, but what would she say? *Avis thinks Coach Keener killed my sister and is wearing a tape recorder on her head to prove it?*

She paced around her room in a tight little circle, trying to decide what to do. Suddenly the phone rang. She jumped as if a gun had gone off beside her. Scooping it up, she clutched the receiver to her ear.

"Hello?" she said, breathless, praying that Avis would answer.

"Is this Kayla Daws?" A woman's voice came over the line, using the same no-bullshit tone teachers used during bomb scares at school.

"Yes." Kayla clutched her strawberry necklace, terrified.

"Kayla, this is Mary Crow, Ridge Standingdeer's attorney. Did you just leave a message on my answering machine and put some tape cassettes under my door?"

"Yes, ma'am." Her voice came out in a squeak.

"I take it those are genuine tapes, not something you've manufactured yourself?" The woman sounded like the angel of death. Kayla's knees were shaking so much, she had to sit down on the bed.

"Yes, ma'am. My sister taped them. My friend Avis Martin and I found them. We think Coach Keener killed my sister."

"Where's your friend Avis now?"

Kayla tried to speak, tried to work her jaws, but no sound came out.

"Kayla?" asked Mary Crow again. "Where exactly is your friend Avis now?"

"She went to trap Coach Keener, she put a tape recorder inside her cap!" Kayla broke down in huge, gulping sobs. "After the game he took Avis up to his house. I think they're still there now!"

FORTY-ONE

Avis sat clutching the armrest of Coach Keener's car. He'd sped her away after practice, before she could even twitch an eyebrow at Kayla, and for the past half hour they'd twisted higher into the mountains on a curvy gravel road. She was pretty sure he hadn't seen the tape recorder. Though he'd acted odd at practice, once they'd gotten in the car to go home, he'd started chatting away just like always. Still, she was going to Coach Keener's house, all by herself. That fact alone made her mouth dry as a cracker, her legs tremble with the urge to get away. As his headlights flashed across the trees that pressed against the road, all she could think about was how much she hated the woods at night! If she could ever just get back home, she would never go outside after dark again. She would just curl up with her books in bed and read for the rest of her life.

"You okay?" Coach Keener looked at her, the dashboard lights giving his face an unnatural pallor. "I know this road's pretty twisty—sometimes it makes people car sick."

She nodded. She was sick, sick to death, but not because of the road.

"Like I said, this won't take long. We can check out my telescope after I get my plans." He glanced up at the dark sky that rushed over the tops of the trees. "It's so clear tonight, you could probably see Uranus."

Your anus. The joke the boys in her fourth-grade class had found so hysterical buzzed through her head. She wished she thought it was funny now. She wished she thought anything was funny now. With clammy hands, she gripped the armrest tighter as Coach Keener drove on. Up they climbed, the pavement growing even more bumpy and rutted. Her stomach flopped as they veered close to the edge of the road and she saw the lights of Hartsville twinkling far below. One of those lights is our house, she thought, tears stinging her eyes. In one of those little dots of light live my mom and dad.

They twisted around two more tight curves, then abruptly he pulled into a drive. With the click of a button on his key ring, a tall, soaringly modern house erupted in bright lights. It was built like a castle—one side seemed to overlook a cliff while the other three sides nestled into a forest of tall black pines. A red light blinked from some kind of tower at the top.

"That's my red winker," Coach Keener explained. "It keeps low-flying planes away."

He punched another button; a great maw of a garage opened. They pulled into a dimly lit basement cluttered with shovels and huge sacks of lime, then he turned off the engine of his car.

"You can stay down here if you like," he said, again smiling. "Or you can come upstairs and have a Coke. This won't take me a minute."

He acted so normal that she wondered if she hadn't just imagined his earlier weirdness. Ever since they'd gotten back in his car, he'd seemed no more threatening than her own dad. Though she didn't much want to go into his house, she also didn't want to stay out here in this spooky garage.

"Okay," she said, slowly opening the car door, careful to keep the cap balanced on her head.

She followed him up some stairs and into a kitchen that looked bigger than her grandmother's whole house. "How about a Coke?" He tossed his own cap on the counter and got two frosty cans of soda from a stainless steel refrigerator.

She wanted to say no, thanks, that she would stay right here in the kitchen while he got his blueprints, but he handed her a Coke and kept talking and walking so quickly that she followed him, not knowing what else to do. He crossed a big living room with a huge fireplace and walked over to a wall-sized bookcase that held more books than she'd ever dreamed of. He paused once to flip on some kind of stereo system. She cringed, waiting to hear the same old tunes she'd heard on Bethany's tape, but classical music, with violins, filled the air.

"Come have a look at the Keener Kats of years past." He pointed to one of the bookshelves that glittered with gold trophies and team photographs. "I'll go get those blueprints and be right back."

Avis held her breath, wondering what he was really going to do, but he turned and trotted up a wide staircase to the upper level of the house. Apparently, he truly did need to pick up something. She considered taking off her cap and hiding the tape, but she was terrified that he'd come downstairs and catch her. She settled for adjusting the thing more firmly on her head and crept over to the bookcase, gazing at his Kats memorabilia. The photographs interested her more than the trophies, and as she heard him thumping around upstairs, she found some players she recognized. Last year Jeannette Peacock had been chubbier, while Kayla had worn her hair long. Three years ago neither had been on the team at all; five years ago a taller, blonder version of Kayla stared out at the camera.

"It's Bethany!" she whispered to the frozen image, recognizing her from the photos she'd seen at Kayla's house. She picked up the picture and held it close. Though Bethany was the prettiest girl on the team, she had not smiled when they snapped her picture, and her eyes looked like she was hiding a great, sorrowful secret.

"Did you ever meet her?" The question came from behind her, so softly that she jumped. Coach Keener had come downstairs without a sound.

"No," Avis said, quickly returning the photo to the shelf.

"She was a beautiful girl." His voice was husky. "I think about her every day."

I do, too, thought Avis, suddenly aware of the cap on her head. And so does Kayla.

Another silence sprang up between them.

"I got what I needed," he said, digging his car keys from his pocket as he held up a long roll of blue paper. "Shall we go out and take a peek at Uranus before we leave?"

Again, he seemed so normal that she felt stupid. Not once had he put his hands on her. He'd given her a Coke, then he'd left her to look at team pictures while he got his stuff. If he'd planned to do something, wouldn't he have done it when they first pulled in the garage? She felt her face flame with confused embarrassment. "Okay," she told him.

He crossed the room to draw back nubby white drapes that revealed a wide flagstone patio that seemed suspended over the outer darkness. At one corner sprawled the biggest telescope she'd ever seen, pointed at some distant light in the sky. He walked out onto the patio and motioned for her to follow.

"Let's see what's showing tonight." He put his Coke down and peered through the viewfinder, adjusting the focus knobs. A moment later, he stood up.

"Have a look," he said. "It's not Uranus, but you might recognize it, just the same."

She stepped over and looked through the eyepiece. The planet Saturn blazed at her from a field of ebony space, its rings hazy purple and pale gold. It was the most coldly beautiful thing she'd ever seen.

"Wow!" she cried, forgetting her earlier resolve to keep her mouth shut. "That's so cool!" She was about to ask if he would show her some other planets when all at once she felt a weight lift from her head. As the cool night breeze caressed her newly exposed scalp, Coach Keener's voice echoed in her ears.

"Why, Avis," he said. "You dropped your cap!"

Trembling, she turned around. He stood just behind her, holding her cap in his hands as if it were a bowl, looking down and smiling.

"You know, I thought I heard a funny noise on the way to the ball park. A little hiss. Like a tape recorder." He turned his gaze from the cap and stared directly at her, his eyes as bright and cold as Saturn. "And son of a gun, I found one! Right inside your cap!"

She realized then that his good humor had all been an act. He'd planned this for hours, and he'd set it up perfectly. Called her parents with a fake story about a blueprint, given her a Coke, gotten her out on the patio with the promise of Uranus. No doubt next he would toss her off this balcony, then call the cops, distraught. *Oh my God, officer! One of my ball players has fallen off my patio! She was standing right there, looking through my telescope. I turned away for just a moment and she fell!* The cops would come, survey the scene, and call her parents. They would cry, heartbroken, and everyone except Kayla would think it was nothing more than a terrible, tragic accident.

He threw back his head and laughed. She turned away, looking up into the sky, at the merciless stars glittering from the dark void of space. *Help me,* she prayed to whoever or whatever might be out there, on the other end of the telescope. *Please help me.*

As if in reply, a sudden cold wind carried the low rumble of a growl. It shook the mind-numbing fear from her brain, making her keenly aware of everything from the newly ashen look on Coach Keener's face to a distant owl, screeching from the trees. Realizing that she was just two steps away from being tossed off the balcony like a sack of garbage, she took a huge breath, then did what they'd taught her to do way back in the fifth grade when they'd had self-defense in gym class. Pointing her toe like a majorette, she aimed, then kicked Coach Keener between his legs as hard as she could. Never had she dreamed of doing such a thing, but she felt a rush of triumph when she felt her foot plunge deep into something soft. As he cried out in pain, she turned and ran. Across the deck and back into the house, back where the classical music mocked her terror with its lush civility.

She fled to the kitchen, desperate to find a phone, but the room was not like her mother's—its high-tech counters held nothing but knives and stainless steel cooking utensils. Frantic, she looked back toward the deck. Coach Keener was doubled over, but he'd recovered enough to start limping after her, his mouth twisted in rage. Forgetting about the phone, she tore down the hall to the front door. She had to get away. If she could just get into the trees before he caught her, she could hide until she figured out what to do next.

"Avis?" she heard him call as she grasped the front doorknob. "Where'd you go, honey? Why did you run away?"

She tugged at the door, but it was locked. Her heart pounding, she fumbled with the deadbolt and tried the knob again. It turned, but now the door stuck, as if swollen. She put one foot against the jamb and tugged as hard as she could. With a great grinding noise, the door finally budged, admitting an amazingly cold blast of outside air. Whimpering, she fled into the darkness, running along a short paved walkway and into the tall pines that surrounded the house. She fought her way through sticky, fragrant needles that scratched her face as she ran, and she didn't stop until she came to a small clearing that allowed a view of Coach Keener's front door. Peeking between the rung-like branches of the trees, she tried to gulp in air silently and still keep watch on what he was doing. No floodlights came on, no doors slammed, no one came out at all. Just as she began to wonder if she'd truly injured him, she saw a figure in the doorway. Coach Keener walked out of the house. He'd changed from his softball clothes into black pants and a black shirt, and he carried a rifle in his arms. There were some funny-looking goggles over his eyes. At that moment she realized in terror that wherever she ran, wherever she tried to hide, Coach Keener intended to find her.

She stood like a statue, praying he'd think she'd taken off down the driveway. If he searched for her in that direction, she might get the chance to slip back inside his house. Then she could find a phone and call the cops. But all he did was stand with his face lifted, like some animal sniffing the breeze. With her teeth chattering like dice, she watched until all at once, like a robot coming to life, he moved. He clicked something on his gun then turned in a deliberate circle, scanning the woods in front of him, looking like a terrorist in his black outfit and bugged-out eyes. As he turned toward her, she made herself small, willed herself to melt into the tree trunk. She waited, watching as his gaze grew closer, then her heart stopped.

"Peekaboo, Avis," he called, laughing. "I see you! You'd better come out now before somebody mistakes you for a bear!"

Grinning, he aimed his rifle straight at her. Without another thought, Avis bolted. Fighting her way through the thick branches, she tore through the trees, plunging headlong into the deeper forest. Still she heard him coming up behind her, giggling as if they were playing a game of tag.

"You can't beat me in the woods, Avis," he called, his voice terrifyingly close. "Nobody can."

She scrambled up a small rise, then along a ridge, her feet skidding on the slick pine needles. A damp, cold mist rose from the ground, chilling her sweat-soaked clothes. She had no idea of how to get to the road, so she just kept running. He followed her relentlessly, his footsteps crackling through the underbrush behind her.

She struggled up another, steeper ridge, her breath coming harder. Her legs burned like fire and she wanted nothing more than to stop and breathe. Heaving herself up the final ten yards, she collapsed against a smooth-barked tree that towered into the night. Wiping the sweat from her eyes, she stared down the ridge below. Coach Keener had not slowed his pace. Already he was halfway up the steep slope. In less than a minute he would be here, pointing his gun in her face.

"Think!" she told herself, looking at the trees that surrounded her. "Think like Nancy Drew, Kinsey Milhone! Figure out where to go!"

She seemed to be standing on the spine of a ridge. If she went left, she would run straight into Coach Keener. If she went forward, she would simply continue along the ridge to who-knew-where. To the right, a sliver of a trail disappeared into even thicker woods. Though it looked like a path from one of her own nightmares, it offered dense foliage that could hide her and a downhill course where she might gain some the hill. She took one more look at Coach Keener, then plunged down the hill.

Immediately she sensed something different. Though the air had been oddly cold ever since Coach Keener had snatched the cap from her head, now it felt frosty. Her breath became visible, and she shook from the chill as well as from her own fear. Further down the trail she began to smell a weird odor—gamey, like an unwashed dog. She'd never smelled anything quite like it before, but she kept on going. When the trail bottomed out, she risked a glance over her shoulder. She gasped. She thought Coach Keener was far behind her, but he'd already crested the ridge. She could see the moonlight flickering in his goggled eyes. Turning, she ran, dodging branches, jumping fallen limbs, desperate to get away. As she splashed through a shallow creek, she slipped on some mossy rocks and fell hard, sprawling on the opposite bank. When the muzziness cleared from her eyes, she saw it. A low, small opening that poked up from the earth like the knuckle of her finger; darker than dark, she figured it must be a cave, or the den of some wild animal. Kayla had told her that deep in the woods you could still hear mountain lions scream. She gulped, trying to decide what to do, then she remembered Coach Keener's eyes and the way his hands had touched her. She headed toward the little cave. If a mountain lion ate her, so be it. Better to be a feast for a mountain lion than to wind up like poor Bethany Daws.

FORTY-TWO

The moment she'd hung up from Kayla Daws, Mary Crow had called 911 and told the dispatcher there was a domestic disturbance at Deke Keener's house. Though it was a lie that could conceivably cost her a career, compared to a child's life, her career was small potatoes. After she hung up from emergency dispatch, she unlocked the bottom drawer of her desk. Though she had not worn her old Glock 9mm since she left Atlanta, she kept it clean, oiled, and ready to go. She loaded it, buckled on the shoulder holster, and threw on a navy blazer she'd been intending to take to the dry cleaners. Though she still only half-believed Kayla Daws' wild story about her friend trying to trap Keener, the tape alone was reason enough to go. The music playing in the background was the same that Deke played all the time; the man on the tape had clearly identified himself as Coach Keener. If Deke was the Pisgah County child molester, maybe she could stop him before another victim "disappeared."

She pulled into his driveway. He lived at the top of King's Mountain, a thickly forested peak honeycombed by logging roads left over from the nineteenth century. She'd passed no police cruisers on the way, nor did any sit with lights flashing at Deke's front door. His house, though, was lit like a beacon in the darkness, clinging to a mountain, seemingly supported by nothing but air. One entire side appeared constructed of glass while the other three sides were guarded by tall pines that stood like sentries around a fortress. How typical of Deke, she thought. A castle for the king.

She got out of her car. The temperature up here was cooler by fifteen degrees, and the damp breeze carried the same woodsy, cedar smell as Little Jump Off. With her breath visible on the air, she hurried to the front door and rang the bell. She heard a deep, Westminster-like chime, but it failed to bring anyone to the door. She tried the bell once more, then began to knock.

"Deke?" she called. "Deke, this is Mary Crow. I need to talk to you!"

Still she got no response. She knew he was here; his Lexus sat parked in an open garage not ten feet away. Cautiously she tried the doorknob. To her surprise, it turned easily in her hand. The tingling in the pit of her stomach grew worse. Deke Keener had obsessed about form and detail ever since the tenth grade. She doubted that he had grown into a man who would leave his front door unlocked, even up here on the top of his own mountain. She pushed the balky door open and walked into a soaring stone foyer that led into the main room of the house. Music played from a stereo—Vivaldi, she thought.

"Deke?" she called as she stepped inside.

Again she heard nothing beyond the music as she walked further into the house. The inside had been designed as strikingly as the exterior, with slate floors, chestnut paneling, and a massive stone fireplace that commanded the single great room. Two leather sofas faced each other in front of the fireplace, and a reading chair sat in front of a wall-sized bookcase that housed the same collection of Keener Kat photos that hung in Sutton's Hardware.

Feeling exactly like the intruder she was, she crept carefully through the rest of the first floor—a sleek space-age kitchen that would make most professional chefs drool and a bachelor-pad sort of bathroom with onyx marble walls. The house boasted a number of state-of-the-art features, but she found nobody around to enjoy them.

She returned to the living room and started to head up the stairs when the white drapes from the patio billowed suddenly into the room. She stepped over, thinking maybe Deke was sitting out there, but instead she found two overturned Coke cans and a Carolina Panthers cap, all clustered beneath a huge telescope that pointed toward the stars.

"Deke?" she called, walking out onto the flagstone structure that extruded into the darkness like the prow of a ship. "Anybody home?"

No one answered. As the lights of Hartsville twinkled below, she walked over to the soda cans. Nothing special about them beyond sloppy housekeeping. She stooped down to examine the Panthers cap more closely, then she gasped. Someone had duct-taped a tape recorder to the inside of the crown, carefully affixing its microphone to one of the air holes on the left side of the cap.

"Oh, my God," she whispered, her heart plummeting. "Kayla wasn't kidding!"

She raced back inside, pulling her pistol as she hauled up the stairs. Maybe Deke had taken the child up here. The second story of the house had several bedrooms that opened off a long hall. Quickly she checked each one. The first was a guest room, the other was painted pink, and held an array of stuffed animals piled on a frilly-looking canopy bed. She remembered Deke mentioning a daughter, though she'd never known the child to visit, even for a day. The third bedroom commanded the other half of the second story. Huge, with a bank of windows that looked down upon the patio and the darkness beyond, this room echoed the same modern, angular look of downstairs. A plasma television faced an oversized bed that stood on a platform. At the foot of the bed lay a pile of clothes—Deke's adult-sized Keener Kat shirt, a pair of black shorts, and sneakers. She looked around for a child-sized version of the same outfit, but found nothing.

"Okay." Mary tried to bite back her rising panic and regard the bedroom as she would a crime scene. What happened here? she asked herself. What does this tell you, so far?

The little girl—what was her name? Anna? Angie?—had come home with him. He'd served them both soda, then they'd gone outside to look at the telescope. Then the girl's cap had either fallen off or been removed from her head. Then what?

Then Deke had changed clothes in a hurry, she decided. But why? And what did he put on? And what had made him so frantic?

Frowning, she walked over to a door that opened off the bedroom, entering a huge closet where at least twenty expensive suits hung with matching pairs of shoes beneath them. The precision with which Deke kept his closet would have made any drill sergeant proud, but what caught her attention was a small armoire along the back wall. Like all the rest of his furniture, it was sleek and modern, except instead of holding shirts and sweaters, it held a collection of rifles. As she stepped closer, she realized that like the clothes at the foot of his bed, Deke had left his gun case in disarray. The door stood ajar, the key still in the lock, and the cradle that should have held the fifth of five rifles was empty. Suddenly it all fell into place. "The little girl managed to get away," Mary whispered. "And Deke's gone to find her."

As if to corroborate her theory, three gunshots rang out from the distant woods, fired at a casual rate, as if someone might have all the time in the world to take aim at his target.

She ran downstairs, through the living room and back out into the night beyond. At first she heard only the rush of her own blood, then she heard a faraway scream, as if some outrage were being visited upon someone in another dimension.

She slipped into the dark, fragrant pines, easily finding a track of trampled weeds and shorn-off branches. Thank God for Jonathan, she thought. She'd spent so much time in the woods with him that she could track most anybody who wasn't trying to conceal their trail, and tonight neither Deke nor his prey seemed the least bit interested in doing that.

"You just think you've got it made, don't you, Deke?" she whispered, her anger flaring again.

She ran on, the Glock heavy in her hand. The trees grew thicker as the terrain steepened, and she had to pull herself up a long, seemingly endless ridge. Wispy clouds scudded across the moon and an unseasonably cold breeze brought the gamey, oily smell of bear.

Oh, Lord, she thought, wiping the sweat from her forehead. *Please not a bear. At best they were unpredictable, at worst, lethal. She didn't need a bear added to the evening's agenda.*

Feeling as if her lungs might burst, she reached the top of the ridge.

The trees thinned out, and she saw that she was standing on the rim of what she knew as a sink—a great, tree-filled bowl made by underground water seeping through limestone. If you made the effort to trek down to the bottom of a sink, you usually found either a creek or a cave. As she paused to catch her breath, she remembered something Jonathan once told her: "Foxes take the high ground, possums take the sink."

At the time, she'd thought he was just spouting more of his cryptic Cherokee wood lore, but now she understood his meaning. No experienced woodsman would seek cover in a such a low place. But a terrified child with an armed man chasing her? She would think it perfect—all downhill, filled with woodsy cover. It would be the first place a scared little possum would go.

She paused to catch her breath, then she started down. The sloping terrain was easier on her lungs, but harder on her knees. Once she slipped on some pine needles, but caught herself by grabbing onto a low-hanging grapevine. As she made her way down, she tried to keep one ear on the gusting breeze. It did not disappoint her. Once more she heard a plaintive cry, floating up from the bottom of the sink.

"You son of a bitch!" she muttered. Knowing Deke, he would have the newest rifle with the sharpest scope while the little girl would probably have nothing but the clothes on her back. She picked up her pace, hurtling downward, trying hard not to trip over a root and blow out an ankle.

Finally the steep hillside leveled off as thorny, waist-high weeds replaced the thick trees. As she surveyed the wide, open area around her, instinctively she dropped to the ground. She was betting that Deke would have night vision goggles, possibly a military rifle scope.

She crept along the ground, quiet, heading toward the distant gurgle of a stream. With every inch she expected Deke to pop up from the tall grass around her, but she crawled on, unmolested. Gradually the weeds began to thin out. Ahead she could see a dark, linear indentation in the earth and the soft glitter of moonlight on water. The sink bottomed out here; this is where the little girl would have come. She stopped behind some laurel and used another trick Jonathan had taught her—owl eyes. Trying to remain still, she softened the focus of her eyes and gazed at everything and nothing, at the same time. Though the nighttime world was arrayed before her in various shades of gray, what she sought was movement—either Deke's or the child's. Once she spotted either of them, she would know what to do.

She watched and waited, like a rabbit frozen in a field of clover, its stalker near. The breeze again brought the smell of bear, but this time no noise rode upon it. Finally, just as she was beginning to think perhaps the child had opted to follow the creek, she saw a pale gray ghost of a thing emerge from the dark little knob on the other side of the water. Too small to be Deke, it moved too hesitantly to be anything other than a terrified little girl, way out of her element, deep in the nighttime woods.

Mary rose to her knees. Somehow she needed to let the child know not to be afraid of her, but she didn't want to risk calling out. She scanned all around, looking for Deke, but she saw no sign of him. Quickly she got to her feet and gave a soft whistle. The little figure spun around and looked directly at her. Mary started to beckon the girl forward, then realized that she might just be luring her right into Deke's gun sights. With one hand held up as a gesture of friendship, she waded quietly across the stream. As she neared the girl, she saw that though she had lost her cap, she still wore the rest of her Keener Kats uniform. She stood a few yards in front of the tiny cave, her eyes huge and terrified.

"Hello," Mary whispered. "Are you Kayla's friend?"

The little girl nodded.

"What's your name?"

"Avis Martin." The child sounded near tears. "Who are you?"

"I'm Mary Crow, Avis. I've come to take you home."

"Take her home?"

Mary's heart froze as a familiar male voice rang out behind her.

"Why would you want to do a thing like that, Mary? From the way I'm looking at things, our party's just about to begin!"

FORTY-THREE

"Drop your pistol, Mary." Deke's voice was sharp as a splinter. "I've got a Browning hand cannon aimed right at the girl. I'd blow her head off before you could fire one shot."

Mary looked at Avis, hoping she could get her to drop to the ground, but the child just gaped at Keener, her eyes fixed in horror. No good, Mary thought. She's too scared to move, much less dodge any bullets.

"Okay, Deke." Extending her right arm, Mary tossed the Glock toward him, slowly easing in front of the child. "I wasn't gunning for you, anyway."

"Oh, really?" He laughed. "I guess tonight of all nights you just decided to drop by?"

"I came up here as your attorney," she said. Deke looked like some crazed white hunter gripping an elephant gun, night vision goggles dangling around his neck. "And I'd still like to advise you on where you stand."

"I think I'm standing at just the right place, as far as this rifle's concerned."

"Deke, I have a tape that clearly reveals you molesting Bethany Daws. I'm guessing that you killed her, too. Probably to keep her quiet."

"Sorry, Mary, but you're wrong. I was home in bed the night that little bitch caught it."

"Deke, come on. Tell the truth. I can't turn you in, anyway. I'm your attorney."

"I am telling the truth, Mary. It wasn't me."

"Deke—"

"He is telling the truth, Ms. Crow." Mary gasped as a high, female voice came out of the darkness. "He did mess with Bethany. But I'm the one who killed her."

Mary turned. In the shadows of the little knuckle of the cave, pointing a rifle just as impressive as Deke's, stood Sylvia Goins. The sweet, fat hardware clerk had killed Bethany Daws? "Sylvia?" asked Mary. "What are you talking about?"

"I was cleaning upstairs when I heard Bethany's sister leave that message on your answering machine." Sylvia kept her weapon aimed at Deke. "It came on so loud, I couldn't help but hear it. Anyway, after that, I figured it was time to come up here and stop him once and for all."

Mary remembered she'd seen the girl getting in her Jeep, alone, when she'd returned to her office, earlier that night. "So you heard that and figured you'd just come up here and shoot Deke Keener?"

"No, ma'am," Sylvia replied, her tone sardonic. "Mr. Keener and I go back a long, long way."

Suddenly Mary recalled her conversation with Sylvia about Bethany and the Keener Kat photo from which both little girls grinned. "Oh, my God," she whispered. "He did it to you, too, didn't he?"

Sylvia nodded. "Me and Bethany both, together, at the same time. Bought me the same pretty things he bought her. Then one day he stopped with me. Told me I'd grown tits and zits and that I wasn't cute anymore. All those presents and pretty things just dried up like an old cow."

Mary said, "But what did that have to do with Bethany? I thought she was your friend."

"She was. She wanted to stop Coach Keener bad, before he took up with her little sister. She had these tapes of them together. She was going to give them to the sheriff, and then make me come and testify in court, about all that happened between the three of us."

"And you didn't want to be embarrassed," said Mary.

"I could've stood that." Sylvia's eyes glittered with tears. "My daddy would have whipped me good, but I'd have gotten over it."

"Then what was it?" pressed Mary.

"If Bethany had told, Ridge wouldn't have cared. And even if he had, Bethany was thin and pretty. She was goin' off to college. She could've gotten another boyfriend just by snapping her fingers. Ruben's all I've got, Ms. Crow. He's all I'll ever have. If he ever found out about them tapes, he'd leave me in a heartbeat."

"So you sneaked into Bethany's house and killed her?"

"I had a key she'd given me way back in the seventh grade. I went there to give her a good talkin' to. I tried to explain about me and Ruben, but she wouldn't listen. She made me so mad, I done took that tomahawk from her bookshelf and hit her on the head."

Death from head trauma, caused by a single blow to the anterior fontanel by a blunt instrument. Mary exhaled the breath she'd been holding. In North Carolina mountain speak, Sylvia Goins had just confirmed Bethany Daws' official autopsy report.

"I never meant to kill her." Sylvia's voice trembled. "I just wanted to scare her . . . to make her forget about those tapes. I wanted . . ."

The crack of a rifle cut the girl off in mid-sentence. Mary grabbed the child who was standing behind her, then watched, horrified, as Sylvia Goins's knees buckled. The rifle dropped from the big girl's hands and she crashed forward, her head thudding sickly on the rocky lip of the small cave. To her horror, Mary heard Deke laughing.

"See, Mary? You're not so smart after all. It's just like I told you. I didn't kill Bethany. The fatty did."

Mary turned to him, wanting to scream her outrage aloud, when an icy breeze gusted up. A low, throaty growl rattled around them and Deke's face paled as a shadow fell over Mary and the little girl. She looked to see what was emerging from the forest, when she felt a rush of cold air. A dark shape, seemingly more noise than substance, roared past her. She pushed Avis to the ground and fell on top of her, tensing her body for the deadly report of Deke's rifle. Instead, the clearing echoed with one long horrific scream. It sounded like someone having their heart torn from their body.

Terrified, she forced herself to look up, to ready herself for what would certainly come next for her and the child. A huge, dark hulk was crouching over Keener. It lifted him up by his neck and shook him. Deke's arms and legs hung loose, as if they were made of rags instead of flesh. Desperately Mary crawled toward her pistol. Trying to ignore the grunts of the creature as it dined on Deke, she snapped the safety off and took aim. She fired—once, twice, then a third time. For a moment the shadowy hulk remained on top of Deke, then, as if annoyed by a gnat, it lifted its head and looked straight at her.

It was a bear. Not a small, brown, garbage-grubbing bear, but a monstrous, magnificent creature that was surely God's own prototype for all bears. Its eyes gleamed like gold; its claws looked long enough to rake furrows in the land. Though bright blood dripped from its snout, it seemed to hold no malice toward her or the child.

"It's the mask!" Mary whispered as her gun hand began to shake. Frantically she tried again to pull the trigger, but her hand simply would not move. Twisting toward her, the creature rose on its hind legs. As it towered over her, she steeled herself for the lethal swipe of the claws that would kill her as surely as Deke's bullet, but the beast just looked down at her. For a moment she felt that awesome gold gaze upon her face, then the bear lifted its head toward the sky. A single, ear-shattering roar came from its throat. Cringing, Mary closed her eyes, waiting for the beast to break her own bones, but nothing happened. When she opened her eyes a moment later, the bear was gone. Where a dark ursine shape had just seconds ago stood, she saw only a dark and luminous sky.

For a moment, all she could do was lie there, shaking. At first she wondered if perhaps Deke had shot her seconds earlier and the bear had been some kind of totemic animal sent to take her into the afterlife. But she felt the Glock's heavy, solid weight in her hand and realized she was still alive.

"Stay here and don't move," she told the child, as she rushed over to where Sylvia Goins lay. She felt for a pulse in Sylvia's neck, but she knew by the size of the hole in the middle of the girl's chest that she would not find one. Already the gash in her head had quit bleeding as her eyes stared, unseeing. Mary shook her head. Though the ME would give Sylvia Goins and Bethany Daws very different causes of death, each had been killed by Deke Keener, years ago, when they were both just two little girls who hoped to have some fun on a softball team.

She turned her attention to Deke. He lay unmoving, his arms and legs splayed like a doll's. Though her senses told her that he'd been badly mauled by a bear, her brain balked at believing it. Monstrous bears with gold eyes simply didn't appear from the woods, rip somebody to shreds, and then vanish without a trace.

"He's probably faking it," she told herself aloud, her voice insubstantial and light. "God knows he fakes everything else."

She trained her gun on him and called to the little girl. "Avis? Are you okay?"

"Yes, ma'am," came a quivery little Southern drawl, polite even in distress. "I think so."

"If you can, honey, I want you to get up and come over here beside me."

"Okay . . ."

"Now I want you to grab on to my jacket and walk behind me. We're going over to see what happened to Coach Keener. If he plays any tricks on us, I want you to run back into those woods and keep running, as fast as you can."

"Yes, ma'am."

Thank God she's calm, thought Mary. A hysterical child along with Deke and Sylvia and an imaginary bear would be more than I could handle. Slowly they inched forward. Part of her expected to find the worst gore imaginable—Keener's chest ripped open, his throat torn out, a bloody, vicious death that would shock Hartsville to its core. Another part of her was equally convinced that the man would rise up, unharmed, and point his gun at them again. But, as they drew closer, Mary couldn't believe what she saw. Keener's clothes were not torn, his body bore not the slightest scratch, and he cradled his rifle in his arms tenderly, as a father might hold a child. Only the expression on his face denied the repose of his body. His eyes stared up into the night sky wild with naked fear, while his mouth twisted in a grimace of utter terror. It was an expression not meant for the living to see. Hastily she removed her blazer and covered Deke's face before Avis had a chance to look.

"Did the bear kill him?" asked the little girl, accepting as only a child could the fact that a twelve-foot bear had killed Coach Keener without leaving a scratch on him.

"I don't know," Mary told her shakily. "Come on, let's have a look around."

Still clutching her pistol, Mary walked a slow, wide perimeter of the scene, Avis following behind her. For the sake of her own sanity, Mary needed to find some spoor of a bear: scat, a footprint, or bushes that a creature that size would have surely trampled in an attack. Instead, she found nothing beyond the neat single track she herself had made just a little while before. She shuddered. She'd tracked bear with Jonathan, had seen many bears penned up as sad little tourist attractions around Cherokee. Nothing indicated that one had been here tonight. As she stood, bewildered and thinking that there must be another explanation, Avis knelt beside Keener's body.

"Look at this!"

The little girl was pointing at Deke's chest. As Mary joined her to get a closer look, her heart skipped a beat. There was something caught in the fabric of his black sweater. She loosened it and held it in the palm of her hand. It was a bear claw, long as her finger, sharp as a razor, glittering like silver in the moonlight.

"So did the bear kill him?" asked Avis again, her eyes wide and questioning.

"I guess it did," Mary whispered, looking in amazement at the lifeless body that bore not a scratch. Carefully she handed the bear claw to Avis. "You keep this. I have the feeling it will bring you very good luck."

Avis frowned. "But aren't we disturbing a crime scene? Isn't this evidence?"

"It's evidence, all right," Mary replied, wanting to laugh at the little girl's use of police lingo. "But I'm not sure what of."

Avis closed her hand around the claw, then looked solemnly up at her. "We probably shouldn't talk about this, should we?"

Mary started to agree that not speaking about the bear would be a good idea, then she realized that nobody would believe them anyway.

They would think that Avis was just some goofy kid and she was a washed-up prosecutor whose one and only client had dropped dead on top of his own mountain. Hartsville excelled at believing the things they wanted to, and ignoring everything else. "You do what you think is best, Avis," Mary said, as she holstered her gun. "I'll leave it up to you."

FORTY-FOUR

One week later

"Hey, Mary! Wait up!"

Mary Crow stood at the bottom of the hundred and five steps that led to the Pisgah County Courthouse, once again dressed in Deathwrap. A hot August sun beamed down upon her as a chorus of cicadas swelled, raspily presaging the beginning of autumn. As she turned to see who'd called her name, a familiar figure dodged a horde of sweating photographers also preparing to climb the courthouse steps.

"Hi, Jerry. What's up?" She noticed that Sheriff Cochran had dressed up today, exchanging his usual jeans and sport shirt for a coat and tie.

He whisked up beside her and whispered in her ear. "Just got Keener's report from Raleigh."

"And?"

"They couldn't find much more than Doc Kennedy. Deke's heart was okay, but his cortisol levels were off the chart."

Mary frowned. For the past week Hartsville had been rocked by the deaths of Deke Keener and Sylvia Goins. Both Mary and Avis Martin had given statements to the fact that Sylvia had been killed by Keener, but everyone still speculated wildly about Keener's death. His demise was attributed to everything from a heart attack to a Cherokee curse invoked by Mary herself. Even so, none of the wildest rumors came close to what she had privately told Jerry Cochran she'd witnessed that night. "Isn't cortisol some kind of enzyme?"

The sheriff nodded. "It floods your body when you're under life-threatening stress."

"Like being eaten by a bear?" Mary recalled the shape that had mauled Keener like a rag doll.

"Yeah. Of course being confronted at gunpoint with all your past sex crimes might spike your cortisol, too."

She smiled at the man who by all rights should be calling both her and Avis Martin insane, but who had not once raised a skeptical brow. "I guess it's a toss-up, then. My bear or your Sylvia Goins."

"Whatever he saw, it scared him to death, although my money's on the girl with a gun."

"But what about the bear claw?"

Jerry shrugged. "Maybe Deke had it with him the whole time. Maybe it fell out of his pocket."

"His sweater had no pockets, Jerry," she said for the hundredth time. "How could something have fallen out of his pants pocket and imbedded itself in the middle of his chest?"

He looked at her, then started to laugh. "I don't know, Ripley," he said, using the nickname he'd given her after she'd given him her official, off-the-record report. "You'll have to put it in your believe-it-or-not museum."

Mary sighed. Over the last week she and Jerry had pieced together what happened that night a dozen times. A police cruiser had responded to her 911 call, but had left after finding nobody home. Sylvia had driven her Jeep up one of the old logging roads on the north side of Deke's mountain. She'd come to kill Keener; Keener was gunning for Avis Martin. All of it made a kind of warped sense until they got to the bear. They'd consulted forest rangers, the state game-and-fish commission, the head of the zoology department at nearby Western Carolina. Twelve-foot bears with golden eyes did not exist in the southern Appalachian mountains. Finally she'd given up and locked the whole incident away in the little "X" file inside her head. There was simply no explaining what had happened. "Let's talk about something else," she told

Jerry, the memory of Deke's final scream even now lifting the hairs on the back of her neck. "How come you're so dressed up?"

"Got to be ready to escort the prisoner one place or the other," he replied. "Should the jury come back soon."

"God, I hope they do."

"You and Ravenel have done a hell of a job."

"I just hope we've done enough," she said, twisting a button on her suit. "I'm feeling pretty edgy about this one."

They started trudging up the steps together. Although George Turpin had read both Mary's and Avis's statements about Sylvia Goins, the prosecutor had refused to alter or drop any of the charges against Ridge.

"That boy's been indicted," Turpin told Ravenel. "That boy's going to trial."

"But you have two sworn statements that another person committed the crime, plus Sylvia's fingerprints were on the murder weapon," argued Ravenel. "That's prosecutorial misconduct."

"I've got a statement from opposing counsel and some little twit kid," Turpin sneered. "It would be prosecutorial misconduct if I didn't go to trial."

So three days ago, the trial had begun. After Ravenel's motion to dismiss was denied, he shredded the state's case with a brilliance that stunned her. Still, Mary had no real sense of which way the jury was leaning. Half seemed impressed by Ravenel's reasoning, the other half just glowered at the handsome Cherokee boy who sat tall in his chair with his eyes straight ahead, his long ponytail brushing the shoulders of his elegant gray suit. Today Ravenel and Turpin were presenting their closing arguments. Soon the jury would decide Ridge's fate.

"So is it you or Ravenel today?" Jerry asked as they neared the Confederate statue.

"It's Ravenel's case," answered Mary. "I'm just the amateur sleuth. Just the same, though," she said as more people rushed past them up the steps. "We'd better get going."

The house was, indeed, full. Both Ravenel and Turpin were already sitting at their desks; the courtroom was packed to the point that the sergeant-at-arms would admit no more spectators. Mary walked up the center aisle, smiling at Hugh Kavanagh, who'd come with young Turnipseed, nodding at Dana and Jen, who discreetly held hands in the fourth row. Bethany Daws' parents sat behind Turpin; Avis Martin's behind Ravenel. If Ridge had any relatives present, Mary did not see them. Opening the gate that allowed her on the other side of the bar, she took a seat between Ravenel and Ridge as the jury filed in.

"How are you doing?" she whispered to the boy as they rose for Judge Wood.

"I'm okay." He looked at her with the same calmness he'd had ever since he'd walked out of Hugh's barn. Though he'd lost weight in jail, his suit still fit his broad shoulders perfectly, and she'd noticed a number of women in the courtroom gazing at him with more than just his innocence or guilt in mind. "Will it be over soon?" he asked.

"Yes," Mary replied, again fighting a feeling of dread. "Very soon."

Barbara Wood took the bench; the trial resumed. George Turpin rose to present his closing arguments. Usually he played the back-slapping, tobacco-chewing country lawyer to the point of parody. Today was no different. He stood up, unbuttoned his coat to reveal red suspenders, and began rehashing his argument, point by point. Ridge Standingdeer had been Bethany Daws' lover. Ridge's fingerprints were in her room, his semen in her vagina. He sneaked into her bedroom, at night, on a regular basis. He wanted her to run away with him, but she wanted to go to college. When Bethany refused to do as he asked, Ridge flew into a rage and bashed her skull in with a tomahawk. If he couldn't have her, nobody could. Turpin wound up with a high, emotional tone worthy of tent-revival preachers. "Now this young, sweet, beautiful girl lies in her grave, with only you to turn to. Not for spite. Not for revenge, but for the kind of justice her wretched, untimely death demands!"

Mary's heart sank as she watched jurors eleven and six wipe their eyes. Although Turpin had a case of dust and feathers, he'd done a hell of a job gluing it all together. Now it was up to Ravenel.

"You ready?" she whispered to the man who sat beside her. She noticed that the only note he'd made about Turpin's summation was a cartoon of a braying jackass, with "Turpin" lettered across his backside. She repressed a smile. Ravenel was one cocky bastard.

"Do you have a compact?" he asked.

"A compact? Like face powder and a mirror?"

"Yes."

"I might." She dug in her purse and pulled out a pretty cloisonné compact her friend Alex had given her one Christmas. "Here."

"Thanks." He slipped the thing in his pocket. "Now watch how criminal defense *really* works."

He stood up. In a soft Charleston accent, he found common ground with the jury by commiserating over the death of the beautiful young Bethany Daws. Then he pulled out Mary's compact.

"Shadows and mirrors, ladies and gentlemen. Shadows and mirrors. Let's see exactly what they have to do with this boy's life."

With that, he took off. Brandishing the small mirror like a magician, he bounced squares of reflected light all over the courtroom—on the ceiling, on the edge of the jury box, once, sharply, in Mary's eyes.

"See how that can blind you? That's exactly what Mr. Turpin has tried to do to you for the past three days. Blind you. Make something appear like something it isn't. Make you see something that isn't really there."

He slipped the compact back in his pocket, then turned to the jury. Point by point, he began taking Turpin's case apart like a cheap watch. "His semen in her vagina? His fingerprints in her room? Well, of course. Those young people were in love. And though they might not have conducted themselves as decorously as you or I, a young man loving a beautiful girl is no crime. And what about motive? There was nothing keeping this boy here. If Bethany wanted to go to college, he could have gone right along with her."

Ravenel went on—inundating the jury with facts about Bethany's abuse at the hands of Deke Keener, and the girl's subsequent tragic and bad behavior. As he sat down, Mary noticed jurors number two and ten were now dabbing at their eyes.

Judge Wood gave the jury their final instructions, then sent them to deliberate. As they filed out, the bailiff escorted Ridge to a holding cell, and Ravenel snapped his briefcase shut and said, "I'll be in my office." Mary turned to watch the courtroom empty behind her. Hugh hobbled out with young Turnipseed, then the Daws, then Dana and Jen, now discreetly not holding hands. All at once she was sitting in an empty courtroom, alone. She went over all the testimony in her mind, both Turpin's and Ravenel's summations. Where before she'd always felt confident when a jury went to deliberate, today she felt sick with nerves.

"You've done your best," she told herself as she rose from her chair. "Now all you can do is wait."

Wanting to avoid the crowds of press and her fellow Hartsvillians, she slipped out a side entrance to the courthouse and sat down on a shady bench in the far corner of the lawn. Earlier, she'd stashed a PayDay candy bar in her purse. As she unwrapped it she thought of Gabe, wondered what he was doing, if he'd found someone new to love. Then she thought of Jonathan and Lily, in Tennessee. She had not heard a word from him in nearly three weeks. She'd called his cell phone a dozen times, but had gotten only a recorded message saying that "the party was unavailable." Finally, she'd given up. Maybe this move to Tennessee was a way to make himself unavailable, at least to her.

And maybe that's just the way it has to be, she told herself, finding the sweetness of the candy oddly comforting. Jonathan had a child to think of now; he had moved on. She was the one who'd been stuck, dreaming of rekindling a relationship that apparently had no more spark than damp twigs or soggy straw.

She finished her candy bar, then leaned back against the bench. All of Hartsville was spread out before her, a bright little multicolored jewel in the lap of the stunningly green mountains. Until she moved back here, she'd considered it home. Now she didn't know where she belonged. Maybe someplace they haven't discovered yet, she thought as her eyelids grew heavy. Maybe some planet, far out in space.

The next thing she knew, her cell phone was ringing, interrupting a dream she was having about Jonathan. She must have dozed off. Hastily she clicked the thing on and held it to her ear.

"Jury's back." Ravenel sounded as if he were speaking from the bottom of a barrel. "In case you're interested."

She switched off the phone and ran to the courthouse. Already people were back in their seats. Ravenel and Turpin sat at their respective tables, both working hard at looking like they weren't nervous. Mary sat down just as the deputy brought Ridge in from the holding cell. They rose for Barbara Wood, then remained standing as the jury filed back into the jury box. Her heart was thudding, and she noticed that even Ridge seemed to tremble as he stood there.

Judge Wood turned to the foreman, a tobacco farmer Ravenel hadn't challenged because he thought the man could relate to Ridge's job as a farm laborer. "Have you reached a verdict?"

"Yes, ma'am." The man handed a piece of paper to the bailiff, who presented it to the judge. She read it without expression, then turned back to the foreman. "How do you find the defendant?"

The man cleared his throat. "Your Honor, we find the defendant not guilty."

Mary had heard courtrooms erupt before, but never like this one. Half the people cheered, the remainder started to boo. The judge gaveled the room to order, then with a glare at George Turpin, thanked the jury and ended the proceedings, quickly returning to her offices behind the bench. As she exited the courtroom, pandemonium broke out all over again. Mary grabbed Ridge and hugged him.

"Do I have to go back to jail again?" he whispered in Cherokee.

"*Tlano*, Ridge," Mary assured him with great joy. "You'll never have to go back to jail again."

FORTY-FIVE

September 30,
One Month Later

After the trial, a stillness fell over Hartsville. September ended the muggy summer's siege of the town, and as the deep green grass began to yellow with autumn, a dry breeze rattled the leaves on the trees, as if beckoning colder temperatures and the high blue skies of fall. Though people still gossiped over breakfast at Layla's and chatted on the sidewalk in front of the barber shop, they spoke mostly about inconsequential things—what teachers their children had gotten for the new school year and which baseball team might win the pennant. The true subject that obsessed everyone was discussed indoors, and in whispers. *Deke Keener had been a killer as well as a child molester.*

When Mary had given Jerry Cochran her scenario as to what had happened to all of Pisgah County's runaways, the sheriff had taken a team of deputies and had gone over Keener's mountaintop home brick by virtual brick. When that had revealed nothing, they'd gone outside. After a search of his ten-acre mountaintop turned up only the bones of a dead fox and three spent .22 shells, Jerry acted on a hunch of his own. He took his men over to old Firescald Campground on Tuckaseegee Creek. There, after estimating the distance a fit, twelve-year-old Scout could cover in an hour, he sent his team to search in a 1.4-mile perimeter around the picnic area. At .96 of a mile, 332 degrees north/northwest of the campground, in a rocky little ravine cut out by the creek, they found six shallow graves. All held the remains of adolescent white females. DNA tests positively identified one as Valerie Fleming; results were pending on the others. Mary gave a sad sigh when Cochran told her that. Now the pink-bathrobed lady with the weepy eyes would finally find out what happened to her child. It would not be the news she'd hoped for, but at least it would be something.

If the revelations about Keener subdued the normally garrulous Hartsville, they totally shattered Glenn Daws. Although Mary first had seen him only when his family went into counseling, as the days passed she ran into him more often. Glenn would trudge up the stairs to Dana's with the look of a man who'd walked away unscathed from a plane crash that had killed everyone else on board. He no longer glared at her as if she were some Cherokee devil, and he became such a fixture at their offices that she asked Dana about it one evening, as they finished a hard-fought set of tennis.

"I take it you're seeing Glenn Daws on a regular basis?"

Dana nodded. "I'm seeing them all. We meet once a week as a family, then I see all three individually."

Mary bounced a ball on her racquet, trying to imagine the layers of guilt and anger the Daws must be sifting through. "You think they'll be okay?"

Dana toweled the sweat from her forehead. "Kayla will. School's keeping her busy, plus she has a very sympathetic and understanding new best friend in Avis Martin."

Mary remembered how Deke had always spoken of Glenn Daws being like his own brother. "What about the parents?"

"Between you and me, I think Paula will probably get back on her feet. If Glenn could, he would tear Keener apart with his bare hands. In a way, it's a shame you can't kill someone who's already dead. Glenn would find that highly therapeutic."

Mary gave a bitter laugh. "Then there would be a long line of people waiting to do Deke Keener in."

Dana dropped her tennis balls back in the can. "So what are you going to do? Have you changed your mind about leaving?"

Mary gazed up at the barn swallows that swooped for insects over the tennis courts. Though her business had picked up and the early morning diners at Layla's were now nodding at her when she came in the door, she had no real reason to stay. Turnipseed had still not found water, her chances of getting on Turpin's staff were totally sunk, and her only communication from Jonathan had been one wild red and purple finger-painting from Lily, enclosed with a note that said, "Hope you are well—will call soon." "No," she finally answered. "I'm going back to Atlanta."

"I really wish you wouldn't," said Dana, her eyes glistening. "I feel like we've become friends."

"I'll come back and visit," Mary lied. She smiled. "When I get my game good enough to give you a run for your money."

After tennis she went home, exhausted. The night was thrashed by thunderstorms, and when she stepped outside the next morning, the air sparkled with a crisp clarity she had not felt in months. When she drove into town she noticed a difference in the people as well. Their steps were quicker and the men wore their shirts buttoned at the neck, their neckties knotted tight. The last visible remnant of all that had happened was a shrine to Sylvia that Ruben Morales had erected in front of the hardware store. A little statue of the Virgin Mary, a small photo of Sylvia, now soggy with humidity, surrounded by sad little bouquets of plastic flowers. Though Mr. Sutton, who was Baptist, disapproved of such garish papist displays, he'd told Ruben he could keep it there for a little while, out of respect for Sylvia. In the past month Mary had grown accustomed to the thing, and she wondered if the sidewalk would look empty when Mr. Sutton finally made Ruben take it down.

"Don't guess I'll be around to see that," she whispered as she walked up her stairs, ready to start repacking all the books she'd brought from Irene's.

Dana's door was closed, as was Ravenel's. One, no doubt, was at hard at work while the other was probably at home, nursing a hangover. Oh, well, Mary thought. At least Ravenel can finally have my office. He and Mr. Henchy can turn it into a combination environmental museum and cocktail lounge.

She unlocked her door and surveyed everything that needed to go.

The books and office supplies she could move herself. Maybe after she got them back to Irene's, Hugh might again loan her his truck to move the bigger pieces of furniture. With a sigh, she took an empty box she'd scavenged from the grocery store and started packing up the first bookshelf. She realized, as she took down Corbin's text on contracts, that she'd never asked Ridge what his plans were. She wished he would stay on and continue to help Hugh, but she doubted that would happen. He's just like me, she thought. Too many memories of this place . . . and not enough of them good.

She packed up one shelf of books and had just started on another when she heard a knock on her door. "Come in," she called over her shoulder, figuring it was Dana. When the door opened, however, Ridge stood there. He wore jeans and a denim shirt, and carried a knapsack over his shoulder.

"*Sheoh.*" He greeted her. "*Ahyole deza?*"

"I'm fine," she replied, genuinely glad to see the boy. "How are you?"

He raised his shoulders as if shrugging off a heavy burden. "Out of jail is much better than in."

She glanced at the pack he carried, surprised, in a way, that this day had not come sooner. "Are you planning a trip somewhere?"

He lowered his eyes and gazed at the floor. When he spoke again, his voice was tentative, as if he didn't trust himself not to cry. "It's time for me to leave here. I've come to say good-bye."

"You don't want to stay the winter with Hugh?" Mary had hoped that he might stay with the old man a few months longer.

He shook his head. "Hugh's a good man, like my father. But his ways aren't mine. I've told Turnipseed what needs to be done."

She studied the boy, knowing that the real reason he'd stayed was gone forever.

"Anyway, I want to pay you for all you've done. Mr. Ravenel told me that he couldn't have won the case without you."

"I did what I could, but I had a lot of help, Ridge."

"Help?" He cocked his head. "Who from?"

"Several people." She thought of Avis Martin and Kayla Daws, then she glanced across the room at the bear mask. Its face brought back that night on Deke's mountain, and she turned to the boy with the one question she still couldn't answer. "Did your people have anything to do with Deke Keener's death?"

"My people?"

"The Ani Zaguhi. Did they send a bear to kill him?"

He, too, glanced at the mask in the corner. Then he gave her a cryptic smile. "That first night at Hugh's, you said the Ani Zaguhi were just old myths. What old myth could send a bear out to do its killing?"

"None, I suppose." Mary leaned against her desk, thinking Ridge was more adept at words than she'd realized. "So where are you headed?"

He pointed out one of her tall windows, to the mountains that glowed purple in the distance. "Hugh says if you walk the mountains and keep the morning sun on your right shoulder, you'll wind up in Canada."

"Yes." Mary nodded. "Why do you want to go to Canada?"

"I want to see the aurora borealis. I saw a program about it on television. At night lights shimmer from the sky like curtains of gold."

She looked out at the Old Men—Dakwai, Ahaluna, Disgagistiyi. The mountains did, indeed, lead north. For one instant she considered joining Ridge on his trek. If they hiked fast, they could perhaps reach the Adirondacks by November, then cross over into Ontario. They were Cherokee—tough, good walkers. They could resupply themselves for winter and skirt Lakes Huron and Superior—surely before they reached British Columbia they would see that curtain of gold. She was just about to open her mouth and ask if he wanted any company when she realized that this was Ridge's trip to heal, not hers. Walking to Canada would not assuage the pain in her own heart. She would have to find her salvation elsewhere. She looked at him and smiled.

"Then Canada's where you need to go. Do you have food? Warm clothes? It gets cold up there—*ooyutla*."

He nodded. "I have enough of what I need."

"Then here." Impulsively, Mary stepped over to the corner and reached for the bear mask. "Take this with you. I have a feeling it's got powers that we haven't dreamed of."

"No." He shook his head. "They meant it for you, Koga. That much I do know." He leaned forward and kissed her cheek. "Now here's part of your payment. I went out to your farm early this morning. If you tell

Turnipseed to drill at half-speed just south of those sycamore trees, he'll find water."

Mary looked at him, surprised. "He's drilled there before, Ridge. He's drilled everywhere. The place looks like an artillery range."

"He's drilling too fast. He needs to drill slow, then the water will come."

She laughed, thinking this was the strangest paycheck she'd ever received. "Okay, I'll tell him. What's the other part of my payment?"

"I'll send it later," Ridge promised, his dark eyes serious.

Suddenly they had nothing more to say to each other. He hugged her once, gave her a wide, brilliant smile, and walked out the door. She listened to his light tread on the stairs, then she crossed over to the window to watch him set out for Canada. She tapped on the glass and waved at him. Already he'd crossed the street. He turned and waved back at her, then a cement mixer lumbered down toward the courthouse between them, for a second obscuring him from view. When the truck passed, she started to wave to him again, but he was gone. Quickly she raised her window and leaned out, craning her neck to gaze up and down both sides of the street, but she saw only Ruben Morales bringing more plastic flowers to Sylvia's shrine and two laughing teenagers going into the music store.

"Golly," she whispered as an unseasonably cold breeze surged up from the street below. "He is one strange kid." She gazed out the window a moment longer, then she turned back inside. Four more shelves to pack up, then her desk, then she could start loading her car. She'd just started on the shelf that held her criminal procedure books when she heard another knock. Ridge must have forgotten something, she decided. She walked to the door, thinking she should remind him to stop at Niagara Falls, but Ridge hadn't knocked on her door at all.

Jonathan stood there, Lily in his arms.

She was stunned. "What are you doing here?"

"Meyliiii!" Lily, who was wearing a bright orange Tennessee cap, squealed as she flung herself into Mary's arms. Mary hugged the little girl tight. How good she felt! How young and strong!

"Hi." Jonathan pulled Mary close. "I'm so glad you're here."

For a long moment she just stood there, loving the feel of his arms around her. "Where have you been?" she finally asked. "I've called you fifty times! All I ever get is this 'your party is unavailable.' "

Jonathan laughed. "A moose stepped on my cell phone."

"A moose?" Mary blinked. "They have moose in Tennessee?"

He looked around her office. "You don't have an appointment with Deke Keener now, do you?"

"No." Mary gave an unconscious shudder. "Deke's no longer a client of mine."

"Good," said Jonathan. "Then maybe you can take me on as a client."

"A client?" She frowned up at him, Lily still sandwiched between them. She didn't like the sound of his voice. "Why do you need an attorney?"

His eyes flashed with bitterness. "Pomeroy's wonderful game preserve turned out to be a canned hunt. I figured it out two days into it, when the animals started coming. Tame deer, hand-fed boars, a moose that Lily could have ridden. Pomeroy wanted to bring his pals up there so they could sip Scotch while they shot deer in a pen."

"Oh, no," said Mary, immediately understanding the reason for his wrath. "What did you do?"

"I put him off for as long as I could—told him the creek had washed the road out, one of the deer had brought in distemper." Jonathan laughed. "For the first couple of weeks, he bought it."

"What happened next?"

"The day before Pomeroy and his buddies were scheduled for their first hunt, I rented a livestock trailer and hired three Mexicans off a horse farm in Chattanooga. We got everything with four legs off that property and relocated up in Virginia. Then I came back and snipped all his fences."

"And Pomeroy found out?"

"Hell, yes, he found out. I told him. I waited until he and his fancy-dan pals drove up the next day. 'Where's my game, Walkingstick?' he asks. You never had any game, I told him. 'All you had was pets, waiting for slaughter.' " Jonathan gave a triumphant smile. "He was pretty pissed when I left. Said he was swearing out a warrant and that I could consider myself a wanted man."

"So did you come up here to find a lawyer or a safe house?" asked Mary as Lily planted a wet, sloppy kiss on her cheek.

"Actually, I was hoping I might find both." Dodging Lily, he leaned down and kissed her. Once more she felt the tingle that she'd felt when they first kissed, so many years ago.

"I was wrong, Mary," he murmured. "You were right. I don't care what you do for a living—I want you to be with me—with us."

"What about all my nasty little criminal law habits?" She needed to be sure before she committed to him this time—she couldn't ride this roller coaster again.

He held her closer. "You never asked me to be something I wasn't when we lived together in Atlanta. I won't ask that of you now."

She laughed. "You must want me to take your case pretty bad."

"The only thing I want pretty bad, Mary Crow, is you."

All at once, she knew with certainty that home had never been in Georgia or North Carolina or even at Little Jump Off. Home had always been right here, in the small charmed circle of his arms. Wherever that was, was where she belonged. "Me, too," she said, glancing at the bear mask that now seemed to grin at her from the corner. "Me, too."

ABOUT THE AUTHOR

Sallie Bissell is a native of Nashville, Tennessee. She currently lives near Asheville, North Carolina, where she's at work on her next novel. You can visit her on the web at www.salliebissell.com.